THE
GAMBLER
WAGERS HER BARON

CRAVEN HOUSE SERIES

Christina
McKnight

Praise for Christina McKnight's Novels

THE THIEF STEALS HER EARL

"When I started reading this book I could not put it down...it caused another book-hangover for me. I wanted to see how things would go when the truth of Judith came out and how Simon was going to handle it...loved it."-*Sissy's Book Review*

"Jude and Cart's story is such a delight! So refreshing to see the hero shy, socially awkward and not super wealthy. I love it...This was definitely one of the best books I've read this summer." -*Reviews from a Thrifty Mom*

FORGOTTEN NO MORE

"This author has made me love historical romance again."
-*TwinsieTalk Book Reviews*

HIDDEN NO MORE

"The storyline was really good, the writing was great. So smooth and engaging, I was able to zip right through the story, it flowed so well. I love finding new to me authors and with this wonderfully written story by Ms. McKnight I've found a new historical romance author."-*Bound by Books*

CHRISTMAS EVER MORE

"*Christmas Ever More* was a wonderfully written festive novella full of hope, renewal, love, and new beginnings. If you're a fan of Christina's Lady Forsaken series, this is a must. Even if you aren't caught up, this stands well enough on its own to be a lovely addition to your holiday reading list."-*Literal Addiction*

BOOKS BY CHRISTINA MCKNIGHT

DEDICATION

For you, my dear reader!

ACKNOWLEDGMENTS

First and foremost, I have to send endless thanks to Marc—the love of my life, my biggest supporter, my rock when doubts threaten to overcome my confidence. Because of YOU, I am able to do what I love.

There are so many people who support my passion for writing. Here are a few I am blessed to call friend: Lauren Stewart, Amanda Mariel, Debbie Haston, Angie Stanton, Theresa Baer, Ava Stone, Roxanne Stellmacher, Laura Cummings, Dawn Borbon, Suzi Parker, Jennifer Vella, Brandi Johnson, and Latisha Kahn. Thank you all for accepting me for, well, me.

Love is having Erica Monroe in my life—she's also an amazing critique partner, friend, confidant, and fellow wine lover. Note: I found her first…you can't have her. (Exception made only for Mr. M).

A very special thank you to my editor, Chelle Olson with Literally Addicted to Detail, your skill and professionalism surpass all that I expected. Chelle Olson can be contracted by email at literallyaddictedtodetail@yahoo.com.

Also, a special thank you to my developmental editor, Jessa Slade.

And to my proofreader, Anja with Hourglass Editing, thank you for embarking on yet another journey with me.

Cover design and wraparound cover design credit to Sweet 'N Spicy Designs.

Finally, thank you for supporting indie authors.

PROLOGUE

London, England
December 1810

HIDDEN IN THE upstairs closet by the family bedrooms, Payton Samuels pulled her knees to her chest and wrapped her arms around her legs as she listened to yet another set of feet enter her mother's private chambers. These were most certainly those of a woman. They lacked the heavy tread of both her elder brother or the man she'd been instructed to simply call Julian.

It hadn't been difficult, even for Payton's nearly ten-year-old mind, to work out that something was amiss in her home lately. No one raised his or her voice, slammed a door, or laughed, which was peculiar for Payton and her four siblings.

For nearly four days, she'd been forbidden to enter her mother's private chambers, and no one would say a word as to why. Arguing and pleading with her older siblings had garnered her only a stern rebuff and a reminder to be a "good little girl" and mind her business.

They, she silently seethed, had given her no other choice but to slip into the upstairs closet outside her mother's chamber and wait, straining to hear what could possibly be keeping her mother locked in her private rooms day and night. Anytime Payton misbehaved or had a terrible row with one of her sisters, she'd sneak into this very closet and listen as her mother debated her punishment.

It was her siblings, Marce, Jude, Sam, and Garrett, who treated her like a babe, not her mother. Never her mother.

She was only two years younger than her twin sisters, Sam and Jude. If she were a babe, then so should they be treated as such.

She scoffed and clamped her cold hand to her mouth to halt the sound. The noise bounced off the wooden walls but drew no notice from within her mother's room.

A sharp pain in her back shot up into her neck at the same time her legs ached from disuse. Tilting her head back and forth, she rubbed the curve on her neck in hopes the pain would recede.

Surely, it had been several hours since she'd snuck inside and hidden in the closet. The cold of the old house had seeped through her thin dress and stockings not long after she entered the tight space. She could not risk leaving her hiding spot to collect a shawl or a blanket—at least not with someone new entering her mother's room. Her stomach growled at the same time a shiver ran down her hunched back, bringing to mind her missed meal.

It was an unwelcome surprise that no one had come in search of her. Not when she slipped from the schoolroom without completing her work, nor when she'd missed their evening meal.

Seven o'clock. Sharp.

The clock chimed, and they were all meant to be in their seats and ready to eat.

Yet, Payton had remained in her hiding spot, breath held, and her ear tuned to hear anything that might come from her mother's chamber.

Perhaps she had not been the only one who'd neglected to arrive in the dining hall. One fact she knew was that her mother hadn't left her chambers, although a meal might have been brought up to her.

Madame Sasha, the *proprietress* of Craven House—whatever that meant—had had two guests that evening. Both men…

Each had spoken in hushed tones, their words indecipherable to Payton before each had left after only a few short minutes.

Payton strained to hear anything happening in the next room.

She hated being cold. She despised being hungry.

But most of all, she loathed being commanded about and coddled as if she were still no more than a baby.

She was clever—her mother told her so.

She was precocious—Julian, whom the servants called the Duke of Harwich, had told her on several occasions when he came to read her stories.

She was vexing—Garrett had insisted more than once.

And she was steadfast. She'd come to learn from Miss Giles, her tutor, that steadfast meant adamant, stubborn, and unwavering in her resolve. Payton wasn't certain what resolve was; however, if she had a bowl of it now, perhaps with warm milk, she'd eat a healthy portion.

Despite all this, no one would tell her what was wrong or allow her to see her mother.

She'd gone so far as to attempt to walk directly through her mother's door; however, Mr. Curtis had turned her away with a kind smile and a regretful shrug. Payton had even mustered a single tear, but perhaps the Craven House servant was as *steadfast* as she.

Something prickled on her bare arms, and Payton

brushed at it, refusing to allow a yelp of alarm to escape. She would have no hope of convincing her siblings that she was not a babe if she gave in to hysterics every time a spider landed on her in a darkened closet.

Lifting her chin from her knees, she pushed back against the frigid wall. Despite her shiver, her neck and back ceased to ache—as much.

She wondered who was in her mother's chambers.

They hadn't spoken in the long minutes since the woman entered, and Payton wondered if she'd departed as quickly as she came, and Payton just hadn't heard the squeak of the hinges on the door.

Suddenly, light flooded the interior of her nook, and Payton's hand rushed to cover her eyes as a single candle blinded her. Her hours in the dark had caused more than aches and pains.

Payton sat numbly, expecting a stern lecture from Marce, or for Sam to haul her from the closet, but the figure, made indistinct by the light, only pulled the door closed and blew out the candle before sinking to the floor next to Payton.

"Whatever are you doing in here?" Ellie leaned close to whisper in her ear.

The tension fled when she realized that it wasn't one of her siblings come to fetch her, but her dearest, bosom friend. As her eyes adjusted to the dark once more, Payton noted Ellie's hallmark red hair, hanging loosely about her shoulders.

"It is dreadfully cold in here," Ellie continued. "I arrived a few minutes ago, and Jude said she hadn't seen you in some time. Mentioned you hadn't been seen in the dining hall." The girl giggled before continuing. "They are all inept, aren't they?"

"What does inept mean?" Payton hissed.

"Oh, it is what my father calls me when I've spilt my milk or sullied a new dress," Ellie said with a shrug. "Last week, he misplaced his jeweled letter opener, and

I called *him* inept. He turned as red as a beet."

"Ellie, you mustn't say such things to him," Payton argued. "You know how he—"

"Do not fret, I ran quickly, and he'd already had far too much to drink for a chase." Ellie's eyes lit with mischief, clear even in the darkened closet. "Besides, I took the bloody opener."

Payton shook her head as concern for her friend's well-being welled within her.

"Now, why are we hiding in the hall closet?" Ellie asked, keeping her tone low.

"It is my mother," Payton confessed. "Something is amiss, and no one will tell me what."

The scraping of a chair across the scarred, wooden floor drew both of their attention as Payton listened closely. She could see in her mind's eye as the chair from close to the hearth was dragged toward her mother's bed.

It was evening time, what was her mother still doing abed?

The creak of bed ropes had Payton's heart beating so erratically, it echoed in her head. Thankfully, she was no longer cold.

She moved to press her ear to the wall, and Ellie followed suit.

"What are we hoping to hear?" Ellie whispered.

"Shhhhh." She held her finger to her lips as Marce's voice sounded in the other room.

Was she crying? Her eldest sister never cried. She lectured, she commanded, she rebuffed. But never had Payton heard Marce cry.

"…Mother, I cannot do this without you," Marce said.

"What will she need to do without your mother?" Ellie asked before falling silent once more.

"What will I do with the children?" Her sister's voice rose with concern.

"You—will—care—for them as—you always— have." Her mother's words were strained as if she were in pain. Perhaps she was hungry, as Payton was. "Keep them together—always."

"But I am not old—"

"You are eighteen, my child." Her mother coughed, and Payton heard several gulps, and the sound of a glass being set back on the table at her mother's bedside. "Remember, you will—move on from this. You, and your siblings will be—strong for your loss. If you keep moving forward—things will be better. Do not give up, Marce."

"What if I fail?" her sister pleaded. It was the first time Marce had ever sounded less than confident. "What if I cannot find the means to support us all?"

"Julian—he has promised to help you," her mother's labored breathing could be heard as if she were in the closet with Payton and Ellie. "As long as you—look to the future—always think about that, you will—do well—by all of them. With time, and distance, they will not miss—me."

"Payton,"—Ellie set her hand on her shoulder, squeezing gently—"do you think…?"

Payton closed her eyes and leaned away from the wall, fearing to hear more, yet needing to know. The cold returned as if it had never left, and her head pounded.

"My mother is dying." What other explanation could there be?

The worst part was that they all knew.

Marce, Garrett, Jude, and Sam. They *knew*, and they'd kept it from her.

As the realization sank in, Payton's breathing became as labored as her mother's, and the pain from her back and head moved to her chest.

Her breath hitched when her mother spoke once more. "No matter how many times it seemed—as if our lives would forever fall apart…" The bed creaked again, and Payton could nearly see her mother pushing up onto her elbows with her need to look Payton's sister straight in the eyes. "We discovered something far better on the horizon. It will be—the same—for all my children. Each of you—shall thrive."

Payton pushed to her feet, unable to listen any longer. She grasped the latch, throwing the door wide as she scrambled from the closet. The door slammed on its hinges and sprang back, nearly hitting Ellie as she followed Payton from the suffocating confines.

She would take any reprimand, any punishment, any lecture—over this.

"Payton…I…." Ellie set her hand on her arm, but Payton only shrugged away and fled down the hall toward her own chambers, her mother's words echoing in her head until her sight blurred from tears.

"*Move on…*"

"*Something far better…*"

"*Thrive…*"

"Payton, wait." Ellie's quick footfalls sounded behind her, drawing Payton to a halt as she spun to face her friend, her chest heaving up and down from her run down the hall and the unexpected news from her mother's chamber.

She couldn't accept Ellie's downcast eyes and soft words.

Payton did not need her friend to feel sorry for her—to comfort her in any way.

Rolling her shoulders back so straight they ached, Payton's *resolve* hardened further. "Do not feel sorrow for me. We all lose people we love. It is a way of life, is it not? I will do as my mother bids…move on from this miserable house, find a life far better than my siblings can afford me, and I shall thrive. You will see, Ellie, I aim to do exactly that."

Her hands clenched into tight fists at her sides, her

nails biting in the palms of her hands until she clamped her teeth shut to avoid calling out in pain.

She hadn't any idea what moving on would mean, if something better than her place at Craven House awaited her, or how to thrive without her family; however, if it were what her mother demanded of her, then Payton would do anything not to disappoint her

CHAPTER 1

London, England
February 1820

DAMON KINDER, LORD Ashford, pressed at his temples, attempting to massage away the endless pounding in his head as the shrieks and stampeding feet outside his study continued to assault the quiet he preferred in his home. Blessedly, the noise receded as his children moved farther down the hall and away from his closed study door.

Glancing down at his desk, Damon's irritation ignited when he noted that everything was in its place, all household matters attended to, and all business correspondence addressed and ready to go out with the late-morning post. Even the missive that had arrived an hour before from his country seat at Falconcrest House was duly reviewed, his response outlining the specific repairs agreed upon by him and his steward.

Falconcrest—the bane of his existence. His country estate, in his family for generations, only caused his insides to churn with guilt each time he had the need to handle anything pertaining to the property. It wasn't the house or even the surrounding land that opened a hole within him that was impossible to close. No, everything about Falconcrest signified his failure as a husband, a father, and a man. He had no interest in overseeing the maintenance of the property nor the repairs still needed for his enclosed carriage abandoned just within his lands all those years ago.

He'd purchased a new conveyance. He'd created a suitable home for his children at his London townhouse. And Damon was resigned to never see his family estate again.

However, that did not diminish his responsibility to the place. One day, his son Abram would inherit the estate, and it would be Abram's decision whether or not to inhabit the languishing house.

Damon's irritation abated at the thought, leaving only his perpetual sense of loss and sorrow—and his tidy desk before him.

To his chagrin, all his work was completed, and the sun had barely risen over the horizon. Most Londoners had just found their beds a few short hours before after long nights out.

The high-pitched, angry cry that pierced the air was one only mastered by that of a young girl. In this case, like many before it, the dreadful, ear-splitting wail was compliments of none other than his youngest child, Joy. A gruff bark of unrestrained laughter followed as Damon's son, Abram, mimicked the tone of a man ten years his senior. At ages six and eight, his offspring were…spirited. At least that was what his sister called them while in polite company.

Damon longed for them to be *spirited* in another part of the townhouse, if only to allow his thundering headache the chance to subside.

His fingers twitched as he pressed his palms flat against the polished mahogany of his neatly organized desk. Perhaps he should have remained in his private chambers and requested his morning meal be brought into the one room where no one dared disturb him. He could have had Mr. Brown, the Ashford butler, bring his paperwork to him there, and Damon would have escaped the nuisances currently bickering in the hall.

A sharp pain seized his chest. No man should insinuate, even silently to themselves in the privacy of their study, that their children were bothersome and that they incited headaches even before he'd taken his morning repast. There had been a time when he hadn't seen the pair as bothersome or so much as an inconvenience—but those days were gone, and no matter how hard he fought to return to that time…he couldn't.

Sarah was gone. His children and his home were without a mother.

And Damon had only himself to blame.

Though he need remind himself, *he* had not been charged with teaching Abram and Joy the proper decorum and manners befitting the children of a baron. He glanced at his elbow, resting upon two single-pound notes. He'd agreed that every month, he'd pay his children's governess two pounds—to educate them, to school them in the art of decorum and manners, and to prepare them for their future in society. Most of all, he was willing to pay twice the normal rate for a servant of her status with the expressed instructions that he not be bothered—and in turn, not be responsible for any future failures. However, the racket echoing throughout Ashford Hall in that moment made it vividly apparent that someone was not earning her keep nor suited to her elevated task.

It was customary for the lady of the house, or a housekeeper when the position was not occupied, to distribute the household wages. Though, after losing seven governesses in four years, Damon had made the decision that his sanity was worth two pounds per month. And how could he explain to Mrs. Brown, who happened to be wed to his butler, that a mere governess was collecting a higher wage than she?

He could not risk having another governess flee the position, however. Word had long ago spread through the agency's gossip mills about the heathens that resided at Ashford Hall in Hanover Square. He'd had to contact his solicitor to secure a governess from a highly dubious location—the famed Craven House. The rumors had spread through London many years ago that the house no longer acted as a brothel, catering to the illicit needs of men, but was operating as a staffing agency—and a safe haven, of sorts.

Not that Damon was one to buy into town gossip. Besides, he'd had little other option. He'd had no other choice but to hastily write the proprietress of Craven House the previous month and had since been rewarded with the appearance of an adequately dressed young woman of obvious genteel upbringing.

Miss Samuels, though Mrs. Brown had told him she barely looked old enough to be out of the schoolroom, came highly recommended and was, in fact, nearing her nineteenth year. The exact age *his* Sarah had been when they wed ten years prior. He'd never thought Sarah too young and unprepared for marriage, so there had been no need to believe Miss Samuels not adequate to serve as a mere governess.

Memories pushed to the forefront of his mind, and Damon's head pounded anew as he tried to keep them from overtaking him. It had been four years since his beloved Sarah passed, leaving their children to grow up without a mother.

To be raised by a succession of obviously unqualified and easily frightened governesses.

The agreement was simple enough—Miss

Samuels would care for the children in a befitting manner, and he would leave them to their tasks. So far, in her month of residing at Ashford Hall, he'd not come directly face-to-face with the governess. He'd watched them pass his study when he neglected to close the door all the way, he'd happened by their schoolroom and took in the sight of his children's heads lowered over their studies with the governess's back to him.

Avoiding the governess was becoming increasingly difficult as the days passed.

Bloody damnation.

Damon craved a drink, his parched throat begging for a long swallow of scotch; however, he was well aware that his aching head was not entirely attributed to the ever-increasing volume of his children but also because he'd imbibed one—or three—too many tumblers the previous night. It had been a rare moment of weakness for Damon...a day when the memories had been too overwhelming, and he'd given in to the dark past that tried at every turn to pull him back into the black days directly following Sarah's passing. He didn't deserve the escape too much drink provided—not after all he failed to do.

A loud thump, followed by Joy's melodic giggle, and Abram's deep, hysterical laughter, shook the windowpanes in their frame as the pair raced past his study once more. At least they were no longer arguing and bickering. Their feuding of late was becoming increasingly worrisome, and though he had listened from afar since their new governess took command, Damon was uncertain how long he could refrain from stepping in to halt their quibbles.

Glass shattered from somewhere near the foyer, and a blood-curdling scream tore through the house, abruptly halted by a deathly silence that descended in its wake.

His entire body coiled with tension, Damon pushed from his seat and strode to the door. It slammed against the doorframe, and he stalked into the hall, his shoulders stiff with a reprimand ready to be shouted at the offending party—or parties.

There was no need to go far to discover the source of the commotion.

A vase had shattered, and its splintered glass lay covering the polished floor with Miss Samuels standing perfectly frozen in the middle of the mess. Though her back was to him, Damon noted the rise and fall of her shoulders as she breathed in deeply and exhaled slowly. It appeared he would no longer be afforded the luxury of avoiding the woman.

"What is going on here, Miss Samuels?" Damon did his utmost to keep his tone level as he spoke her name aloud for the first time. "Please, tell me that is not my dearly departed mother's prized vase shattered on the floor...and that you are not ruining my hardwood with pooling water."

Damon took in the mess littering the foyer. He didn't care a whit about the broken vase, the ancient thing was atrocious and should have been tossed away a decade before; however, he also did not relish the notion of things being broken and destroyed at will within his home.

His children's muffled laughter rained down from the landing above the foyer as Miss Samuels' fists clenched at her sides, and her shoulders straightened, but she remained quiet, his question going unanswered.

"Miss Samuels?" Damon prodded, his tone turning severe at the woman's continued silence.

With aching slowness, the governess turned to face Damon as another round of laughter burst from above. His pointed glare pivoted to his children to keep from settling on Miss Samuels' clinging, soaked bodice.

Joy and Abram hastened from view and moved into the shadows of the first-floor landing.

He brought his glare back to the governess as he took in everything about her. Her eyes lit with irritation, and her long, dark tresses were matted and wet hanging over her shoulder.

Damon wasn't certain what he'd find when he came face-to-face with the woman for the first time, but this was nothing close to what he'd expected. It was as plain as his white linen shirt that she was young—though not too young to take on a position in a baron's household; however, something in the way she glared at him, her chest laboring as she breathed deeply in and the air gushed from her lungs with each exhale, had him taking notice. She was far taller than he'd thought, her hair not a simple dark brown but laced with both lighter strands and hints of red that should seem out of place but only accentuated the blue of her eyes.

His immediate instinct was to avert his stare and return to his study; however, his better judgment won out, and he remained stoic with the precise amount of disdain lingering in his stare.

When her eyes finally met his, the woman was barely restraining her fury as her face burned red with a mix of what could only be deemed shock…and a healthy dose of embarrassment. Her eyes sparkled in a way he hadn't thought possible before that moment.

"Do explain what is going on," Damon gritted through clenched teeth.

"Your *children*"—her fists tightened at her sides with each word—"thought it comical to drop a vase full of—"

"We thought it downright hilarious, actually," Abram all but sang from above. "Cook had red cabbage brought in from Suffolk, and the color was…"

"Quiet!" Damon slashed his hand through the air, cutting off his children's latest burst of giggles. His glare never left Miss Samuels where she stood doused in blue dye from her bodice to the toe of her half boots, peeking out from under the hem of her morning gown. Her white apron was saturated, and droplets of blue-colored liquid fell to the floor from her tightly clenched fists.

He could not halt his appraisal as his stare landed on her bodice and slowly traveled to her waist. Her dress was stained and soaked and clinging to her shift below as the distinct stench of ammonia travelled through the air. Apparently, his son had taken heed of his chemistry studies and was employing the lessons learned.

With much effort, Damon lifted his eyes, thankful that despite the havoc wreaked on her dress and boots, her face was stain-free. Her dark tresses were pinned high atop her head with a single curl hanging over her shoulder, luckily impervious to the blue coloring.

Despite his children's many governesses, none had even remotely resembled the lady before him. Miss Samuels was far younger than any governess he'd had as a child or any he'd employed for his own children. And the uptick of her chin as her eyes held his, said that she belonged in a ballroom instead of his foyer.

Clearing his throat, Damon was hard-pressed to determine who was more deserving of his reprimand: his wayward, unruly children or the woman who'd been hired to make certain his children were not wayward and unruly. He did not risk the wrath of his other servants to pay a governess twice the normal wage for a job that was not being successfully accomplished.

It was not his responsibility to tame his children. Bloody hell, that was exactly why he'd hired a string of governesses after his wife's death. Sarah had tended to Abram and Joy as if it were her lifelong dream to raise children. She had provided them with love and nurturing, holding their small family together. And after she was taken from them, Damon had struggled to find his way. Raising a family without Sarah had never crossed his mind.

As with any hired post, there were certain expectations to be met—both his and society's. Joy and Abram were far from the orderly, polite children of other *ton* members. And as much as he could be blamed for their lack of decorum, Damon was unwilling to accept censure.

Damon's deep breaths mirrored the governess's labored inhales and exhales.

"Miss Samuels," he said before pausing to think through his next words. He could not, *would* not, allow the woman—as inept as she appeared—to flee her post before he'd secured another governess. "I would've thought twice the going wage would be incentive enough to handle two small children."

Her fists landed on her hips. "Twice the going wage for *each* would not adequately cover it."

"I hadn't thought our first opportunity to meet would be under such circumstances, Miss Samuels." Damon worked hard to keep his tone even, reminding himself that this was not a conversation to be had before his staff, and certainly not with the children present.

"I hadn't thought to take a post for an absent lord, either. If you took any interest in your children, perhaps employed a firmer hand with them, there would be no need for such a meeting between us." Her chin lifted a notch, and her blue eyes darkened. "Certainly, they would be better behaved, at the very least."

"Are you criticizing my position as their father?"

"I have never witnessed you in such a role, however—"

"How I conduct myself, care for my children, and hold my place in this household is none of your concern, Miss Samuels," he retorted. "I love my children very much. *You*…I must merely tolerate for the time being. They shall go nowhere, while governesses come and go."

Indignation widened her stare before she lowered her gaze to the floor.

His severe tone was necessary. There were important issues that needs must be voiced, matters to be addressed and edicts adhered to. If not by his children, then at least by this staff. "It is your responsibility, as their governess, to teach them manners and decorum. If they possessed such skills, they would not be acting the heathens they are at present."

Joy and Abram had not evolved into the troublesome beasts they were under her watch, but rather his own. The knowledge of that fact did nothing to diminish Damon's ire. His temper flared when he came face-to-face with his own failures. As simple as it would be to cast the blame at Miss Samuels' feet, his children's behavior had been something of a thorn in his side for some time, and chastising the governess as he was, was not the ideal first conversation for them.

"Joy…Abram…you will come down here at once and clean up this mess. Next, you will apologize to Mrs. Brown for sullying her freshly polished floor," he said, mustering every ounce of sternness he possessed. His tone softened with his next words, and he pinched the bridge of his nose as the ache in his head pounded ever more insistently. "Miss Samuels, you will join me in my study for a private word."

Why was his household, and everyone under his roof, not as easily maintained as his business endeavors?

CHAPTER 2

MISS PAYTON SAMUELS closed the baron's study door behind her—with a bit more force than necessary or proper truth be told. However, she refused to add any further embarrassment to her situation. Was it not enough that Lord Ashford had spoken harshly to her in front of her charges? The last thing she desired was Abram and Joy overhearing their father lecturing her on the proper conduct of children and her duties as their governess. She'd been at Ashford Hall for an entire month, and this was the first time the baron had troubled himself enough to address her or interact with his children.

Payton could only imagine what would have happened if her mother had left her and her siblings to fallow for such an extended period of time. It was surprising the children were not far more lawless than they were. When she took the position as their governess, it had been explained by the housekeeper that Payton would be responsible for the children from the time they woke until they found their beds each evening, with one day off per week. She'd viewed the post as a spot of fun. She'd be away from her elder sister's watchful eye and staying in a grand London home.

Unfortunately, spending most of her days teaching two young children was a chore she'd quickly discovered she was not exactly qualified to handle.

The baron's absence from daily life only seemed to make matters worse. He stalked the halls during the night and slipped unseen into his study during the day. Once, earlier that week, Payton had sensed someone watching her as she worked with Joy on her ciphering. When she glanced toward the open schoolroom door, a shadow had been the only thing she saw, but it too had disappeared in an instant.

She glanced down at her saturated dress and apron, praying the blue dye hadn't splashed higher to blemish her neck and face. Since taking the post, she'd tried to understand the baron's children, to attain a companionable relationship with them; however, they resisted at every turn. After an entire month, she no more understood them than she did their absentee father.

The troublesome duo was mischievous and exasperating. Her elder siblings would no doubt find immense satisfaction in the sheer amount of frustration—and the limitless problems—Joy and Abram inflicted on Payton on an almost hourly basis. Most nights, Payton barely made it to bed without falling asleep at their evening meal first. Forget all the evenings she'd thought to enjoy herself about London without having to answer to her siblings regarding her whereabouts.

This morning, early as it was, had gone from unpleasant to completely dreadful, and all before they'd even settled down for their morning meal. First, Abram had tossed something at her as she escorted them toward the dining hall. Payton was one to anticipate such things, coming from a family of five children herself, and had deftly caught the object…only to discover it was a mud-soaked toad.

Her skin crawled at the very thought of the large, lumpy, slimy creature wiggling from her grasp as it leapt to the floor and attempted its escape.

Despite Mrs. Brown scooping up the toad and hurrying with it to the kitchen, the damage had been done, and her new gloves were utterly ruined by the mud.

The children had taken off back up the stairs, laughing the entire time, leaving Payton to strip her stained gloves from her hands and tuck them into her pocket as she shouted for the children to return.

In the next instant, glass had shattered at her feet, sending a cascade of wetness up the length of her.

Payton wished to flee from her charges and escape her responsibilities at Ashford Hall, but she kept the picture of her future at the forefront of her mind. She would do her job, save her wages, and would one day be free to live where she wanted, do as she pleased, and answer to no one but herself.

But now, Payton had to deal with Lord Ashford's wrath. The baron's anger was not that of most men she'd been told by several servants; instead, it was a quiet, seething disappointment. Much akin to Marce's way of dealing with Payton when she misbehaved in her youth. Through the years, she'd learned how to deal with her sister, and Lord Ashford would likely be no different.

Why couldn't he still be abed? Or better yet, not home at all to witness her humiliation.

Why had he chosen today, of all days, to leave his study?

Joy and Abram were little more than children, and yet they foiled her at every turn. Even in the classroom, they openly and mercilessly jested and teased her. Payton had behaved no better in her younger years. However, her mother, and then her sister, had been there to chastise her unruly ways. The Ashford children did not have that—they only had Payton.

She lifted her gaze to the baron as he took his place behind his desk, sinking into his chair, his head falling into his open palms. He sighed as he scrubbed at his freshly shaven face.

Disappointment. As if it should be Payton's sole purpose at Ashford Hall to *not* disappoint the baron. Yet, he'd not given her the benefit of a proper meeting before now, and she suspected that this conversation would not come close to the appropriate discourse.

How was she supposed to keep from disappointing him when he'd never spoken of his expectations?

But with him sitting still and silent, Payton had no choice but to wait, her bare hands clasped before her. How should one look in this situation? Contrite? Apologetic? Stern? Downright furious?

When she vexed Marce, contrition worked the quickest to dispel her sister's anger.

But what did the baron expect?

Payton looked within. Unquestionably, at present, it was fury coursing through her, her skin blazing hot under her soaked, stained gown. She *was* here for a purpose, and the baron's children sought to thwart her at every turn. Her employment should be simple: tend the children, tutor them, and put them to bed. After that, she was free to come and go as she pleased during the late-evening and nighttime hours, and receive two pounds per month as her compensation. It wasn't an excessive amount, but it did allow Payton enough funds to join many card games—with the hope of growing her savings quickly.

But the torment she was forced to undergo daily

seemed worth far more than a mere two pounds.

"Miss Samuels…" His voice was deeper than she'd assumed it would be, his eyes more intense. And his presence…it was large, for lack of a more suitable term.

She waited for the baron to continue, but he remained silent, his brow furrowed, creating thin lines at the corners of his eyes and mouth. She halted from proclaiming aloud that the action made him appear far older than she'd heard him to be. Heavens, the baron was only four years older than her brother Garrett, yet his shoulders held the weight of a man thrice his age. Perhaps that was his reason for hiding in his study all day, only to depart for his bed.

She knew it was only after the children had found their beds that he left the solitude of his office for his private chambers because she heard his footsteps outside her own quarters as he paused before each of the children's rooms.

If she'd known about the baron's ragged and seemingly exhausted demeanor before now, she might have thought twice about accepting a position in his household. There was little doubt there was more beneath the surface than she knew. Likely, a troubled man hiding from a household in shambles. But she hadn't suspected anything before joining his employ, and it was only after a week at Ashford Hall that she'd questioned the housekeeper about the baron's aloof nature. She'd been told it was the way of things, and that she should complete her tasks and accept her wages without further question.

She would be lying if she said the mystery behind the man didn't pique her interest. However, the man sitting behind the desk presently was not hiding some grand secret, he seemed to be wallowing in solitude.

Honestly, it was none of her business what burdened him, nor if anything could be done to alleviate the weight. The other servants at Ashford Hall had been clear about that from her first hour of employment. Meddling in the master's personal affairs was not done—under any circumstances. Which suited Payton well enough as she would not relish anyone interfering in her business either.

His shoulders straightened, and his vexation returned. She couldn't help but notice the hardening of his jaw, a distinctly aristocratic jawline that only served to highlight his full lips and large, green eyes.

She pushed those thoughts from her mind. She had every right to be as angry as the baron right now. Payton's position within the baron's home had been rather difficult to adjust to. This was not Craven House, her sister was not the master at Ashford Hall, and Payton was nothing more than a paid servant—the lowly hired help, as it were—without even the courtesy of an audience with Lord Ashford before this moment.

"Do you find yourself unqualified to serve as my children's governess, Miss Samuels?" he asked.

Miss Samuels. Another thing she'd been forced to acclimate to. Anywhere else, she was Miss Payton, or more commonly, simply Payton—no prefix or surname at all. If her brother, Garrett caught her cheating at the gaming tables or swindling her sisters, it was merely Pay. A moniker of familiarity, and also a demand for his coin to be repaid.

Of course, she wasn't qualified to be a governess, though she'd be damned if she would admit that to Lord Ashford—or her siblings. She *needed* this position. She would never return to Craven House and live under her sister's constant watch; though it was not lost on her that the baron's autocratic behavior was remarkably similar to her sister's. With one startling difference. When Payton was not caring for the children, she was free to do as she wished, without her sister's disapproving oversight.

She'd need to be contrite, apologetic, and enthusiastic about improving in her duties if she hoped to remain in the baron's household and not get banished back to Craven House.

"Lord Ashford." She kept her stare focused on his impressively organized desk, hoping to portray an outwardly humble appearance...though her temper remained red-hot. She wasn't sure what to expect from the baron's study, but organization was not it. "The children and I are still getting acquainted with one another. I can assure you, I am indeed qualified to serve as the Ashford governess. If you need any further confirmation of that, I request you contact my references."

It was all poppycock. Pure bluster.

Her references entailed directions to Lady Cartwright and the Marchioness of Ridgefeld. The pair of highly regarded ladies also happened to be her elder twin sisters. However, Payton had kept that bit of information to herself as the housekeeper had contacted both women and had not questioned them beyond Payton's suitability for the post. The position would have never been given to her had the baron known her upbringing and the simple fact that she'd never worked a day in her life outside the few chores she'd been given at Craven House. She was educated, though; her eldest sister, Marce, having hired the finest tutors in all of London. She hadn't outright lied about her skills, only kept a spot of secrecy about her family name.

The baron's pensive stare turned critical as he took her in from head to toe.

Did he relish making her look the fool; standing before him drenched as the chilly morning air began to seep through her dress? The fire against the far wall of the study was little more than glowing embers at present and did little to ward off the chill.

"That will be all, Miss Samuels." He waved his hand in dismissal and turned his attention to his work as he collected a ledger from the corner of his desk. "Please make certain another episode like today does not occur again."

That was all? He was dismissing her without…without…Payton wasn't certain what she'd expected when he summoned her to join him in his study for the first time, but this was not it. Perhaps it would have been easier if he had shouted at her, chastised her for her ineptitude, or simply released her from her duties and sent her on her way.

The curt dismissal annoyed her.

"My lord, before I go—"

"What is it?" he mumbled, keeping his stare on the open ledger, pinching the bridge of his nose between his thumb and forefinger. "I have much work to do, as you can see."

"It is my dress, Lord Ashford," she prodded, the acidic stench of ammonia had followed her into the study. The dress was not anything special, but one of the few she'd brought with her to Ashford Hall. "My gown is ruined. I am but a simple governess with limited means. How do you expect me to replace it?"

If she were attempting to muster an apology from him, she had seriously underestimated him— and her own skills at playing the contrite, reserved, and meager governess.

"You worry about your frock, whilst I am concerned with my children's education and future, miss?" In no way could his words be construed as an apology or even an understanding of her position, and for a brief moment, Payton worried she'd pushed him too far. Overplayed her hand, as it were. "Return to your room, change, and give the gown to Mrs. Brown. She will certainly find a way to remove the stains."

Payton wanted to snort at the absurdity. Was Lord Ashford's sight failing? There was no amount of scrubbing by the finest laundresses in all of England that could remove the blue pigment.

"Is that what you would do if you found yourself coated in dye, my lord?" She regretted speaking out of turn, though the man before her was but a stranger—a stranger who seemed unperturbed by his children's antics. She noted the orderliness of the room once more, and her interest grew. A man that demanded order and routine but did not seem upset by his wayward children. With the question posed, all she could do was hold her shoulders steady and wait for his reply.

"I can assure you, Miss Samuels, I would not continue to stand there dripping the foul liquid all over the expensive rug beneath my feet." His brow rose as if challenging her to continue down the path she'd chosen.

Very peculiar indeed. He cared about the floors in this room but seemed oblivious to the disarray of his household.

The man was lucky Payton had no intention of being released from her position, or she would show him what it felt like to be doused in frigid water, dyed or not. One day, yes, but today was not that day.

"Is that all?"

She relaxed slightly, allowing her anger to abate. "Yes, my lord."

"Very good." His stare drifted to the corner of his desk, and he reached for something, holding it out to her.

Payton leaned over the wooden surface, several droplets landing on a stack of parchment paper, the water and color instantly spreading and soaking into the document. Taking the two pound notes he held out to her, she retreated. The catastrophe of her morning had nearly made her forget that wages were distributed today. She'd expected to collect from Mrs. Brown as the other servants did, not from Lord Ashford. Did the fact that she did place her higher in the household hierarchy, or did it simply mean the baron thought he needed to keep a closer watch on her?

"Do see that the children are abed promptly tonight, and find yours, as well."

"Tomorrow is my day off, my lord."

"Yes, Sunday," he mused quietly. "Find your room, or take your leave until tomorrow evening, whichever you prefer."

Payton nodded. "I will see the children are in bed and be off, my lord."

"Very well." Lowering his head, his light brown hair fell forward, covering his face as he returned to his work. "If you'd be so kind as to close the door on your way out."

She slipped the notes into her pocket, the wet fabric sticking to her bare hand as she did, and departed the room before her stare stayed on the baron a moment longer. He hadn't inquired about where she might be headed when she left Ashford Hall, and after a month in the baron's household, she wondered if he knew her secret.

But there was little chance of that. Moreover, Lord Ashford had more important things occupying his mind than the whereabouts of his children's governess, made all the more noticeable by his lack of involvement in Payton and the children's daily activities.

And his disapproval would go from minor irritation to outright anger if he learned that her first time in his home hadn't been when she became his children's governess.

CHAPTER 3

DAMON'S MIND WANDERED as he leaned against the wall of the Ashford ballroom, his eyes trained on the servants working diligently at their duties. The preparations were always the same—tables, chairs, linens, and not much else. Refreshments nestled in the corner against the far wall, closest to the terrace doors, while the dais for the musicians was set up in the opposite corner. Unobtrusive and truly not necessary, but the musicians were a welcome distraction Damon was hesitant to do away with. They provided enough noise to keep his conversations to a minimum—the parties were not for his enjoyment, but a penance of sorts.

Not many hours after nightfall, the room would be filled to brimming with several dozen of London's wealthiest men and women, each plying their hands at cards. Shillings and pounds would flow more freely than the sherry. His guests would partake of his food, wine, and gaming tables until near daybreak before departing into the early morning hours to find their beds.

Some with heavy pockets, and others empty-handed.

Debts were satisfied before anyone took their

leave.

One thing Damon knew for certain was that they would return the following week, ready once again to wager their luck.

For him, the nights kept fresh in his mind how quickly life could change—like the mere flip of a card. With luck, a player could be granted a sizeable purse, or a stroke of bad fortune could strip a person of all they held dear.

Damon had found himself in the latter category.

Each week, Damon was prepared for a few brief hours in the company of the peerage, as he relived fate's cruel hand without the endless condolences and pitying looks of his peers.

"My lord?" His valet, Everett, stood at his elbow, a mask in each hand. "Do you prefer the blue and silver, or the red and gold this eve?"

Every week, Everett asked for his opinion. And every week, he gave the valet the same answer.

"Whichever you prefer." The domino disguises had been purchased at Mademoiselle Ottum's shop in Pall Mall, each identical save for their color—at least a dozen resided in his dressing closet. The clock in the hall chimed, echoing seven times before falling silent. At that precise moment, Miss Samuels would be seeing the children fed and put to bed, bringing to mind his chaotic morning. "Not the blue, Everett."

"Very well, my lord." With a quick bow, the valet turned to leave.

"One last thing," Damon called, stopping the servant. "Can you speak with Mrs. Brown regarding the governess's dress?"

"Of course."

He listened to his valet's retreating footsteps as he went in search of the housekeeper.

It vexed him that he cared about Miss Samuels' gown. If the frock were ruined, Damon would replace it. It was the right thing to do.

She was but a servant, and one he'd easily avoided up until that morning. Despite how beguiling she was with her dark, cascading hair and blue eyes that darkened when she was angry or annoyed. Her reproach after the children had ruined her gown had only drawn his notice—she'd been angry, and rightly so, but she hadn't stormed away nor threatened to leave his employ as other governesses before her had. Miss Samuels had a stark, resolute streak about her that he envied. As far as first meetings went, Miss Samuels had caught his attention much more rapidly than any governess before her.

Damon shook his head. He shouldn't be thinking of the woman, not her appearance or her character— at all. She was his governess—his *children's* governess—a servant earning a wage. Beyond her aptitude for her duties, Damon should allow Mrs. Brown to manage the woman.

Bloody damnation.

She was insufferable, yet an unavoidable necessity in his home. He needed her. Likely, that was what made her presence so intolerable. She was unlike any woman he'd ever met.

His children's governess, like Joy and Abram themselves, did not fit into the ideals Damon had for them and his life.

His children should be a delight to him—to his entire household—joyful, attentive, and bright; yet due to Sarah's absence, nothing was as it had been meant to be. Nothing was as he and Sarah had planned.

His wife—a hollow ache seized his chest—had been a quiet, patient, and reserved woman and mother. She'd never fallen prey to any form of anger or annoyance, nor acted with contrary behavior. Not with their children, their servants, or him. However,

Miss Samuels appeared peeved with his children's mere presence. It did not bode well for the longevity of her employment.

Upon her arrival, he'd been told by Mrs. Brown that the new governess had determined the children were fed and abed too early for her liking, and so, it was seven in the evening now, and they were only just finishing their meal. He knew because the sound of their voices drifted through the house to greet him in the ballroom, much liked the unwanted call of a raven. Damon preferred they complete their school work, take their meal, and see themselves to their chambers for the evening much earlier. Yet, he was willing to admit, if only to himself, that he was the least knowledgeable about when children should be fed and put to sleep. That had been Sarah's role in their family, and without her, he was adrift and overcome with uncertainty.

Perhaps it was best if Mrs. Brown oversaw the governess and her tasks with Damon remaining free to focus on other—more important—matters. Things that he was more familiar with.

Which did not include Miss Samuels' soaked bodice clinging to her bosom as her chest rose and fell with barely restrained anger. Nor his suggestion that she disrobe and don a fresh, dry gown. For that…that simple musing brought to mind images worse—or better?—than a drenched, stained bosom.

Damon huffed, pushing away from the wall. His sudden movements halted the two footmen, who busily arranged tables as they glanced in his direction before returning to their tasks.

The uptick of his pulse at the thought of Miss Samuels disrobing was a spike of betrayal aimed directly at his heart—or the place where his heart had once been. It was alarming that a man could exist without such a vital part of his being. Despite that, here Damon remained, while his heart was buried with his lost love.

There was actually a day, around the time that Abram was born, when his dearest Sarah had patiently explained how all-encompassing love and matters of the heart were. How could Damon fracture his heart enough to afford a sliver of love for his babe that was to be born? Sarah possessed all of his heart; but indeed, she'd been correct. Damon's heart had swollen to include Abram, and eventually Joy.

However, including a new child in his heart was nothing close to the devastation of having his heart ripped from his chest when Sarah was gone. As the light and life drained from her, so did she take with her his ability to love. If not his ability than his drive to extend any amount of care that would see himself or his children hurt once more. He hadn't known love before Sarah, and he feared he was undeserving of love after her.

Four bloody years. It had been the longest—and also the shortest—years of his life. Desire and passion had no place in the world he'd created around himself. Even a sense of contentment hadn't come to Damon yet. Each morning dawned, and he was secure in waiting for the sun to set once more…bringing him one day closer to a time when the possibility of seeing his wife once again drew near—and he'd be whole again.

Forevermore, his desire would lay dormant. No, not dormant, extinguished completely. Snuffed out as a candle was before bed. Yet, the fire of his passion and desire was never to be lit again, not even with a new day dawning.

Perhaps it would be wise to heed his sister's advice and return to society, if only for a distraction. Anything to calm his melancholy and pass the years as swiftly and painlessly as possible. However, the pitying glances and murmured condolences would start once more. No doubt every Londoner with even the most basic amount of humanity would be remorseful with regards to Damon's loss. Yet, reminding him of his wife's passing at every turn would not bring her back, would not give his children a mother, and would not repair the massive void left within him. And if Damon did agree to venture out more, how long would it be before Flora was parading a new crop of young debutantes before him? His sister, Viscountess Wittenbottom, had good intentions—somewhere deep, deep inside. Her way of expressing her love for her younger brother verged on parental dominance, however.

His own heart notwithstanding, Damon would not risk causing his children more hurt by bringing any woman into their lives who would eventually be taken away. Governesses, yes. Any woman who meant more, never.

Light footsteps, followed by a set of heavier ones, rushed past the open ballroom doors.

Damon ducked farther into the room as Joy's laughter rang out in the hall, followed by Abram's irritated shout. When the pair continued on, their voices receding, Damon relaxed.

Their governess would soon see them to their rooms and ready for sleep, leaving him to his own devices and free to move about the house without being waylaid.

He hadn't crossed paths with the trio since that morning, and he'd come to the ballroom knowing his children wouldn't stumble upon him there.

"Master Abram," Miss Samuels' stern yet exasperated call followed in the children's wake. "Miss Joy. How many times must I instruct you to walk whilst indoors?"

Likely another ten thousand times, he thought to

himself.

His children had been born running, at least that was how Damon remembered it.

He inched closer to the door and caught a glimpse of his children's governess stalking by the ballroom. She didn't pause to glance into the room. Before she strode out of sight, he noted that she'd donned a fresh, simple, peach gown and let loose her long waves of hair, pinning the fall at the base of her neck.

Massaging his temples, Damon suppressed the urge to think back to the brief years of happiness he'd known within these walls—and this room. If he'd known it would be all he had before his entire world crumbled, Damon would not have worked so tirelessly, visited his club so often, or spent as many hours away from home and his family. He'd grown accustomed to the leisurely way of *ton* life, and it had come back to hurt him.

Any hope Damon had for a happy, content future was gone. The sound of Sarah's uninhibited laugh on Joy's lips, or the toss of Sarah's glossy, golden curls on Abram's willful head were knife-sharp reminders that his beloved wife was gone forever.

The best Damon could hope for was a present that was not altogether intolerable.

To achieve that, he'd need to keep clear of Miss Samuels and her contrary nature. As long as she watched over his children, attended to their education, and stayed out of his way, she would do for the time being. And, as every governess had before her, Miss Samuels would eventually move on to another house, another family. And when that occurred, Damon would charge his housekeeper with the task of finding a replacement.

For now, he need only concern himself with preparing for this evening.

One long night at a time—followed by an even longer day.

During the gaming parties held at 14 Saint George Street in Hanover Square, Damon was not the widowed baron with two small, motherless children. He was simply a lord enjoying himself, at least that was the image he attempted to portray. For those limited hours, no one saw behind his mask to the empty shell he'd become. And he could act normally, despite never *feeling* it.

"Ashford!" A familiar, shrill voice thundered down the hall and into the ballroom. "Ashford? Where in heavens are you hiding?"

His stomach tightened, dread coursing through him. Damon had managed to convince himself that the worst of his day had passed. Yet life—and its cruel irony—seemingly hadn't been able to afford him even a few hours of peace.

As if his simple musings about society had conjured her, his sister's labored breathing drifted toward him as she stomped down the hallway.

Lady Wittenbottom swept into the ballroom, her assessing glare scanning the room before finding him in the shadows. Her pungent, floral perfume permeated the air and would have likely announced her arrival long before he saw her. It was the smell of his childhood—an offending odor that drove away anyone that came near.

"Why are you hiding in the dark?" she snapped, flipping her fan open and waving it a mere inch from her face. Over a decade older than he and wedded since her seventeenth birthday, Flora had long ago assumed the role of the matronly and dour lady, feeling the need to impart her wisdom upon her younger brother and chastising him for every small infraction—actual and perceived. "Are you not going to offer me a refreshment?"

"I am not hiding, I am overseeing my household," he retorted. "And you can well see that we need to retire to the salon for refreshments."

"Certainly, if you had any sense in you, you'd wed and run a proper household." Her chin notched higher, causing her headpiece to tilt precariously to the left. "It would serve everyone well. You would have a companion, and the children would have a mother. I simply do not possess the time nor the energy to run this household and my own."

As if it were that easy. Everything being mended by marrying again and replacing the one lost after a mother died. Replacing someone of that importance in one's life was not at all similar to securing a new governess. Though his sister likely thought there was no difference.

Damon scoffed. However, it sounded more like a strangled cry.

Flora slipped her fan into the bag on her wrist and hurried toward him. "You know I only care about you and the children, Damon. Despite my feelings for Sarah, it is you I think about. Poor Wittenbottom says I fret in my sleep, I am so plagued by worry for you. I simply cannot imagine you being alone"—her voice dropped to a whisper—"forever."

It was always *the children*, never Abram and Joy.

Similarly, it was always *despite my feelings for Sarah*, never that the world had been a better place while Sarah was in it.

"We manage well enough, Joy, Abram, and I—"

"But the children need a mother," his sister retorted.

"I was unaware that you had any notion what children—mine or otherwise—were in need of."

Her stare narrowed, and she took a step back as if he'd lashed out physically and not vocally. "Simply because Wittenbottom and I never longed for children, does not mean I am ignorant to their ways and needs. You know perfectly well I did my best raising you."

She appeared affronted, not hurt by his words in the slightest, confirming what Damon already held as truth where his sister was concerned.

"Please excuse my manners." Damon leaned forward, placing a light kiss on her cheek. "I fear I am a bit unnerved. Joy and Abram have once again decided to test the merit of their new governess."

"Perhaps we should revisit the topic of boarding school," Flora mused. "St. Agatha's in Dorset, and Winchester Boys Academy in Manchester have places reserved for both of the children."

We.

As if Flora had had any hand in raising his children, any interest in their studies or their preferred pastimes. If it weren't for the long list of governesses he'd employed, the children would be left fallow.

"They are not old enough to be away from home," Damon responded, shaking his head. "I may one day reconsider, but not today…nor tomorrow." And he hoped by then, his sister would have taken to other interests and no longer think of him and his children as her charity project, a good deed that would see her raised further in society as a pillar of kindness and compassion.

"I implore you to keep my suggestions in mind. My dear friend, Lady Carmichael, has fifteen grandchildren, and as soon as they no longer required a nursemaid, they were sent to live at a boarding school. The two eldest, both girls, were both wed before the end of their first Season." Flora nodded, further dislodging the pins that held her hat in place. "However, as you so kindly reminded me, I am not one to know about children and their upbringing."

"As I said, I promise to consider it once they are

a bit older," Damon agreed.

"See that you do"—she patted his cheek as if he were a good boy worthy of a reward and not a thirty-two-year-old widower—"now, where are the children?"

The way her shoulders hitched and her brow furrowed, Damon suspected that she didn't actually care where Joy and Abram were, nor would she remain long enough to see them.

Despite his sister being their only living relative besides himself, the children were not fond of Flora, and the familial bond was non-existent on both sides. "They retired for the evening a few minutes ago."

Flora exhaled. "Well, I would not wish to interrupt their sleep."

"That would not be wise." Did he so readily agree because he didn't want to journey above to his children's side-by-side rooms, or that his sister had only asked after her niece and nephew because it was proper? "Is there a reason you came?"

It was after evening meal, and most of London was preparing for their nightly outings: the opera, Covent Gardens, routs, or even Ashford Hall for a night of gaming. His sister, ever the esteemed lady, would likely be attending a ball with Wittenbottom before retiring early because, as she was wont to say, "Only heathens and ne'er-do-wells would dare be caught out after the witching hour."

"Certainly, yes." Her lips pulled back into what Flora likely thought was a genuine smile; however, her thin lips and narrowed eyes gave off no warmth. "You remember the Duchess of Catherton, my dearest bosom friend?" Flora barely paused for him to nod. "Of course, you remember Her Grace. Well, her husband asked after your famed game evening."

"I do hope you did not issue an invitation without speaking with me first."

Catherton was the type of lord Damon should want in attendance at his gaming nights: deep pockets with many friends who wagered vast fortunes on a regular basis in seedy gaming hells. Yet, the man's cruel reputation made him someone Damon did not wish to host in his home.

"I would never—"

"However, you did?" Damon prodded.

Flora picked at the string on her reticule as she avoided Damon's glare. "I may have…well, the duchess—Evangeline—she said her husband had heard word of your entertainments and desired to know when you would hold your next gaming evening. He is a duke, Damon, a *duke*! With a son little older than Joy. Think about a match made between our families."

Damon took several deep breaths as his hands clamped tight behind his back. "Joy is six. *Six*, Flora. I am not—nor will I in the next ten years—be promising her to any man, duke or otherwise."

"Of course, not." Flora attempted light laughter, though it sounded a bit shrill to Damon. "Nevertheless, I gave Evangeline your directions and let her know you'd be hosting this very evening. I assumed"—she glanced around the ballroom as several servants continued preparations—"tonight would be no different than last Saturday night."

Damon tensed. "You did w—?"

"As always, very good to see you, Damon." She nodded before her eyes grew round. "Wittenbottom is awaiting me in the drive. We are dining at Wiltons. Wiltons! I dare say, I cannot believe we may very well sup at the very same table Queen Caroline favors. Well, before all the divorce nonsense began, that is."

She clapped her hands in excitement, her unease at angering Damon forgotten as she spun around and headed for the door.

"Enjoy your evening." He remained in the shadows of the Ashford Hall ballroom until he heard his butler close the door behind Flora. Only then did he allow his exasperated sigh to escape.

His children were unruly, his governess had the audacity to rebuff his place as their father, and now the Duke of Catherton, known for his ruthlessness in both business and his personal affairs, would be joining his gaming night.

Damon's cherished few hours outside the hell that was his life suddenly vanished before his eyes, turning into a nightmare of his own making.

CHAPTER 4

PAYTON CREPT FROM Joy's room on silent, slippered feet, careful not to disturb the slumbering child. With her golden tresses and moss-green eyes, the girl would one day be a true beauty, a diamond of the first water. London—and likely all of England—would know Miss Joy Kinder. Whether for her beauty or her hellion ways, Payton was not certain. Often, she wondered how a child so peaceful at rest could cause the sheer amount of chaos Joy did while awake. Had Payton been the same in her youth? An angel while abed but a hellion when awake?

She couldn't help the hint of a smirk that pulled at her lips. Likely, she and Joy had more in common than either thought, though the difference was that Marce had known how to deal with Payton, while Payton was still learning how to handle Joy and her brother.

Pulling the door closed behind her, Payton hurried toward her own room, pausing outside Abram's chambers to listen. No sound escaped. Both children were tucked in and had found their rest. Payton's duties for the day were complete, and it was now her turn to escape, though not into slumber. She had a long night ahead of her. Thankfully, the following day—Sunday—was her day off.

The room next to Abram's had been assigned to Payton when she took the position as the Ashford governess. The chamber was sparse, previously given to Joy's wet nurse, but it suited Payton well enough. They were her own quarters, and no one intruded on her. The most welcome advantage to her room was the view.

The drapes hadn't been drawn for the evening, and Payton hurried to look out the double windows to the street below.

Saint George Street, nestled in one of the finest squares in London, was nearly always quiet—unlike her own home, Craven House, which resided in the far less desirable neighborhood of Leicester Square. The carriages coming and going in the Saint George Street area were well maintained and driven by livery in the colorful uniforms of the local households. Her windows faced the street, giving her ample view in both directions. This night, she did not linger at the window, relishing the sights of the cityscape, nor did she focus on the clouds drifting in to cover the moon.

She searched for only one thing; namely, the Craven House carriage.

As it was each week, the enclosed landau with Mr. Curtis holding the reins, waited outside the townhouse three doors down from Ashford Hall. Mr. Curtis, the only male servant employed by Craven House, was tasked with all duties ranging from tending the grounds to attending the door and even driving Payton and her sisters about London in the family's decrepit coach.

Payton collected her cloak and her wages for the week and rushed from her room, heading down the servant's stairwell and out into the hall leading to the foyer, which kept her far from the baron's study. She paused outside the ballroom, watching as two footmen adjusted palm plants close to the dais. In a few short hours, the room would be teeming with lords and ladies—and some wealthy businessmen—as Lord Ashford hosted an evening of cards. Nothing about the baron's townhouse felt the same during those hours when its normally empty halls filled with the sounds of merriment, laughter, and good cheer. Once a week, this was not a home shrouded in despair and eerie silence.

A shadow shifted in the recesses of the large room as the baron himself came into view.

Payton took a step back, the frame from the doorway blocking her as she watched Lord Ashford assess the room. He appeared as out of place here as he had in the foyer that morning. Odd that he could give his time to something so trivial as preparing his ballroom, but couldn't be bothered to see to his children's upbringing.

In fact, after she'd left the baron's study that morning to change her dress, Payton hadn't seen him again. She'd fully expected him to seek a word with his children, perhaps during their morning studies or at their noonday meal, but he hadn't come. Things had continued as they had each day before: she tended to the children, and he retreated to his study.

Lord Ashford had proven gruff, contrary, and distant. At times, Payton wondered if he even remembered that he *had* children. Despite her mother's early passing, Payton had never gone a day unloved by her older siblings. Marce had also seen to their discipline and upbringing. If not for Payton, who would take responsibility for Joy and Abram?

It appeared she needed Abram and Joy as much as they needed her, despite everyone acting to the contrary. She could at least give them a bit of the notice that should come from their father, not a governess.

As he walked around the ballroom, the baron called instructions to the footmen, pointing out a lopsided table and questioning the placement of the refreshment stand. The men hopped to each task given by Lord Ashford, each seeming happy to do the baron's bidding.

The servants at Ashford Hall had made no attempt to gain any familiarity with the baron's new governess, and she'd overheard the whispers surrounding her presence more than once. Payton would tend the children for several weeks, perhaps a couple of months at most, and then she would leave—either relieved of her position by the baron or run off by the children. That was what everyone at Ashford Hall predicted for her.

Payton had little doubt she would see the same fate as the last half-dozen governesses; however, she planned to leave of her own accord.

And that would happen as soon as she saved enough money—for housing and...other things.

Working tirelessly for a mere baron with two quarrelsome, unmanageable children was not all her future held. Her sisters, Judith and Samantha, had wed an earl and a marquis respectively. While Payton hadn't set her sights on marriage, she was confident that she would do better than living as a servant in a baron's household. There were places she longed to see, people to meet, and experiences to have. Though she didn't have it all figured out, Payton knew she longed for a place of her own, like her mother before her. She knew that living under the edicts of another was not in her future. But beyond earning enough to secure a suitable residence, Payton was still figuring everything out. Her mother had bidden her to strive for something better, yet she hadn't imparted to Payton precisely what *something better* was. Was it mere independence? A home of her own? The means to travel the world at will?

She feared if she allowed herself to remain in Lord Ashford's employ—to gain a sense of comfort—those accomplishments would be stifled and eventually forgotten altogether. Over the last month, a small amount of comfort had been found in the lavishness of Ashford Hall and the continued presence of Joy and Abram. Unless Payton sought out solitude, she was never alone.

The clock down the hall chimed, eliciting a startled yelp from Payton. She'd spent too long lost in her thoughts, staring at Lord Ashford. The baron pivoted toward the door just as she hurried by the opening and continued to the foyer and out the front entrance.

There was nothing better to regain her focus than the crisp, cold London air. As heavy with soot as it was, it reminded Payton of her goals. Much like her mother before her, Payton was confident great things lay in her future.

She pulled the collar of her cloak high to ward off the breeze as she hurried down the street to her waiting carriage.

Her time at Ashford Hall was not all her future held. It was merely a few hard months of work that would enable her to live the life she truly desired.

And that future would begin all the sooner if she could win a few sizable hands at the baron's card tables tonight.

Payton didn't try to temper her grin as she arrived at the Craven House carriage.

"Good even'n, Miss Payton," Curtis called as he hopped down from his perch to open the door for her, a bit too agile for a man of his age. "How ye be this night?"

"Wonderful." She gave her trusted servant a wide smile. Why could the mere anticipation of a night spent gambling fill her with such good cheer, even after her disastrous day? "Let us be off for"—Payton hesitated to call it what it had always been: home—"Craven House."

PAYTON STOOD BEHIND Marce's desk in her private study where the madame of Craven House conducted all her business. The cabinet doors were all open, and the desk drawers nearly pulled from their places.

Her sister's money box was gone.

The key not in the top drawer.

"Bloody bad nuisance," Payton mumbled to the empty room. The red and gold chamber had always been a sanctuary of sorts for Payton. When her elder siblings had taken to teasing her during her childhood, she would escape to this very room. She would bring her deck of cards and practice her shuffling and dealing skills for hours. She'd play loo, piquet, and even vingt-et-un, challenging herself to be each player. When her brother, Garrett, stumbled upon her hiding behind the long, low lounge one day, he'd joined her and instructed her in the art of whist, though they needed another team of players to have a real game.

Today, Marce was gone, away on another of her mysterious trips, and Craven House was empty.

Payton had thought to borrow ten pounds from their household's funds box kept in Marce's desk, but after searching the entire room, it was nowhere to be found.

There was nothing left to do but collect her gold mask and be off on her way back to Ashford Hall. The four pounds and several shillings she'd managed to save over the last month would have to do.

Perhaps a few well-won hands would double—or triple—her meager savings.

Payton hurriedly closed the drawers and doors on the cabinet.

The hour was growing late, and if she did not arrive soon, many of the men would have already lost their coin to other players.

"Whatever are you doing, dear sister?" Payton spun around to see Garrett, brow raised in question, standing in the open doorway. "I imagined you'd be at Lord Ashford's by now."

"I was hoping to borrow a few pounds from Marce, but Mr. Curtis told me she is not in residence." There was no doubt that Garrett saw right through her lie; however, Payton would rather perish in a fire than admit any such fib. Besides, if she borrowed the funds for gambling, she always made sure to replace it before anyone noticed it missing. "I was just leaving, actually. Will you be joining me?"

She sincerely prayed that Garrett had other plans this evening, and her luck—the little she'd had of late—held.

"No, not this evening." He glanced over his shoulder, and Payton couldn't help but wonder what distracted him. "I have other matters to attend to this night."

"Very well." Let him keep his secrets, especially since Payton preferred to keep hers, as well. "I must collect my cloak and be on my way."

She started for the door, prepared to push past Garrett and find her escape, but his hand landed on her elbow, halting her.

With a firm tug, she attempted to sidle around him, but his hold did not give. "Are you forgetting something?"

Payton turned, fearing she'd left open a drawer or cabinet, betraying her real purpose for being in

Marce's private study.

Her mask, gold with a red ribbon to keep it secured, lay on the desk where she'd forgotten it.

"Dear brother," she smiled. "Whatever would I do without you?"

"Do not even speak the question."

Collecting her mask, Payton gave Garrett a quick peck on the cheek. "Are you certain you cannot come with me?"

"Fear not, you will survive without me for one evening." He stared into the room, and for the first time, she wondered what he was doing at Craven House. As a second son and therefore without benefit of a title and the coffers that came with it, Garrett had insisted upon setting up lodging at the Albany not long after he reached his majority. With Marce away from London and Payton living at Ashford Hall, there was no reason for him to be home. "Do enjoy yourself. I will come round tomorrow during your day off."

It had been Garrett who'd told Payton of the baron's masked gaming evenings, even risking Marce's wrath to escort her to her first proper event. The night, nearly a year prior, had gone off without a problem, and Payton had returned with pockets brimming. Garrett's only rule: no cheating. She would not use her card counting skills nor her sleight of hand tricks.

She'd promised and kept her word.

In return, Garrett had made certain Marce never learned of Payton's late-night adventures.

"What is that on your arm?" He pointed to her elbow, where her glove had slipped when he'd held her arm. Blue tinted her skin, one of several spots she'd hoped to cover with her full-length gloves and wide sleeves. "Why is your arm blue?

Despite thirty minutes spent scrubbing the area,

the dye had held fast to her skin.

"Just a small mishap."

"A small mishap?" He chuckled, and Payton remembered her discussion with her sibling from the week before—an hour she'd spent in this very room complaining about Lord Ashford's headstrong, rebellious children.

"Truly, brother, it is nothing of consequence." Yet certainly something he would find great merriment in hearing. "A vase broke, and the contents splashed me. That is all. Besides, I must be off…or risk all the fat purses being won."

He waved his hand as she moved past him, her mask in hand.

Glancing over her shoulder as she strode away, Payton watched Garrett enter the study and close the door behind him. She would question him about his presence at Craven House when he visited her on the morrow. At the moment, she had a card game to attend—and money to win.

Or fear being stuck in the baron's employ for far longer than she could bear.

CHAPTER 5

DAMON WALKED THE perimeter of his ballroom, noting that his guests were well cared for: no glass unfilled, the refreshment table laden with fruit, cheese, and pastries, and no group lacking friendly conversation. He'd applied himself far more tonight than most evenings when he hosted, mainly as a distraction, but partly to keep his attention from the Duke of Catherton where he sat at a table crowded by onlookers. The man was easily identifiable, if not by his finely tailored evening attire, then by his two footmen that remained close by at all times, proudly wearing the Catherton's burgundy and blue livery.

The room was dim with the chandeliers above only at half-light, though bright enough to see one's cards and the person sitting across the table. The terrace doors were thrown wide to allow in the evening air and help the music escape into the night. The gathering was slightly larger than usual, yet the room was big enough to host several dozen more guests.

A group of men debated the merits of ventures to the Americas. Another table, mostly women, conversed in hushed tones about a new musical instructor who was known to teach his pupils' mothers far more alluring lessons than the harpsichord or the pianoforte. Each table was full. And, by all accounts, his guests were enjoying their evening.

Yet Damon lurked on the fringes, never taking a seat at a table nor joining any conversation, though he'd overheard many that interested him. His feet made no sound as he moved about the room unnoticed. It was one of the boons of hosting masked card games. Damon could remain unobserved unless there was trouble.

Would he ever enter a room and escape his misery in a friendly debate or idle chitchat? Would the sight of his offspring ever stop bringing to mind everything he lost—*they'd* lost? He'd managed to break free of his crushing troubles when he began hosting gambling parties, but the reprieve hadn't lasted nearly long enough, and Damon soon found himself feeling more and more alone in his crowded ballroom, just as he'd been alone for the last four years despite his children's presence.

Raised voices caught his attention as a chair skidded across the polished floor.

The Duke of Catherton stood and ripped his black half-mask from his face, his nostrils flaring as he held his gaming opponent with a pointed glare. The crowd made it impossible for Damon to see who was on the receiving end of the duke's anger. This was exactly what Damon feared would happen if the duke took to attending the weekly Ashford affairs.

Damon stepped to the duke's side when he arrived at the table.

"Is all as it should be?" He glanced at Catherton, focusing his efforts on calming the lord before his temper flared brighter, and the entire evening was brought to a halt—or, worse yet, fists were thrown. "May I do something for you, Your Grace?"

The duke didn't take his glare from his opponent as he spoke. "This trollop…this uncouth harlot…this brazen-faced cheat has bilked me of ten pounds."

A woman?

He turned towards the recipient of the duke's scorn to see a woman he'd noted several times before at his parties. She had hair of the darkest, rich brown, always pinned at the base of her neck with a single curl hanging over her shoulder and down her low-cut bodice. This night, the lady wore a gown of the deepest red with gold beading. Perhaps it was due to seeing her several times at his parties, but he could not dispel the increased feeling of familiarity with the woman. He'd never attempted to look beyond the masks of his guests, just as he prayed they did not long to see past his.

To say she hadn't caught his notice on several previous occasions would mean Damon was blind. He admired her for both her reserved beauty and her skill at the gaming tables.

"It is not my fault you are a bottle-headed ninny who has trouble counting his own cards." She laughed with a wide smile.

Damon's guests gave an uneasy chuckle, and he found himself smirking, as well.

Perhaps the duke would think twice about attending another game at Ashford Hall.

Catherton slammed his open palms against the table, causing coins to scatter, and the other players to reach for their winnings at the same time his two footmen stepped forward.

"Your Grace." Damon attempted to shift the man's focus—and rage—away from the lady. "May I offer you a drink in my study? We can discuss this matter privately and allow my guests to continue with their evening. I am certain this has all been a misunderstanding."

Catherton scoffed, shrugging away from Damon as he began to move around the table.

"Your Grace, is it?" The dark-haired beauty's blue eyes sparkled behind her mask. "I think we can solve this here and now before our host. One final hand. If I win, I will depart immediately with my coin. If you win, I will return your ten pounds plus the rest of my winnings from this evening"—she glanced at the stack of notes and coins on the table before her— "another three pounds and four shillings."

"You, my *lady*, are a thief and a swindler."

Damon couldn't see the woman's expression behind her gold mask; however, she seemed rather unaffected by the duke's claims.

Did he have a grifter in his house?

"Come now"—she paused to glance around the table—"we have the eyes of everyone on us. I certainly cannot cheat with so much attention."

Damon should put an end to their scuffle and ask the duke to depart.

She reached across the table, gathering all the cards, and held them out to Catherton.

"You may shuffle and deal, Your Grace." When the duke didn't make a move to return to his seat, she leaned farther across the table, her glove slipping down her arm. "We do not wish to disappoint our waiting audience…unless you are a coward."

Catherton's face flooded crimson at the woman's prodding and, had his opponent been a gentleman, there was no doubt the duke would have challenged him to a dawn meeting in Hyde Park for the remark.

A hush fell across the room, even quieting the musicians as no one made any movements. The seconds ticked slowly on as the woman stared up at Catherton, her head tilted ever so slightly to the left.

Damon reached forward, determined to put an end to the debacle by taking the cards and announcing that their evening had come to its conclusion; however, something on her exposed arm drew his scrutiny. The cards were forgotten as Damon recognized what stained the woman's upper arm. Blue dye.

Miss Samuels? His children's *governess*?

"One hand, but I will have more than what you have wagered on the table." Catherton's voice was a low hiss as he collected his chair and sat. "My ten pounds, your three pounds and four shillings, plus an additional twenty pounds."

The crowd erupted in applause.

Did they not realize the threat and consequences of Catherton's declaration?

Miss Samuels did not possess twenty pounds. The woman had fretted over her ruined gown that very morning, demanding it be replaced if his housekeeper could not remove the blue dye from the fabric.

Damon should be utterly stunned beyond words and command her to his study; however, he also wanted her to best Catherton and send the man scurrying home…without his precious coin.

After a lengthy pause, Miss Samuels nodded. "An additional twenty pounds it is, Your Grace."

"Piquet?" Catherton asked, not waiting for Miss Samuels to agree before shuffling the cards. "When partie is reached and six deals complete, the player with the most points wins the prize of thirty-three pounds, plus the shillings, forgoing the usual payout for scoring."

The game was one of memory, skill, and strategy. His governess could not seem to muster the skill and strategy to handle two small children; certainly, there was little hope she'd best the duke at piquet. However, her history in his very card room spoke to the contrary. He'd witnessed her, week after week, besting some of London's acclaimed gamesmen.

"I shall keep the scores," Damon said.

The first hand was dealt in short order, and Miss Samuels laid down five cards and exchanged them for five from the talon pile. The duke scanned his cards, holding them close to his chest before similarly trading three of his cards from the remaining talon stack.

Damon listened closely as the players declared their cards, back and forth, paying special attention to the points, sequences, and sets.

After five deals, it was Miss Samuels who was ahead with ninety-eight points, while the duke wasn't far behind with eighty-seven.

One last hand, and the match would be over. Both parties had agreed to adhere to the outcome, accept their fate, and continue the evening without another mention of cheating.

It was his governess's turn to shuffle and distribute the cards—twelve each with eight in the talon stack. The crowd inhaled sharply when the duke exchanged five cards, leaving three for Miss Samuels. However, she didn't exchange a single card for a new one. It was rarely done, holding the originally dealt hand.

What was the woman thinking?

She'd played a strategic partie so far, expertly knowing when to hold certain cards and when to play them to their best advantage. Her lead was not so great that she could risk allowing those cards to go unseen.

However, when her chin notched up an inch, she declared, "Carte blanche."

Miss Samuels flashed her cards briefly to verify, and Damon noted her added ten points.

"Five," Catherton declared, his smug grin giving off the impression he'd already determined himself the victor.

"Good," she replied.

"Forty-eight," the duke said, declaring his score.

Thankfully, the set was far from over, as the last declaration gave the duke a clear advantage.

"No sequence," Catherton divulged, his stare trained on his cards.

Miss Samuels spread her cards before her. "Quint." Her eyes narrowed behind her mask as she tallied her score. "Fifteen."

One hundred and twenty-three, to one hundred and thirty-five.

"Declare."

"Quatorze," Catherton proclaimed.

Damon's guests exhaled. It would be a difficult declaration to best.

"How much?" Miss Samuels called, sending several women into fits of laughter behind their raised fans. A woman besting the Duke of Catherton at the piquet table would certainly cause a fair amount of gossip among the *ton*.

Could she have it?

The conviction in her tone clearly made the entire gathering think the mystery woman behind the gold mask had vanquished the vile duke.

"Aces." Catherton laid his card face-up before him and pushed from his chair, issuing a curt bow to the many guests watching the players. "Even with adding the play phase points, I am the victor."

Damon quickly tallied the final phase points in his head. Six hands with three tricks per round equaled eighteen points. Neither Catherton nor Miss Samuels had won all eighteen tricks. No bonus points for rounds seven through eleven as neither had won all the rounds. One point for Catherton for winning the final trick.

The duke was the victor with one hundred and

fifty-seven points scored.

He double and triple checked his addition, somewhere deep he was unwilling to acquiesce that she'd lost to the duke.

Damon's stomach twisted, and he turned to Miss Samuels, thinking to see dejection and dread, but her shoulders remained squared, her chin high, and her mask in place. His stomach roiled yet she remained composed. Did Miss Samuels utterly lack any hint of self-preservation?

"If you will both join me in my study to settle your debts." Damon stood. His only hope was that he could see the debt paid without Miss Samuels' identity being discovered. "This way please—"

When Damon started for the open double doors, two blond heads peeked around the frame. Matching sets of green eyes widened before disappearing from sight as two pairs of feet could be heard scurrying down the hall. Blessedly, the musicians launched into a new piece, covering the sound.

Joy and Abram should be asleep in their beds, above stairs, and at the opposite side of the townhouse. He'd even glanced into both rooms before going downstairs to greet his guests. They'd been tucked in bed and fast asleep—a book lying open on Abram's chest as if he'd fallen into slumber while reading. Joy had been curled into a tight ball on her side, facing away from the door.

Damon increased his pace and exited the ballroom, but his children were out of sight. Behind him, the duke collected his winnings, and Miss Samuels stood from her seat, glancing about the room. His heart pounded in his chest when she watched the duke tuck a stack of notes into his coat pocket. A mere governess did not have the funds to pay such a steep wager, and neither was a woman of her ilk suited to care for his children. Without her position at Ashford Hall and the meager wages he paid, there was no possibility she'd ever repay her debt to the duke.

He should have requested a private word with her as soon as he discovered her identity. It would have saved her from the fate awaiting her in his study. His throat tightened at the thought of what Catherton would do if he learned the woman could not make good on her wager.

"My lord?" Mr. Brown cleared his throat at his elbow. "Can I be of assistance?"

Damon had never been more relieved to see his butler. "Yes, yes," he said, glancing down the hall towards the main stairs. "Can you see the Duke of Catherton and the golden-masked woman"—he'd nearly divulged her ruse to his servant—"to my study? Ask them to await my arrival." He needs must see to his misbehaving children before taking up the matter of the large sum owed the duke. "Do not leave the pair alone together."

Despite Miss Samuels' provocative words and the duke's accusations, Damon would not tolerate any woman within his home being the recipient of Catherton's wrath. If only he could have a few moments to speak with the governess and assess her capability—and willingness—to fulfill her debt, Damon would be able to dispel his unease.

But first, his children were in need of proper discipline.

He should have seen to their unruly behavior earlier in the day after they'd ruined Miss Samuels' dress. As the years passed, he found it easier and easier to keep his distance from the pair. It was as if he resided in a completely different house. Damon took his meals in his room or after the children had gone to bed. He locked himself in his study during the day or remained at his club in the evenings to avoid Joy and Abram.

It was the simplest way to assuage his guilt. His children had lost their mother because of his carelessness—his previous tendency for moments of impulsivity.

Impatience coursed through him. He should be focused on the matter between his guests; instead, he was distracted by his offspring. His backwards thinking was not lost on him—he knew he focused on the trivial in hopes it would distract him from the important.

Damon took the stairs two at a time and started down the hall that housed the children's rooms— along with Miss Samuels'—just as the pair disappeared into Joy's chamber. The door slammed in their wake.

The sound echoed in his head as he stalked down the hall.

Damon rubbed the back of his neck to dull the ache before pushing the door open.

It took him only a moment to spot Joy and Abram in the dim light where they ducked behind the unmade bed.

"Come out, now!" His command boomed in the larger room.

The pair stood behind the bed and crawled over the unkempt bedcoverings and then eased themselves to the floor several feet in front of Damon. Abram's mussed hair stood in every direction, and his long nightshirt hung open at his throat, his stare solidly leveled on Damon, while Joy kept hers trained on her feet.

"Have I not told you to remain upstairs when I am hosting guests?" he demanded, keeping his voice low, but stern.

"Yes, Father," they chimed in unison.

"Than what, may I ask, were you doing below,

sneaking about the ballroom?"

"We wanted to see—" Joy halted her explanation when Abram poked at her.

Abram's stare hardened, barely noticeable in the light given off from the dying fire and the candelabra next to the bed. "We wanted to see what occupied so much of your time, if it is not us."

"Pardon?" Damon wondered where the steel in his son's tone came from at the same time his every decision over the last four years flooded him.

Both children remained silent, but hostility fairly filled the room. After a few moments, Joy's lip trembled, and Damon's breath hitched at the sight of her hands clenched tightly before her. For possibility the first time, Damon realized his children were hurting as much as he was. They felt his pain despite the distance he'd created between them.

"Do you not miss her, Father?" Her strangled cry dispelled his irritation. "Do you not think about her at all?"

Damon searched their matching green eyes, at a loss for what to say, how to react, and utterly devoid of ideas for how to flee the room. While Abram's glare held only reproach and scorn, Joy's were filled with hurt.

Why now?

Of all nights, why had the pair brought up Sarah tonight?

"Did you love our mother?" Abram set his fisted hands on his slender hips. "Huh? We deserve an answer."

A million moments spent with Sarah—many including his two small babes—floated through Damon's mind. Days spent on the expansive lawns at his country seat, Falconcrest, with the sun shining brightly overhead. Nights spent with his arms wrapped securely and comfortably around Sarah.

Afternoons attending dreadful and boring London musicales at Flora's behest—but having his wife by his side had made the long hours bearable. The time their carriage had broken a wheel an hour outside of London proper when Sarah was heavy with child.

Every moment had held one thing above all else…love.

After a childhood shrouded by a lack of love and affection, Sarah had come into his life and changed it all. She'd made the impossible possible.

How could his children question his feelings for their mother? She was all he thought about, all he dreamed of at night, and the only person he longed to see again.

He fell into fitful sleep every night, only to wake suddenly and reach out for something—someone—to hold close. But Sarah's side of their marriage bed would forever be empty.

And they *dared* ask him if he loved their mother?

Yet, they knew nothing of his struggles, his nights spent in dark musings, or his days barricaded in his study. They were not privy to his innermost thoughts, his great regrets—or his immense guilt.

His throat tightened, but he refused to allow his children to see the weakness that afflicted him every time he thought of Sarah, remembered their many years together…and how unexpectedly she'd been taken from him.

Damon swallowed past the lump that had formed in his throat and pinned Abram with his hard stare. "You will both find your beds and not leave them again until you are called down for breakfast." He turned to Joy, her stare once again on her tiny, bare feet poking out from under her long, white nightgown. Her twin golden plaits hung over her shoulders. "Am I understood?"

Reluctantly, Abram nodded.

"Miss Samuels has tomorrow off," Damon continued. "I expect the pair of you to look after yourselves and not cause another scene like this morning."

Without another word, he pivoted and strode for the door.

He needed to be away from his children and locked in his study before the waves of anguish, hurt, and loss overtook him. Only alone would he give in to the memories, relive the moments, and cry until there were no tears left.

As he closed the door, Abram shouted after him, "You act as if she never existed. That you are better without her!"

Damon's steps faltered. Better without her?

No one was *better* without Sarah. There was no more joy to be had now that she was gone from his side. Damon had simply adjusted to a life that didn't require him to live within it.

CHAPTER 6

PAYTON HUDDLED IN the shrubs bordering Saint George Street in Hanover Square, waiting for Mr. Curtis to arrive and collect her. The dew from the leaves soaked the satin of her gown—borrowed from Samantha's dressing closet—ruining the delicately sewn fabric. Not that it mattered overmuch as her sister had bid Payton take whatever she wanted after she wed a most wealthy lord and purchased a townhouse full of satin, silk, and muslin gowns. It did not stop Payton from worrying over the expensive garment, however. It cost more than she'd earn in an entire month at Ashford Hall, and she would not be able to replace it easily.

The bitter night chill seeped into her bones when a gusty wind pushed between the three-story townhouses flanking her on either side of the street. She'd had to depart Ashford Hall without her cloak or risk being caught by Catherton sneaking off without settling her debts.

Her bottom lip trembled, and she bit down to stop the sob that crept up her throat. It was the way of things, she reminded herself. The flip of a card, a bad hand, or the skill of another took her coin as often as she won. It was disheartening to be set back another month, but life was not always easy, and moving on to *something better* would undoubtedly have its setbacks. Things hadn't been easy for her mother, and Payton was not deluded enough to think that her own independence would be easily won.

Carriage wheels sounded on the cobblestone street, and Payton peeked from the bushes, only to pull back sharply, gaining a poke to the back of her head. Another pointy branch pricked her elbow. Whistling drifted on the breeze as yet another coach traveled away from Ashford Hall, taking their occupants home for the night for a few hours rest before they started the day anew.

Bloody bugger. Yellow-livered cod monger. Caper-witted bounder.

Payton thought of every insult she'd heard in her short, sheltered life. Mutterings she'd overheard at the market or in the mews that ran behind Craven House. She'd even gained a few unladylike retorts from her dearest friend Ellington, now Lady Chastain. Suddenly, they were all too tame to express her feelings for a certain duke.

Because of that dull-witted, arrogant dandy, Catherton, she'd lost everything. All her hard-earned wages and the coin she'd won at other gaming tables. She wasn't sure if she was madder at him for besting her or allowing him to bait her into such a high-stakes hand.

Either way, it was gone. All of her winnings and salary…gone.

And the duke had dared accuse her of cheating.

Cheating!

If she'd employed her deftness at card counting, she would have taken the pompous duke for far more than a mere ten pounds—and a lot quicker, too. Truth was, she hadn't needed to bamboozle him. The Duke of Catherton was a dull-witted, arrogant dandy who thought himself above all others just because some ancient ancestor had garnered the approval of a long-dead king.

The worst part of it all was that she'd no longer be welcome at Ashford Hall, at least not during the baron's weekly gaming nights. She would most certainly have no other recourse but to return to the townhouse as Miss Samuels, governess to Ashford's quarrelsome children.

Perhaps angering Catherton hadn't been her wisest decision. However, the man was insufferable. Why had he been permitted into Lord Ashford's townhouse with his sordid reputation in the first place? Payton had never seen the man in attendance before. Despite the masks every guest wore, she recognized several lords and a few ladies from her limited outings among the *ton*. The guises were more of a lark, not to properly hide one's identity.

The wind whipped through the underbrush, twisting her skirts between her legs and sending a draft between her thighs. If she'd had a few shillings to her name, she would have hurried down the block and hailed a hackney cab.

She cursed the Duke of Catherton once more.

The moon lay hidden behind dark, ominous clouds, ready to let loose a torrent of rain. Hopefully not before Payton made her way back to Craven House.

"Damnation." Why hadn't she thought to hide *within* Ashford Hall until closer to dawn when Mr. Curtis came for her? She could have scurried to her own room and hidden there until more of the guests departed—or at least until the duke took his leave. But she'd seen Lord Ashford stalk up the stairs and couldn't risk him discovering her nighttime masquerades.

Or her embarrassment at losing to Catherton.

The baron would release her from her duties

without a moment's thought.

And then how would she ever earn the funds she needed?

Twenty pounds.

Payton Samuels owed the Duke of Catherton twenty pounds.

Her hands shook, and her head spun with dizziness at the sheer amount. She rarely possessed such large sums of money—and when she did, it usually went to pay her other debts.

She'd had no option but to flee Lord Ashford's house. The duke was persistent enough to have the entire house searched for her. Marce had remained steadfast that she would never settle Payton's debts again. Any notion of earning a sum that large without risking her own skin by bilking players at a gaming hell was out of the question. Payton needed funds, but not at the hefty price of her safety.

At least neither the baron nor Catherton suspected her true identity.

If she were lucky, as she hadn't been tonight, the duke would never again make the acquaintance of the woman in red and gold, and her employer would never learn that his children's governess had a weak spot for high-stakes card games.

Payton wrapped her arms around her midsection in hopes of trapping her waning body heat as her teeth chattered and her skin prickled with goose pimples. She could feel her mask, safely hidden in the folds of her gown. To keep from thinking about the cold dampness soaking into her dress and skin, Payton trained her eyes on the townhouse across the street. When she'd taken to her hiding spot earlier, there had been five upstairs windows alight. Now, there was only one. Soon, it would be snuffed, and there would be no candles casting a faint glow on the street before her.

How late had the night grown?

Midnight had surely come and gone. Carriages had been departing Ashford Hall for over an hour now. There could not be many guests remaining. Had Mr. Curtis forgotten her? Perhaps he'd fallen asleep in the stables and would awaken in the morning with the lingering thought that he'd forgotten something of import the previous night.

If there were anything Payton knew, it was that every circumstance was only temporary and open to change. At the moment, she was crouched in the shrubs in London's finest neighborhood. But tomorrow would be a new day with new experiences. Not long ago, she'd been lorded over by her eldest sister with no freedom to do what she desired, and no ability to be the woman she longed to be. Marce was to be admired for her dedication to her siblings. However, her way of showing her love left much to be desired. If Payton needed proof of all she believed, she needn't look any further than her own family. Both of her sisters had accomplished exactly what they wanted with no help from their eldest sister.

Judith had been apprehended as a thief by the night watchmen only a few years prior. Now, she was wedded to Cartwright. Samantha had been labeled a ladybird by the London gossips, and now she was a marchioness. Even gaining the position as a governess in the baron's home was a huge step up for the illegitimate daughter of a madame and a lowly country blacksmith.

Not that Payton knew much about her father besides his name, and how he earned his living.

Her own mother had changed her circumstances for the better after her husband had died, and she'd been cast out of her home with two small children: Garrett and Marce. In the end, she'd had a fine home and five children who loved her dearly.

The clopping of hooves and the turning of carriage wheels sounded in the opposite direction of the baron's home. The familiar creak and groan of Craven House's neglected conveyance was a sweet melody to Payton's ears—her freezing ears. She said a quick thank you to whoever was watching over her as she leapt from the bushes, gathered her skirts, and sprinted across the street, her mask hidden in the generous folds of her gown.

Before the driver had even pulled the coach to a complete halt, Payton opened the door and threw herself inside.

"Go, go!" she called, slinking to the carriage floor.

"Right away, Miss Payton." Mr. Curtis's forehead scrunched in confusion. He'd worked for the women of Craven House since long before Payton was born and knew it was better to act first and question later—at least when it came to the sometimes unseemly requests of Payton and her siblings. "Hope'n ye didna wait too long for me. Blimey cold out an' all."

"Shhhh," she hissed as they pulled past Ashford Hall and continued down the street to the next corner before making their way back to the main road.

Once they reached Regent Street, Payton was able to ease up onto the seat. There was little traffic this time of the early morning, but they'd traveled far enough from Hanover Square that she no longer feared being noticed.

With all her savings gone, Payton couldn't jeopardize losing her position as a governess by bringing any scandal to her name. It had taken her weeks to collect the measly amount of coin.

Payton must keep her head down, work diligently to please the baron and his children, and only accept a card challenge when she knew she could win. If she held to those promises, she'd one day find herself in exactly the place she longed to be.

The children didn't have to accept her, nor did she have to be particularly fond of them—or their father. But she did *need* the position.

CHAPTER 7

AFTER A DAY off spent alone at Craven House—
sleeping in a bed that no longer felt like her own—
Payton returned to her position. She'd never thought
that seeking her independence from Marce meant losing
her sense of home and feeling like a stranger in two
houses.

Ashford Hall was silent, every footfall echoing in
the abandoned hallways. After being greeted by Mr.
Brown upon her arrival, she'd not seen another
person. The household had found their beds. Every
light in the front of the townhouse had been
extinguished when Mr. Curtis had deposited her at
the stoop earlier, the only glow was from the pair of
sconces on either side of the front door.

Now, she stood silently inside Joy's bedchamber,
watching the girl breathing deeply, in and out, lost in
a dreamland that only a sleeping babe could escape to.
The room around her was decorated in pale yellow
with cream drapes and a four-poster bed. In her
youth, Payton would have given anything to have
such a finely adorned room with dolls neatly arranged
on a shelf, and a miniature dressing table made
specifically for a young girl. Payton could have done
without the demure pinafores with polished black

boots and ribbons matching each dress. She could have done without the pearl-handled brushes and eyelet bed covering that perfectly matched the draperies.

Even the beeswax candles lighting every room had taken some getting used to given how they differed from the tallow ones used at Craven House. Despite the unappealing aroma tallow candles were known for, beeswax was a luxury Marce never allowed within their home—at least anywhere but in her parlor on the nights she held events.

Food over extravagance.

Education above travel.

And tallow candles with their sooty gray burn over the clean, fresh smell of beeswax.

It hadn't mattered that the smoke from the wicks left horrible stains on the walls, or that their gowns, after years of exposure, always held the lingering scent of smoldering cotton.

Ashford Hall even appeared brighter when lit by beeswax over the sputtering of tallow flames.

Unfortunately, Payton did not know how Craven House appeared when lit by expensive candles. Such luxuries were not within Marce's budget as she preferred to spend their money helping others, not only themselves. Payton agreed with her elder sister's frugal spending habits; however, her time at Ashford Hall had her growing accustomed to certain extravagances.

Her day off had passed quickly, and she'd found herself longing to return to Ashford Hall if only to be away from the quiet of Craven House. She'd returned less than a day after her hurried escape from the gaming tables.

The hour was growing late, and she knew she should find her bed before she risked waking Joy, but she couldn't seem to take her eyes off the tranquil, serene girl. Did she know how lucky she was to be born into a noble family? To have the luxury of such contented slumber, knowing a hearty meal awaited her when she woke, complete with hot cocoa and marmalade for her toast. Those were things rarely offered to Payton and her sisters.

The baron, though aloof and distant, would surely do everything in his power to make certain Joy and Abram were cared for. Payton couldn't even go to her sister for the funds to pay her debt to the duke. That was something she'd realized over the last day. She would need to repay Catherton. The lord was a powerful man and would—if needed—discover her identity.

If not today, then tomorrow or the next.

She was a gambler…never a thief.

Living with such worry hanging over her head would be too much to accept.

Even if Marce hadn't been away from London, Payton wouldn't have had the nerve to ask her for twenty pounds to repay her gaming debt.

Joy mumbled in her sleep, rolling to her other side and curling into a tight ball with her knees close to her chest. Did Lord Ashford realize how thankful he should be to have his two children—hellions that they were? If not for them, he would have been left utterly alone after his wife's passing; his melancholy and heartbreak easily taking him down. She'd heard the servants' whispers around the townhouse as they spoke of the baron's crushing despair after his wife's death. Though she knew nothing firsthand, it was not a secret.

She eased out the door and quietly closed it behind her.

It was long past time she retired to her own chambers.

Yet, she was not tired after her day of rest.

Perhaps a warm glass of milk, another extravagance not commonly found at Craven House, would help soothe her to sleep.

Pausing at the head of the main stairs, Payton listened for any sounds from below to signal that someone was still awake, but nothing could be heard.

Her half boots made no sound as she hurried down the stairs, her footfalls silenced by the rug covering the hardwood. Making her way through the darkened hallway toward the kitchen at the back of the house, she paused before the open library door. If she had more free time during her day, she'd likely slip into the shelf-lined, cavernous room and search the rows of books until she found the perfect story to lose herself in. It would be one of adventure—or mystery. Instead, her days were filled with geography, arithmetic, and history. Joy applied herself to learning her letters, while Abram enjoyed reading about the bloody battles in England's past. Thankfully, Lord Ashford had not required her to tutor the pair in Latin or Greek or chemistry, for her shortcomings in languages and the sciences would have been apparent, even to a person unfamiliar with the subjects.

Before she realized it, Payton had stepped into the room and wandered toward the row of books closest to the waning light given off by the hearth. On a table near the fire, rested an unlit candelabra with three tall candles—and a cup of spills at its side. Deftly, she retrieved a spill and leaned close to the hot embers in the hearth. Once burning brightly, she lit the three candles and tossed the spill into the hearth.

The added light illuminated the dark, glossy wood shelves and reflected off the gold leaf-embossed titles of the leather-bound books. Craven House had an adequate collection of books, but Ashford Hall's library housed too many to count. She ran her fingers down the length of a spine, relishing the texture of the aged binding. If she leaned close, would she breathe in the scent of leather, ink, and parchment?

Careful to hold the flaming candelabra away from the volumes, Payton walked along the shelf, reading titles as she passed.

History.

Philosophy.

Architecture.

The library was bursting with every subject imaginable.

Still, she kept moving around the room, nothing catching her notice and holding it for any length of time. Perhaps it wasn't sleep she longed for but distraction. Great tomes detailing the history of rock formations in the Swiss Alps would not do.

A shelf filled with small, thin novels, close to the large bank of windows on the far wall drew Payton's attention. Titles including *Gulliver's Travels*, *Robinson Crusoe*, *The Monk*, and *Moll Flanders*, but her stare landed firmly on *Love in Excess*. Marce had a copy on her own personal shelf in her private chambers—a book she allowed no one to borrow.

Payton slipped the novel from its place and held the candle close for a clear look at the small book. The binding was well worn as if it had been read a thousand times over.

A throat cleared behind her, and she nearly dropped the novel as she spun around toward the door. The sudden movement extinguished two of the three candles in the candelabra, shrouding her in a murky, dim glow. The wall sconce lit the figure in the doorway but kept his face in shadows.

"Miss Samuels." The baron stepped into the room. "I had not been told you'd returned. I hope your time away was…pleasant."

"Lord Ashford," she breathed.

"May I help you locate something?" The tread of his boots was muffled by the ornate rugs covering the library floor.

"I—I—was going to see about getting a drink from the kitchen," she said in a rush, her face heating as she tucked the book under her arm.

The baron glanced about the room, suddenly feeling far smaller than it had felt a few moments before. "This does not appear to be the kitchen, though I have been known to be wrong."

Her throat tightened as he walked closer to her, stopping to light another candlestick on a table, flooding the area around him in a muted glow.

Lord Ashford wore only his breeches with a loose, linen shirt—no jacket or neckcloth. His sleeves were rolled up above his elbows, exposing his forearms. Never had she seen him in such casual attire, despite her having lived in his household for over a month. When outside his chambers, he was always properly attired as he'd been the other morning. Even his sandy brown hair hadn't seen a comb in recent hours, as it spiked in every direction much like Abram's when he first awoke in the morning.

Her stare lingered on him far longer than she should allow. Something about him, especially surrounded by the dim candlelight, made him appear exposed. Vulnerable. He wasn't hidden in his study behind mounds of paperwork and a locked door. He wasn't hurrying out of the townhouse for an evening of…oddly, Payton didn't know what the lord did when he was outside Ashford Hall. Besides his gaming parties, she had witnessed no friends or business acquaintances coming or going from the townhouse. He sulked, unseen, around the townhouse most days.

The baron spent little to no time with his

children, yet he'd claimed to be busy the prior day.

"I decided to borrow a book to read before bed. I hope that is acceptable," she said, breaking the silence between them.

He ran his fingers through his hair before tucking them into his trouser pockets, as if uncertain what to do with his hands. It was a boyish gesture she hadn't expected of a lord such as him. "It is a library, the books are for reading, and I fear since Sar—my wife's passing the room is most often forgotten. What have you chosen?"

He took a step closer, his focus alighting on the book nestled under her arm.

Payton hoped the dim glow masked her heated skin.

"*Love in Excess.*" She held out the book to him, but he made no move to take it. "I've noticed it on my sister's shelf and wondered why she kept the book for so many years."

"A favorite of…some distant relation from the past," he murmured, his arrogant detachment no longer clinging to him like an oversized coat. "You will certainly enjoy the tale."

"Have you read it, my lord?" Her pulse fluttered at the thought.

When he flinched at her question, she couldn't help but wonder if she'd crossed some line she hadn't known existed. The baron was a private man, but his reading interests could not be so personal in nature, could they?

He shook his head with a light chuckle. "No, I have not. I much prefer tales of war—and triumph."

"As does Abram," she offered with a shrug.

Ashford's stare widened. Was he unaware of his own son's interests?

Her heart ached for his neglected children as she remembered Joy's peacefully sleeping form, nestled in her bed.

With it came a twinge of sorrow for the baron, as well. He missed so much but seemed oblivious to the fact.

Before her was not the lord who'd scolded her the previous day. Gone was the baron who'd questioned her capabilities as a governess. In his place stood only a man, his eyes heavy with exhaustion as if whatever kept him from his children during the day also tormented him in the night.

Even during the gaming party, she'd noticed something different about him as he hovered here and there around the room, never partaking of a game nor pausing long enough to speak with anyone. Until she and the duke had come to their battle. Only then had Ashford stopped pacing on the fringes of the ballroom and sat at their table to keep score during their piquet game.

He hadn't known it was she. Couldn't have known it was his governess hiding behind the mask.

Never had he addressed the duke's accusation of cheating.

Nor had his stare lingered on her as she played.

Now, Ashford seemed distracted, his focus trained on nothing, yet he gave off the impression that he was deep in thought.

She should find her chambers immediately before anything else about the man had her rethinking her desire to collect her wages and move on as soon as opportunity allowed.

Her body tensed. She wasn't rethinking or forgetting her chosen future. The baron—nor even the duke—could cause her to do that. Lord Ashford's happening upon her in the library was only a misfortune of fate, not an indicator.

"I was just on my way to my study. I have a few matters that need to be handled before I retire."

"I will not keep you, my lord." Payton could not think of anything so pressing that it would—or could—be handled this late into the night. "It is past time I return to my room anyways. The children will be awake early."

His moss-green eyes glowed in the candlelight as he remained in front of her, blocking her path to the door. His mouth opened several times but closed again without him saying anything.

"Miss Samuels." He swallowed, his lips pressing into a firm line before the tension in his shoulders relaxed, causing her own body to stiffen. "Miss Samuels, if you find yourself still parched, I can offer you a drink in my study before you continue to your chambers."

Her pulse leapt with panic. Alone with the baron in his study… in the middle of the night? Pair that with it being the first time he'd spoken to her in any other tone but with annoyance and disinterest, and it was perplexing to say the least. Especially since, more often, she believed he saw his children—and her—as nothing more than an inconvenience.

Despite her place as a servant in his household and the warnings from the other Ashford servants to keep out of the baron's private affairs, she desperately wanted to know why. So she accepted.

CHAPTER 8

DAMON RUBBED AT his temples as he faced the sideboard in his study. His private domain. The place he was free to allow himself to dwell on the past without prying eyes scrutinizing his every move, his every word, his every expression.

And he'd invited the bloody governess in.

For a damned drink. At nearly midnight.

He wasn't sure which was worse: his offer, or her acceptance.

Stalling time for him to reassess his bearings, Damon lowered his head and inspected the crystal decanters on his sideboard. Scotch whiskey, gin, cognac, arrack, rum. No wine or sherry. Why did his servants not stock his sideboard with an appropriate drink for female company?

The answer was glaringly obvious. After Sarah's death, there hadn't been another woman in his study. After several months, Damon had noticed that his space no longer had his wife's favorite drink, a honeyed wine that he'd imported from France. It had been a relief at the time. He wasn't reminded of her absence every time he sought out his study. She would never curl up on the lounge close to the fire while he worked late into the night, nor would she join him early in the morning before the household woke for pastries pilfered from Mrs. Eleanor's kitchen pantry.

He'd lied to the bloody governess, too.

There hadn't been any reason for the deception except that he longed to hold the memory to himself…a secret that only he knew about.

The book, *Love in Excess*, was not, in fact, the favorite of a past relation but Sarah's cherished novel.

How many nights had they lain in bed or secluded themselves in this very room as she read aloud from the book?

Of all the thousands of titles precisely arranged in the library, why had Miss Samuels selected the one novel he never wanted to set eyes on again?

His fingers shook, causing two decanters to clink together.

He listened as the rustle of the governess's skirts revealed her position across the room. She seemed as hesitant to enter the study as he'd been to invite her.

Closing his eyes and steadying his rapidly beating heart, Damon gripped the edge of the sideboard. There had been no reason for his invitation, except Miss Samuels had appeared so alone and lost in the library, dwarfed by the massive shelves that reached all the way to the ceiling with the impressive Italian chandelier hanging unlit overhead. He'd watched her as she ran her fingertips along the spines of the books closest to the hearth, but then she'd spied the low row of books that had belonged to Sarah. Only Sarah.

He'd needed to be away from that shelf, out of the room entirely; yet here they were, in another room the governess had no place in.

His children's rooms, yes. The breakfast hall, of course. The schoolroom, absolutely. But in the library, and his study, no. One thousand times no.

There was no need to learn anything about the

woman—her history, her intentions, her dreams. They belonged to her, not him.

After discovering her last night, adorned in gold and red, sitting at his gaming tables, Damon couldn't help but wonder about the woman. He couldn't so much as remember her given name. Something starting with a *P*. Prudence. Penelope. Pricilla. Pearl.

None of them fit the dark-haired, confident woman who'd escaped his townhouse the night before without settling her debt. Neither did the names fit the quick-tongued, reserved beauty he'd hired to look after Joy and Abram.

Just that afternoon, he'd requested Mrs. Brown collect the governess's paperwork—including her references; however, she'd yet to deliver them to his study.

He cleared his throat as his eyes focused on the wall behind the sideboard. "I must apologize, my selections are not what I thought. I have everything from cognac to gin, but nothing suitable beyond that."

"I will have scotch." Though spoken quietly, her words were not hesitant in any way.

The drink was entirely unsuitable for a governess, but did it fit the masked woman who'd been attending his gaming evenings? When had he seen her for the first time? He could not recall a party she hadn't attended, not that he allowed himself the freedom of noticing her or any woman.

He poured scotch into two tumblers and turned, freezing where he stood.

Miss Samuels had taken a seat on the very chaise Sarah had favored. Damon needn't even close his eyes to imagine the way she'd cast her slender body across the lounge, her blond waves cascading over the edge of the backrest and almost touching the rug below. Even heavy with Joy, she'd taken her place on the low-slung seat, and he'd had to assist her to stand.

But this woman, Sarah's children's bloody governess, sat upright, her single long, rich brown curl hanging over her shoulder, her hands relaxed in her lap as her gaze traveled about the room—landing on everything but him.

Miss Samuels and Sarah were like night and day.

Bright light and midnight darkness.

Sarah had been easily read and even simpler to love.

This woman had secrets that teased at far deeper things.

However, Miss Samuels could not hold even a portion of the depth her exterior hinted at. She was a governess, a servant in his home. He had no knowledge of her background besides her letters of recommendation that she'd brought with her when they first met. Damon had no reason to know anything beyond her qualifications to care for and teach his children.

She wasn't a mystery to be solved or a woman who should hold any amount of his attention.

"Your drink." He stepped forward, and she took the tumbler from him.

Settling in the chair across from the lounge, he brought his own glass to his lips but did not drink as he watched her over the rim, the firelight bringing out the red in her dark brown hair.

She brought the tumbler to her mouth, taking a small sip. No expression crossed her face as the liquid slipped down her throat.

Damon would have expected a grimace—or at least a widening of the eyes as the scotch burned its way down.

Yet, she remained passive and disinterested.

He knew insouciance when he saw it, for it was the mask he donned to keep others from seeing what lay beneath. What did Miss Samuels hide?

The opportunity to voice his questions about her activities the evening before was upon him. However, he said nothing, asked nothing, demanded nothing. He was hesitant to give up this private moment—a spot of intimacy, no matter how forbidden it was, he hadn't experienced in many years. He felt an uncanny kinship with Miss Samuels he couldn't begin to explain, let alone understand.

"I am pleased to see you were able to remove the dye from your skin."

When her glare snapped to meet his, Damon feared he'd misspoken.

Damon glanced down into this glass, swirling the liquid before taking his first sip. "I have spoken with the children." Why did his use of *the children* make him think of Flora? "They have been duly chastised for their antics."

The last thing he wanted was to have another conversation with Joy and Abram. Even this discussion, alone in his study with Miss Samuels, was preferable to seeing the unease and betrayal in his offspring's matching green eyes. Their angry accusations had barely left his thoughts since the night before, and he had no urge to repeat the exchange. It went so far as to overshadow his confrontation with the duke after his gaming party.

"I appreciate that, my lord." He glanced down at her elbow, where the dye had given her away the evening before, but it was gone. In its place, her skin was red, likely from her scrubbing.

She appeared an unrecognizable woman from the lady adorned in red and gold. Returned to the simple, reserved attire of a governess, her finely beaded, satin evening gown had been replaced by one of muslin with a high waist and a modest neckline. The muted gray was nothing like the vibrant red from the evening before, yet the unassuming dress did little to detract from her beauty. For the first time, Damon found himself longing to ask why she'd taken a position as a governess and not sought to wed and have her own family. She was certainly alluring enough to catch any man's eye, and her demeanor, though a bit forthright, was not displeasing.

His thoughts did nothing but bring back his many other questions regarding the previous night; where had she fled to, why had she sought to make a fool of such an important man, and why had she kept her secret from him?

A cry broke the silence in the room, penetrating the walls from above. The quiet of the night was shattered, forever gone as reality invaded.

Damon's heartbeat thrashed in his ears, nearly drowning out the all too familiar bellow at the same time his fingers dug into the arms of his chair.

"Joy," they both said at the same time.

"She has nightmares," Miss Samuels said, setting her tumbler on the table beside the lounge. "I will see to her."

Damon clamped his mouth shut to prevent the remark that hung on his tongue. He knew damn well that Joy found it difficult to fall asleep—and remain asleep—without awakening on a scream. Just as he knew he should change, be there for his daughter when she needed him. Yet, he still cultivated the distance between them, and it grew nearly as quickly as his regret.

"No, I should go." Damon stood quickly, but Miss Samuels was already making her way to the door. "I can see to her—"

"I will care for Joy." She gestured toward his desk. "You have work to finish."

Work? Yes, he'd used his responsibilities to the Ashford title as his excuse for being below stairs at such an hour.

Unwanted relief flooded him at the woman's insistence on seeing to Joy. Damon wanted to care for his daughter, soothe her pain; however, he could not make things better for her when he was helpless to do it for himself.

Damon was grateful for the governess's assistance, despite his own remorse for not doing more for Joy. How many nights had he listened to Joy's cries when they woke him from sleep? How many times had he stilled himself from going to her, stopped himself from wrapping his little girl in his arms and whispering that everything would be well? How many times had he kept to his own room, knowing that any promises he made to his children would go unfulfilled? If he went to Joy, if he gave her and Abram all the love and adoration they deserved, it would only lead to their heartbreak when he ceased to exist. That day would come as it had for Sarah, though he prayed it was several decades away.

Nothing would be all right again.

And Damon would be damned if he ever pledged any such thing to Joy and Abram when he knew, without a doubt, that with Sarah gone, nothing would ever be as it should be. He'd let his children down once, and he would not allow himself to do so again. They deserved far more than a father who could not keep his promises.

Instead, he would allow his never-ending succession of governesses to placate his children, whisper sweet murmurings of a bright future to come in their ears, while he alone knew the real cruelty of the world.

The unfairness of life.

The follies of fate.

"Thank you," he called to Miss Samuels as she slipped from the room, closing the door behind her.

The echo of his daughter's quieting sobs continued to punctuate the air around him.

His entire body shook along with Joy's continued cries, his eyes clenched tightly shut as he sent a silent prayer into the night. If only he could absorb his daughter's pain, her suffering, and return them all to the happy family they'd once been.

If anything even remotely resembling a normal, happy life presented itself to Damon, he would grasp hold of it, if only for his children.

Damon was willing to give anything to gain the satisfaction of letting his hurt, his sorrow, and his despair go. Though it was only in the dead of night he allowed the overwhelming emotions to overtake him.

But in the morning, when he awoke, they remained—haunting him yet again.

CHAPTER 9

PAYTON DEPARTED THE study, the baron's reticent "thank you" at her back with Joy's heartbreaking sobs pulling her down the hall and up the stairs to the girl's closed door. If anyone understood the pain the baron's children experienced it was Payton. She'd lost her mother at roughly the same age. One day, Sasha Davenport, Payton's mother, had been alive; and the next, she was gone, taking with her every ounce of security Payton had.

Unlike Damon with his children, Payton's sister had stepped in and filled the void left by their mother's death. She'd held Payton for hours until she slept, and when Payton awoke during the night, her sister lay in the bed next to her, her arms open and ready to offer comfort.

Lord Ashford wasn't there to hold his children and make certain they knew he loved them. Nor did he insist that things would get better. He had the power to truly make their lives better, but he didn't— or perhaps he couldn't. While Payton had never known the love of a father, she suspected what the baron gave his children was greatly lacking.

The entire family had suffered a massive loss.

How did Ashford continue on, seemingly

unaware of the hurt that burrowed deep within his children?

It was clear he was not oblivious to their anguish, he merely chose to ignore it. Anger bubbled inside Payton, but she tamped it down and saved it because she needed to see to Joy. Later, there would be ample time to curse the baron and his hardened heart. She could explore his reasoning for keeping his children at arm's length and decide if it was a choice or something much more complicated.

She'd seen the pain that crossed his expression when Joy had cried out, but his impassive mask had returned within the blink of an eye. His offer to see to the child had been a hollow one.

Payton didn't pause at Joy's door; instead, she grasped the latch and pushed into the girl's private chamber, the child's weeping louder than in the hall. There were so many things she longed to share with the baron's children. Despite her penchant for trouble, she and Joy had much in common. Payton had lost her mother when she was young, and she too had woken many nights in a cold sweat as she attempted to fight her way out of a confined dark space. Perhaps it was why the children had caused an irrational irritation within her. They were, in essence, the same, except Payton had been left with siblings who lorded over her, while Joy had been stuck with an absentee father. Empathy for the children's plight filled Payton, though it may be a journey with no plausible resolution. She'd been with Joy and Abram for weeks, and understanding of the situation had eluded her the entire time.

Payton lowered herself to the edge of the bed and gathered the girl into her arms.

Life would not always be what it was at this moment for Joy, Abram, or the baron. The pain would never disappear, but one day, they would realize it was manageable. Even further ahead, they would use their own past to make certain they achieved a future that pleased them. Payton had been on her way to achieving that final accomplishment—or she had been until the duke took her at piquet.

The here and now was always changeable.

The realization of how much Payton had lost to the duke suddenly didn't have the crushing weight of defeat it had before. Here, in Joy's delicately decorated room, outside troubles seemed of a smaller magnitude.

As she did most nights, Payton murmured in the child's ear, soothing her as she stroked her long, golden plaits and let the tears seep into the fabric of Payton's dress. Joy clung to her, and her sobs slowed to faint whimpers with time. Her grip on Payton loosened until she fell back into slumber. During the day, they kept a strict divide between them, but in the dark of night, Payton allowed herself to comfort the child, to act as if forming a connection with the baron's children was not terrifying. Mothering had been so natural to Marce after their mother died, but Payton wasn't a mother and had no notion of where to begin, even if only to fill the role as a governess. And so, Joy persisted in her vexing ways, and Payton continued in her role as the irritated governess. Some days, she didn't have to playact—much like the morning they'd doused her in blue dye. But other days, it was difficult.

That terrified Payton even more. What if she made a mistake? What if the children refused her kindness? What if they had no desire to care for a governess?

Payton rocked Joy's tiny form back and forth long after the need was past. Soothing the girl's pain was something Payton had never expected to excel at, yet she did, and that surprised her.

No doubt come morning light, Joy would return to her precocious, troublesome self, and Payton would once again take her place as the stern governess…these brief moments forgotten.

Their day would be filled with schoolwork, meals, lessons on decorum, and outings to the park with little time to dwell on the intimate nature of this moment. If the time ever came to speak about these late-night bouts of terror, Payton would ask after what pulled Joy from sleep so violently. What had the girl sobbing in the arms of a stranger?

And the question that nagged the most, what kept the baron from comforting his own children?

However, the time to ask those questions had not yet come, and Payton feared it never would. The cause of Joy's nightmares was likely the same thing that burdened the baron. It should be discussed with the girl's father, not the hired help.

Just as it should be the baron holding his daughter, not Payton.

Yet here she was with Joy while he remained detached in his study.

Joy nestled closer in her sleep, the whimpers now forming unmistakable words.

Mum. Father.

The girl called to them in her slumber. Payton was helpless to offer any further comfort. She would never be Joy's mother and was unable to bring the baron to her. For now, Payton's embrace would have to do. It was all she had to offer the grieving child.

Joy's brow furrowed, and her eyes moved behind their closed lids as her nightmare returned.

With a jerk, Joy's eyes sprang open again, and she searched the darkness as her cries started anew.

Payton's chest seized as she gripped Joy tighter to keep her from tumbling from the bed.

Gradually, Joy eased back into her arms.

"Can I tell you a story, sweet girl?" Payton wasn't sure what had made her speak, but when the girl burrowed closer, she continued. "When I was a child, no older than you, I lost my mother, too. I was lost, aching inside, without the urge to leave my bed for days on end. I didn't eat, just slept all day long. Never would I allow the drapes to be parted and the bright sun to enter."

She wasn't sure the child listened, but the tension eased from Joy's small body.

"Everything I loved was taken from me when my mother passed away. You see, I hadn't a father, only my mother...and my siblings. I was so young and scared. Who would care for me? Who would tuck me into bed, read me a story, and extinguish the candle at my bedside when I fell asleep? I worried I would burn our home down because the candle would shrink until the flame found wood. I fretted about who would make certain I woke for my lessons in the morning. I cried over who would select the perfect ribbon to match my pinafore. Such trivial things to fret over, I know." Payton couldn't help her small laugh. How innocent and guileless she'd once been. "However, as a child, those were the ways I knew my mother loved me, and without her, who was there to fill that place? My siblings teased me mercilessly, as Abram does you, and I mistook their jests for dislike. But it was they—Marce, Sam, Jude, and Garrett— who came together and proved our family...our love...was not ruined with our mother gone. We were strong, we were resilient...we have thrived, just as our mother taught us to."

The words left her in a rush, feelings she'd never shared with another soul, not even her siblings, but Joy needed to hear them, needed to know they were true for Payton and would be for her, as well. Her mother's words from that long-ago night had been seared into Payton's every desire and need. There wasn't a day she didn't remember her mother's final musings, heard through the thin wooden walls at Craven House, and know that she would do exactly as her mother bid.

"Until the day you find your strength—which I know is within you—I will be here to blow out your candle at night, to read you a story before you find your slumber, and to select your ribbons come morning. That I can promise you."

Even as the words left her, Payton feared it was a promise she wasn't fated to keep without giving up a part of herself and the path she was forming for her future.

The deep, even rise and fall of Joy's chest told Payton that the child was once again asleep and had likely not heard her governess's promise.

It was a commitment Payton had no right to make, and one she could not be sure she could keep. If the baron ever discovered her deception, she'd be relieved of her post and would have no way to fulfill her promise to Joy.

But for this night, Payton was here. And come morning, Joy would find her pretty, pale pink gown laid out for her…with matching pink ribbons for her hair.

DAMON PRESSED HIS back into the wood paneling of the hallway, the shoulder-high railing biting into his flesh through his thin linen shirt as Miss Samuels' voice fell silent in Joy's room. A stranger was soothing his child's pain. A governess was the one holding Joy close, rocking her until she fell once more into sleep.

All because Damon was not strong enough to do it.

No, he was strong. He just kept his hurt from his children in hopes that they would not fall into the despair that relentlessly clawed at him. He remained distant to protect them. He wasn't blind, Damon knew how their mother's death had affected them, how deeply they were both scarred by it. He had hoped to save them from another such event, were he to suddenly be no more. They would mourn their mother, but if they knew him naught, they would be free from pain when he was taken.

The absurdity of his thinking had never been more apparent than it was in that moment.

He'd misguidedly stumbled through the last several years genuinely believing his children would heal faster, more thoroughly, without his overwhelming despair shadowing their recovery. He held on so tightly to the belief that he had nothing to offer them on their course to healing that he hadn't realized that the tie binding their family had frayed and unraveled, sending him plummeting, while his children clung to what little strand of promise was left.

That minuscule thread was Miss Samuels.

It should be him holding his little girl, soothing her back to sleep with tales of her mother and promises for the future. Instead, it was a governess that would likely be gone in a month's time, leaving his daughter to mourn the loss of yet another woman she'd come to care for.

What would become of them all when the governess left them? Did his children care for Miss Samuels?

Could her story be true? Surely, she was only saying what needed to be said to calm Joy and return her to bed.

Damon was the only man who could understand what his children had been through and the loss that plagued his household. His grief seemed wholly and innately his own, not to be experienced or understood by any other person. How could anyone know the depths of losing a woman such as Sarah? Damon had a decade of memories with his late wife. Every moment since his eighteenth year was colored by her presence. She'd been by his side when he gained his majority. She'd held his hand after each of his parents' deaths, and when Damon took his father's title. Their quiet wedding, their yearly journeys to Bath and Dorset, their winters at Falconcrest, and the births of their children.

Those were memories only Damon shared with Sarah. No one else.

His children ached for their mother just as much as Damon did. Why should this utterly shock him? They'd had fewer years with her, but that did not diminish her value to them or the memory of her.

The creak of Joy's bed drifted into the hallway.

Damon should seek his own chambers before Miss Samuels caught him in the hall, listening to her private conversation. Or, worse yet, take his presence as his belief that she was incapable of fulfilling her responsibilities. Despite everything, Damon needed Miss Samuels—not for himself but for his children.

He was incapable of being there for Joy and Abram, but despite all of Miss Samuels' flaws, she was the only one who could soothe his children's pain.

"Good night, Joy." Miss Samuels' hushed whisper held a quiet compassion he'd never heard in her tone before, especially when she was speaking with his unruly children. "Sweet dreams. I will be waiting in the morning."

Damon froze when footsteps started his way. The governess would step into the hallway in but a moment, and there was no place for him to hide, no excuse for his eavesdropping.

"Miss Samuels?" his daughter's sleepy voice called out.

Though he couldn't see into the room, he knew the governess turned back toward Joy.

"Yes?"

"Why doesn't my father love us?"

Damon trembled, his knees buckling, barely keeping himself upright, and he leaned heavily against the wall. His fist pressed to his mouth in an attempt to remain silent. He should inch his way down the hall to the stairs and return to his study—and his waiting decanter of scotch.

Instead, he remained outside Joy's door, longing to hear how Miss Samuels responded, as if somehow it would answer his own questions about his love for Joy and Abram. He did love them, with all his heart— at least what little was left with Sarah gone.

He held his breath and listened as Miss Samuels made her way back to his daughter's bedside, her skirts rustling, and the bed creaking as she sat once more.

"Why do you think he doesn't love you and Abram?" she asked.

"I don't know about other mums and fathers, but ours only seems irritated at us all the time." She paused, and Damon could imagine her tiny, angelic face scrunching as she tried to put into words something that was far too mature for her to reconcile. "He is home, but he doesn't tuck us into bed or eat his meals with us. Even when we are horrid to you, he doesn't scold us."

"Mayhap your father thinks it is my responsibility, as your governess, to handle such things."

"But you are not our mum."

"No, I am not," the governess agreed.

"Soon, you will leave—"

"I am not leaving anytime soon," Miss Samuels said. "However, one day, you will be a grown woman—smart, beautiful, and confident—and you will not need me any longer."

Damon pushed away from the wall and risked a glance into the room. The embers in the hearth gave off barely enough light to see Miss Samuels perched on the edge of Joy's bed, stroking the child's brow. His stomach twisted, knowing it should be him at his daughter's bedside. The only thing to do was announce his presence and tell Joy that he did love her and her brother. Nothing would change that. But, instead, he sank back against the wall.

It was best he not disturb Joy. She'd found some semblance of peace, and he was loath to take the moment from her. Tomorrow…there would be time enough tomorrow to speak to the children.

Damon prayed the governess's words held truth. She would not leave him…er, his children. She would remain in his home and show Joy and Abram the love they so rightfully deserved. The love Damon had for them but could not bring himself to express. *One day*, he swore to himself, one day he would be free of his guilt and regret over the past and everything they'd lost because of his actions. One day they would be a family again.

He wanted that time to come. More than anything.

For now, he needed to make certain nothing stood in the way of Miss Samuels remaining as his children's governess for as long as they needed her…for as long as *he* needed her.

"You must sleep now. Tomorrow, we will learn all about Egyptian history and the hidden tombs their lands have kept a secret for many of centuries."

"I do not want to study, I want to—"

"You must learn all you can, or you'll become

one of those feather-brained misses who cares for naught but fancy gowns and speaking only of the weather," Miss Samuels said with a quiet laugh. "Now, to sleep with you."

Yes, Damon could use a good night of rest, though he suspected a fitful slumber awaited him.

He inched back down the hall as Miss Samuels sang an unfamiliar lullaby.

Damon didn't deserve the indirect kindness the governess had shown him at Joy's question. He had neglected his children, he had grown the distance between them, and he despaired that he'd never be able to mend the rift he created. How could he soothe his children's pain when he was helpless to overcome his own?

CHAPTER 10

DAMON HAD THOUGHT his exhaustion could not possibly worsen; however, after hurrying away from Joy's bedchamber—the melodic melody of the governess's voice chasing him—he slept late into the morning without a hint of restful respite. He walked briskly down the hall and past the schoolroom door, not risking a peek inside through the portal that stood ajar. Abram's stern tone warned Joy against knocking his inkwell over. As if in response, Miss Samuels cautioned Joy against her plan by outlining the consequences if she were to spill the onyx ink on the wood floor.

His steps faltered, but he decided not to interrupt Miss Samuels and his children. They needed to learn to obey their governess, and Miss Samuels must assert her authority over the pair. Otherwise, Damon's household would continue to be disrupted. After the previous night—the stark honesty between his daughter and the governess—a bond had obviously been formed…or had it been formed long before last night? At the very least, it had been reinforced in their private exchange.

He took the stairs two at a time, more to hurry to his study than any amount of lightness to his step.

Mr. Brown nodded when he reached the final

step and waited for his master to address him, his face pinched with a certain measure of pain.

"Good morning, Mr. Brown." Damon greeted, his voice lacking its usual gruffness.

The butler bowed, then straightened quickly to glance over his shoulder toward Damon's study. "My lord—"

"Out with it," Damon sighed, glancing at the hall clock. Nearly midday, and he hadn't even made it to his work yet. "I have a long day ahead of me."

"Ummm—" Brown stared at the floor. "You have a visitor."

"A visitor?" Damon asked. "Why was I not summoned?"

Was it Flora again, stopping by unannounced to badger him and create unease in his servants? It had been less than two days since her last visit. Even when she was upset over Damon's refusal to conduct his daily life according to her edicts, Flora was not known to call on him more than once per week. Had he done something unusual to incur her wrath?

Mr. Brown cleared his throat as he was accustomed to doing when he was nervous and feared inciting Damon's ire. "After what happened at the party, I had hoped he would take his leave if you did not attend him directly."

The only thing that had happened at the party was…

"The Duke of Catherton is here?" Any lingering tendrils of exhaustion fled as a new alertness coursed through him. "How long has he been made to wait?"

"Only ten minutes, my lord."

"Thank you, Mr. Brown." Damon couldn't be upset with his butler. After Damon had gone upstairs to see to his misbehaving children the night of the party, Brown had been charged with escorting the duke and Miss Samuels to his study. At some point, the governess—still masked—had slipped from the gaming room and absconded into the night, leaving the duke enraged with an unsettled debt.

"Shall I have tea brought round?" the butler asked.

"Heavens, no." Damon had insisted he would send word to the duke as soon as he located the mystery woman who owed Catherton twenty pounds. He hadn't any notion where she'd gone that night, but he knew where she was now, and handing over her identity to Catherton was not an option. "We shall not endeavor to make the man feel any more welcome than he is."

Damon needed the governess to remain in his employ. If not for himself, then for Joy and Abram. With her in residence at Ashford Hall, she cared for his children in a way he'd been unable to all these years—something he longed to learn.

"Please make certain the children remain above stairs." He couldn't risk the duke spotting Miss Samuels, nor chance his children creating a scene his sister would surely hear about.

"Of course." The butler nodded stiffly and turned to make his way upstairs.

There was nothing left for Damon to do but appease the duke.

With a casual grin, he entered his study to find the duke pouring himself a healthy tumbler of brandy. If his guest had been any other man, Damon would have laughed and asked him to pour him a drink, as well. Though it wasn't another man.

"Your Grace." The greeting was cool as Catherton pivoted to face Damon, his chilling, cold blue eyes nearly cutting him from across the room. "Do have a seat."

Catherton ignored his offer; instead, he turned to study the portrait above the sideboard.

"My father with his favored hound," Damon offered.

Still, the duke remained silent. Damon couldn't help but wonder if it was a tactic the lord regularly used to unhinge his opponents. Not that Damon was in any way the man's adversary.

Perhaps it was best to discuss the issue at hand and have it finished. "I thought we decided I would—"

"It has been over a day, Ashford…over a day." The duke drained his tumbler and set it on a nearby table then sauntered across the room toward Damon. "I was under the impression you would handle the matter with haste and have the debt paid."

"I have been unable to locate the woman in question. My man of business has taken up the search, and will no doubt be contacting me with information soon."

Catherton's stare narrowed on him. "I would hate to think you allow such unsavory characters into your home and go so far as to assist them in bilking your friends."

The only unsavory man in his home was Catherton, and *friends* was something Damon would never be with the duke.

Reflexively, Damon moved toward his desk, putting Catherton closer to the door.

Damon stalled himself from running his hand through his hair before pivoting to stare over Catherton's shoulder and out the open door as a wisp of green ducked from view.

The duke moved back toward Damon, grabbing his tumbler from the sideboard and refilling it.

Outside his study, Miss Samuels' dark hair could be seen as she leaned around the door frame. Was the woman determined to be noticed? If it hadn't been for the blue dye on her elbow, Damon might have continued on, oblivious to the mystery woman's identity.

Damon turned in her direction, his brow raising in question before he sauntered across the room and shut the door in her bewildered face before moving to stand behind his desk.

"My home—and my gaming tables—are open to many, Your Grace." The woman was a fool and certainly should pay for her mistake, but never would he allow Catherton to know her identity. He opened the drawer near his elbow and retrieved the small box he kept his household funds in. Each week, he gave Mrs. Brown enough for the market and his servants' wages. "If I am not mistaken, you received an invitation from Lady Wittenbottom, my sister."

"That is of no consequence," the duke retorted. "I will have the lady's name and directions immediately. If you cannot be held responsible for those gaming in your home, then I am certain the magistrate will handle the matter swiftly."

"My sister informed you of my rules. Identities always remain secret." Damon opened the box and counted out the twenty pounds Catherton was owed. "Even I do not know all my guests. That is why many come to Ashford Hall. I afford them both privacy and safety. That being said, I do agree you should have your debt settled."

The sum was not significant for Damon, nor would it affect his household accounts. However, such a debt for a mere governess would be impossible to repay.

"Here is your due." Damon held the notes out to the man. "I will assume the debt marker and collect."

"I don't want your money, Ashford," the duke hissed. "I want the name of the woman who dared flee before making good on her losses."

"Even if I knew her name, I would not give it to

you." Damon straightened, sending his haughtiest glare across his desk. "If I were you, I'd take the money, consider the debt settled, and be gone."

Catherton's eyes narrowed, and his face reddened at Damon's audacity.

His brow rose. "And what, may I ask, would you do if you found her name and directions?"

"That is my concern." The duke snatched the notes and slipped them into his coat pocket, never removing his cold stare from Damon. "Ashford, do not expect me—or any of my friends—to attend Ashford Hall again."

"I never presumed you would, Your Grace." There could be no mistaking the intent behind Damon's retort. "I will bid you good day."

Behind them, Mr. Brown opened the study door as if he'd had his ear pressed to the wood and gestured for the duke to follow.

Catherton swung around and departed the room without so much as a farewell, not that Damon expected one.

He only hoped Miss Samuels had found her way back upstairs and out of sight.

Damon rubbed his face as he slumped into his chair. He'd settled Miss Samuels' debt for a selfish reason. Damon needed a governess, particularly someone who understood what his children were going through, and she was that person. He couldn't help Joy and Abram. Damon was as lost in his own grief as they were. However, if what he'd witnessed the previous night told him anything, Miss Samuels could help them. And in so doing, she might save Damon, as well.

If he hadn't paid Catherton, there was little chance the man would forget the debt or allow Damon to continue his gambling parties without issue. If he could not maintain his gaming evenings, he would need something else to occupy his mind and his time.

He needed the brief reprieve from what his life had become. It was only when he donned his mask that the pain and anguish did not threaten to overtake him with each breath he took. He did not long for the woman he lost. He did not languish over the void that separated him from his children.

And he had no need to face his failures, at least for a brief few hours.

PAYTON DIDN'T HALT until she was safely returned to the schoolroom, the door closed at her back. When Mrs. Brown had delivered their midday meal to them while they continued their studies, Payton had thought it a good time to speak privately with the baron.

About their time in his study, and also his children.

It was a matter she was ill-equipped to handle. The baron's children were not unruly because they were naughty children. No, they were misbehaving because they were hurting. Payton was disappointed in herself that she hadn't spotted it before. It had been her recourse when she lost her mother. Joy and Abram needed more than Payton could offer them.

They needed their father. Someone who'd experienced the same loss.

When she heard the voices coming from the study, she should have known better than to eavesdrop. In fact, she should've been wise enough to sense the danger that lurked ahead and return to the schoolroom immediately.

Yet, she'd ventured closer.

And closer still until she spied the man meeting with Lord Ashford.

The Duke of Catherton.

Had he come to discover Payton's identity?

The baron had slammed the door in her face without a word, which was favorable. If Lord Ashford had known she was the mystery woman who'd lost to the duke, he likely would have called her into the room and demanded she settle her debt.

Payton would have had to admit that she did not possess the funds to repay the duke.

What would have happened next?

She shivered at the thought of Lord Ashford handing her over to Catherton. She'd been a fool to allow the duke to bait her into such a grand wager. And now the baron was involved. She'd ruined an advantageous situation and lost her meager savings in the process. Her chest tightened at the thought of starting over—without her money or her post at Ashford Hall.

Hopefully, Marce would return from her trip by her next day off so Payton could throw herself on her sister's mercy and beg for the funds to settle the debt. Never again would she gamble…at least not more than she could afford.

But she couldn't tell Marce that part. It would be akin to giving up a large portion of her newly found freedom—a piece of herself. She would need to promise never to ply her hand at cards or any wager again. Perhaps it was time she put her gambling behind her, find a new way—a sensible way—to secure the future she intended for herself.

"Miss Samuels?" Joy stuck her head into the room from the sitting area. "Are you going to eat with us?"

She smiled at the child, her mood lightening at the sight of the young girl, free from her nightmares. "Only if Cook sent enough for us all."

"Cheese with jam and fresh bread."

She didn't normally luncheon with the children, favoring a brief few moments to herself before their afternoon lessons commenced; however, Joy had awoken in a delicate mood—finding Payton straight off and remaining close all morning.

"Oh, that sounds delightful," Payton accepted.

They hadn't spoken about the previous evening, but from the soft pink that blossomed in Joy's cheeks each time Payton noticed the girl watching her, Payton knew she too was thinking about the private moment they'd shared. But how to bring up the subject?

Was it better to leave the topic alone for now?

If the child had more she longed to talk about, she would eventually bring it up when she was ready. It was undoubtedly a difficult thing to speak about with someone as unfamiliar as a governess. It had taken years for Payton to accept that Marce could help her heal; that losing their mother did not mean the end of their family.

The loss of Baroness Ashford shouldn't have meant the end for Joy and Abram. Yet each day, she witnessed their father pulling further and further away from his children. Where Payton and her siblings had banded together, the baron and his children had drifted apart, allowing a void as vast as the English Channel to open between them.

"Hurry up!" Joy shrieked.

"Or what?" Payton countered, pushing away from the closed door. "The cheese will turn moldy and the bread stale?"

With a giggle, the child spun on her heels, her long braids whipping behind her as she fled back to the table and her meal.

Something was different about the child today…more to the point, *everything* was different. Before, Joy had been a child with the weight of the world's troubles upon her. Holding her down and dispelling any sense of calm. Maybe it was Payton who'd changed, not Joy. She'd told a story, her own personal nightmare, for the first time—ever. There had been no expectations surrounding her confession, nor had she believed that Joy was fully awake and listening; however, the simple retelling of her past heartbreak had shifted something within Payton. It had brought back the importance of her mother's words—the truth of them.

Payton followed the girl into the adjoining sitting room. A table had been set up by a footman with the meal atop. She watched in stunned silence as Joy bounced to her brother's side and gave him a loud kiss on the cheek.

"Yuck!" he exclaimed, wiping the offending spot. "I do not want to think about where your lips have been."

"I kissed a horse's rump," Joy teased. "A mangy horse's behind."

Payton covered her mouth to hide her smile and stifled a chuckle. Odd that such a ruckus would have irritated her before, but now she saw the endearing connection between the pair. It was the same kinship she shared with her own siblings.

"Miss Samuels," Abram whined. "Make her stop."

She swallowed, morphing her face into an impassive stare. "Joy," she scolded, her tone rising a notch to betray her mirth. "Apologize to your brother and sit down."

Joy plopped down into her seat, her elbows landing on the small, circular table with a thud. "Sorry you are more sensitive than Auntie Flora."

"That's not an apo—"

"Joy, that is quite enough," Payton warned, taking her own seat. "And, Abram, it would behoove you to tamp down your gullible side, or you will surely be taken for every shilling you have."

"I am not gullible." Abram crossed his arms with a huff and slunk down in his chair.

"Elbows off the table," Payton said in Joy's direction, mildly surprised when the girl complied. "And you should sit up straight, Abram, or you'll end up with a crooked back by the time you are my age."

"I don't plan to live past forty," he scoffed.

"Forty?" Payton said, allowing her laughter to fill the room. "How old do you think I am?"

"With how dour you are, certainly as old as Father."

Payton turned to look at Joy, who giggled at her wide-eyed expression.

"What of you?" Payton asked. "Do you think me decrepit, too?"

The girl's brow furrowed, and her smile vanished as she bit her bottom lip in thought. "At least fifteen," she announced, obviously pleased with her guess as she grabbed a hunk of cheese and popped it into her mouth.

"Well, I can tell you that neither your father nor I are close to our fortieth year," Payton declared. "However, I am a bit older than fifteen."

"Told you." Abram poked Joy in the side.

"Why on earth would the pair of you be discussing my age?" Payton asked, turning her attention to the display of cheese, bread, and cold pheasant, making light of her question. "If you spent more time at your arithmetic, Abram, you'd be moving on to your next-level coursework."

"Can we go to Pall Mall and see Xavier's Traveling Menagerie?"

The question came from Joy, throwing Payton off their original topic. The child's expectant yet hesitant smile had Payton longing not to disappoint her. In her time at Ashford Hall, she'd never taken the children farther than the townhouse garden.

"Yes, Miss Samuels." Abram bobbed in his chair, the most excited she'd ever seen him. "Can we go? I am certain Father will give us the two shillings each for the show. Can you believe they have a real bear…and a monkey?"

She glanced between the pair, their matching green eyes staring up at her in anticipation. Two days prior, they were playing horrid jests on her; and today, they wanted her to take them gallivanting about London. Was it a ploy to be out of the townhouse where they could escape her watch and cause the baron to dismiss her? If she were honest, she did think the children spent far too much time cooped up in their drafty home, and Payton was blessed enough to have her day off each week where she could return to Craven House and go about her business. Joy and Abram didn't have that privilege. Even the baron tended to remain locked away at Ashford Hall most days.

"I…and the pair of you…out alone?" Payton's skeptical tone had the smiles falling from both children's faces.

"Not alone," Abram grunted, sounding far too much like his father. "We will have our driver. And a footman. Father can not deny us. You will tell him it has to do with our lessons."

The boy smiled triumphantly as if he'd secured the answer to all the world's problems.

Joy gasped. "Mayhap Father will come *with* us."

She clapped her hands as she bounced in her seat, nearly knocking her plate to the floor.

"Your father is a very busy man," Payton hedged. There was no sense misleading the pair. The baron would never accompany them on an outing to see a traveling menagerie, no matter how many bears and monkeys the show boasted. The man couldn't even be bothered to dine with his children, let alone be seen in public with them. "I don't think—"

"Please," the pair whined in perfect unison.

Payton glanced between their pleading stares. "Well, your father has not been particularly happy with the trio of us of late."

"We are sorry we ruined your gown," Joy moaned.

"And put the ants in your bed," Abram continued.

"Ants in my bed?" Payton set her fork aside, suddenly itching at her scalp. "When did you put ants in my bed?"

Joy waved her hand at the question. "Oh, ages ago. I am sure they are all gone—"

"—or dead."

"—by now," Joy finished with a giggle.

Payton wanted to ask who in their right mind puts ants in someone's bed; however, she'd done far worse to gall her older siblings. Not that she planned to share any of that with the children.

"Mayhap I can have a word with your father tomorrow or the next day," Payton promised. What would she tell them if the baron said no? In her younger years, she would have gone anyways, consequences be damned. Unfortunately, she didn't possess the funds to take the children, nor the transportation needed. They could signal a hack, but again, where would she find the money required to pay for the conveyance or the entry fees. But it was only a brisk twenty-minute walk to Pall Mall. "Yes, I will do my best to speak with him; however, if we are to be allowed out of the townhouse, the pair of you must promise to be on your best behavior from this moment until we return."

Abram poked Joy again, and the pair shared a

look, an unspoken message. It was similar to the conversations Sam and Jude had growing up, never exchanging a word but communicating everything through a simple glance nonetheless. A pang of jealousy hit her, but Payton refused to entertain the feeling. She was no longer a child, nor should she be privy to whatever silent conversation the siblings were entrenched in.

"May I please be excused?" Abram asked.

Payton's brow rose at the question. "But you have yet to finish your meal."

He glanced back at Joy before continuing, "I have something I need to tend to immediately."

"Very well, but do hurry back," Payton said, waving the boy off. "We will start our afternoon lessons in ten minutes."

"Would it be all right if I go with him?" The apprehension in the girl's voice was unmistakable, and Payton suddenly faced the hopeless, hurt child from the night before.

"Of course. Go ahead," Payton murmured. "I suppose it will be up to me to finish all this wonderful food Cook prepared for us."

The pair slid from their chairs with uneasy smiles and fled the room, their voices making their way back to Payton.

"…I told you the flour wasn't a stellar idea."

"How was I to know she'd agree to speak with Father so readily," Joy retorted before the door slammed behind them.

Payton focused her attention on the meal spread before her, determined not to dwell on what exactly the pair had concocted with the flour. They'd turned a corner, the trio of them, a new understanding recognized between them. Perhaps continuing on at Ashford Hall would not be as dire as she'd anticipated, at least for the time being. Nothing was forever—and the future was ever-changing. Deciding to remain here, with Joy and Abram, was not entirely forsaking her chosen path, only a slight detour.

And gaining another private moment with the baron didn't seem as displeasing as before either. She'd noticed—seen with her own eyes—a side of the man not many people were privy to, at least not any in his household.

However, when next they met, would he be the man from the previous night? Or the withdrawn, forlorn lord she'd witnessed since her arrival in his home?

Payton wondered if sharing her past with him would bring about the same change she was noticing in Joy.

Her truth for his.

CHAPTER 11

DAMON STARED INTO the blazing hearth, the crackle from the burning log the only sound disrupting the peace of his study. With all his business handled for the day, there was nothing else to fill his time until Mrs. Brown brought him his dinner.

The quiet was nearly deafening.

No shrieks from above. No slamming doors. No bickering.

He hadn't heard a single footfall besides that of the servants going about their chores.

An entire day without incident. It had seemed inconceivable only a day before.

The muscles in his neck hadn't eased, though. He was not fool enough to believe the tranquility of his home could last more than another few hours.

He'd passed by the schoolroom during the afternoon to find Joy and Abram busy at their studies, heads lowered while his daughter scribbled on some paper and Abram read a large tome. Certainly, the book was too advanced for his son. Hesitant to disrupt them, Damon had moved on and returned to his study…where he now sat.

Odd that only an hour before, he'd even wondered if Flora would be coming for a visit soon.

His boredom due to his self-imposed reclusive lifestyle had reached a new level. He'd spent years hiding in this very room, and now he longed for a distraction from his solitude.

Five long days until the next gambling evening. It seemed a lifetime away.

And even the idea of that gave him no thrill.

Damon sighed, glancing at the sideboard where his tumbler lay empty. Not even the prospect of getting thoroughly drunk held any appeal.

Why could his children not come running down the stairs, yelling at one another? Or perhaps switch Cook's sugar for salt? Or fill Mr. Brown's pantry with stable cats. Better yet, ruin another of Miss Samuels' gowns.

The image of his children's governess standing before him, red with indignation, filled his thoughts, followed quickly by the sight of her sitting on Sarah's favored lounge. Damon shook his head. He wouldn't allow himself to think of Miss Samuels at the same time as Sarah. They were completely different women, from two opposite stations in life. One was the mother of his children, while the other…

Damon clamped his eyes shut as the unfamiliar lullaby echoed in his head.

The damned governess had given him a gift he didn't deserve. She'd soothed Joy's pain in a way he never could. A way he never imagined possible. He'd settled her gaming debt with the duke, but it was Damon who owed *her*. He'd been a fool to think he'd paid off Catherton to keep the man from spreading gossip about his gambling parties. That hadn't been the reason at all.

He'd done it to repay the governess's kindness.

Though she'd never know he did it, or his motives behind the deed.

She'd given Joy comfort from her pain, loss, and

grief.

Damon had been swallowed whole by his own despair. He would never be the same man who'd cared for his wife and children again. That part of him had left with Sarah. Any hope for healing for Joy and Abram would come from another…Miss Samuels. She would be the key to their moving beyond their suffering even if Damon never found his way out.

A future untainted by his past was unimaginable.

What would life have been like had fate not dealt him such a cruel blow?

He pushed from his seat and strode to the sideboard, pouring himself another tumbler of scotch. It was not worth even pondering life without the massive hole that ate at him every single day. He desperately wanted to heal, but where and how to begin was beyond his comprehension.

But his children… Despite Miss Samuels' flaws, maybe she could make them whole again. They deserved more than Damon could ever give them. But what did that mean for him, having the governess close? Was it possible to heal his children but also keep far from Miss Samuels? Perhaps if Abram and Joy had time away from him, they would flourish. Flora had been pressuring him to send the pair to boarding school, but up until this moment, he'd thought he hesitated because he wanted to keep the siblings together for as long as time allowed.

Now, he realized that he kept them at Ashford Hall for not only that reason but also so *he* wasn't alone. They were held down by the loss of their mother, as was Damon. Without his children close, he would suffer alone.

Swirling his glass, Damon focused on the smooth, heavy feel of the tumbler clenched in his fisted hand. He'd taken to drinking often since Sarah's death. So much so, even the stiffest liquor failed to burn as it made its way down his throat and into his stomach now.

He set down the drink and turned away from it. No matter how many tumblers of scotch, gin, or absinthe he imbibed, it would never mend the fracture within him. It would never fill the void that consumed him. It would never bring a sense of life back to his existence.

Sarah was forever gone, and he'd diminished her memory by allowing a stranger to offer their children the solace that should have come from their father.

His head fell into his hands, and he rubbed at his eyes, hoping to lessen the ache that persisted behind them. How long had it been since he'd been afforded a single night of uninterrupted slumber?

Perhaps he should inform his butler that he would not be eating his evening meal and retire to his room early. A long night's sleep—even a fitful one—would see his mood improved by morning.

Damon pulled at this cravat until it hung untied around his neck and unclasped the buttons of his shirt at his throat. Breathing in deeply, he pushed the air from his lungs. If only it were so simple to expel all his worries.

A knock sounded on the door.

Likely Mrs. Brown with his evening meal. Though he wasn't hungry, he'd eat whatever was brought or risk injuring the Ashford cook's—Miss Eleanor's—feelings when his plate returned to the kitchens untouched. In recent days, he'd felt he disappointed everyone around him—his children, his sister, the governess, and his servants.

"Enter." He glanced in the mirror on the wall close to the hearth. The darkened circles under his eyes were far more prominent than they'd been that very morning. His linen shirt was no longer pressed but wrinkled from sitting all day. And now his cravat hung limply at this throat, his shirt buttons undone, exposing his neck. "Please, leave my meal on my desk."

He couldn't bear to turn and face his housekeeper. What must his servants think of their erratic, reclusive lord after all these years?

"Lord Ashford?" Miss Samuels whispered. "I thought I might have a word with you."

He rubbed his forehead. "Miss Samuels—"

"I can return another time if you are otherwise occupied."

When he remained quiet, the creak of the closing door sounded at this back. "Wait," he called. Despite his mood, the governess hadn't done anything to deserve his dark demeanor. "Come in. I have a few minutes before my evening meal arrives."

He pivoted slowly as she eased into the room, silently closing the door behind her. Her shoulders tensed before she exhaled and faced him.

Something was different about her, far more than the night before. He was used to her irritation, annoyance, and anger. Last night, he'd glimpsed a rare moment of calm conversation with her. Now, she appeared deep in thought. Had she come to give her notice and vacate her position at Ashford Hall? Perhaps she'd come to confess her suspicious activities and beg for the funds to repay the duke.

Damon was prepared to deny both. His children needed a governess—specifically Miss Samuels—and she was no longer indebted to Catherton.

He gestured to the seat he'd been slumped in the last several hours. Having a coherent conversation with Miss Samuels sitting on the lounge would be impossible. He'd need to keep his wits about him if he thought to dissuade her from leaving his employ.

Miss Samuels moved across the room on silent feet and lowered herself into his chair. Her eyes widened before her lips pressed into a firm line.

He couldn't help but wonder if the seat was still warm, if the soft cushion molded to her back as it did his, if the chair gave her the sense of security he'd found while in it. Yet that was something that marveled him about her; she appeared secure and confident in all she did, whether in the schoolroom or in his study. Damon envied her that above all else.

She stared down at her hands, folded on her peach-colored skirts. Even with her eyes cast toward her lap, her elegant neck was visible, swathed in pale, creamy skin seemingly untouched by the rays of the sun.

Her hesitation had Damon convinced he could change her mind if she meant to resign her position.

"The children have been quiet today," he mused. "I do hope they are not giving you any more trouble."

She gave a slight shake of her head. "No, my lord."

He took the chair next to her, sinking into the plush, brocade back. "When I stopped by the schoolroom this afternoon—"

"You came by the schoolroom?" Her tone was suspicious, and her blue glare snapped to meet his. "I mean…"

He held up his hand with a chuckle. "This is my house, and occasionally I do go so far as to leave my study."

Damon could not understand where his light jest came from but relished the moment nonetheless.

Her head dipped forward, hiding her grin. With her otherwise occupied, Damon took the time to look at the woman…truly *see* her. Though he'd had the opportunity the previous night, his reason for assessing her had been different. That was before the kindness she'd shown his children, and before she'd spoken of her own family. He longed to know more but did not want to betray his eavesdropping. Perhaps with the correct questions, they'd arrive at the subject he wanted to hear more about. Still, a large part of him hated that he'd learned anything about her at all. He did not miss any of the other governesses for the simple fact that he hadn't taken any time to get to know anything about them beyond their qualifications.

Yet everything was different with Miss Samuels. She was everything his children needed, but her flaws were damning in the extreme. A gambler, a thief, and a liar. Those were not the traits of a woman he should want around his children.

But last night, in those brief moments of comfort, *she* had been everything Joy needed. No matter what had transpired with Catherton, Damon could not help but look past Miss Samuels' indiscretions. Perhaps if they had the opportunity to become more familiar with one another, he would discover the reasons behind her actions.

"In all seriousness, though, I happened to be walking past and glanced in, nothing more." He returned his stare to the hearth, begging his body to relax. "You are good with the children. Do you have younger siblings at home?"

"No, my brother and sisters are all older," she confided without trepidation. "Though I am experienced with children and tutoring if that concerns you."

He wanted to say outright she shouldn't fear losing her position, that she actually held the upper hand because, no doubt, he needed her far more than she needed her place at Ashford Hall.

Miss Samuels' back was rigidly straight, despite the voluptuous cushions, and a single long, dark curl fell over her shoulder. Its glossy texture reminded him of silken bolts of fabric, laid out to view at a modiste's shop. Would it be smooth to the touch?

If Damon had learned anything since Miss Samuels' arrival in his home, it was that things were not always as they seemed. Despite his attempts to the contrary, many things could still surprise him. And not all surprises were bad.

He asked no other questions, just waited. The governess had come to speak with him, and he feared she'd come to tell him she was leaving. It would be his duty then to convince her why she should remain at Ashford Hall.

It was not difficult to note that something was at war within her.

"The children would enjoy the opportunity to see the traveling menagerie at Pall Mall tomorrow." The words burst from her so quickly, Damon needed to listen closely to understand them all. "We can walk. Or, if you'd prefer, we can take the carriage and a footman for protection. The fee is two shillings apiece, which is exorbitant; however, I think it important the children explore areas outside of Ashford Hall…at least every once in a while."

The speech ended with a deep inhale as she attempted to catch her breath.

It wasn't what he'd expected at all—and in no way a bad surprise.

When he remained silent, she continued, "Pall Mall is safe enough. My siblings and I have visited the area on many occasions. The children have promised to behave and heed my rules. The weather is mild for this time of year, and there is no fear of them catching a cold or being caught in the rain. *The Post* declares no rain for the next three days, actually. If we leave directly after lunch, we will return in time for our evening meal."

Damon smiled, a genuine, teeth-bearing grin at her methods of persuasion. "You have certainly researched the excursion, Miss Samuels."

She gripped the arms of her chair, and her breathing hitched. "It is very important to them, and they pleaded with me to seek your approval."

"Well, there is no need to fret, you have my approval…even if it were to rain tomorrow."

Her mouth fell open. "Wait, you mean we can go see the menagerie?"

"If it is important enough for my children to plead for you to ask my permission, I cannot find any reason to deny them—or you."

She leapt from her seat. "That is wonderful, my lord. I will hurry and tell them the good news. They should be waiting for me in the dining hall."

"Mayhap I will join them," Damon replied before he thought better of it. "I can give them the good news and solicit their agreement to act accordingly."

Her head tilted to one side, and her lips pursed. If he hadn't caught the look firsthand, he never would have believed his decision to dine with his children and their governess could incite such confusion.

"Unless you think it best I dine here," he said, gesturing to his desk. Miss Samuels' surprise had him all the more determined to accompany her to the dining hall, yet he also needed to hear her say that she wanted him to dine with them. It was ludicrous; however, Damon could not stop himself from prodding. Since when had he needed confirmation that his presence was wanted?

"I understand—"

"No, no. Of course, you should eat with the children." She smiled, her confliction disappearing. "I will let them know to expect you and find my meal in the kitchen."

"You do not eat with them?" he asked.

Surely, there was no rule against a governess

breaking her fast with her young charges.

"Yes. Of course, I do. However…" her words trailed off as she searched for what to say. "I thought perhaps you'd enjoy some privacy—just the three of you."

"Come now, Miss Samuels. You went through all the worry and trouble to ask me about the excursion. You shall dine with us and be there for the good news." Why was he so hell-bent on keeping the woman in his sights? Perhaps if she saw him making an effort with Joy and Abram, even something as small as sharing a meal, she would know he appreciated her presence, as did his children.

CHAPTER 12

THE ROOM WARMED to a stifling degree around Payton, and she blinked several times to make sure she saw things for what they were. She would have pinched herself if she'd been alone, but she was not.

Had she fallen into a dream, her mind finding it comical to play tricks on her?

Lord Ashford, neckcloth hanging untied around his neck and the buttons undone at his throat, stood before her—his arm out.

Waiting.

Waiting to escort her, Payton Samuels, to the dining hall.

She looked between his outstretched arm and his smiling face. Had she ever seen the baron smile before? The simple change transformed him from the detached, dour lord into a man ten years younger. His shoulders were straighter, and his eyes sparkled. Was it mischief they held?

The look was all too familiar as it mirrored his children's sly glances when they were causing trouble.

"Shall we?" he asked. "If we do not hurry, I fear they will eat everything before we arrive."

After nearly five weeks in the baron's employ, Payton had never witnessed Lord Ashford in any state except vexation and annoyance—besides their brief reprieve in his study.

She placed her fingers at the crook of his elbow, just below his rolled-up sleeve. The warmth of his skin heated her hand through her white glove, and her fingers tensed. For a man who rarely left his study, muscles corded his forearm.

Payton tilted her chin up, her reply on the tip of her tongue. "You have a dusting of freckles across the bridge of your nose."

Instantly, she longed for the floor to open beneath her and swallow her whole.

Embarrassment flamed within her, making her already heated skin boil.

The baron brought his free hand to his nose. "Yes. Yes, I do."

How had she never noticed the freckles before? They matched the light brown hue of his hair exactly.

"The children do not have any freckles."

"I suppose it would not be fair if they inherited my eyes *and* my freckles."

"My apologies, my lord." Payton lowered her gaze. No longer looking into his eyes, she was now focused on his chest—another mistake. Without his coat, the material pulled tight across his pectorals, giving her a hint of what lay beneath his shirt. Her cheeks flushed as images of his bare, muscled chest sprang to her mind. "I think you are correct. If we do not hurry, Joy and Abram will start without us."

Payton kept her stare trained on the floor as they made their way from the study to the dining hall, her skirts brushing against the baron's leg with each step. While she was taller than the average woman, Lord Ashford still stood a head above her. She risked a glance up at him. His angular jaw tightened, and the muscles along his neck twitched.

Perspiration beaded on his forehead, betraying

the confident tilt of his chin.

He was nervous. But why?

Laughter rang out as they entered the dining hall. The lighthearted sound went silent immediately as both children turned to face them as they made their way to the table. Joy's wide-eyed stare traveled back and forth between her and the baron, while Abram's expression had turned solemn.

"Father?" Joy's tiny voice quivered.

A footman stepped forward and pulled Payton's chair out for her to sit, and another hurried into the room with a place setting for Lord Ashford.

Abram shifted in his seat when the baron took his place at the head of the table—his children at his left, and Payton on his right. Table etiquette wasn't a topic she'd explored with the children as of yet; however, the place she sat was typically reserved for the lady of the house. She glanced at the chair next to her, one farther away from the baron, and debated switching seats.

"Are you dining with us?" Abram asked.

Lord Ashford cleared his throat, his smile thin with unease. "Yes, I thought it would be a nice change."

The children gaped at her from across the table, and she merely shrugged. She could no more explain their father's change in behavior than predict when the first snows would fall come winter. As if sensing their father's unease, both children sat quietly as a footman delivered a steaming tureen of soup, followed by roasted pheasant with hearty vegetables, and finally, fragrant, spiced pudding.

Everyone ate in silence with only a murmured "thank you" here and there in appreciation of the servants' work.

Payton barely touched each course as she waited for the baron to make his announcement.

Instead, he focused on his plate, finishing each course with gusto only rivaled by Abram.

Joy and Abram glanced in their father's direction as if they could not believe their eyes. How long had it been since the baron had shared a meal with his children? She'd always assumed they dined together on her day off each week. It was apparent how wrong she'd been.

Thinking back to her own youth, Payton remembered every morning and evening meal taken with her mother and all her siblings. They spoke of their days, laughed at Garrett's outlandish jests, and commonly discussed much more serious topics when the need arose. After her mother's death, while they still ate together regularly, it was not every day as her brother and sisters forged their own paths in life. Garrett moved to the Albany, while Marce was often too busy to join Payton and the twins.

The baron's children did not have such fond memories to hold close.

"Abram," Payton said, breaking the silence in her eagerness to spark their conversation. "Why don't you tell your father about the book you've been reading."

The boy's fork clinked against his plate, and he looked at his father.

"I—I—it is an analysis of the Ottoman wars, starting with their strike against the weakened Byzantine Empire." Abram paused, glancing at Payton. With her nod of encouragement, he continued. "I've only made it as far as the wars in Venice, but I cannot stop myself from moving ahead to read about the conquest of Cyrus."

It was a subject the father and son should bond over, yet Payton doubted the baron knew the depth of Abram's interest in the subject.

"I am reading a picture book about ponies," Joy chimed in, not to be outdone or overshadowed by talks of wars and ancient battles. "I've decided that when I am older, I am going to have an entire stable full of ponies—white ones, grey ones, and even midnight-black ones."

Their father smiled, and as quickly as that, the tension fled the room.

"So many ponies? How will you remember all their names? And who will feed all those horses?" the baron asked with mock seriousness.

"They are ponies, Father. Ponies," she said the word slowly. "And I shall care for them myself. I am going to be a grand opera singer. I will make more money than Prinny himself and hire a stable master who will assist me."

"A singer and a pony collector?" Payton marveled aloud. "I had no idea you'd set your cap on two such prestigious aspirations."

The girl had never so much as mentioned a love for ponies or singing since Payton had been at Ashford Hall.

"My mother was a grand singer," Joy continued, a measure of pride in her voice. "Wasn't she, Father?"

The trio turned to the baron, who trained his gaze toward the far end of the table, drawing deep, measured breaths. She knew Lady Ashford's death affected not only the children but also the baron; however, she'd never been confronted with the reality of it all—and neither had the baron, it appeared.

"I am certain she had the voice of an angel," Payton replied, taking the children's attention off their father. Lord Ashford appeared frozen in his seat, his body present but his thoughts somewhere far away—and likely long ago.

"She sang me to sleep every night."

"You can't remember that," Abram cut in. "You were just a babe, still in nappies."

Joy's tiny face reddened. "I do so remember. Tell

him, Father, Mother sang to me all the time."

Payton held her breath when the baron remained silent, his eyes unfocused. She wasn't sure that she nor the children would be happy to see him revert to his distant, dour mood.

As if a candle had been lit, the baron turned to his children, his smile returning, though a bit more forced than before. "Yes, Joy, your mother sang to you often, but that was the only time I can remember her singing."

"She didn't sing to me?" Abram asked, his expression clouding.

"No." The baron shook his head. "You would wail so loudly when she sang. To you, my son, your mother read. Books filled with adventure—pirates, explorers, and faraway places."

"That must be why I love stories about battles," the boy mused.

"I think it is," his father replied.

The baron's gaze met Payton's, and they both knew it was exactly what the boy needed to hear. Something that could form a connection with Abram's lost mother. Lord Ashford's interest in the same subjects mattered not a whit in the moment, only his remembrance of Sarah.

When the last plates were removed, both children groaned with satisfaction as the baron pushed back his chair as if, with the meal done, he was ready to return to his secluded study.

However, he didn't move toward the door but stared down at his two fair-haired children, a gleam in his eye.

"I have an announcement." He punctuated the word *announcement* with a clap of his hands.

"An announcement?" Joy squealed with delight, bouncing in her seat. So quickly, the child forgot the years of avoidance and distance at the mere mention of something special.

"Yes." He leaned slightly forward and held his arm out wide. "We are going to see the traveling menagerie at Pall Mall tomorrow."

"We?" Payton exhaled. Her stomach fluttered with—anticipation? Unease? Confusion?

Perhaps all three…

The baron turned to her, his smile broad as he nodded. "My dear sister has been berating me of late about my cloistered lifestyle. I think an adventure will be grand for us all."

If Payton had been taken aback by the degree of the baron's announcement, the children were outright stunned—and seemingly skeptical—as they both froze in their seats, their excitement fleeing. A meal with their father was one thing, but an entire afternoon in his company?

Payton had thought about more time with Lord Ashford, but an afternoon outside the townhouse was far more than she'd expected.

She could not show her surprise and risk adding to the children's hesitancy around their father. That would benefit no one. If the baron insisted on accompanying them to Pall Mall, then she would do her best to appear enthusiastic.

She smiled. "Isn't that a wonderful announcement?"

Joy nibbled at her bottom lip. "You mean to spend the entire day with us?"

The girl's tone made it clear that the baron had never spent an entire day in his children's company, at least not within their memory.

The baron's eyes narrowed, and the tenseness returned to his shoulders. "Most certainly."

"It has been some years since we've enjoyed an outing together." Lord Ashford's voice was strained, as if he heard the meaning behind Joy's question, as well. "The excursion will be fun. Your governess has explained how much you both want to go."

Joy and Abram shared a familiar, silent glance, neither looking confident in their father's use of the word *fun.*

"Very well." Abram shrugged, his indifference mirroring his father's nature.

"Wonderful." Payton infused as much joy as she could into the single word. "Now that everything is settled, I think the children should find their beds and get a good night's rest before tomorrow."

Abram and Joy slid from their chairs.

"Say goodnight." Payton gestured toward their father, and the pair obediently mumbled goodnight before starting for the door. "Have a pleasant slumber, my lord. Thank you for agreeing to the excursion."

He glanced over Payton's shoulder, likely watching the children depart. "They don't want me to come, do they?" he mumbled low enough to keep the children from hearing.

It had been what she was thinking, but she'd never thought to verbalize it, especially to the baron. "I think they are anxious, Lord Ashford." She paused, knowing if she chose the wrong words, it would hurt the baron. Or worse, return the distance between him and the children. Payton thought back to the way Joy had asked why her father didn't love her or her brother. It had broken her heart to hear the uncertainty in the child's voice. "I think they are just hesitant. You are not accustomed to having them underfoot, and neither are they overly familiar with you."

He grimaced and averted his stare. She'd hurt him. Perhaps there was no other way to put into words Joy's and Abram's adverse reaction to the news of him accompanying them on their outing.

"We will depart at eleven o'clock. Sharp." His gruff tone did nothing to hide his disappointment. "I will have the carriage ready and a meal prepared. Do you think they would enjoy a picnic in St. James's Park?"

"I think they would enjoy that very much, my lord."

He rubbed the back of his neck. "It is that…"

"What?" The question came on a breathless whisper, and for a moment, Payton longed to be back in the baron's study without the listening ears of servants.

"I fear that no matter what I do, this outing will cause Joy and Abram disappointment." His head lowered as he fell silent.

"How so?"

Lord Ashford appeared resigned to some unknown fact. "Because what if I speak out of turn? What if the day is marvelous, but when we return home, I…?"

When his words trailed off, unfinished and looming in the space between them, she prodded, "You what, my lord?"

He ran his hand through his hair, causing it to fall haphazardly over one eye. "It matters naught."

"Can I ask you a question, my lord?" Gaining the baron's approval before she made a disparaging comment was unfair, but this moment was a long time coming. She'd noted the distance that separated him from his children the first day she arrived at Ashford Hall. When he nodded, she said, "Why did you offer to accompany us tomorrow? After all this time, why now?"

He showed his palms with a shrug. "They were happy. I haven't seen them excited about anything in a long while unless they are up to some troublesome behavior. Is it wrong for me to want to be a part of that, even when I know I have no right, and they are better off without me close?"

Payton couldn't understand how the baron had come to believe that his children would fare better without him. They had no mother...only Lord Ashford. Had her presence at the townhouse over the last month taken away the baron's chance to deepen his connection with Joy and Abram?

"Do forget I mentioned anything," the baron sighed. "I bid you goodnight, Miss Samuels."

Without a backwards glance, he strode from the dining hall. She remained frozen in place as his heavy footfalls faded.

Perhaps it was Payton who should forego the outing to Pall Mall on the morrow. If she were not as readily available, would he take more notice of his children? If she left him no option, would he build his relationship with Joy and Abram?

There were too many questions to have them all answered so simply.

However, there was one thing she was not questioning: Payton hadn't been overly enthusiastic about the outing until Lord Ashford announced that he'd be joining them. It might be a selfish decision, but Payton now looked forward to witnessing the baron outside of Ashford Hall. Without his study to seek refuge in, and without his mask to hide behind, she—and the children—would likely encounter an entirely different man.

The baron could not possibly keep up his stoic demeanor with both of his children clamoring for his attention at Pall Mall. And there was little chance that Joy and Abram would *not* be demanding their father's much-needed notice.

She wondered if any of them would recognize the baron outside the townhouse.

Surely, there was more to Lord Ashford than

Payton had seen in their short acquaintance. Was there a time when he had been a charming young lord? A dashing rogue? Mayhap even an enticing scoundrel?

CHAPTER 13

THE ROOM HAD become his prison.

It was his haven while holding all that haunted him. The more Damon retreated, the more he found himself isolated in a place that held so many memories for him. Some good. Some bad. Most heartbreaking.

The more he glimpsed how life could be free from his past, the more he knew that he needed to find a way to release himself, though the draw of his reclusive ways continued to tempt him.

It was more than just this room, it was the entire house. And yet, he remained. Forever fortifying himself in his own personal hell. The decorative trappings, the muted hues of blue and grey, and the books... Lord above, help him, all the bloody damned books.

Everything was a constant reminder of what he'd loved and lost.

Even his children.

He kept them close, yet he could barely hold himself together in their presence.

Escape. Damon needed to escape, though he suspected it would not grant him the freedom he frantically sought.

But where could he flee to? His country seat at Falconcrest? He'd journeyed there only once since Sarah's death, and he'd lasted a mere fortnight before the past drove him back to London. The house, the lands, the mere smells of the winter blossoms brought back that fateful day—and his failure.

Maybe Flora had been correct. Damon should send the children to boarding school. Allow them a normal upbringing far from their haunted father. They'd been so tiny when Sarah passed...why should they not have the chance to forget the pain and move on?

Because he was weak. He was broken.

And he greatly needed to keep his children close because they were all he had left of Sarah, even though the sight of them made the agony everlasting.

Damon stood before the hearth, begging its flames to leap from the logs and singe away his pain. Burn it from his very skin.

Closing his eyes, he allowed the heat to overwhelm him. To saturate his exposed flesh and heat the fabric of his trousers until the burn was nearly too much to bear.

This was what he craved, what he deserved.

His fingers tightened around the tumbler clenched in his hand, the throbbing in his head keeping rhythm with the ache in his knuckles. The glass was empty, had remained as such since he'd fled the dining hall and closed himself back in his study. At present, the sight of the bottle that had become his only companion over the years made his stomach turn.

He was so pitiful, he didn't have the nerve to drown himself in scotch and bring about a few hours of blissful reprieve. Instead, he'd chosen to wallow in the situation of his making. His sister—and his friends, when they still came around—had told him it wasn't his fault; yet Damon knew it was his impulsive nature that had taken him and Sarah away from Falconcrest in the Ashford carriage that night. Off on one of Damon's many larks—a late-night, winter sleigh ride through the snow to May's Brewery for a New Year's mead while Joy and Abram's nurse looked after them.

The horse stepping off the hidden ledge under the snow drift and injuring his leg hadn't been Damon's fault.

The damaged, unmovable sleigh stranded in the increasing snowfall hadn't been Damon's fault.

Their inability to find shelter from the coming storm hadn't been his fault.

Sarah and him, stranded during the frigid winter night out in the open hadn't been his fault.

Her following sickness hadn't been his fault.

But Damon knew it was all a lie. *Everything* had been his fault, especially every misfortune after Sarah's death.

He'd retreated from life, his children, and society.

Damon had convinced himself that his children would heal faster if they did not fear losing him. At some point, their hurt and anguish had festered into something far graver, and he'd failed to notice. Instead, he'd paraded a never-ending line of governesses before them. The women each left without fail, and every time, he'd blame his children or the inept servant…when the fault lay squarely on his shoulders.

That wasn't something he could change. It was too late.

Joy and Abram had been telling him—in the only way children knew how—that they were hurting, that they needed someone to step in and make everything right. He couldn't even make it right with himself, so how was he to help them?

Where he'd failed, Miss Samuels had stepped in, caring for his wayward children in a way that Damon couldn't.

Tomorrow…tomorrow he would be better. Try to be who his children needed him to be.

There had to be time to make things right for them. Sarah was gone, but they were not. If he tried, genuinely tried, he could fix his family. He loved his children—more than he could ever imagine. They could not go on without knowing they were loved, without him showing them his affection—even if he could not bring himself to speak the words.

Miss Samuels had shown him actions were sometimes more powerful than words.

For now, he needed to find his bed and pray that a few hours' sleep would diminish the ache in his head and relax the tension in his shoulders.

His back slumped as he set the empty glass on the table beside the lounge, careful to keep his eyes away from the familiar spot. He should have the piece of furniture removed, but even with it out of sight, the memories surrounding it would not disappear.

Ignoring them only made the images more painful when they broke through.

Damon left his study, exhaustion reaching every inch of his body as he made his way to the stairs.

"Good evening, miss," Mr. Brown's deep voice echoed from the foyer. "Going out?"

Damon was so close to making his escape up the stairs and the solitude of his private chambers. Instead, he halted, desperate to hear the woman's response.

"Yes, I shan't be overlong." The sound of rustling drew him closer until only the shadows of the darkened hall hid him from view as he watched the governess slip into her cloak, and the butler hand her a muff. She slipped her hands inside and waited for the servant to open the door. "I will let myself back in. There is no need to wait for my return."

He'd never before wondered how she spent her evenings or her days off. Before he'd caught her at his gaming tables, at least.

"I can summon the coach for you, or perhaps send a footman to hail a hackney?" Mr. Brown offered. His tone was untroubled without any hint of concern for the governess's well-being, as if the woman often left with little explanation. "Or is your carriage coming for you?"

Her carriage? Miss Samuels was a governess without the means for her own conveyance. She'd lost a healthy amount to the duke and slipped away without making good on the debt. How could she have a carriage? And if she did, how was he unaware of it?

"No, it is only a short walk." She smiled at the elderly servant, bringing a new light to the man's eyes. He imagined it was how Mr. Brown looked upon his own daughter. "I donned my wool stockings and sturdy boots"—she patted her cloak—"and I've brought my key. Do not fret over me."

"It is not my place to worry over you, Miss Samuels." With a stiff bow, the butler opened the front door. "However, my missus claims I sleep more soundly when all the household is accounted for."

The governess slid her hand from her muff and patted the aging butler's cheek. "I will be gone two hours, at most. Please, do not cause my absence to keep you awake, Mr. Brown."

She swept out the door with her chin held high, as regal as if she were the lady of the house.

The butler held the door open and watched her walk down the steps before closing the portal behind her.

"Mr. Brown." Damon stepped from the

shadows.

"My lord," the butler sputtered, adjusting his coat. "Can I assist you with something? Perhaps I can collect you a pot of tea before you retire?"

Damon ignored the servant's question. "Where is Miss Samuels going?"

"I do not presume to know, my lord." When Damon frowned, Mr. Brown glanced toward the front door and then back to him. "I can catch her and ask, if that is your wish."

Their agreement, as with every governess before her, left no questions about responsibilities. She was allotted one day off per week, and evenings were to be spent however she saw fit as long as the children were asleep, and she returned before sunrise. Neither Damon nor the butler had any right to question the governess's private comings and goings. There was a certain amount of freedom afforded to governesses that was not given to other servants.

"It appeared she was going for a walk," Damon mused, keeping a close watch on his butler. Did the man know more than he was sharing? There was not much the old butler missed, and it was quite possible the servant was well aware of Miss Samuels' penchant for gambling. "Mayhap a turn about the square will do me well. A spot of crisp, fresh air."

The butler shot Damon a narrowed glance as he collected Damon's greatcoat. "I cannot attest to anything on the matter, my lord. My old bones freeze with the winter weather. But do enjoy your…walk."

Damon pulled the limp cravat from his neck and handed it to the butler before fastening the buttons at this throat and donning his coat. It would have to do, or he'd risk losing Miss Samuels to the night if he dallied a moment longer.

"Very well, I will be off." Damon stood awkwardly, expecting the servant to question him further; instead, he nodded and opened the door.

Part of him hoped Mr. Brown would attempt to convince him to remain at Ashford Hall, tell him the weather was too unpredictable for an outing at this ungodly hour, or at the very least give him a reproachful glare.

But his trusted family servant would never lower himself to such behavior.

For once, Damon longed for a butler who overstepped his position.

He walked into the night, realizing that this was his first jaunt out of Ashford Hall in nearly a week. The cold air burned his lungs as he breathed deeply and pulled his coat tighter around himself to ward off the chill. There was little telling how far Miss Samuels planned to travel, or if she'd spoken the truth to Mr. Brown. She could easily make the short walk to Grosvenor Street, hail a hack, and disappear into the night.

Lamplight from the row of townhouses on either side of Saint George Street cast a hazy glow on the walk, making it easy to spot Miss Samuels walking briskly toward the main street. Her steps were sure, and she kept her eyes trained straight ahead as if she hadn't a care in the world. It was entirely possible that she departed his townhouse each evening and embarked on these suspect *walks* about the square every night. Merely strolling to and fro, no matter the time of day, was not the gravest sin one could commit.

Hanover Square was as safe a neighborhood as to be found in London proper; however, that did not mean that cutpurses and thieves did not lurk in the passageways, waiting for an unsuspecting victim to happen down their walk.

Did the woman not possess even an ounce of self-preservation? And why hadn't his butler insisted that a footman accompany her?

Damon waited until she reached the sixth townhouse down from his before he began his pursuit, hoping the noise from Grosvenor Street would be loud enough to drown out the ring of his boot steps on the walkway.

His apprehension lessened when she reached the main street and didn't hail a hack but instead turned right and continued on down Grosvenor Street on foot. When Damon reached the corner, he paused as she crossed the street at the next intersection and disappeared between a row of houses on Mill Street.

Where in the bloody hell was she going at this time of night?

As the hour grew later, so would the frigid London cold settle across the town, burrowing into every alley and thoroughfare. She'd been in his employ only a short time, did she know her way about the area? Would she grow lost or be targeted by a vagabond up to no good?

He darted down Grosvenor and hurried between two slow-moving carts to the corner of Mill Street, where he lost sight of her. Pushing up against the stone facade of the corner house, he crept along in the darkness, making sure to keep his steps light.

As much as he kept to the shadows, the governess walked in the little light that could be found from the street lamps and uncovered windows to her right—no hiding, no sulking, no fear.

Damon could never imagine allowing Joy to traverse the dangerous London streets, no matter her age. The risk, even in Mayfair, was too great—the late hour notwithstanding.

Miss Samuels slowed her pace, forcing Damon to crouch low to remain unseen.

Glancing up at a townhouse, she pulled something from her pocket and held it close in the dim lighting before returning it to her cloak and walking up the two steps. Before she even had a chance to knock, the door opened, casting a bright light over the governess and onto the walk below. Whoever resided inside had been expecting her.

"A simple walk," Damon scoffed.

Common sense told him to turn around and return to Ashford Hall.

His ineptness at listening to his own good sense had Damon moving swiftly down the walk to stand before the townhouse at 10 Mill Street. It was nothing as grand as the townhouses in Hanover Square or Grosvenor Square, with no overhang and only an unlit sconce above the single door. The rough stone wall was worn from years of London drizzle, marred by the soot from the tall chimneys dotting the tops of every home. All in all, this townhouse was no different than the ones that flanked it on both sides.

A voice cleared behind him. "Pardon, my lord."

Damon pivoted to catch an elderly gentleman approaching on foot from behind him, his smile wide and his footfalls matching the strike of his cane against the walk. When he stepped to the side, the man continued up the steps to 10 Mill Street and, once again, the door opened without the newest arrival knocking.

This time, Damon was afforded a quick glimpse inside as the footman paused to take the gentleman's coat. The interior was lit by a massive silver chandelier, the walls covered by rich, orange silk swaths trimmed in silver. A servant passed the open doorway, a platter held close to his chest. The newly arrived guest took a flute and moved farther into the townhouse.

Miss Samuels had already moved out of view, deeper into the dwelling.

Laughter and music floated out into the night

before the door swung shut.

Damon was left alone, in the cold of night.

He hadn't but a moment to wonder what his children's governess was doing at 10 Mill Street before an expensively adorned, enclosed coach halted at the curb. With two footmen at the rear, a driver high atop his perch, and four blazing lamps swinging at each corner, the conveyance's occupant was undoubtedly a lord of means. Damon's own unkempt, wrinkled attire was not only unsuitable for the chilly night but also made him appear the ruffian. He pulled the collar of his great cloak high to mask his lack of neckcloth and to hide his wrinkled linen shirt.

The driver remained on his perch as the footman at the coach's rear hopped to the ground, straightened his coat, and brushed the dust from his uniform before opening the carriage door.

A lady grasped the footman's outstretched hand as the servant assisted her to the walk.

"Flora?" Damon asked.

"Brother?" His sister's stare met his, and her face paled as if she were seeing a ghost—or, more accurately, as if he'd spotted her in a place she was not supposed to be. "What in heaven's name are you doing here?"

She looked him up and down, her stare settling on his bare neck.

"I was—am"—he swallowed, collecting his senses—"I thought a brisk walk would do me well before bed."

"It is several blocks to your townhouse." She couldn't disguise her suspicion.

"Yes, well, once I was out of Ashford Hall, I continued to walk. The evening air does wonders for my mind."

Flora's gaze traveled over Damon's shoulder to

the door of 10 Mill Street.

"Where is Wittenbottom?" Damon made a display of glancing toward his sister's waiting carriage. "I should say hello before I am on my way."

"He, um," she said, "he is having a meal at his club before meeting me later this evening."

Damon glanced over his shoulder to where the door stood ajar, waiting for Flora to enter. "I can accompany you inside," Damon offered.

"You hardly appear presentable," she retorted. "Besides, it is not necessary. I am only here for an hour or two, then I will be on my way to meet Wittenbottom."

Miss Samuels had said the same thing to his butler. That she should be gone for only an hour or two.

"Whose residence is this?" he asked. "Someone I know?"

Flora huffed, her patience with his questions expired. "Sir Galment hosts a few select…ladies…for evening entertainment. Music, lectures, and the like. Wittenbottom, as you know, is not the most educated man."

Educated, no.

Wealthy as a Prussian prince, yes.

"And the evening is for women only?" he prodded. A man had entered directly after Miss Samuels. He waited for Flora to deceive him and for a reason as to why his governess would attend such an affair, let alone who she secured an invitation from.

"Heavens, no," Flora laughed. "There are spirited debates and cultured conversations. Sir Galment invites several scholarly men to lead the discussions."

"Ladies attend such gatherings?"

"With zeal, I can assure you." She waved her hand as she said, "As a boon, Galment offers a spot of cards for those interested. I do not waste my time or funds at the gaming tables but find interest in the conversations to be had."

Gaming tables.

Damon should have suspected as much. However, what Miss Samuels chose to do during the hours she was not caring for his children should not concern him. If she were determined to set upon such a path, it was hers to take. Squandering her meager earnings at the card tables only involved him so much as it interfered with her duties as the Ashford governess. If he'd known her tendency to frequent the tables before his children grew attached to her, Damon would have relieved her of her position. But now, what option did he have but to overlook it?

"I must get inside, Damon." Flora stepped forward and pressed her lips to his cheek. "I will call on you and the children in a couple of days."

He was helpless to do anything but watch as his sister entered Galment's townhouse, and the door closed in her wake. He'd done his best to keep his position on the outskirts of those around him, and now Damon had the sense to realize that he'd achieved precisely what he set out to do. Any malcontent with his life was solely due to his choices. He worked tirelessly, pushing others away—and now, it appeared, he'd succeeded.

Slipping his hands into the warmth of his coat pockets, he stared up at the house before him. A home he would not enter. A place that did not want him.

Joy and Abram had one another.

Flora had society involvements and her husband.

And Miss Samuels had her secrets—not well-kept secrets, but secrets all the same.

PAYTON GLANCED DOWN at her cards with an amount of confidence she hadn't felt since her disastrous game with Catherton. Despite her steep loss at Lord Ashford's card table, this night, she was ahead. Winning one more sizeable pot would mean replacing nearly all the money she'd lost to the duke. With another couple of weeks of luck, she could collect the twenty pounds to repay Lord Catherton. Then, and only then, would she be able to consider her future plans once more.

Perhaps she could gain a position as a lady's companion. The responsibilities would surpass those expected of her by the baron, but if she chose her mistress wisely, there would be many nights spent enjoying house parties and entertainments.

With that came the opportunity for more elusive card games.

Sir Galment's nightly salon gatherings, while a successful enough place to find a rousing game of cards, did not put Payton in the company of London's elite lords. It was mostly a gathering of lonely wives who fancied themselves in need of spirited conversations and time away from their families.

Payton had become accustomed to the serene gatherings. No one bothered with her name—nor asked questions about her arrival and departure. She did not partake of the libations nor fall prey to the spats regarding governmental overreach or the romantic movement currently enthralling most poets. She stayed only long enough to win a few rounds and depart into the night without bringing notice to herself.

Her gown was simple, though refined. Her dark, mahogany hair was pinned tightly, not so much as a single curl breaking free. Payton kept her voice low and calm and avoided their host at all cost.

This evening's game was vingt-et-un—the most basic of card games that relied solely on Payton keeping track of the cards played and reading her opponents. A house full of ladies with endless funds and no ability to hide their enthusiasm at a winning hand meant Payton knew exactly when to hold and when to double down. This particular game only had her besting the dealer, a Galment servant who'd been charged with the task.

With a triumphant smile, Payton flipped her card, showing a twenty-one value between three cards. The dealer had held at eighteen.

Another twenty shillings added to her stacks.

It was time to depart.

After less than two hours, she'd managed to win over four pounds. She'd suspect the dealer was losing on purpose had it not been for their host's disapproving glances as Payton, as well as two other women, collected their coins.

Payton took in the room, reassured that no one paid her any mind. However, her stare settled on a matron across the card room. The woman's name eluded her; however, the resemblance was evident. Lord Ashford's sister stood in the far corner and spoke animatedly to an elderly, robust gentleman. As she flapped her hands, the man squinted and nodded vigorously.

How did Lord Ashford's sister know of Lord Galment's salon? While Lady Wittenbottom was wed to a lord, she did not seem the type to frequent either gaming parties nor intellectual gatherings. Payton had never encountered the lady at the baron's weekly gatherings or at Galment's townhouse previously, though Galment's parties were not a secret or exclusive in nature.

Would Lady Wittenbottom recognize Payton if they came face-to-face? Payton had seen the woman from afar during her infrequent visits to Ashford Hall. She could not risk being discovered by the baron's sister.

Deftly, Payton collected her winnings and slipped the notes, as well as the small stack of coins, into the pocket sewn into the exterior layer of her skirts. The many layers and undercoats hid the pocket adequately enough. Next, Payton stood, nodded to her host, and made her way to the foyer to collect her cloak and muff for the walk back to Ashford Hall.

When she left for the evening, she'd been focused only on escaping the baron and his children. With each day, she sensed the tie binding her to Ashford Hall growing. At first, she'd felt pity for the baron and his children, but as time passed, those feelings changed and evolved into something far more powerful. An unmistakable kinship to children who'd experienced a loss much like her own. No matter how fervently Joy and Abram—and even Payton—fought against the draw, it was still there. Despite their pranks and Payton's irritation. Even before she'd rocked Joy to sleep, reassuring her that the baron loved her, the change had begun.

And now, Lord Ashford was to accompany them on their outing the next day. If she had any sense, she'd claim ill and send the trio on without her; however, the baron would likely cancel the entire excursion, leaving Joy and Abram hurt and upset.

It would not be their father letting them down, but her.

The butler helped her slip into her waiting cloak and held her muff out to her.

"Good evening, my lady," he said as he opened the door for her to depart.

"Good evening to you, too." She didn't correct his use of the word *lady* before stepping into the night. The air had grown even colder than when she arrived. The sky overhead was devoid of clouds, allowing the moon to shine brightly as she started her return trip to Ashford Hall. Her skirts, heavy with her winnings, bounced against her thigh, but thankfully, the coins did not clink.

No carriages or pedestrians loitered in her path as she crossed Grosvenor Street and turned onto Saint George.

Few candles were lit in the townhouses bordering the street. The hour was late, and the lack of lighting didn't surprise Payton.

Keeping her head lowered, she quickened her pace—only four townhouses to go.

She slipped her hand from her warm muff and wrapped her fingers around the key in her cloak pocket.

Shuffling sounded behind Payton, and her feet faltered.

Was she being followed? Of all the nights she'd come and gone from the baron's home, never had she encountered any trouble. This street was one of the safest in all of London, far safer than her own home where it sat nestled on the fringes of a suitable neighborhood. With time, Craven House would not be considered situated in an area fit for polite society, while Saint George Street would only grow in respectability.

She couldn't dwell on that. The footfalls behind her echoed, breaking the silence of the hour. Whoever was pursuing her did not bother to keep their presence a secret. If the thug thought her an easy mark, he was gravely mistaken. If she, along with her dear childhood friend, Ellington, had learned anything, it was how to protect themselves when walking the streets of London.

Attaining the upper hand was vital. Throwing the lout off guard was a close second.

Thirdly…get away.

Payton knew the likelihood of remaining safe majorly diminished if the man gained a hold of her. She was tall, but her slender frame didn't hold as much muscle as a grown man.

Unfortunately, gaining the upper hand and remaining out of reach sometimes conflicted with one another. With the rapid movement behind her, there might not be the option to get away without a struggle.

Everything Garrett and Marce had taught her came to mind at once.

Upper hand. Keep him off guard. Run.

Simple enough, at least when you weren't in the middle of being accosted.

The blood rushed in her ears as her heart beat erratically. She fingered the key in her pocket, positioning the metal object to be used as a dagger of sorts.

It had been easy enough to learn to defend her person, but when an imminent threat lurked a few feet away, courage was difficult to muster with any amount of conviction.

Payton took a deep breath, sent a quick prayer to the heavens above—not that she deserved anyone's benevolence—and pulled the key from her pocket as she pivoted to face the man who pursued her.

"I am armed, sir," she yelled into the open air behind her. "Come out and state your business."

Upper hand gained. Whoever stalked was now aware Payton had spotted them.

When no one stepped into the lighted walkway, Payton retraced her steps until she heard breathing coming from up ahead. Whoever it was stood in the doorway to her right, sunken into the shadows, waiting.

"I can see you," she prodded, hoping to throw

the man off guard. "Come out before I raise the alarm for the night watchman."

She was deluding her pursuer. Certainly, the night watchman patrolled the area. However, Payton had never spotted the man during her nights out.

The man's heavy, labored breathing broke the silence of the night.

"I said, come out." When no one answered her call, Payton knew it was time to run. If she hurried, Payton would make it to the baron's townhouse before the man, but what if the key did not turn quickly? No, she would be caught and taken before she could open the door. Why had she insisted that Mr. Brown not wait up for her?

She watched, fist poised with her key for defense, as her pursuer stepped from the shadows into the dim light that barely lit the walkway.

Confusion coursed through her as her hand fell to her side. It was only then that the tremendous fright sent wave after wave of shivers through her. She could have been gravely harmed, taken, made to disappear without anyone the wiser, all because she'd not told anyone at Ashford Hall where she was going.

"Lord Ashford?" Payton resisted the urge to fling herself into his arms, her relief was so overwhelming. "What in the heavens are you doing out"—she forced the final words—"at this time of night?"

The baron, fully visible now, slipped his hands into the deep pockets of his coat while his stare settled somewhere below her eyes. "I saw you depart without a footman. It worried me—"

"And you followed me?" It was what she'd left her home to avoid. The constant watchfulness of her elder siblings, each thinking they knew what was best for her. At least at Craven House, they made their actions known. It was far more upsetting to realize the baron had been following her, keeping track of her whereabouts, without her notice. How closely had he kept watch on her since she'd joined his household? A chill ran down her spine, and she stopped herself from reaching up to pull her collar higher. "My lord, I do not need a caretaker."

He shuffled closer, his regret visible. "I did not mean to insinuate that; however, as a member of my household, I was justified in my concern for your safety."

Her relief quickly dissipated as her anger took over.

She clenched and unclenched her fists, and her skin heated despite the cold air.

"I am a grown woman," she snapped. "During the hours when I am not overseeing the children, I am free to come and go as I please. Was that not our agreement when I took the position in your household?"

He nodded, but his green eyes flared. What right did he have to be angry with her?

Never would she have left her home and taken a post as a governess, only to find the freedom she sought elusive once more.

"Mayhap we should return to the townhouse and have this discussion."

For the first time, Payton noticed the baron's breath in the frigid night at the same time her nosed ached with the cold.

"There is nothing to discuss, my lord. Yes, I am a servant in your household. However, that does not give you the right to question my whereabouts at every turn." She paused in an attempt to collect her thoughts, to express what truly angered her. "My duties for the day were done, the children are abed, and it was my understanding that I am free to do as I wish in the evenings."

He took the final step, coming to a halt before her, and she glanced up into his remorseful face. His cheeks were hollow, emphasizing the dark circles under his eyes as his gaze begged for her forgiveness. He was exhausted—barely standing, if she were to guess. She'd often noticed his disheveled appearance, even suspected nights of fitful slumber, but it appeared the man before her had not slept for a long, long time.

"I think it best we return to Ashford Hall," she mused, refusing to allow all her anger to slip away. "Seek our beds. Tomorrow will be a busy day for the both of us."

Lord Ashford, his light brown hair falling to cover one sparkling green eye, stood so close, she caught the scent of the Albany: a blend of lavender and citrus mixed with something wholly unfamiliar. Her eyes drifted shut as she attempted to place the aroma. Every instinct in her told her to retreat, make haste for the townhouse, find her room, and bar the door until morning—or at least until her good sense returned.

He was not a lord to be trifled with—or a man she should allow to trifle with her emotions. Everything about the baron was confusing, vexing, and continuously changing. One minute, he was aloof and quiet; the next, he was inviting her into his private study only to push her away before inviting himself to dine with her and the children…even dangling the prospect of an entire day together. She'd lost track of how she felt about it all. Her path, only a few short weeks prior, had been set in stone: gain her independence, earn enough funds to support herself, and live any life she wanted. At that moment, Payton could think of nothing beyond the present, these precise few minutes alone in the London night with the scent of the baron carried on the breeze. His green eyes holding hers, asking an unspoken question that she had no answer for before she lowered her lids, fearing what he might see in her gaze.

Surely, her good sense would return come morning light.

Her eyes still closed, his hand brushed a wayward lock of hair behind her ear, and she felt the warmth of his touch through his glove. If she concentrated, she could almost imagine the feel of his flesh against hers. In her mind, his skin was smooth, his touch tender, and his words nothing more than a whisper.

His ragged breath broke the silent hold the moment had encapsulated her in, and Payton's eyes sprang open to see the baron's soft stare taking in the sight of her.

Pivoting, Payton pushed her muff higher on her arm and gathered her skirts, her winnings still heavy against her thigh. Without a backwards glance as her heart beat erratically, and her pent-up breath rushed from her lungs, she hurried back toward Ashford Hall. The baron's footsteps trailed behind her, keeping pace but not daring to come any closer.

CHAPTER 14

"PULL OVER HERE," Damon called, rapping his knuckles on the side of the carriage.

"I thought we were going to the park and having a picnic?" Joy asked, lifting her head from Miss Samuels' shoulder. "You promised—"

"Yes, but we have one small stop to make before we arrive at the park." Damon kept his focus off his children's governess and on the row of shops bordering Piccadilly as Rigby halted the carriage. "I promise to be quick, and there is a treat in it for everyone."

"We can wait in the carriage while you attend to your errand, my lord," Miss Samuels said, stroking Joy's hair. "I am certain Joy would not mind a few minutes' rest before the park."

Their day had started with an early afternoon at the menagerie. Seeing his children in such awe at the spectacles within the traveling show had Damon longing to give them more occasion for jubilation. Though their day was not yet complete, and he'd taken it upon himself to schedule a special treat for Miss Samuels and Joy. More a surprise for his daughter and something he *owed* Miss Samuels.

"What is it, Father?" Joy pulled back the fabric

covering her windowpane. "We haven't traveled far from the menagerie. Are we going to see the show again?"

"I'd rather eat." Abram crossed his arms, and Damon heard the corroborating statement of his own stomach growling.

Damon saw the shop out his window. It had been many years since he'd visited any establishment beyond those necessary for a lord. Even Joy's pinafores and half boots were seen to by Flora when the child grew out of her dresses.

"Madame DelFortaine's Shoppe," he proclaimed, hiding his smile by reaching forward to open the door before the footman set down the steps. "A new dress for you, Joy, and a replacement gown for Miss Samuels."

"I don't want to go into any ladies' dress shop," Abram grumbled.

Damon hopped down from the carriage and reached his arm in to assist Joy and Miss Samuels down.

Helping both alight, he waited for Abram to disembark.

"Abram, do hurry." Joy bounced from foot to foot, glancing over at the row of shops. "I do so ever want a new gown." She paused, tapping her finger against her chin. "I think purple…no, yellow. What do you think, Father?"

"Either would look splendid." Damon smiled at the child's delight.

"Abram," Miss Samuels' stern tone rang over the sounds of the many people hurrying to and fro, and several sets of prying eyes landed on them. "You will exit the carriage now."

Damon expected a sharp rebuff from the lad, but his son slumped to the walkway, his glaring stare focused beyond Damon to the shops at his back.

"Do calm yourself," Damon chuckled. "There is a bookstore two shops over with an entire shelf dedicated to wartime battles."

Abram did his best to keep his frown in place, but Damon knew the boy's interest had been piqued.

"Madame DelFortaine is expecting you." Damon gestured to the modiste's shop. "Abram and I will be at Oliver's Bookseller. You can send Rigby for us when your shopping is complete."

"My lord, I cannot accept—"

Damon had suspected she'd turn down his offer of a new gown, but he'd prepared for the argument. "Joy and Abram ruined your dress the other morning. The gown is not from me, but a way for the children to make amends for their troublesome behavior. Isn't that correct?"

Joy had the sense to at least appear sheepish while Abram's frown turned to a scowl.

"Very well, we will see the pair of you as soon as you are finished." Damon set his hand on Abram's shoulder and guided him down the walk to Oliver's.

He could not remember the last time he'd been afforded any time alone with Abram that did not include a scolding for misbehaving. Any other time, Joy was present, and the pair seemed far more connected to one another, as if Damon were the outsider in their trio.

"I've visited Oliver's Bookseller since I was a child, no older than you," Damon said, pushing through the door as a bell rang overhead to alert Oliver that a customer had arrived. "The shop owner is a collector of rare volumes, and every time I come in, I find myself stumbling upon a new book—or subject."

Abram pulled from his father's side, stumbling to a halt as his head swiveled from side to side, taking in row after row of books.

Regret pooled within Damon. It was his fault his son hadn't experienced the excitement of a bookshop before today. It was Damon's fault that now, a moment his son might remember always, he could think of nothing to say.

"Can I have a look around?" Abram whispered.

"Of course." Damon spotted Oliver, the bookseller, behind his counter. "Mr. Oliver, this is my son, Abram."

"Master Abram!" the bespectacled proprietor called, hurrying around the desk to greet them. "It is lovely to have you in my shop."

"Where are the books on great battles, specifically the Ottoman Empire's rise and fall?" Abram asked breathlessly.

Oliver glanced at Damon with a grin. "Your boy doesn't waste any time, my lord."

"No, he does not." Damon clasped Abram on his shoulder. When the boy took a step away from him, Damon's hand fell back to his side. "Please, Oliver, show him around. Books and knowledge, a boy can never have too much of either."

"Very good, Lord Ashford." The man's chin bobbed up and down at the prospect of a large sale.

With the pair disappearing into the stacks, Damon was free to wander the shop and find a volume of his own. Unfortunately, it wasn't books that interested him at the moment. After she'd fled inside the townhouse the previous evening, Miss Samuels had been distant with him. She was attentive and jovial with the children but refrained from any interactions with him that were not completely necessary. Bringing her to Madame DelFortaine's hadn't only been to replace her ruined gown but to repair the damage he'd caused when he followed her to 10 Mill Street.

Bloody hell, he wasn't sorry he'd loitered outside

and made sure she returned home safely. He would never apologize for that. It was *being caught* he regretted. She was correct. She was in his employ, and Damon had no right to insert himself into her personal affairs. What was far more puzzling, was why he cared. Yet again, he knew why her safety, the safety of everyone in his household, was so important to him.

Soon enough, Damon pushed from the bookshop and ambled two shops down to the modiste's. Inside, he could see Miss Samuels looking through a mountain of fabrics while a seamstress measured Joy. His daughter seemed happy, her smile stretching from ear to ear, much as it had when they saw the monkeys in the menagerie. Her face was alight with wonder at the workings in the shop as the seamstress and her assistants hurried to and fro. He'd witnessed Joy smiling more in the last several hours than in the last few years.

Contrary to Joy's exuberant nature, her governess looked perplexed. Her forehead was scrunched as she shook her head and laid a bolt of muslin aside to pick up another.

Miss Samuels' lips pulled back into a smile, and she held a yellow silk high, gesturing for Joy to come and see it. His daughter hurried over, and both ran their hands along the fine fabric. The child had only been a toddler when she lost her mother. However, Damon couldn't help but imagine what the last few years would have been like for her had her mother not passed away. Would she always be the precocious child he'd witnessed today? Happy, carefree, and quick to offer a kind word?

What of Abram? Soon enough, he would need to learn all there was about running the Ashford Barony: the estate landholdings, business ventures, managing the account ledgers, meeting with his stewards and man of business. There was much Damon would need teach his son if the estate were to thrive and provide for future generations.

Beyond the glass, Joy nodded vigorously, and Miss Samuels handed the bolt of silk to the modiste and returned to the table of fabrics. Would Joy have relished shopping outings with her mother, if she were still with them?

Damon shook his head and turned back toward Oliver's Bookseller. The question didn't merit further thought. Miss Samuels would go the way every other governess had. She would tire of the position and move on, leaving Damon and the children alone once more. Perhaps he should have remarried long ago, taken another wife for the reassurance that his children would have someone permanent to care for them. He couldn't imagine another woman beside Miss Samuels holding Joy close while she cried, rocking her to sleep, and tucking her into bed. There had been no other who'd treated his children with the care they needed and deserved: stern when their antics grew out of hand, yet compassionate when their sorrow overtook them. Even Flora, his dear sister, hadn't found any special place in her life—or her heart—for Joy and Abram.

"Father, Father!" Joy skidded out of the dress shop, her half boots clicking on the walkway as she ran to him. "Payton found the most perfect yellow for my new dress."

"Payton?" His brow pulled low. He should have known it was her given name as he'd briefly reviewed her reference before having Mrs. Brown contact them. Yet acknowledging her name meant a familiarity he hadn't been comfortable with at the time.

In his mind, governesses came and went. This one would be no different.

"Miss Samuels, silly," Joy giggled, yet another sound that should be familiar to him but wasn't.

His children were changing before his very eyes, and Damon was finding it difficult to keep up.

"Miss Samuels says I can have a proper evening gown made from the yellow fabric," Joy continued. "She called it silk. I wonder how long it'll take to get my dress. Do you think it'll be ready before Mama's birthday?"

Damon froze, searching his memory for what month it was. February. There were still several weeks until Sarah's birthday came and went.

"I'll ask them to hurry. We should get it in, say, two days?"

Joy looks doubtful. "What if it's *not* ready?"

"I promise."

She brightened. "Truly?"

"Truly."

Damon's stare drifted back to the shop window where Miss Samuels—no, Payton—pointed to one of two fashion plates the modiste held up. Payton? An unusual name and one Damon should have been quick to commit to memory. If he'd heard the name before, it was for a man, not a woman. However, it was as unique as she was—and unexpected, as well. Much like her hair, long and curling, had come to symbolize her. Or the way her eyes sparked with the changing of her moods.

"Father." Joy tugged at his coat sleeve. "Do you really promise?"

"Of course, dear one." He wasn't sure where the endearment had come from, but the moment the words left his mouth, Joy stopped tugging at his sleeve, her mouth fell open, and her shoulders tensed. "Did I say something wrong?"

Her bottom lip trembled. "Mama called me *dear one*."

"She did, didn't she," Damon said, remembering Sarah's melodic voice as she sang Joy to sleep all those years ago. "As did I."

The bell from Oliver's chimed, and Abram exited, his arms laden with several massive tomes.

The smile on his face was worth the invoice Damon would receive from the bookseller.

"Can we go now?" Joy's voice hitched.

"Certainly." Damon waved to the Ashford footman waiting by his coach. The servant hurried over. "Rigby, see the children inside the carriage. I will collect Miss Samuels and return."

"Very well, my lord."

The children followed the footman, Abram focused on the top book, while Joy shuffled alongside her brother.

He'd been caught up in his daughter's happiness, and he'd unwittingly caused her pain with his thoughtlessness. In the future, Damon would be far more careful when he spoke to his children. Rigby assisted Joy into the carriage and held Abram's books while the boy found his seat.

"Are the children ready, Lord Ashford?"

Miss Samuels stood behind him, fastening the buttons on her long cloak before touching her perfectly pinned hair.

"Yes, they are hungry and cannot wait for the park." He held out his arm, and she stared at it as if debating whether to place her hand at his elbow. Something about the woman, her speech, her manners, her way of holding herself, spoke of a past spent among society. She had the poise of a woman raised with privilege. Could she be the daughter or relation of a nobleman? Before he could ask, she set her gloved hand at his elbow and then started for their waiting carriage. "I hope you selected a suitable new gown."

She kept her stare trained straight ahead. "You were under no obligation to purchase me a new dress. I should have kept a better watch on Joy and Abram's antics…"

"You are welcome, Miss Samuels." He knew full well that he wasn't only under obligation, it was something she'd expected.

"I did not thank you, my lord," she hissed.

"Are you unfamiliar with accepting a kindness?"

"A kindness?" she asked, her stare meeting his. "Mayhap it *was* more of an obligation."

"A kindness, a gift, or a mere obligation, regardless, I hope you selected a lovely new gown." He handed her up into the carriage, bringing their brief moment of privacy to an end, though he suspected he'd touched on a subject she was wholly uncomfortable with. "To St. James's Park, Rigby."

Climbing into the carriage, Damon found Abram reading a book as Joy rested her sleeping head on his shoulder. The only available seat was beside Miss Samuels.

PAYTON COULDN'T BE out of the carriage fast enough after Rigby had opened the door and set down the steps. Now in the fresh air of the park, with wide-open, rolling lawns in one direction, and a small pond in the other, Payton allowed herself the first deep breath she'd taken since they departed Ashford Hall that morning.

Anger still churned deep within her at the thought of him following her to Lord Galment's and then waiting outside for her to depart as if she were a child in need of a nursemaid. It hadn't mattered that she feared falling prey to a ruffian. It had only been Lord Ashford, not a cutpurse. She would have had no reason to feel uneasy had it not been for him trailing her on her walk home, despite his noble intentions.

The baron was being too nice, too accommodating, and nothing like his usual stoic self.

Today, he'd organized an entire morning and afternoon for his children: the menagerie, the dress shop for Joy, and the bookseller for Abram. And now the park.

And he'd had enough foresight to arrange a fitting for her, to commission a dress to replace the one ruined by the children. In her younger years, she would have expected the gown replaced—with a dress of superior quality.

Payton had matured in the time she'd lived at Ashford Hall. She was a grown woman in charge of herself. If her charges ruined her gown, she could very well purchase a new one without the baron's help, despite her recent loss at the gaming tables. Very soon, if her luck at the tables held, she'd have the money to repay the duke and enough to start on a different future. On her next day off, she planned to preview a room for rent in St. James's Square. It was farther from Craven House than she'd like, but the area was acceptable and wasn't far from The Strand. The time to move on was approaching.

The simple fact was that she'd actually come to enjoy Abram's and Joy's company. The girl's infectious delight in the modiste's shop had reminded Payton of her own misguided youth when she'd thought the world—and her family—perfect.

The world was not perfect. Payton's siblings were not close to perfect. The baron was not perfect.

And Payton, no matter how long she stayed at Ashford Hall, would never find her path if she chose to remain.

"Stay close, children," Lord Ashford called from behind her.

Joy and Abram ran past her across the lawn and along the riding path toward the pond beyond.

Which left Payton to watch over the blanket that the Ashford footman had spread out on the grass, a basket with bread, cheese, and cold meats holding one edge down as the light wind played with the other corner.

She'd expected Lord Ashford to follow the children, but when she turned, he lay upon the blanket, his face turned upward, and his eyes closed. His chest rose and fell as if he'd dropped into quick slumber. Seemingly at peace. A serenity, despite his stoic demeanor, that she'd never witnessed before. The only thing that betrayed him was his eyes moving behind his lids.

Did he attempt to lull her into sitting with him?

Surprisingly, she realized she desired to lower herself down to the blanket beside him, to recline and close her eyes to find her own brief seconds of peace. Separate, yet together. Their individual burdens and concerns were far removed from one another. However, as people, they both had their own troubles.

Payton crossed her arms and paced toward the pond and back.

A never-ending slow precession of carriages and gentry on horseback passed close to where their picnic sat untouched. Ladies and gentlemen promenaded at the fashionable hour, showing off their new stallions or recently adorned coaches. Ladies wore elaborate gowns and outlandish hats, while men sat tall upon their horses or in their carriages, displaying their wealth in a manner no less reserved than pinning hundred-pound notes to their lapels.

The park was little different than parading livestock at Tattersalls.

She sniffed. Peculiar that no one but she saw it.

"A shilling for your thoughts, Miss Samuels?" Lord Ashford pushed from his reclined position, propping his chin on his fist and crossing one outstretched leg over the other.

He did strike an appealing pose with his relaxed demeanor, his hair ruffled by the breeze, and his face turned up as he watched her pace.

"The peerage baffles me, my lord."

His brow furrowed, and for a brief moment, she realized her statement may very well have insulted him.

"And here I thought you belonged to the peerage," he mused, glancing past her until his eyes focused on the children.

"What would make you think that?" She'd been careful not to expose her lineage when she met with the baron about the governess position.

"Your poise, your cultured tone, your education," he paused, tapping his chin much as Joy did when she was pushed to make an important decision. "Also, the tilt of your chin."

"The tilt of my chin? What has that to do with anything?" Her hand immediately came to her chin, and she tilted her face from side to side.

"You hold yourself like a woman who is used to moving about in society, and that means holding your chin a notch higher than those around you."

"Is that a polite way of saying I am haughty?" She'd always kept her chin high because her eldest sister said it stopped the trembling caused by nerves. "Before you answer that, I will have you know my father was a blacksmith."

"Hmmm." He dropped down to his back, lacing his fingers behind his head.

That her mother was once wedded to a marquess was of little import to this conversation. It did not make her nobility, nor did it make her lofty.

"Do you not believe me?" She couldn't help her eyes widening. She'd never spoken of her lineage with another, besides her siblings, and to have Lord Ashford pushing the information about the circumstances of her birth aside like it meant nothing in the grand scheme of things was…startling, to say the least.

"I said nothing of the sort," he said with a chuckle.

The man seemed to enjoy angering her.

"So, tell me, why does the peerage baffle you?" He returned to their original topic, and Payton had a difficult time remembering why, exactly, they puzzled her.

She bit her bottom lip and sank to the blanket beside the baron. "They only leave their homes to parade themselves before others to make certain all and sundry know their status. They select gowns of the latest fashion, not because they are taken by the cut and color, but to show that they have the coin to afford extravagant things. Lords gamble away their fortunes to prove money means nothing to them because they possess far more than any man needs. All of this while so many in London and beyond go without food, without proper education, without things as simple as shoes or a warm coat."

Her ramblings were more akin to her sister Judith's thoughts. However, telling the baron that being surrounded by lords and ladies satisfied to strut before their peers much like peacocks seemed a juvenile thing to say. And completely out of the ordinary for her, especially after the fine gown she'd selected at the modiste's shop earlier that day. She was not prone to fits of hypocrisy, or at least she hadn't thought so. The baron was certain to rebuff her jaded outlook on societal life; his position within it demanded that he defend his peers.

He turned his head toward her. "You are very wise, Miss Samuels."

"Thank you. I think," she murmured, eyes turning to him to see if his words were truth or a way to placate her churlishness.

"If there is one thing I pray you teach my children, it is compassion."

They'd never, even once, spoken of his wishes for Joy's and Abram's education. "You can, just as easily, teach them."

While many nobles she'd met lacked compassion, Payton wasn't certain Lord Ashford did.

They both fell silent, lost in their own thoughts as the warm afternoon sun shone down on them. The baron's light brown hair had golden strands weaved through it. His cheeks, pale from spending too much time indoors, were already turning a rosy pink from the sun.

His ability to relax galled her.

Was it his position as a baron, a wealthy one at that, which gave him the ability to look thoroughly at peace? Since they'd departed the townhouse, he'd released the tension that normally bound him at home and even appeared several years younger. Perhaps gaining distance from his burdens was a benefit.

Payton huffed, closing her own eyes, determined to not allow the baron to distract her from enjoying her time outside Ashford Hall. The park was not the place she would pick to spend her afternoon, but at least they were not shuttered in the schoolroom.

Anyone on the outside looking in would think them a normal family.

A father. A mother. Two children.

But they were not a family, normal or otherwise.

No matter how many outings they went on, no matter how many meals they ate together, no matter how long they all resided under one roof. Longing filled her, a wholly unfamiliar longing to belong to something great, something permanent.

Payton had never been part of a typical family unit. Her mother, after falling from grace, had become London's famed madame of Craven House. Her sisters' reputations, while intact now, had been similarly tarnished not long ago.

What would it have been like if she'd followed in Sam's and Jude's footsteps and found a suitable man to wed? It had been easier for them; their father wasn't a lowly blacksmith, he was a viscount. At that thought, a familiar feeling coursed through her: determination. She would rise above her circumstances, just as her mother had.

No, Payton was on a clear path to follow in their mother's footsteps. To live each day waiting for the chance to better her circumstances. Today, she was a mere governess; but tomorrow, she could earn enough coin at the gaming tables to afford her own townhouse and be free to explore her choices for her future, beholden to no one.

The children's laughter floated toward her, followed by a loud splash.

Heaven help her if Joy had pushed her brother into the filthy pond. It would mean a swift end to their day. A day she was loath to admit reminded her of her own childhood—the ease with which they'd traversed the menagerie, their stop at the Piccadilly modiste and bookshop, and now, their time in the park.

She squinted into the bright afternoon sun, turning her head toward the pond where she hoped to find the children playing. But all she saw was Abram, holding a stick extended over the water.

"Abram?" she called loudly to be heard over the pedestrians on the carriage path.

The boy turned to her, dropping the stick and waving his arms wildly.

Payton pushed to her feet, her gaze darting from the edge of the water back to the carriage path. No sign of Joy anywhere.

It was then that she saw Abram wade into the water.

"Lord Ashford," she screamed before gathering her skirts and running toward the pond's edge. "Joy! Joy!"

Payton didn't hesitate before flinging herself into the cold, murky pond, rushing past Abram deeper into the water, her body threatening to freeze from the sudden, unexpected chill of the water as it enveloped her. Her head dipped below the surface, and her gloved hands clawed at the water, searching for Joy.

The commotion beside her said that the baron had followed her into the pond. She adjusted her position, bringing her head above water to scan the area for any sight of Joy. She gulped air, polluted pond water sliding down her throat and making her cough.

"There, there!" Abram called from the shore, but Payton didn't take her eyes off the water as she continued to search for Joy.

"I've got her." The baron threw himself farther into the pond, swimming about ten feet toward the center before ducking under the surface.

Payton held her breath, waiting for him to resurface, knowing she'd never again be able to draw air if Joy did not.

Finally, Lord Ashford broke the water's surface, Joy clinging to his chest, and waded toward the shore. Payton's entire body trembled at the sight—the baron, as soaked as she was, clutching his child to his person as his knuckles whitened from his hold. While

Joy clung to her father, shocked from the surprise of it all, Ashford gripped the girl with such fierceness and terror, it was like he hadn't realized he'd saved her.

Payton's hair hung limply about her shoulders, and her gown and cloak were molded to her body as she followed them from the water. Her half boots sloshed. She shivered from the cold when the afternoon breeze assaulted her as it whipped off the pond and across the park.

A group of onlookers had gathered during their brief time in the water, but Ashford pushed past them, stalking toward their blanket, leaving Abram and Payton to hurry behind. Rigby arrived at the picnic blanket at the same moment the baron did and pulled the cloth free before wrapping it around both the baron and Joy.

Lord Ashford didn't pause as he continued on to their carriage.

Payton pushed Abram to enter the coach before her and then pulled herself up, not caring that she dripped water all over the baron's cloth seats.

"Is she well?" she asked in a whisper.

"She will be." He lowered the blanket until Payton could see the girl, her skin tinted slightly blue with cold. "She needs to warm up, but I am soaked to the skin, too."

The carriage surged into motion, throwing Payton forward slightly as she latched on to the handle looped above the windowpane.

The baron didn't so much as budge. He remained unwavering, his head tucked against Joy's neck as he mumbled something in her ear. Payton couldn't hear what he said, but the child's eyes fluttered, and she turned her face into his shoulder, burrowing closer to her father.

It had all happened so quickly: Payton realizing

something was amiss, Abram standing alone, and golden hair disappearing below the water's surface.

Neither she nor Lord Ashford had hesitated for even a second before plunging into the frigid pond in search of the child.

Her exterior was freezing, and her heart beat frantically.

She squeezed her hands tightly in her lap to stop her shivering, though her wet hair hung over her shoulder, droplets of water hitting her fists. Her knuckles turned white before she released her hands and wiped them down her skirts, pushing her soaked, discolored gloves to the floor.

Joy was safe. She was alive. They were headed home.

Not her home, *their* home. Ashford Hall.

"Thank you."

She glanced up to find the baron staring at her, his eyes meeting hers without reservation. The intensity there was something she'd never witnessed before.

Payton shrugged, attempting to hide the trembling that wracked her entire body. "I am her governess, I should have been watching her more closely. If I had, this wouldn't have happened."

"We could not have foreseen this." He shook his head. "And it is I who should have been paying closer mind. They are my children…my responsibility. I should have kept her safe."

He spoke the truth, but it did nothing to assuage Payton's guilt.

Payton watched as he gently rocked Joy, much as she had after the child woke from her night terror. With his other arm, the baron pulled Abram close to his other side.

Part of her wished he hadn't accompanied them today, that he'd kept this side of himself hidden from her.

However, all of her wished she hadn't allowed herself to become invested in the baron and his children. If her mother's past had taught her anything, it was to remain level-headed with her thoughts trained on what was to come. Focused on what came next for her. Something better. Moving on. Thriving.

It wasn't about settling, finding comfort in what she had and losing sight of her independence and future in favor of a few months—possibly a year—with Lord Ashford and his family.

At what point had her goals altered to such a degree that she'd fallen into the false security of everyday life at Ashford Hall?

CHAPTER 15

DAMON RESTED HIS face in his open palms, listening to the deep rumbling of Joy's breathing. Bathed, hair dried, and tucked into bed, she once again appeared the angel she always was in his eyes. Only in sleep was his daughter at peace, her forehead smooth and without worry lines. As her father, it was his responsibility to remove all her burdens. A duty he'd failed to do.

And he hadn't only failed at the park, but every day since her mother had passed.

Their day had been wonderful. It had even given him hope that he'd begun his climb out of the dark place he'd lived in the last several years.

It wasn't until he saw his daughter's head slip under the water that he knew—*knew*—how utterly he'd failed his children. Joy could have been lost forever—and thinking he didn't love her.

He'd told her...over and over on their ride home.

When she awoke in the morning, he'd tell her again. And then he would go to Abram and repeat the words that hadn't escaped him for so many years.

A throat cleared behind him, and Damon turned to see Miss Samuels standing in the doorway, her candle casting a soft glow about her. As soon as they'd gotten home, he demanded she return to her chambers and change while he saw to Joy and Abram with Mrs. Brown's assistance. He'd made sure his daughter was well and that the hearth in her room was stoked until the heat reached every corner of her chambers before he allowed himself to find dry clothes himself.

His tight shoulders eased at the sight of the governess.

If he hadn't been there, he knew she would have saved Joy. He was positive. His children meant as much to her as they did to him. It was obvious.

It had taken only a second, Joy lost in the water of the pond, to bring back the helplessness he'd felt all those years ago with Sarah. He would have risked everything in that pond if only to not repeat his failures from the past.

Safety. Security. The two things he'd strove to provide for his children. And he'd nearly failed them.

"How is she doing?" Miss Samuels whispered, stepping into the darkened room.

Mrs. Brown, with the help of a maid, had pulled all the curtains tight, blocking out the waning late-afternoon light.

"She is asleep. But her breathing is labored, and her chest sounds heavy," he confided. "The water was dreadfully cold. Mrs. Brown made her a tonic to ward off illness after the doctor saw to her. Pure fright, he proclaimed. Nothing more. She needs rest now. And warmth."

Damon had been petrified to think of Joy falling prey to the fevers and chills that had overtaken her mother.

"And what of you?" She pulled a chair close on the opposite side of Joy's bed. "You will likely face sickness, too."

He grimaced at her concern. "I will be well."

His shoulders tensed. Just as he'd remained well as Sarah battled for her life.

Damon watched the woman smooth Joy's blond hair away from her face and adjust the blankets at her throat. How had she gone from battling his children to this affection, this seemingly innate connection?

Perhaps it was the governess who'd fallen under Joy's and Abram's charms.

Either way, it didn't matter. Miss Samuels truly cared for his children, and that brought him a measure of peace he hadn't felt in a long, long time.

"Abram is reading in his room," she said. "Cook will bring a meal to him shortly."

"Thank you for tending to him." Gratitude filled him. Damon had seen the boy to his room, quickly changed into dry clothes, and then returned to Joy.

"My wife passed four years ago."

As if he needed to share this detail—or bring up the topic at all with everything that had transpired at the park. It was difficult to live under his roof without being reminded of Sarah's absence. It was likely the same for everyone living at Ashford Hall.

"It is the reason I've hired governess after governess," he said, turning to stare at Joy, a new tenderness blossoming within him. "I am not the right man to care for my children, to teach them, to be…anything."

"I think you are the *only* man to do all those things. You are their father."

His heart pulled in his chest, and he fought against the tears that blurred his vision. "After Sarah died, I retreated. My grief was all-consuming. It still consumes me. Every day. Every hour. And my guilt over it all is far more severe. I let Sarah down, and I let my children down." He sighed. "However, today, for just a few minutes, I forgot my hurt, my pain, my loss. We visited the menagerie, we stopped on Piccadilly, and we rested at the park. For once, my children and I were away from Ashford Hall and the constant reminders of everything we've suffered.

"I think they forgot, as well. Yet with a blink of an eye, we were all reminded of how fragile life can be. I've spent so many years wallowing in my own shattered dreams, burdened with my own regrets and guilt, that I've neglected to realize my children still have a future ahead of them—even if mine was ripped from me. It took you, a most unlikely woman, to come into my household and begin to mend the damage Joy and Abram have lived with since Sarah's death."

Damon lifted his gaze back to Miss Samuels when she remained silent. Unease and trepidation flooded him. He shouldn't be telling her any of this. If she hadn't been frightened off by the disaster at the pond, his candid confession would surely send her running for new employment.

"How did you manage to break through their anger and change their troublesome ways?"

The hint of a smile touched her mouth, and he noticed the plumpness of her bottom lip. "I have my own siblings, and we are a very quarrelsome bunch. Fortunately for you, they *want* to love you. They *want* to forgive and forget the past—although they are too young to express it."

He zeroed in on her initial statement regarding her family. It was the first she'd shared about herself with him. "You've mentioned your siblings before. Do they often give you trouble?"

His question was meant to distract them both from the colossal mistakes he'd made with Joy and Abram.

"No," she said, her eyes darting to her hand that rested on the side of the bed. "I have always given *them* trouble. You see, I was an unruly child my whole life. Heeding another's rules has never been a strong suit of mine, and that has never sat well with my sisters and brother. I was the youngest, I was the baby, and they knew what was best for me—or so they told me over and over."

Joy's head lolled to the side, and she sighed in her sleep. Damon hoped she found herself in a beautiful dreamland and not amidst the terrors that had awoken her the other night.

Damon watched Miss Samuels look upon Joy with a degree of tenderness he hadn't seen before.

"You will make a wonderful mother one day," he muttered.

She shook her head. "No, I do not think that is in my future, my lord."

"Why ever not?" He should have ended the conversation long before this point. What she had planned for her future was none of his concern, only that she remained in his employ for the foreseeable future, at least until Joy and Abram reached an age suitable for going away to school. However, he did know that becoming a mother had undeniably changed everything about Sarah, similar to how it had altered him as a man. "My apologies. You needn't answer that."

Damon shoved to his feet, attempting to push from his thoughts the way the governess had changed in the short time she'd been in his life as a part of Joy's and Abram's lives.

"My siblings and I—five of us in all—have three different fathers," she confessed. "My mother was never one to settle or remain in a situation if it no longer benefited her. In turn, none of us had any relationship with our sires. I never met mine before I was told he passed away."

"Again, I am sorry—"

She waved away his words, also pushing to her feet. She glanced over her shoulder at the door. "Do not fret about my upbringing. My mother taught me strength and perseverance. I am, and always have been, steadfast in my resolve: that a woman can live a life of her own choosing…on her own terms. She can run a business, raise children, and still find contentment and happiness."

She'd shared more than she planned, he could see it written on her face: remorse, regret, and no small amount of annoyance. But if that final emotion were aimed at herself or him, Damon did not know. Her openness had him thinking of all the things he hadn't shared with her during her stay at Ashford Hall.

He moved around Joy's bed to where the governess stood. "As I would tell my daughter," he whispered with a small grin, "yes, a woman can do anything she sets her mind to. And that is no different for you, Payton." He started inside at how natural it felt to use her given name. "However, having children and a family is not an inferior path in life. Some days, I do not know what I would do without Joy and Abram…they are all I have."

"What happened with your wife? If you don't mind me asking," she whispered, glancing at Joy, sound asleep in her bed. "I—I know she passed when the children were very young, but nothing beyond that."

No one spoke of Sarah; not him, not the servants, and rarely Joy and Abram.

Damon squeezed his eyes shut, begging the tears to remain at bay and not fall as they commonly did when he thought back to that night. "I convinced Sarah that an early evening sleigh ride to a neighboring town would be a grand adventure. It was nearly the new year, and the children were safely nestled in their beds, their nurse close by. And so, Sarah and I started out, unwittily oblivious to the storm pushing toward Falconcrest, my country seat. Our horse took a misstep, and our sleigh was caught in a rut with the snowfall increasing."

Damon opened his eyes to find Payton intently watching him, her focus on the set of his jaw before moving to his eyes. He couldn't go on, couldn't admit his failures aloud. Not here, and not to the woman standing before him. Their recently established relationship would dissipate and disappear before he even had the chance to finish telling his story—Sarah's story...his family's story.

The resolve in Payton's stare pushed Damon on. "We walked in the storm for hours with no shelter and only the warmth of our coats and huddled bodies. Until first light crested, breaking through the storm. By the time we found our way home, the chills had already begun to wrack Sarah's body. Her teeth chattered uncontrollably. And then the fever set in. The doctor was summoned, but it took nearly a day for him to make his way through the snowfall to reach the estate. By that time, it was..."

Damon swallowed the final words—*too late*.

He'd thrown himself into the pond because he refused for it to be *too late* for Joy. And in the depths of his mind, he knew he'd followed Payton the other night for the same reason.

He reached out and took hold of Payton's hand—her bare hand—when she looked away, her brow knitted. The feel of her skin against his warm palm was unlike anything he'd experienced in years. It felt right, yet so very wrong. Why was it so important to him that she understand the magnitude of his past failures, his damage?

He pulled her toward the door and the safety of the hallway beyond.

"My lord—"

"Damon," he corrected, halting only when they stood outside Joy's chambers, the child blocked from view. "I think here—with just the two of us—you can call me Damon."

Her blue eyes widened before she looked away again, pulling at her single long, dark curl with her free hand.

She did not pull her hand from his or put distance between them.

Surprisingly, her skin warmed within his grasp.

"My children are blessed to have you as their governess." Damon took a step closer. Payton's willowy height made her nearly as tall as he was. "And I will be forever grateful that you came into our lives when you did." *Before it was too late*, he thought.

She blushed and turned to stare at their clasped hands.

"I think your siblings are wrong to believe they know what's best for you," he murmured. Just as Flora had been wrong to think she knew what was best for him and his children after Sarah's passing.

The memory of Payton, masked and elegantly gowned, losing to the duke at his gaming table pushed into Damon's thoughts. He'd taken care of her debt, and she'd have nothing to fear from Catherton. He'd made so many mistakes over the years, but settling Payton's gaming debts was not one of them.

That was something he would never regret.

As he looked into her deep blue eyes, her long, ebony lashes lowered, threatening to break the connection between them. Damon suspected that he might regret not releasing her hand in that moment, saying his good night, and fleeing to the solitude of his private chambers. At least if he did that, he'd have this small memory to relive without remorse of what came next.

Instead, his fingers held fast to hers, his thumb massaging a circle on her palm.

How had he never appreciated her beauty before this? Of course, he had noticed her stunning eloquence and graceful poise. How had he never observed that her floral aroma had invaded every inch of his home? How had he resigned himself to such a desolate future without considering all he'd be missing?

She nibbled at her bottom lip, worrying it between her teeth.

Their thoughts—and longings—seemed to align, and she took the final step toward him, bring her soft, delicate body against his rigidly tense chest.

Damon knew he should pull back, put distance between them, apologize for his ungentlemanly behavior; however, the simple comfort of her against him had the tension draining from him. It was as if he'd taken a deep breath four years ago and held it until he could do nothing but focus on the burning within him.

The raging fire he held inside was suddenly not so unbearable.

For once, he wanted to surrender to the flames, not extinguish them.

In her eyes, he saw certainty, a confidence that had fled him years before. No longer did she glance away in doubt. She held his stare as if they were both in a raft, adrift in a sea that threatened to rip them from safety and send them both tossing and turning into the midnight waters.

"I want to be ripped away," he sighed.

She tilted her head to the side, and her tongue darted across her plump lower lip.

Her eyes closed before she lifted the mere few inches to press her lips to his. Damon yielded to her, allowed her control. And bloody hell, it was everything he needed. Her soft, insistent, rhythmic kiss set the pace, allowing Damon to revel in the feeling of her pressed against him, the heat of her mouth covering his, the security of her hands coming to rest on his shoulders.

The years of pain, guilt, and remorse within him broke, shattered, and he sensed the pieces within him fusing back together, creating a deep longing, a desire, the unmistakable need to hold Payton close and not let go.

Not fail her.

In this moment, and the many to come.

A groan escaped him as her fingers tightened on his shoulders, digging into his coat.

Damon brought his hand to her cheek, his fingers trailing down her neck as she inhaled sharply.

He thought she'd pull away, but instead, she pushed close to him, her slender body fitting perfectly against his.

Intoxicating need gathered at his manhood, the rigid length hardening until pain shot into his stomach. He hadn't experienced such heady desire since…

Much like an ocean of water extinguishing a single flame, Damon's hands dropped to his sides, and he stepped away from Payton. Cold air rushed between them, smothering the final remnants of their brief but fiery passion.

What was he doing?

Miss Samuels was his children's governess. His heart, all his desires, belonged to Sarah—and no one could replace her.

Payton stared up at him, hurt and confusion furrowing her brow, the appearance of an unvoiced question upon her lips.

Damon cleared his throat as he took another large step back, fisting his hands at his sides.

"I think it is time I retire." His voice was thick with an emotion he couldn't identify. Didn't want to name.

Desire, longing—need.

Or remorse, regret—and betrayal?

"Good evening, Miss Samuels," he stuttered. "I am sorry I kept you. I can care for the children for the afternoon and night. Do continue with your evening plans."

He stared over her shoulder and down the deserted hall, not daring to meet her eyes and see the hurt he'd created. It was not enough that his children were growing attached to Payton, now *he* was falling under her spell. They would all suffer the loss when she left them.

Damon could not risk losing another person he cared for.

He felt lighter, an increasingly prevalent weight having been lifted from his burdened shoulders. Yet, at the same time, his past collided with their kiss. Payton had offered him a piece of herself, and he was faltering, terrified to accept it for fear of what might come of it.

"Good evening." He gave her a stiff bow and brushed past her, his stare trained down the corridor and focused on his escape.

CHAPTER 16

PAYTON STUMBLED ALONG the hallway outside Joy's bedchambers, her fingers pressed to her hot, swollen lips, and glanced up and down the hall. Lord Ashford had disappeared. Somewhere deep in the townhouse, a door shut with more force than was necessary. Had he fled to his study, the library, or his private chambers?

She exhaled the breath she'd held since he—*Damon*—had pulled away from their kiss.

What had she been thinking?

Blood rushed through her veins as the knot in her stomach loosened. She hadn't been thinking...not at all.

She'd kissed the baron.

Kissed him while his daughter slept just out of view...after nearly drowning in a pond.

While her heart slowed, her lips still pulsed in time with the beat.

They'd shared a private, emotional experience, and she'd misread his intentions. His desires. His wants.

The last thing she'd been thinking about was her *evening plans.* For once, Payton hadn't been dwelling on departing Ashford Hall to find a gaming house, nor escaping the baron and his children. She'd actually longed for him to hold her close, even if it were only for a short time. Instead, he'd pulled away and told her to leave.

She hadn't wanted to leave with Joy in such a state—the child was her responsibility. She should be at her bedside.

When she made no move, he'd fled.

Her time in the baron's household had finally become bearable. She and the children had come to understand one another. She'd settled into a companionable relationship with the other servants. And the baron had blessedly begun to spend more time with his children; which they desperately needed. And through all of this, she was earning a decent wage.

And she'd ruined it all.

There was no way she could stay in the baron's household now.

It would be surprising if he didn't release her by morning. She'd known the time would eventually come for her to move on, but she wasn't ready. Hadn't thought this moment would happen so soon. What had happened to her? She'd been planning her departure from Ashford Hall since the day she'd been given the post. Never was the thought of what was to come next far from her mind. When had she stopped looking toward her future?

Perhaps Damon was correct. She should continue as she'd planned, act as if their kiss meant nothing. They'd both been overwhelmed with fright over Joy. They'd both shared a piece of themselves. They'd both found themselves lost in their own vulnerability.

It was as simple as that. Their intimacy wasn't born of any innate connection, but their own personal hurt and anguish.

Perhaps an evening away from Ashford Hall was exactly what Payton needed. She could only hope that by morning, the baron would have put behind him what happened and not release her from her position.

She hurried to her chambers to retrieve her cloak and her meager stash of coins. She had no urge to find a gaming table. Not this night. The distraction of the baron's kiss would be enough to have her so unfocused she'd risk losing what little she'd saved that week.

No, she would return home.

Craven House.

A sound night's sleep in her familiar, childhood bed would bring everything into clear focus. The heat that had gathered within her was nothing more than a base need and had nothing to do with her feelings— or her lack thereof—for Damon.

The baron and his children did not belong to her. Would never belong to her.

She was a hired servant in the Ashford home.

The only place she could always count on returning to was Craven House. No matter where she went in life, no matter how many situations she ran from, that was her true home—despite her need to escape, it was the place she was always drawn back to.

She would never be a part of Damon's family, beyond her usefulness as a governess—just as the many men her mother had taken to her bed had never become part of her family. Time passed, and people moved on.

Her kiss with Lord Ashford meant nothing. Promised nothing.

There was no unspoken declaration on his part, as she would proclaim none herself.

Payton slipped her small purse of coins into the hidden pocket in her skirts and made her way downstairs.

Mr. Brown only nodded to her and opened the front door.

Stepping into the early evening twilight, Payton walked away from Ashford Hall, her footsteps not the confident ones from the evening before but slow and hesitant.

She didn't want to leave the baron's townhouse; however, after their embrace, the decision might not belong to her any longer.

At the corner of Saint George and Grosvenor, Payton paused before hailing a hackney. Instead of returning home, she could walk the short distance to Regent Street and settle in an alehouse until the gaming house on Mill Street opened for the evening. At least if she were surrounded by strangers, she would be able to forget the disastrous predicament she'd created at Ashford Hall.

But, no, while there was much she was willing to risk, losing her meager stash of coin was not one of them. She might very well need the money sooner than she thought if she were cast from the baron's employ as she feared.

Raising her hand, she signaled a passing driver, who pulled quickly to a stop but made no move to assist her into the conveyance.

"Where ye be headed, miss?" the driver called from his seat, the reins hanging loosely in his grip.

"Leicester Square." When the man frowned, she continued, knowing her family home was nestled close to the edge of the respectable district. "Craven House, if you don't mind the long drive."

He nodded agreement, and Payton took hold of her skirts, climbing into the back of the hack.

As the driver sped toward the only place she knew as home, Payton didn't fret over the dust coating her cloak from the filthy streets, she didn't dwell on what was to come next for her, and she couldn't allow herself to think about the baron's lips pressed to hers.

It had apparently been a moment of pure yearning for Damon. He had been overwrought with concern for his daughter, worried to utter exhaustion, and she'd been there. Payton had been there with him through it all. It had created some invisible bond between them, but not one that would last. Come tomorrow, she'd need to forget the few private moments she'd had with Lord Ashford—not Damon—and return to the townhouse ready to serve as Joy's and Abram's governess. Nothing more.

She was not part of their family.

Blazes, the baron and his children were barely a family themselves.

But she suspected that they'd begun to heal if their day at the menagerie and the park were any indication. However, Payton had no place in their trio. That she knew.

Even in her own home, she was the odd sibling out. Marce had Garrett. Sam and Jude, as twins, had one another. And that left her…

Yes, living within but never truly a part of a family was something Payton knew very well.

Tears stung her eyes, and she told herself it wasn't her self-pity taking over but the wind whipping at her face that caused her eyes to moisten.

The stark circumstances of her life had never been more apparent than in that moment. It was the reason she was determined to make a life of her choosing, even if she had to do it alone and leave the baron, his children, and her siblings behind.

DAMON WATCHED OUT his bedchamber window for what seemed like hours after Payton had disappeared down Saint George Street. He'd wanted to go after her, to tell her to stay, beg her to sit with him in his study or perhaps return to their places on either side of Joy's bed. And yet, he stood in his darkened chambers and watched as the sun completely set and the evening dusk turned to full night.

She did not return.

Without his noticing, Mrs. Brown had delivered his evening meal. It remained untouched on the table close to the hearth.

At some point, his valet had turned down his bed and stoked the fire.

Still, Damon watched for the woman's return.

She would return. *She must return*, he repeated silently.

He glanced at the hearth, the fire waning but still enough to keep the room warm, before glancing back outside to the street below. In the hall outside his study, the tall clock chimed twice.

Two in the morning.

Where had the hours gone? Had Abram fallen asleep? Had Joy awoken to find him gone from her bedside?

And where in the bloody hell had Miss Samuels disappeared to?

He'd stopped himself several times from going to 10 Mill Street. Indeed, that must be where she was. Gambling.

He wondered if it were a habit or an addiction for her. Did she gamble out of necessity or was it merely for the thrill of it?

It didn't matter why she did it—or even that she gambled at all. It was none of his concern, as she'd pointed out to him quite bluntly when she caught him following her the other night. She was a servant in his household. However, he could not forget the memory of her plunging into the water alongside him. She had been affected by the incident with Joy as much as he had.

If it didn't matter—if *she* didn't matter—why had he settled her debts with the Duke of Catherton? Far more than that, why hadn't he told her that he'd paid her debts? Payton hadn't any notion that he knew she was the mysterious, masked woman at this gaming nights. Hell, until the previous week, Damon hadn't known either.

If it weren't for his children's horrid prank and the dye that had stained her arm, he might never have made the connection. Perhaps that would have been better for everyone involved.

Damon pulled the cord, releasing the drapes, and they fell over the window, blocking out the street below. If she didn't return by morning, it was his own fault.

Kissing his children's governess.

He tensed, remembering the desire that had coursed through him at the mere touch of skin against skin. He'd forgotten how all-consuming a physical connection could be. Add to that the empathy in her eyes when he spoke of his past, and everything within him craved her—the connection of an honest conversation, the press of her soft body against his, the security of his arms holding another.

What had come over him?

But it hadn't only been that moment. No, something had drawn him to her even before he learned her secret. He'd known when she stood before him dripping blue-tinted water all over the expensive rug in his study.

He shook his head, clenching his fists at his sides. He stalked toward the hearth, past his waiting meal, and back toward the covered window.

He could never betray Sarah in such a way, yet he knew he'd done precisely that when Miss Samuels had appeared at his door with references in hand. He hadn't done his due diligence when hiring her to care for his children. Her letter of recommendation and references still resided in Mrs. Brown's care, and though he'd read them, Damon hadn't been in a place to be overly fastidious with his selection. He'd neglected his responsibilities where the governess was concerned, similarly to many other aspects in his life. It had been only Payton who applied for the position.

It was little wonder the woman had turned out to have unsavory habits not fit for a governess.

If he dared tell her about paying her debts, she would demand to know why, just as she'd questioned why he followed her to Mill Street. Could he convince her that it was for his children that he'd done it and not for himself? Hell, he wasn't wholly convinced either way.

No, he couldn't tell her. *Wouldn't* tell her.

If he did, she'd expect an explanation to follow—and he had none.

He slumped into the chair facing the fire and stared into the flames, allowing them to soothe his aching chest and calm his pounding head while begging for sleep. For years, he'd been tortured by nightmares of losing Sarah all over again. But, for some reason, he suspected when he did find sleep, the terrors would be new…and not what he would expect.

His worst nightmare, that of losing one of his children, would roll through his mind over and over again…overshadowed only by his absolutely horrifying lack of sense when he dared kiss Payton.

…and liked it.

No, he more than liked it, he'd been devastated by it. It changed everything, yet nothing.

After all his years with Sarah—their love, their companionship, their joys and heartbreak—this dalliance with Payton was different. It hadn't held the comfortable familiarity of an intimate moment shared with a woman he knew innately, likely as well as he knew himself, but that did not mean it was any less poignant.

But it had only been a kiss, their bodies pressed close for no more than several breaths.

It shouldn't have happened, nor affected him in such a way that he couldn't bring himself to find his bed until she returned for the night.

Damon scrubbed at his face, his eyes strained and dry from exhaustion.

Sleep would be impossible.

He pushed to his feet and exited his chambers. If he were going to feel trapped in a disaster of his own making, he would at least do it in a room with plenty of scotch.

On his way to the study, he paused briefly at Joy's door and pressed his ear close, listening for any signs that she was awake or finding sleep difficult, but the silence that greeted him was deafening. Next, he opened Abram's chamber door, but his son was similarly asleep.

Damon stepped into the room, noticing that one of the drapes had been left partially open, allowing a stream of moonlight into the room. Before long, the light would reach Abram and awaken the child.

Something about the sleeping boy drew Damon to his bedside. His sleep had been restless from the tousled, tangled nature of his bedsheets. He moved to the window, releasing the drape to cast the room into shadows. Abram shifted, turning onto his side to fully face Damon and settled with a contented sigh.

Damon longed for even a mere speck of his son's newfound peacefulness.

Unfortunately, that was something he feared he would never have.

Though peace and serenity, safety and security, were the few things he would always work toward giving his children.

He turned, departing Abram's room and making his way downstairs to his study.

CHAPTER 17

HURRIED FOOTFALLS SOUNDED as his children entered the room, already mid-banter as the import and gravity of the previous day had been long forgotten. Peculiar how resilient the pair was to such grave occurrences, while he could hardly stop himself from dwelling on the disastrous way their time at the park could have turned out.

"You did no such thing," Abram said with gruff indignation as he entered the dining hall. "Tell her, Miss Samuels. Tell Joy she did not best me during our history lesson."

Joy followed close behind her brother, her hair plaited down her back, and her black boots scuffed from her tendency to not lift her feet high enough in her hurry to beat Abram up the stairs.

"I very well did thump you good, Abram," she said with an arrogant grin. Where had she learned that the confident upturn of a smile could bring her opponent to his knees?

"Miss Samuels." Abram's wail was commendable if it were meant to repel others away from him; however, they were all in the same room, and the dining hall was not large enough to swallow the grating cry. "Tell her. Joy's questions were meant for a child, while mine were far more advanced. And I only missed two out of ten, while she missed one very important question."

Joy huffed and shoved Abram from behind, causing him to stumble farther into the room, nearly colliding with the back of a chair.

"Ah-ha! So you admit it," Joy announced victoriously. "I missed one question, while you missed two."

"Children." Miss Samuels' voice could be heard a split second before she entered the room behind his children. "I am certain your father does not want to hear you arguing after he's been working all day."

Damon kept his eyes trained on *The Post*, raising it a bit higher to stop himself from giving in to the urge to gaze upon Payton. What gown had she donned that morning? Did she wear her hair with the long, single curl that hung over her shoulder? Was she looking at him as he longed to look at her?

He'd resisted the urge most of the day to stray down the hall that would take him within hearing distance of the schoolroom. It was startling and utterly bemusing that instead of locking himself within his study for the entire day, he'd actually longed to spend time with both of his children and Payton.

However, he'd never been a man to allow his wants to overshadow his responsibilities.

"Good evening, my lord." He heard the scrape of Payton's chair as a footman pulled it out for her to sit. "Children?"

"Good evening, Father," Joy chimed, mimicking Miss Samuels.

"Good evening, Father." Abram took his seat next to his sire. "I would implore you to tell Joy that not knowing that King George II ruled over England in 1740 is a major disservice to our country. It is akin to treason, I should think."

"But you could not name the first Egyptian king, nor the father of democracy."

"You can neither spell democracy nor locate Egypt on a map," Abram retorted.

Joy merely stuck out her tongue at her brother, sending him into yet another fit of anger.

Damon made a show of rustling his paper before folding it neatly and tucking it under his elbow on the table as he glanced between his children, his expression serious. This had been the way of things for the past several days. Damon joined his children and Miss Samuels for meals—but, beyond that, he kept his distance.

Clearing his throat, he settled his hard stare on Joy, gaining a giggle of excitement from her. "Now, Joy Kinder, what is your defense for such an accusation?"

Her eyes rounded, and she nibbled on her bottom lip. "My defense is...I was not born at that time and do not care much for stuffy, wigged, old men who likely smell worse than the Thames."

She nodded on the last word, and Miss Samuels broke into laughter.

Damon couldn't help but allow his stare to stray to the governess. Her face was alight with merriment as if she were enjoying herself as much as he was.

"Miss Samuels," he grunted. "You think to support Miss Joy Kinder's treasonous declarations?" When Payton covered her mouth and nodded, Damon continued, "What shall be done, Master Abram?"

"The gallows, I fear," Abram responded with all seriousness.

"You would send your sister and your governess to the gallows, good sir?" Damon asked.

"King Henry VIII had two queens beheaded."

Abram lowered his voice to a hushed whisper as if he spoke to his father in privacy. "It would set a bad precedent if I were to be lenient with this pair."

Damon leaned close to Abram. "What do you know of leniency and precedent? You are only eight."

"I know that if King George III had been less lenient and set a precedent with the Colonies, we would not have lost so many lives," Abram retorted.

"Very true." Damon rubbed his chin as if thinking through what fate Joy and Miss Samuels would face. "However, the good peoples of the Colonies did not deserve the oppressive rules forced on them by a king who would just as readily leave them all to perish in the New World."

Joy smiled, sensing she'd won her reprieve, while Damon nodded to the footman over Abram's head, signaling for the meal to be served.

Several servants swept into the room, placing plates on the table and retreating, effectively putting an end to Joy and Abram's banter.

Damon would be lying if he didn't find a measure of satisfaction in his children's love for history, and Miss Samuels' willingness to educate them in all respects of the past, not just those deemed proper for young children. Damon was a firm believer in the past predicting the future. If things did not change, then history was doomed to repeat itself. How that pertained to him—or his children—he did not know.

Focusing on his plate, Damon felt Payton's stare on him as he did at each meal they shared.

It was as if she waited for him to look at her. That they'd share a private moment in the presence of his children. But Damon couldn't allow himself that intimacy with her. Bringing about a closer bond between them was not something Damon could afford.

He could keep watch over his children without making it known, just as he'd visited the schoolroom several times over the past several days and remained unnoticed by Payton and the children.

Distance.

It was best for them all.

However, their bantering—and the jovial mood it brought—certainly wasn't distance. The realization filled Damon with a speck of hope. For what, he wasn't sure, but hope nonetheless.

"My lord," Payton said, demanding his attention, though her tone remained relaxed. "The children have asked about a possible trip to the British Museum. It would be beneficial to their studies and give them a day outside of the townhouse if—"

"You needn't list the benefits of a day at the museum, Miss Samuels." Damon paused with a bite of pheasant nearly at his mouth. "You are free to take the children places whenever you deem they have behaved well enough for the excursion. Mrs. Brown will give you the coin needed for entry, and Mr. Brown will have a carriage at your disposal."

"But, Father, you will not come with us?" Disappointment hung heavy in Joy's tone.

"Your father does not sit idly about all day," Miss Samuels tsked.

Damon set his utensil next to his plate with a little more force than necessary. "You do not have to come to my defense, Miss Samuels."

"I did not mean—"

"It is all right." He paused, focusing on his food to calm his nerves. With only a few words, all of the light, jovial mood fled the room, taking with it his children's smiles. "Joy and Abram are children. I am an adult—with responsibilities. I cannot neglect said responsibilities to frolic in the park or visit a museum I've been to over a dozen times before. However, if

Joy and Abram wish to see the exhibits, you can accompany them."

"Very well, Lord Ashford." Payton lowered her head and set about finishing her meal, as did his children.

He hadn't meant to be difficult or brash, nor could he allow himself to give in to the hope and anticipation swirling within him after their kiss.

It was just that there were boundaries to adhere to, and propriety to maintain. Gallivanting about London with his children's governess was neither proper nor acceptable. It was better for them all if he remained at Ashford Hall while they ventured out.

He'd relished—reveled in, actually—the changes taking place in his household. Though he feared them, as well. On his way to the breakfast parlor, he'd heard Mr. Brown whistling—*whistling*. Yet, it was Damon who needed to remember how quickly things could change. The household's air could turn silent just as swiftly as it had turned cheerful.

His children's dejected and sullen glances in his direction were not something he'd anticipated. It was as if the last couple of days had undone the past four years of distance. Even Payton appeared unhappy with his decision to remain home instead of accompanying them on their outing.

"Miss Samuels." Damon pushed back his chair, his appetite gone, and his headache returned. "If you'd be so kind as to attend me in my study when you are done with your meal."

She didn't so much as take her eyes off her food when she spoke, "As you wish, my lord."

As he wished? Damon wished for many, many things. Another private moment with Miss Samuels was at the top of that list, although he had no right to desire her company. It had been a mistake to invite her to join him, one he'd resisted since their kiss.

"Enjoy your meal," he grunted before departing the room.

The fact that neither of his children met his stare shouldn't injure him as it did.

THE BARON WAS going to release her from her duties, Payton was certain of it. Why else would he demand her presence in his study after ignoring her for so many days? Letting her go after agreeing to their museum outing would hurt Joy and Abram greatly, possibly more even than their father turning down their invitation to join them.

She stood outside the closed study door for several minutes after the children's voices had faded as they made their way upstairs. She smoothed her hands down her skirts, wishing she'd changed her gown before their evening meal. Chalkdust clung to her bodice, and a spot of ink had found its way onto her sleeve. At least her hairpins still remained solidly in place.

In her mind, she heard her sister Samantha's voice, chiding her for neglecting her appearance. "*If your dress is pressed and wrinkle-free, your hair is in place, and your gloves pristine, you can command any room, Payton.*"

She wanted to laugh at her sister's irrational thinking.

A woman's dress, hair, and adornments did not speak for the woman within.

"Miss Samuels?"

Mr. Brown, the Ashford butler, watched her intently where she stood frozen in the hall.

Payton smiled, knowing the elderly servant felt responsible for everyone under the baron's roof, not just her. He was kind and caring to all the staff, along with the baron and his children. "Good evening, Mr.

Brown. The baron asked to speak with me after I finished my meal."

His lips pursed. "Shall I have Mrs. Brown bring tea?"

"I do not think that necessary but thank you." It was enough that she'd ruined her place at Ashford Hall, making it impossible to continue on. But to have the housekeeper witness her disgrace was unthinkable. "I am certain whatever he has to say will be completed in swift order, and I will be dismissed...to my chambers."

The butler nodded, his chin falling at a slight angle due to his age. "Very well, miss."

Nothing was *very well*; however, there was no need to share that with Mr. Brown.

"Do have a restful night if I do not see you again this evening," she said with a smile.

Payton faced the door, her hand poised on the latch. Everything her mother had taught her during their short time together was before her. It was time to move on. She should not *fear* doing so. Life improved with each new opportunity.

Releasing the latch, she raised her hand and knocked to announce her arrival.

"Enter." The single-word command should have irritated her, but there was no bite behind it.

She pushed the door open and stepped into the study—so familiar after her many conversations with the baron over the last month, yet it remained his private domain. She surveyed the room, finding the baron sitting in his favored chair, facing the open fire.

"Have a seat, Miss Samuels," he said, his stare never leaving the hearth. She expected to find a tumbler in his hand, filled with liquor—or empty, depending on how long she'd tarried in the hall. No glass rested between his fingers nor on the table near his elbow. In fact, his hands were clenched in tight fists on the armrests of his chair.

Had she upset him again?

"Drink?" he asked, tilting his head toward the sideboard as if inviting her to collect her own.

"No, thank you, my lord." She lowered to perch on the lounge.

"Not there."

Payton quickly stood, taking in her other option—a matching chair to the baron's seat, also facing the fire. Perhaps that was best, at least she wouldn't have to see the relief on his face when he stripped her of her duties.

She sank into the overstuffed chair, instantly knowing why Lord Ashford preferred the seat over the lounge. The cushion contoured to her bum and back, cocooning her in a softness she'd never experienced before.

The silence between them was almost comforting. He didn't speak; therefore, he hadn't told her that she must leave her position.

The minutes stretched on and on, seemingly endless as they both stared into the fire, its warmth wrapping them in its embrace. She longed to ask why he'd requested her presence but was loath to break the quiet stillness around them.

Was this how he spent his hours locked in his study? Staring into the open flames and merely existing. Her own upbringing was rarely peaceful with a house full of siblings. There was always bantering and bickering, slamming doors and pounding feet. Despite Joy's and Abram's childish episodes, the household was orderly and quiet most of the time.

When she first arrived, the overwhelming silence had unnerved her.

Now, she wondered if she could return to the chaos of Craven House—or more importantly, if she wanted to. Despite knowing that she shouldn't *want* to return home, there was a sense of comfort in the chaotic nature of her childhood home. She'd spent the last several months preparing for her future—a future outside the bounds of her family—yet the lure of home picked at her subconscious.

Obviously, with no money to her name, and her debt with the duke still unsettled, she had no other choice.

Perhaps that was what made it all so troubling: the idea that the choice was once again being stripped from her.

At her side, the baron's brow furrowed, his fists clenching and unclenching as if he worked through something in his mind. His breathing was shallow and quick, tension evident in the set of his shoulders and back.

He'd appeared at ease and almost jovial in the dining hall despite his mood turning solemn after she'd spoke out in his defense. At the moment, he seemed to have returned to the man she'd met when she first came to Ashford Hall. Burdened and...almost defeated. The crushing weight of his indiscernible troubles threatening to finally overtake him.

Payton had been foolish enough to think that their outing and their kiss would change things— *anything*.

It had certainly changed everything for her. No, not changed, but it had altered her perception.

Perhaps too much time had passed, too many issues remained unsolved, and the damage was far more profound than she'd imagined. Did he struggle with things that she was unaware of?

The clock on the mantel above the hearth chimed seven. She'd asked Mr. Curtis to come and collect her at half past the hour. That left her thirty minutes to have the children abed and herself waiting down the street for the Craven House servant.

The baron had asked her here for a reason, to speak about something, but his silence continued.

"My lord?"

He flinched at her words but kept his narrowed stare focused straight ahead.

"Will you be going out tonight?" His question was unexpected. Besides the night she'd discovered him following her home from Galment's, he'd never queried her about her comings and goings.

"Yes." There was no reason to lie.

"I will also be leaving for the evening," he said. "I will have a carriage readied for your use."

"I do not need—"

He turned sharply to face her, his entire countenance heavy with something akin to fatigue. That was not something new.

"I will not spend my infrequent evening away from Ashford Hall fretting over you walking the dark streets," he said in a rush before his lips pressed closed. "Is it not enough I have to worry about my children's welfare that you will add yourself to the burden?"

"I am a grown woman. A hired servant in your home, my lord," she replied quietly. "Do you worry when the maid goes to the market? Or a footman out on an errand?"

He remained silent.

"I am no different than a maid or the footman."

"The bloody hell you are not," he huffed. He rubbed the back of his neck, but his built-up tension did not leave, even Payton could see that much. He breathed in and exhaled, the sound louder than the crackle of the fire. "Never have I worried over the whereabouts of another governess or maid for that matter, and there have been many with likely more to come. Yet, with you, I…"

The silence stretched between them once more as the tension inside her twisted tightly at the insinuation in his words.

"I do not want to care about you," he whispered, so softly she wondered if she'd heard him correctly. "When will you return?"

She would not admit that she was fleeing Ashford Hall for Craven House. It was none of his concern—her past, her present, or her future.

"Before the children awaken." She couldn't bear to look him in the eyes.

"Very well." His words sounded flippant to her, but his tone conveyed that things were not well at all.

"I will see to the children and depart for the evening." Payton stood and started for the door, expecting the baron to stop her. To call for her to return. To command her to remain here, with him. To say or do…something before she crossed the threshold into the hall beyond.

But he remained silent. And still.

If this were how her mother's entanglements ended, Payton would be happy to leave Damon behind. To hollow silence. The playacting that what had transpired between them had been forgettable and not worth mentioning. The feigned laughter and jesting from the dining hall.

With a sigh, Payton fled the study, keeping her steps measured and unhurried as she made her way to the stairs. The last thing she was willing to do—and she was willing to do many things—was allow the baron to know he'd hurt her as well as his children.

CHAPTER 18

PAYTON PULLED THE pins from her hair, allowing her gathered waves to hang freely down her back before she threw herself on the chaise in Marce's gold and red office. Her long, mahogany curls trailed on the rug below where she lay, but she paid it no mind.

The room was startlingly empty without her eldest sister on her throne behind the feminine desk. How many times had Payton been summoned to this very room while Marce held court over her younger, impertinent, disobedient siblings? She'd been beckoned to attend her sister when she was caught pickpocketing with Ellie when they were only twelve. She'd been hauled into the room by Garrett when he found her cheating at cards at a dinner party. She'd been taken to task in this very room when Marce discovered her slipping into her upstairs window after a night wandering Covent Garden.

It all seemed a lifetime ago. And childish.

She'd been so contrary in her youth.

Difficult to believe that she'd changed so much since her arrival at Ashford Hall.

When had her actions begun to have such severe consequences? When had her words taken on such import? Her plans for her independence, her life to come, had developed since she'd moved out of Craven House. They'd become more real and encroaching, if that were even possible; as if she were only now coming to understand the gravity of her choices.

And why had the baron taken any interest in her?

He'd all but ignored her since their kiss, only joining her and the children for meals. Nothing more.

She scoffed at Damon's earlier declaration. He planned to spend his evening away from Ashford Hall, as well. The man hadn't spent so much as a single evening outside his townhouse in all the weeks she'd lived there. He rarely even left during the daytime, but he thought to go out tonight. But why even speak of it to her?

She ran her hands through her loose hair, her fingers tangling in the long waves, and she had to tug several times to free them.

Footsteps sounded in the hall, likely Mr. Curtis coming to collect her to return to the baron's house. It was as they'd done over a dozen times since she'd taken the position as the Ashford governess, the only difference being that she knew that Damon would not be home when she returned.

Where could the man have gone?

The door to the office opened without a knock, and Payton twisted on the chaise, her head hanging off the side.

"What in heavens are you doing?" Her brother filled the open doorway.

From her vantage point, Garrett was upside down…the entire world topsy-turvy.

"Wallowing," she offered. "You?"

"Hiding," he mused, sinking onto the chaise beside her.

"I never thought I'd say this, let alone admit it to you. *However*," she paused, shifting her head back onto the chaise, "I miss Marce...and Jude."

"What of Samantha?" he jested.

Payton wrinkled her nose. "She can remain abroad with Ridgefeld."

At that, Garrett chuckled, setting his hand on her outstretched legs. "Sam is a bit of an oddity, is she not?"

"We are all peculiar in our own way; however, she lacks Jude's empathy."

"What do you know of empathy?" he asked.

"More and more as the days go by, I fear," she mumbled, lifting her neck slightly to clasp her hands behind her head.

"Is my little Pay growing up?"

"I have never been *your little Pay*, Garrett," she retorted but laughed when he feigned injury. "It is only that life is difficult, and decisions are not always easy. Do you think Jude's choice to wed Simon was something she labored over?"

"What has you pondering marriage?" He pinched her leg through her skirts, and she kicked at him to stop.

"Not marriage, but change." She wasn't certain what she hoped Garrett would say. "What of you? Was it difficult to make the decision to move on, to leave us, departing Craven House for life at the Albany?"

"I wasn't moving on or leaving you," he grunted. "I am a man. Despite my meager inheritance from my father, I cannot expect Marce to take care of me forever. I have to find my own way in life. But I did not move on from my family. I hope to one day have something to give the four of you. At the moment, I can give Marce some semblance of contentment knowing that I can care for myself."

"Jude is wed to Simon, and Sam to Elijah. You are living at the Albany and doing Lord only knows what during your time away from Craven House." She snuck a glance at him, hoping he'd share a bit of what he was up to when he was not with her, but he remained silent. Every time she attempted to gain a peek into his London life, he said nothing…or evaded her questions with comments such as *hiding* with no further explanation. "I suppose it is only I who Marce has to fret over now."

"Not true." He shook his head. "She is pleased that you are doing well in the baron's employ. Perhaps that is why she left so unexpectedly for one of her mysterious trips. She is satisfied we are all cared for, Perhaps, she will find a husband herself before long."

Payton snorted, and Garrett broke into unrestrained laughter.

The thought of their eldest sister…with a man…was preposterous.

"Marce will wed the same day I swear off the gaming tables," Payton chuckled, her stomach aching from her deep laughter. "Besides, she can't marry. What would happen to Craven House?"

"I suppose she'd have no use for the property."

"What if I moved home?"

His brow rose before his stare narrowed on her. "Are you leaving your post at Lord Ashford's?"

"Of course, not." She sat up, swinging her feet to the floor. "I only meant, what if I ever needed to return to Craven House?"

"You are not the young girl you once were. With time, I have no fear you'll figure things out without having to return home." He shrugged. "Beyond that, it is not my concern. Men only at the Albany. Do not think to cast yourself at my feet for housing."

Her brother jested, as was his defense when conversations took on a serious tone.

"Thankfully, I'd rather throw myself on Sam's

mercy than request lodging with you, dear brother."

He wiped his forehead in mock relief. "That is wonderful news, as my paltry funds would not last long with both of us at the tables."

Payton had thought several times of taking her fifteen shillings and returning to 10 Mill Street in an attempt to triple her savings, but since her kiss with Damon, the thrill of a high-stakes game had lost its luster. Perhaps the allure hadn't diminished, per se, but she longed for something entirely different. Not the adventure that came from laying all she'd acquired on the line with the threat of losing it all. Perhaps she'd discovered other activities—or people—who gave her the same thrill…posed the same risk.

"If you have your own funds, my friend Davenport and I are attending a party this evening— with a card room. I am certain he wouldn't mind if you joined us." His eyes widened. "In fact, you might lend an air of respectability."

"That is ever so kind of you, but I should be returning to the baron's house." She pondered remaining at Craven House for the night and having Mr. Curtis return her before first light. "The butler, a most kind man, does not take to his bed until the entire household is accounted for."

"If you must," Garrett mused, pushing to his feet.

"Who are you hiding from?" she asked, almost as an afterthought.

He eyes flitted toward the door—his escape— before he turned back to her with an easy smile. "Did I say hiding earlier? I meant picking up an old coat I left here a few nights ago."

"Good evening, Garrett," she called as he departed the room.

"I'll inform Mr. Curtis you are ready to return to Ashford Hall," he tossed over his shoulder.

Suddenly, she longed to be back at Damon's residence, if only to make sure *he* arrived home safely.

CHAPTER 19

DAMON STOOD OUTSIDE the schoolroom doorway. The room had initially been Joy and Abram's nursery, but it had been converted for their use as a classroom as soon as they were old enough to no longer need a wet nurse. The pale-yellow draperies had been replaced by muted grey fabric. The twin cradles were moved to the Ashford attic, and the chest of toys transported to Falconcrest for future generations of Ashford children. Even the charcoal drawings and the neat row of nursery books had been done away with in favor of two desks, a tall shelf full of textbooks, and a chalkboard mounted on the far wall.

The transformation had been something he'd been proud of, though that did not stop him from wondering if Sarah would have felt the same had she still been alive. Were the colors too drab, the furniture too masculine, or the books not arranged as she'd like? She'd been a learned woman with a family who prided themselves on knowledge, similar to Damon's way of thinking.

Joy leaned over her primer book, sounding out words as her finger traced the letters. He could almost picture an older version of the girl, diligently bent over some large tome, reading aloud the new progressions in medicine or the sciences.

Abram, on the far side of the room, had abandoned his desk for a cushion on the floor, three books open and spread out before him as he hastily made notes on a piece of paper before glancing at one of the books, turning a page, and nodding as if he'd found something unexpected yet enticing.

Damon's sister might think that his children would flourish if given a chance to study outside their home; however, Flora was not their parent. Damon was their father, and despite all the years of uncertainty, he knew they belonged here, with him. At least for another few years.

Once Miss Samuels taught them all she knew, he would hire other tutors. They would study the ancient languages, foreign lands, and more of the sciences. Perhaps music and art if they desired.

Speaking of the governess, she paced at the front of the room, her own nose stuck in a book. He could not tell from the distance if the volume were of an educational nature or for pleasure. He lurked in the shadowy hall outside the door, confident that his presence wouldn't be noticed.

After he'd ventured out the previous night, demanding Rigby drive him around town for several hours, Damon was pleased to hear that Miss Samuels had arrived home before him—safe and unharmed. It was inconceivable that he'd been forced out of his home for the simple fact that he couldn't seem to collect his thoughts with Payton close. One moment, he desired nothing more than to go to her. And the next, he remembered the hardship of loss when someone he cared deeply for was no longer there. It was a constant struggle between his wants and his needs.

He wanted to hold her, touch her, kiss her.

However, he needed to remain separate and not

allow his emotions to dictate his actions. Letting her close, allowing her in, would only make the hurt of her leaving more piercing.

Damon's emotions were at war with his common sense—with neither finding clear victory.

He'd tiptoed down the hall housing her room, pressing his ear to each door as he passed, but no sounds had been heard. He knew she was within; however, a part of him needed the comfort in confirming it for himself. In the end, he'd continued to his own chambers and fell into a fitful slumber. Truly, he wondered if there were ever to be any other type of sleep for him.

They were all awake now.

Had Payton wondered about his whereabouts the night before? Had she fretted when she came home and found him still out?

He scoffed. It was likely she hadn't noticed his absence at all.

The noise brought a trio of stares to him— Payton's questioning glance, Joy's excited bouncing, and Abram's suspicious glare.

He deserved each reaction. He'd acted uncouth and pompous the previous night, and now he desperately wanted to make it up to his children…and their governess. He was at a loss for how, but he couldn't allow that to stop him from attempting to make amends.

"Father." Joy rushed from her seat and threw her arms around his legs, burrowing her face against his side. "Come, see my letters."

It appeared his youngest had already forgiven him and completely recovered from her ordeal at the pond. From Payton's and Abram's reserved watchfulness, Damon had no doubt they would not be as easily persuaded.

He allowed Joy to lead him to her small desk,

where she pointed to her slate. In a delicate hand, she had written the first five letters of the alphabet. The curve of the *B* precise, while the *E* was a bit less neat.

"Wonderful," he marveled. He turned to Abram. "What are you working so diligently on, Abram?"

He wasn't as excited to share his studies as Joy had been, but he pushed to his feet, bringing his stack of papers with him. "I am outlining the movements of soldiers during the Trojan War." He held out his notes. "In Greece."

Damon accepted the paper, impressed with Abram's detailed accounting, as he kept his expression serious in an attempt to hide his grin. "I am well informed about the Trojan War—I am older, but I remember my studies at Eton well enough."

"Miss Samuels was telling me all about Helen of Troy." Joy closed her eyes, clutching her hands to her chest and swaying from side to side. "Ever so romantic. She was married to a great king but loved by many. She caused the war, did you know?"

"Helen of Troy cost her people many lives." Abram snatched his papers back and slunk back to his place on the floor. "Besides, I am not convinced the woman ever existed. She is a fabled Greek myth, that is all."

Damon remained quiet. He hadn't sought out the schoolroom to partake of their lessons but invite them on a lesson of his own.

"I thought today might be a good day for the pair of you to discover all the hidden wonders of the museum." He rocked back on his heels and waited for their ready excitement at the prospect of another excursion…and so soon after the disaster at the park. "I thought we might leave within the hour. Spend all day studying the exhibits."

Damon glanced between the pair. From Joy's vigorous nodding, she was prepared to depart that very moment; however, Abram stared between his books and his notes.

"I am in the middle of my lesson," Abram mumbled. "I do not think—"

"Come now, son," Damon prodded. "It will be great fun, and you can finish your lesson tomorrow. I'm certain your governess will allow you an extra day."

Abram narrowed his stare at his father. "Great fun? The museum is a place of learning, not a playhouse."

"Abram," Miss Samuels warned. "I think the pair of you will have a wonderful time at the museum with your father. He can teach you many things."

He huffed, crossing his arms. "I much prefer your tutelage, Miss Samuels. Father holds such archaic notions about history."

"Well, I only visited the museum under duress when my sisters forced me to accompany them. In this matter, the baron is far superior." She smiled. "I will remain here and prepare your lesson for tomorrow."

Damon's heart sank when he realized Payton would not be accompanying them.

"You do not mean to come with us?" Joy turned away from Damon, but he'd already spied her disappointment.

Damon met Payton's stare. Did she seek to escape their outing, worried it would be as calamitous as the last? Or was she avoiding him?

"Miss Samuels works tirelessly every day with the pair of you." Damon leaned down and swooped Joy into his arms. It was such a foreign gesture that his daughter stiffened in his hold for a moment before clasping him around the neck with a giggle. "I think she is very deserving of a day off, even if it is only an afternoon. What say you, dear one?"

Joy's expression turned serious as she nibbled her bottom lip. When had the girl taken on such a habit? "Oh, I think that is a positively lovely idea."

"Unless Miss Samuels wishes to accompany us to the museum…"

Damon trailed off, hoping she'd indeed insist on joining them.

Utterly shocked, he realized he *wanted* her to *want* to accompany them. His stomach twisted as they awaited her response. Since the moment he'd seen her in his foyer doused in blue, he'd struggled with his need to be close, yet keep his distance from her. Had his internal war been won without him noticing?

Payton closed the book in her hands with a sharp snap. "I do have a few personal matters to attend to, if you do not mind, my lord."

His chest seized with disappointment, but his smile remained. Even if Payton didn't wish to accompany them, it would still give him precious time with Joy and Abram, in a place Damon much enjoyed.

Abram appeared downright dejected at the prospect of being alone with him.

They had become too attached to the governess…which would eventually make her departure all the more damaging to them all. That did nothing to stop him from desiring her company, despite the damning consequences he knew would follow. He'd been too long in his grief to know where to go, what to do, and, most importantly, what to say to convince her to remain at Ashford Hall.

"VERY WELL." THE baron set Joy back on her feet and tapped the girl's button nose with a familiar affection Payton had never witnessed from him. "It is settled. I will take you two to the museum while Miss Samuels attends to her own affairs."

Tucking the book under her arm, Payton smiled and nodded.

What other choice did she have? She could have accepted Damon's invitation, voiced her opinion that the baron was not suited to an outing without her, yet it was obvious he could care for his children without her present. He was a capable man despite his reserved nature.

Time alone with his offspring could not do anything but strengthen the baron's bond with Joy and Abram. It was what she'd hoped to achieve and would leave fewer feelings of guilt when she left Ashford Hall. It was what they needed, all of them. The three of them were a family, after all.

When the time came, they needed to hold strong together after she moved on.

Payton could not always be there between a father and his children. Someone shouldn't have to be there to keep Damon connected to his offspring. She was not the tie that bound their family together. Payton was an outsider—one destined to leave.

She notched her chin higher. "I know you and your brother will enjoy the museum, Joy, even more so without me tagging along."

It shouldn't hurt that Damon had insisted she take the afternoon off, but the truth of the matter did not make the spike to her chest any less painful. In fact, she'd turned down his invitation to accompany them because she was uncertain if it were a genuine offer or if it had only been made to appease the children.

It was Saturday. Tomorrow was her usual day off, and perhaps some distance and time to evaluate her precarious position in the baron's household would do her good. She'd thought she'd come to terms with the circumstances separating her and Damon and the implications of their shared kiss; Damon was her employer, and his children were her charges. But each time she saw him, it only brought more questions to mind. When he first suggested taking the children to the museum alone, she'd thought she'd seen a question in his eyes. Almost as if he silently pleaded with her to reject his offer and accompany them. However, the look disappeared, and Payton wondered if she'd imagined it entirely.

"I suppose nothing will change with the Trojan War timeline if I do not complete it today." Abram slipped his papers into one of the books and closed it, trapping his notes and saving his page. "I will collect my coat."

Abram departed the room, pausing to take Joy's hand and lead her out.

Payton turned toward the chalkboard, busying herself by rubbing the wall with a rag to remove their daily lesson. They would not return to the schoolroom until Monday, and that left her plenty of time to explore lesson planning.

"Payton?"

She lowered her head and let her hand fall away from the wall.

She'd prayed the baron would follow after the children, leaving her to her own devices, but he remained behind.

She cleared the lump from her throat before she spoke. "Thank you for escorting the children, my lord."

When there was no sound behind her, Payton lifted her chin—and the rag—to continue with her chore. She didn't need an explanation of why he preferred that she remain at the house while they went to the museum. She did not need to see the regret in his stare over their brief, intimate encounter outside Joy's room. Blast it all, but she could not be made to forget the entire night if he continued as he was.

She was not part of their family, would never have that luxury—nor did she want it.

Her place at Ashford Hall was merely temporary.

She was replaceable to the baron and his children, just as she could replace them and her position as a governess with another household—if she so chose.

She'd been begging herself to believe all this, to grasp the truth of it and hold it close, if only for her protection. For her, it didn't matter what her place was with the baron and his children, nor that it was temporary. Never in all her years had she dreamt of a future as a governess. There was no freedom in that fate, and if she accepted that her life held nothing else, then it was where she would remain.

She sensed his eyes on her back, watching…waiting.

What was he waiting for? Her approval at his decision to leave her out of their outing even though it had been her idea to take the children?

The baron didn't need her approval on any matter, least of all his children, and especially *his* comings and goings.

She squeezed her eyes tight, remembering her foolish idea from the night before. Directly upon returning to the townhouse from Craven House, she'd sought out the baron in his study, thinking if they spoke—really discussed what had happened in Joy's room—they could put it behind them. Marce had always been a firm believer in communication. If a person spoke of something enough, clarity would follow. In this case, Payton would listen as he admitted that their kiss had been a mistake, that any private time between them was best avoided, and they'd both laugh with relief and go on about their duties.

Unfortunately, or fortunately depending on how she looked at it, that hadn't happened.

Damon hadn't returned from his evening out.

Worse yet, Mr. Brown had caught her leaving the baron's study. The butler's knowing look had made Payton wonder if news of their master kissing the hired help had spread through the servants' quarters already.

What if Joy and Abram heard the rumblings of scandal?

She could not bear to hurt them any more than they'd already been harmed by their mother's death.

"Are you certain my taking the children without you is wise?" he whispered, suddenly closer than she'd expected. His footsteps had made no sound as he walked across the schoolroom. "They would prefer you join—"

"My lord." She pivoted, and the book slipped from under her arm and thumped to the floor. Neither made any move to collect it. "I agree it is best that I allow you to take the children."

"I never said it was best," he sighed.

He was a mere two feet from her. So close, his scent traveled toward her, a familiar blend she'd come to expect when he was near.

"Payton, I..."

"Miss Samuels," she sighed. It had to be Miss Samuels to him. There were no more private moments, no more stolen kisses in the dark. She was his children's governess—nothing more. "Joy and Abram are your children. You are quite competent to escort them to the museum without my accompaniment, I assure you. Do enjoy your day."

His shoulders sagged. Had he expected something different from her?

She had expected something entirely different from him, as well. Going on about his usual tasks, especially taking Joy and Abram out was nearly unbelievable. Life was not always what a person expected, though. She knew that well enough, as should the baron. Life was unfair and normally unpredictable.

He reached out, taking her free hand and rubbing his thumb across her palm.

"Miss Samuels—"

She pulled her hand from his grasp and clasped both behind her back, the rag wadded up in her fist. She hadn't any idea what game he played at, but she was tired of playing along. One moment, he pushed her away, And the next, he stood far too close for her to keep her thoughts in order.

"The children will be back any moment, my lord." She narrowed her eyes at him and straightened her shoulders. "It would be unwise to allow them to see us standing so close."

They both took a step back at the same time the children raced back into the room. Joy had chosen her black, knee-length coat with the brass buttons and a bonnet, while Abram had his jacket slung over his shoulder but had donned his small Hessians that matched his father's.

"Children, I think it would be wise to bring your notebooks," Payton called as the baron turned away from her. "In case you learn something interesting or want to sketch an exhibit to discuss later."

Joy's grin dimmed, but Abram readily collected his notebook and pencil nub from his desk.

Damon held his arms wide and boomed, "Are we ready?"

"Yes," both children called.

Damon ushered the children from the room, throwing her an expectant look, his eyes begging her to stop him, to reconsider accompanying them. When she remained silent, he disappeared from sight, his footfalls matching his children's pace as they headed for the stairs.

Pinching the bridge of her nose, she leaned over and collected her book from the floor and slumped into Abram's empty desk chair. There was little hope they could return to the way things had been. They'd crossed some invisible boundary, with no chance of negotiating their way back.

The slam of the front door below stairs signaled the family's departure.

Perhaps she should spend the day outside of Ashford Hall. There was an errand she'd been putting off. She needed to collect the gown the baron had purchased for her at Madame DelFortaine's Shoppe. She'd debated accepting the dress; however, after their recent situation, Payton had determined that the baron owed her. Joy and Abram had ruined her other gown, after all.

She hurried to her room and collected her cloak and handbag.

Perhaps after picking up her new dress, she'd call on Garrett at the Albany and insist that he accompany her to Paxton and Whitfield for afternoon tea. After that, maybe she'd convince him to continue on to 10 Mill Street as he was seen as an educated lord and his attendance at Galment's townhouse was viewed favorably. Tomorrow was Sunday and her day off, after all.

CHAPTER 20

"MY LORD." MR. BROWN stood at his elbow, a single letter on a silver tray in presentation. "This arrived for you only moments ago."

Damon set the morning *Post* aside and retrieved the letter, holding it above his half-eaten meal. Flora's bold, heavy-handed script was as familiar as his own across the missive as well as her stationery scent—roses. The offensive aroma of old flowers wafted about the room, and he slipped his finger under the wax to break Wittenbottom's signature seal.

If anything, a note from his sister would distract him from musings about where Payton had gone. He'd given her the afternoon and evening off the prior day, and today was Sunday; however, he'd expected her to be around the townhouse. To his chagrin, he'd been informed by his butler that the governess hadn't returned since departing the previous afternoon.

"Who is the letter from?" Joy tugged at his sleeve. She'd taken to sitting in Payton's seat—formerly her mother's seat—when the governess didn't join them for meals. "I wish I could receive a letter."

Damon smiled. "It is from Aunt Flora."

His day with the children at the museum had been taxing but worthwhile. Abram and Joy had remained close to his side and listened to his every word as he guided them through the exhibits. They'd laughed many times. He and Abram had sat before a display of archaic, crude weapons and debated the merits of hand-to-hand combat versus ancient weapons. They'd even strayed into modern warfare. The discussion had been inspiring, at least for Damon.

Joy had been less talkative as she remained steadfast by his side while they traversed the museum. Damon suspected her quiet demeanor had nothing to do with boredom, but rather a sense of overwhelming interest.

They'd eaten a simple meal after returning home, and then Damon had walked Joy and Abram to their chambers for bed.

With the children asleep, he had naught to do but pace the halls as he attempted to hide his anxiety.

And now, the children flanked him at the table, with Miss Samuels nowhere to be seen.

Oddly enough, the children hadn't asked after her either.

Could it be only he who noted her absence, or had the children grown accustomed to caring for themselves on Sundays? Most Sundays, Damon was busy preparing for his gaming evening.

"Open it, Father!" Joy said, falling into her chair as if the excitement of it all were too much for her tiny body to bear.

As soon as he unfolded the letter, she was behind his shoulder, attempting to read.

"Hmmmm," he mused, holding it close. "Very interesting."

"What? What?" Though she was behind him, Damon could sense Joy hopping from foot to foot.

"It appears that Aunt Flora has procured a tiger for Abram and an elephant for you, dear one," he jested, making certain to keep his tone steady and without any hint of laughter.

"I am not interested." Abram hadn't taken so much as a bite of his morning meal as he scribbled in his notebook. "Tigers are dangerous and belong in their natural environment, not in London."

Damon gave up and chuckled at the boy's oblivious demeanor. Perhaps he'd done a disservice to Abram by not jesting with him more often.

"That is just silly." Joy swatted his arm playfully. "An elephant and a tiger would never suit in the gardens. Where would they sleep, and what would Cook feed them?"

Damon turned to Joy with a smile. "I am happy to see at least one of you has a sense of humor." Or more accurately, one of the three of them. Years ago, he and Sarah had often laughed at inane anecdotes and obtuse *ton* members. His merriment was another part of himself he'd thought long gone. "But, alas, Aunt Flora has not written about anything as exciting as zoo animals."

Joy pouted, pushing her lower lip forward. "Then what?"

He glanced down at the missive. If he'd been alone when it was delivered, he would have slipped it into his desk and forgotten about it. Unfortunately, his daughter's zeal at receiving a letter, even though it wasn't addressed to her, was infectious and impossible to ignore.

"We have been invited to dine with Aunt Flora this afternoon at Wexfestor's on Piccadilly." She'd never sent such an invite before and rarely requested the children's presence.

This did bring Abram's attention away from his work, his brow furrowing. "Aunt Flora does not ask

Joy and me to meals. In fact, I have never heard her speak either of our names. You may go without me."

Damon had been thinking the same exact thing. He reread his sister's note. *I find myself free this afternoon. You and the children shall attend me at Wexfestor's for my afternoon meal.*

It was everything he'd expect from Flora.

A summons, not an invitation. He was her servant ready to do her bidding, not her brother.

"Mayhap you are correct, Abram," he mused, refolding the letter. "I am certain you are both very busy today."

"*I* have nothing to do," Joy screeched.

"You want to dine with Aunt Flora?" The girl's enthusiasm had his chest tightening. Had he neglected to give her something she truly longed for?

She returned to her chair, folding her hands in her lap and tucking her crossed ankles under her seat. "Oh, yes, please."

Perhaps Wexfestor's would be another welcome distraction. His gaming night was later that evening; however, Mr. Brown, with the assistance of a couple of footmen, could see the room prepared.

"It is settled," he said, placing his palms on the table. "We shall go."

"It is not settled at all." Abram frowned.

"We will attend your aunt, eat quickly, and return home," he rebutted. "But you will go."

"I will stay here with Miss Samuels."

"Miss Samuels has the day off and is not at Ashford Hall."

"Then summon her back," Abram said, crossing his arms as if that were the end of things.

"Did Aunt Flora invite Miss Samuels to join us, too?" Joy asked.

"She did not." Damon reclined in his chair. It appeared the governess's absence would not remain unnoticed.

"That is quite discourteous of Aunt Flora." Joy rubbed her chin. "I suppose we should send our regrets."

Discourteous? Send our regrets?

The girl was barely six and spoke like a lady thrice her age.

"It is one meal without Miss Samuels," he argued.

"Three," Abram said before returning to his notebook once again. "Last night, this meal, and now afternoon dining with Aunt Flora."

"I am certain Miss Samuels would not want the pair of you to remain indoors just because she is not here to accompany us." Why had he thought their good cheer from the previous day would extend to the next? "We are going, and that is all."

"Very well." Abram collected his notes and stood, leaving his plate untouched. "What time will we depart?"

"One o'clock."

He nodded before leaving the room.

"What could Aunt Flora possibly want?" Joy mumbled.

"I haven't any notion." Damon picked up his fork and speared an egg on his plate, popping it into his mouth.

If she thought to bring up the subject of boarding school—with the children present—she would be sorely peeved when he gave her the same answer he'd given for years now. What other reasoning could she have for demanding they meet her?

Could she know of the disastrous card night with Miss Samuels and the Duke of Catherton? No, the duke would never admit that he'd been swindled and left owed a debt.

Maybe it was long past time Joy and Abram spent more time with Flora. She was their only other relation besides him. With Sarah gone, Joy would one day need a woman to guide her in society, and Damon knew of no other for the task. A relationship between Joy and her aunt would not harm his daughter, and could only do a world of good for his sister. If there was one thing Flora was gifted at, it was making her way in society. Indeed, if she spent some time with Joy—and Abram—Flora would come to care for them, much like an aunt should for her niece and nephew.

Joy bent over her plate, her blond hair brushed and hanging freely down her back as she finished her toast with orange jam. The same orange jam he favored.

His heart squeezed with affection. He wanted the best for her—both now and in the future. If that meant a closer relationship with her only female relation, then it was what needed to be done. Damon had spent so many years neglecting his children's needs while feeding his own despair. It had to end.

If—or more accurately, *when*—Payton left them, Joy would benefit from Flora's presence. No matter his sister's aversion to children, at least she could be a constant in Joy's and Abram's lives—something he couldn't expect of Payton or any governess that might follow.

"Do you have a pretty frock to wear?" he asked.

Joy's sparkling, moss-green eyes caught his as she bit her bottom lip. "Perhaps. Do you think Aunt Flora would prefer a light green dress or peach?"

"I would assume"—he leaned toward her as if captivated by the conversation—"peach. And would you like to know why?"

When she only smiled and nodded, he continued.

"Because you are as sweet as a peach."

"Oh, Father," she giggled, slipping from her seat. "I will be ready on time."

She flitted from the room, dancing the entire way until all he could hear was her humming as she skipped down the hallway to the stairs.

Damon longed for even a fraction of Joy's lighthearted nature. Perhaps then he would not dwell so much on the past or fret so intensely about their future.

PAYTON WALKED BRISKLY down Piccadilly, the early afternoon sun warming her skin and invigorating her spirit. An entire night at Craven House without any of her siblings in residence had been almost too much to bear. Quiet, without a thing to attend to, she'd languished about the house with nothing to occupy her time but her own thoughts.

The moment she left Craven House, her spirits had begun to lift.

It made little sense. Freedom and independence would mean periods of time spent alone. Solitude was something she should relish. Nevertheless, she'd done nothing but think about those she'd rather be with. Namely, Damon and the children. She'd wondered who'd selected the perfect frock for Joy or if Abram ever left his studies long enough for a spot in the sun. What of Damon? Had he returned to his study? Did he wonder where she was and if she thought of him—their kiss.

Damon's maudlin mood, which had lifted over the last several days, had instead settled on her.

Mr. Curtis had deposited her on Piccadilly and promised to return for her a few hours later.

She hadn't anything to buy, nor the funds to spend; however, her new gown, along with Joy's, should be ready at the modiste's shop. She could imagine the girl's excitement when she arrived back at Ashford Hall with their new frocks.

Perhaps they would don the finery and dine together in the schoolroom.

Payton laughed, her arm bumping a passing gentleman.

"Pardon, miss," he called over his shoulder but kept pace as he continued away from Payton.

The walk was busy for the time of day; however, the warm weather was likely a draw to tempt everyone from their residences.

Snippets of conversation floated around her as she walked. The creak of carriage wheels and the clop of horse hooves passed her on the street. It was almost enough to keep her mind from wandering back to Damon—errr, Lord Ashford, and his insistence that she take the previous afternoon and evening off. Never, in the several weeks she'd been the Ashford governess, had the baron given her time off that wasn't her regular day. Even more confusing, he planned to spend time with his children—away from the townhouse.

Why should she feel left out? Hadn't it been her goal to have the baron connect with his children?

She hadn't expected it to happen so swiftly. That was all.

She took a deep breath. The smell of fresh bread and savory meat drifted on the air, and her stomach let out a loud growl. Glancing around, she set her hand against her midsection, hoping that no one had heard the noise.

Before her were large windows beyond which was a fancy restaurant.

Perhaps a small meal—alone—would take up a bit of her time, and then she could collect the waiting dresses and meet Mr. Curtis. Despite it being her day off, she could have him deposit her at the baron's house. Joy would be beside herself with excitement.

And, if Payton were being honest, she missed the children.

This evening would be the baron's gaming party; however, she had no intention of attending. She had yet to gather enough coin to repay her debt to Catherton and the possibility of encountering him at Ashford Hall was too great a risk, even for her.

The clink of fine silverware and jovial, spirited conversations floated out to greet Payton, along with the delicious aroma of food.

Inside, nearly every table was taken.

Cupping her gloved hand above her brow, she scanned the interior of the dining hall. Eating at such an establishment had been a luxury her elder sister had never afforded them, and Payton had often stopped in front of such places when she and Ellie were out in London to imagine what it would be like to sit amongst the finely dressed patrons. A large table toward the back of the main room caught her notice, but not because the group sitting at it was causing a scene. Two blond-haired children sat focused on a young woman.

Her stomach twisted at the sight of Abram and Joy, their heads bent toward a red-haired woman, a few years Payton's senior, her hair pulled into a tight knot at the back of her head, her dress a muted blue so deep it was nearly black. Her collar rose to nearly her chin with a line of pearl-white buttons leading down to the sash at her waist. Her mouth appeared an angry slash across her face as she spoke. The group's conversation couldn't be heard from the walk outside, but the woman's words appeared clipped, and her eyes glared between the children.

What had the baron spoken of at Ashford Hall?
There have been many with likely more to come…

If he'd thought his meaning had escaped her notice, he was gravely mistaken. As he'd been correct to state, a governess *was* replaceable—simply and swiftly.

Along with Joy and Abram, Lord Ashford sat with an elder woman, her gown and hat richly adorned with lace. Payton had seen the woman at Ashford Hall once or twice, though never at the baron's gaming nights. But Payton did recall seeing her at Galment's recently.

When Payton saw the woman at the Ashford townhouse, she'd made a lapse in judgement by questioning Mr. Brown about the woman's identity. He'd clucked and blustered, informing her that it was the baron's elder sister, Lady Wittenbottom—a viscountess, and a deplorable lady, indeed. The viscountess was rumored to despise the baron's children, or so the household staff insisted. All children, in fact. At the time, Payton had sighed and commiserated with Damon's sister as it was a morning that Abram had decided to switch her salt with sugar, thus causing her to ruin three hard-boiled eggs. Though if the children's aunt ever put any effort into gaining familiarity with her kin, she would find Joy and Abram spirited yet sweet.

It had taken Payton some time to gain Joy's and Abram's trust and, therefore, their respect. However, as their family, Lady Wittenbottom was required to care for her kin. And it was even easier now that everything was different. The wall Joy and Abram had constructed around themselves had quickly crumbled. Even Payton had gone against her better sense and grown attached to the children. Affection for the duo was no longer lacking in the least.

Was Damon aware of his sister's disdain for children?

In the dim dining area, the baron shook his head

with a frown and laid his fork beside his plate. Payton did not think the family meal progressing well at all until the baron turned to the younger, red-haired woman and…smiled. Damon spoke to the woman and the children, shifting his seat over a few inches to be closer, and his mood appeared to lighten.

It could not be.

Payton narrowed her glare on the baron, his children, and the two women as a servant appeared and collected their empty plates.

The day was suddenly overly warm, and beads of perspiration broke out on Payton's forehead at the same moment her lungs ached. She held her breath without realizing it.

Damon said something that had Joy breaking out into a fit of giggles, while Abram cracked into a much more sedate grin. Even the auburn-haired woman eased a bit, and the hint of a smile spread across her face before her expression returned to her previous stern countenance.

There was no other explanation for the meeting, or for giving Payton the prior day off. It had all been a ruse. She was being replaced.

The woman inside the restaurant with Damon, his sister, and the children bore a striking resemblance to every tutor and governess Payton had had in her youth. She had a severe, reserved nature only possessed by those who dedicated their life to instructing the young.

The baron was hiring a new governess for the children, and from how well the meeting was going, it appeared he planned to give Payton no notice of being let go.

There should be a considerable measure of relief at the sight. The children would fare well without her, and the baron could continue to grow closer to his children if he allowed himself to do so. However, it was only disappointment…and a sense of coming loss that coursed through Payton. She'd become too lax and comfortable at Ashford Hall, despite reminding herself daily that she should set her sights on what came next for her.

She couldn't entertain the option of permanently returning to Craven House and falling once more under Marce's watchful eye. Perhaps she could implore Samantha and her husband to allow her to travel with them? However, that much time with Sam would quickly fray Payton's nerves. There was always Jude and Simon, though Jude's mother-in-law, the Dowager Countess Cartwright, was an ogre of a woman, and even Jude found her tolerable in only small doses.

Payton set off down the street, her aching stomach forgotten as she made her way to the modiste's shop.

If she remembered correctly, Lord Cartwright's younger sister, Lady Theodora, was studying at a girls' boarding school in Canterbury. What was the school called? Miss Emmeline's School of Education and Decorum for Ladies of Outstanding Quality. Such a silly, cumbersome name for a school, but perhaps Payton, with the aid of Jude, could secure a position teaching at the institute. There was not much in the way of social engagements in Canterbury, though it was something she could become accustomed to if there were no other choice.

She stalked down the sidewalk, her reticule hanging from her clenched fist. Holding her chin high, she swallowed the lump that rose in her throat. She would not cry over such a trivial matter. She'd planned to move on, leave the baron and his children behind, and secure a more superior position. It should please her that Damon had the foresight to do the same.

The bell over the modiste's door chimed as she pushed through it into the bustling shop.

"Miss Samuels," Madame DelFortaine greeted her with a smile. "Are you here to collect your gowns?"

"Only my gown, please." She suppressed her guilt at the modiste's wide-eyed stare. "Have the child's dress delivered to Ashford Hall on Saint George Street."

"Very good, miss."

Payton waited as the modiste sent her servant to collect the cream-colored, off-the-shoulder ball gown she'd had commissioned on the baron's account. The gown had been an extravagant purchase, costing three times as much as the morning dress Joy and Abram had ruined. At the time, Payton had been taken aback by the modiste's insistence that she replace the ruined dress with a gown of such fine quality and cut; however, Madame DelFortaine and explained that the baron had given strict instructions as to the cost of the gown. And now that he'd seen fit to replace Payton, the extreme cost of the dress seemed more of a parting gift than an extravagance.

CHAPTER 21

PAYTON LEAPT DOWN from the Craven House carriage, startling Mr. Curtis with her unexpected and unladylike jump onto the Ashford walk. She hadn't bothered to instruct the Craven House servant to park down the street. It would not take her long within the townhouse.

"Do wait here, please, Mr. Curtis," she threw over her shoulder as she stalked to the front door. "I shall only be a few moments."

She didn't wait for his response but raised her gloved hand to knock. The door swung open to reveal Mr. Brown's grinning, wrinkled face.

"Good morn, Miss Samuels." He stood back and allowed her entrance. "I was beginning to worry."

It had taken all of Payton's resolve not to return to Ashford Hall the night before and tell the baron precisely what she thought of him. He was aloof, cold, distant, and highly unqualified to be raising two children.

However, she'd adjusted her plans by the time the sun rose.

"Good morning, Mr. Brown." The hour was ungodly early at only seven o'clock. It would be best if she collected her things, left the letter on the baron's desk, and departed before the household was fully awake. "Is the baron in his study yet this morning?"

Payton started for the stairs, and the butler fell into place beside her, matching her long strides. "He is, in fact, up early this morning and already at work."

Her step faltered. "Lord Ashford is awake and in his study already?"

The butler nodded toward the baron's office where the door stood ajar.

She hadn't expected to find him up and already below stairs. In fact, she'd hoped he'd be having a lie-in after hosting his gaming evening the previous night, giving her another thirty minutes at least to pack her room, leave her letter, and escape before Damon or the children came downstairs to take their morning meal.

Her hopes had been dashed, though her anger had yet to ebb.

Grasping her skirts, she held them up from the floor and started for the study.

Speaking directly to the baron would have to do as he would certainly hear the commotion if she attempted to remove her trunk from Ashford Hall and move it out to the walk where Mr. Curtis waited.

"Shall I announce you, Miss Samuels?" The elder servant attempted to keep pace with her but was falling behind.

"No need." Payton slipped into the study and closed the door at the same moment the butler scoffed at the brashness of her entering unbidden.

"Miss Samuels?" Confusion laced Damon's voice, and her shoulders tensed at the softness. "Good morning. It is lovely to have you back. I do hope you enjoyed—"

"Stop," she commanded, taking a deep breath before leveling her narrowed stare on the baron. She needs must think of him as *the baron* or better still, Lord Ashford if she had any hope of making it through this without showing the bloody man how much it hurt her. She took her painstakingly neat letter from the pocket of her cloak. It had taken nearly three hours to write it as she attempted to collect her words yet keep her emotions out of the situation.

He stood from his desk, his eyes trained on the paper clutched in her hands.

"What have you there, Payton?" She detected a hint of unease in his tone.

Payton glanced down at her hands before raising her chin and pointedly staring at him across the room, attempting to keep her irritation at bay at his insistence on using her given name. Why had she kissed him and allowed him to kiss her back? If it hadn't been for that brief lapse in judgment, she would be able to continue on as Joy and Abram's governess.

That wasn't true.

The boundaries had been crossed long before their kiss.

What of the night he'd invited her into this very room and offered her a drink? She'd accepted without a second thought. It was in that moment that things had changed between them. He was no longer the aloof, reserved baron who all but ignored his children, and she was no longer the ill-tempered governess who couldn't bring his children to heel.

They'd come to an unspoken agreement as they shared a scotch. He'd told her of the woman he'd lost, and she'd shared a bit about her past.

Now, there was nothing of the quiet, intimate moment remaining.

By the light of day, everything was different. *He* was different, and she most definitely was.

She walked toward his desk and held out the letter. "My resignation letter, my lord."

After he'd taken the paper from her, she could do nothing but twine her fingers, squeezing them so tightly, her knuckles surely turned white beneath her gloves. She could not look at him—did not want to see the satisfaction on his face to know that he did not have to release her and commit to severance pay. Payton was undertaking the difficult task herself.

She heard, rather than saw him unfold the letter.

It would be wise for her to pivot and depart the room. She hadn't many possessions at Ashford Hall, mainly a handful of dresses, two pairs of slippers, boots, underpinnings, and her brushes. A few hairpins and ribbons—but not much else.

When she'd taken the position as governess, she'd arrived with only her traveling trunk. In truth, she could have carried all her possession if the need had arisen. Thankfully, Mr. Curtis waited just outside the townhouse.

"You are leaving?" he whispered.

She glanced up to see Damon's questioning stare.

"I think it best I move on," she replied. Her voice remained steady without so much as a waver in her tone.

"Best for whom?"

"For all considered." She'd expected this to be the easy part, giving her notice and collecting her things.

"You think to know what's best for me?" Almost as an afterthought, he added, "For my children?"

She cleared her throat. "My apologies, my lord. Best for me, this is best for my future."

"Where will you go?" he demanded.

Belatedly, she realized he had no intention of making this easy for her, even though they both knew this was what they both wanted.

Of all the questions, why would he be concerned with where she went after departing his employ?

"Home, though that is none of your concern." She bit out the words with more force than intended.

"What of the children?" Was it hurt that etched his face? "They need a governess, Miss Samuels."

"And you shall find another. If you haven't already."

"What is that supposed to mean?"

"Come now, my lord—"

"Damon," he all but growled across the desk.

"That is improper and far too informal, Lord Ashford." Every word was like a dagger to her chest. She wanted to call him by his given name, just as she wanted to hear her name from his lips at least once more. "We both know after what happened, this is best. You will find another suitable governess, and the children will continue to thrive. Of that, I have no doubt."

"Nothing has changed." He pounded his fist on the desk, causing Payton to flinch. "You know that as well as I."

She shook her head. "We both know it is impossible to return to the way things were."

"Damnation," he hissed. "I do not *want* you to leave, and my children need you."

Payton laughed, though the sound rang false and hollow.

Was she using their kiss as an excuse to escape? Certainly, she was not misreading everything that'd transpired since that night. The baron had all but demanded she leave that night and proceeded to give her the next afternoon off. They both knew what'd happened between them was a mistake and could never happen again. The only way to make sure it didn't was for the baron to be rid of her and hire another governess.

He was pushing her away.

She was not fleeing.

And it was all for good reason.

She remembered his words from before. That he didn't want to care about her or any servant to come.

"Be that as it may"—she shook her head ruefully—"I must. Wants and needs cannot outweigh everything else. Besides, you know it is for the best. You've already started the process of finding someone to replace me."

"That is ludicrous," he snapped, his entire body tense, even as his eyes softened.

Payton slipped her fists into the pockets of her cloak to hide her clenched, aching hands. This was for the best...she knew that, and Damon knew that, despite his denial. This arrangement had never been meant to be permanent. It had come to its natural conclusion, and she would not mourn it, only look to what would come next for her.

"It is not ludicrous, nor unexpected, my lord." She took a step back at the same time his eyes lightened with...what? Anger? Betrayal? Confusion?

There was nothing to be angry over. She couldn't allow any feelings of betrayal as they owed one another nothing. His confusion was what kept her in the room. Damon had no right to be confused about her leaving her position. He was the one meeting with another governess. He was the one relieving her of her duties and granting her days off. He was the one avoiding her at every turn.

"If you will allow me to pack my things—"

His glared burned feverishly into her as he rocked forward. "Do you think I would have settled your gaming debt with Catherton if I expected you to pack your things and disappear into the night?"

His confession was akin to a slap across the face. All these weeks, she'd been set on earning her own way, taking care of herself, and truly living a life free from oversight. How had she not noted that hadn't been the case at all?

"I am not disappearing into the night, Damon." Her voice was a near shout before she fell silent, every nerve in her body on alert. She'd been a fool, harrying to and fro in an attempt to find a way to repay the duke, when Damon had already seen to the matter as if she were the baron's charge. "You paid my debt to the duke? How did you…why would you…I cannot…"

He held his hand out between them, palms up. "You, obviously, did not have the means to settle your debt."

"That is not for you to judge, Lord Ashford." Fury rolled under her skin, and her face grew heated at his highhandedness. "How dare you."

"How dare I?" he demanded. "How dare *you* enter my home on a lark, disguised as a proper lady of the *ton*, only to abscond when your debt grew too large to handle."

She sucked in a breath as if he'd physically struck her. He knew her ruse as the masked woman. He'd overstepped his bounds by settling her debt with the duke. And now he challenged her standing as a proper woman. She may be little more than the daughter of a blacksmith and his whore, but never had she lowered herself to crying off when her debts seemed insurmountable. She was a gambler, but never an outright thief.

"You go too far," she hissed, suppressing the urge to stomp her foot in fury. "No man will ever own me."

Was this what her mother had feared most? When a man thought himself above his position and misguidedly assumed that a woman needed to be cared for. Payton could take care of herself. She might owe money, but no one controlled her. Except, now, the baron *owned* her.

It was no longer Catherton who held her debt but Damon.

CHAPTER 22

DAMON WAS AROUND the desk before he had time to think, standing face-to-face with Payton, his stare pleading with her to understand. He should be the angry one. He should be the one questioning her motives. He should be the one unsurprised by her determination to leave him.

He was always the one left behind.

"You do not understand," he said. "Catherton was prepared to call the magistrate, to start a manhunt—a womanhunt—for you. You fled without making good on your debt. He would have scoured the streets of London until he learned your identity. He would not have stopped until you paid dearly for your actions. Catherton's arrogance and pride would have demanded it of him, even if the debt were a mere shilling."

"I did not ask for, nor do I want a protector."

"And I did not ask for a masquerading governess with mounting debts." He paused, staring down his nose at her attempting to muster a bit of disdain, but failing miserably. "But despite that, here we both are."

"No, I am leaving." She pivoted toward the door, and he sneaked out a hand to clasp her upper arm.

"Wait—"

"I will have someone come to collect my things," she bit out between clenched teeth.

"It was meant as a kindness, nothing more." The fight left him with those words. Each true and meant to his core. "This is not a debt I expect to be repaid."

"No debt goes unsatisfied, my lord. I can assure you of that." She pulled from his grasp and crossed her arms, her pointed glare stopping him from attempting to keep her any longer. "You have overstepped."

"Overstepped what?" he asked, his hand falling to his side as he fought to urge to clench his fingers into a fist.

She might be angry, but he was not.

"Propriety." Her face reddened. "You have overstepped your place in my life. You are not my guardian, nor do you make any decisions for me, especially those concerning my financial circumstances."

He wanted to reach out to her and explain the unexplainable. But he held himself still, knowing that once she walked out, he might never see her again. He needed her to remain.

"I will repay my debt to you," she proclaimed, lifting her chin, yet the action did not hide the glisten of unshed tears in her eyes. "You can begin by keeping my final wages."

"Payton, I do not…" Damon didn't want her bloody money, nor any pledge to settle her debts. This was why he'd kept to himself all these years. This was why he'd never taken another wife as his sister had pushed him to do. This was why he kept distance between himself and his children.

With connection, came dependence. With care, came attachment.

And when that connection and care were severed, only loss remained.

He and his children had mourned the loss of Sarah all these years, and the most important thing he'd taught Abram and Joy since then was that distance saved the heart. Governesses came and went. No attachment, no loss.

He'd held on to his misguided notion for so many years, it was difficult to let it go. But since Payton had come into their lives, he'd lost sight of his long-held belief.

When had he—and the children—accepted Payton as part of their family?

When had they decided, without vocalizing it, that this dark-haired woman was different from all the rest?

Despite his best efforts, she had indeed become part of their family. A significant portion if he were being truthful. And they would all suffer from her absence. He'd fooled himself into believing that he needed her for the children.

The truth was, Damon needed Payton for himself.

He'd told himself, year after year, that he'd learned his lesson. He'd given himself entirely to Sarah, reveled in their love, and he'd lost her. She'd left him and the children behind. She'd died and taken his heart with her.

Or at least that was what he'd thought.

But letting Payton go, allowing her to walk out of his home, was something he was unprepared to face.

"You can collect your things, but, I beg of you, allow me to tell Joy and Abram." The words came out like his last wish.

At her slight nod, Damon knew it was for the best—for both him and his children.

When Payton hesitated, new hope sprang up within him, and the words begging her to stay nearly tumbled from his lips. He would apologize, and she would forgive him. They could move past it all and forget. Everything would return to normal. She would reprise her position as the Ashford governess, and he'd return to his place as the sulking lord. He would not dwell on their kiss. He would not languish over their severed attachment.

If he promised, would she remain at Ashford Hall, or was she determined to leave him?

Not him, this was not about him. Joy and Abram would be devastated if Payton left. It was for them that he clung to the small sliver of hope.

"I will repay you, Lord Ashford," she bit out, her tone cold.

"That is not necessary nor needed," he replied, his hands trembling as he held himself back—from going to her, from holding her close, from not letting her leave. He wanted to keep her but wasn't sure how. He'd thought settling her debt with Catherton had been the right thing to do, but she'd seen it as a presumptuous act intended to form a new debt. If he begged her to stay, to reconsider, would she see it as him overstepping his place once more? He hadn't paid her debt as a means of controlling her. The thought had never crossed his mind.

"Unfortunately, I must." She turned, her single curl falling over her shoulder to hang down her back as she strode from the room.

Damon listened to her retreating footsteps as they disappeared when she climbed the stairs.

He'd made a colossal mistake; however, he wasn't sure if it was bringing Payton into his home all those weeks ago or allowing her to walk out now.

It took all his willpower to move to the sideboard and pour himself a drink before slumping into his chair in front of the fire. He set his scotch on the table, forgotten, as he closed his eyes and leaned his head against the back of the seat.

He knew what he listened for—even though he begged himself not to.

The light footsteps of her leaving...for good.

Would she pause in the foyer? Would she return to give him a final goodbye?

Was he strong enough to let her go? Or sufficiently weak if he begged her to stay?

Bloody hell...he wanted her to stay, no matter the cost to him.

He was a fool to think he could fix whatever had gone wrong between him and Payton. At each step, it only grew worse. He *made* it worse; with his words and his actions.

Damon sat frozen and waited until he heard her coming down the main stairs. Her attempt to slip from the house silently was made impossible as he heard her struggling with her trunk as she slowly made her way down.

To halt himself from rushing from his study to assist her, he grabbed his tumbler and took a long pull. The scotch burned its way to his stomach as his insides roiled against the spirits so early in the day. Yet, with what was to come when the children awoke and learned of Payton's departure, he shouldn't turn away from the anesthetic provided by the scotch. It would undoubtedly diminish the ache that would remain after she was gone.

The front door opened to several voices, both male and female.

Likely Mr. Brown and the other servants giving the governess a final farewell.

What seemed like an eternity later, the door closed, and his household fell silent once more.

Miss Samuels was gone.

Relief should lessen the tension in his shoulders. Annoyance at Payton's sudden departure from her position should flare his anger. It was over, she was gone, and he no longer need fight the urges within him, the draw to take her into his arms, and the desire in his heart to hold her tight.

Yet, he could neither grasp his relief nor anger.

The stark realization that he'd need to start his search for another governess was enough to have him draining his glass.

"My lord?" The partially ajar study door opened behind him. "The Duke of Catherton is here to see you."

"Tell him I am still abed," Damon mumbled, massaging his temples.

"I do not think that will do."

"Tell him I have already departed for a morning meeting."

"Again, my lord, that will—"

Damon slammed his empty tumbler on the table, refusing to turn toward the butler. "I am in no mood to see the vile man. Get rid of him."

"Vile man?" The sound of the duke's Hessians rang across the floor until he stepped on the carpet. "I think I shall endeavor to embrace your words as a compliment, though I dare say they were not meant as one, Ashford."

"What do you want, Catherton?" Damon stood, turning to face the unwanted duke. "You have your money. We have no other business together."

The duke gave a gruff laugh before waving Mr. Brown from the room. "I have my money but not the masked lady's name."

"What does that matter?"

"It is the only thing that matters, Ashford," Catherton hissed. "I will have her name and see her punished."

"We have been over this, Catherton. You have your money…the woman will not be allowed in my home again. It is the best you can hope for."

"You are more of a simpleton than I thought if you assume this is only about money."

"I do not know the woman's identity." Damon strode to his desk, putting the large expanse of the surface between him and the duke. "If I learn it, you will be the first to know."

The duke paced farther into the room, picking up Damon's empty glass and smelling it. "Scotch? This early, Ashford?" His tsk-tsk was as disapproving as possible. "Who was the woman I passed when I arrived?"

The hairs on the back of Damon's neck stood on end, but he managed to keep his stance from showing his alarm. "My children's governess."

"Early to be departing without the children," Catherton mused. "Not that I am afflicted with children...or the need for a governess."

"Just as my actions are none of your concern, neither are those of my servants or children."

"The trunk she carried appeared quite cumbersome." He set Damon's glass back on the table, trailing his fingertip along the rim before turning toward the door. "She was very familiar. Perhaps we are acquainted. What is her name?"

Damon would rather shave a pound of his flesh than give the duke so much as Payton's first name. There was no trust between them nor any kinship lost by denying the duke's request.

"I think it best if you depart before your line of questioning offends me further." Damon sat at his desk in an attempt to hide his fury.

"I will have the swindler's name, Ashford," the duke said, pivoting back toward Damon. His nostrils flared, and he narrowed his glare on his supposed adversary. "Even without your help. I do not take kindly to being bilked, especially by a woman."

Damon flipped open a folder on his desk and

lowered his head as if to read, signaling that their meeting had come to its conclusion. "I wish you all the luck in your endeavor to locate the mystery woman. Again, I will send her directions to you immediately if I discover her identity."

"Did she attend your gaming night last eve?"

"No." There was no reason for Damon to share that he hadn't been of a mind for cards either and had remained in his room while his guests enjoyed themselves. "I do not think she'd risk it if she has any sense."

"Women are not known for their sense," Catherton chuckled snidely.

"The same is true for many men I know." Damon didn't bother looking up at the duke. His meaning was clear. "I do wish you a good day, Your Grace."

Damon was likely to get an earful from Flora if she heard about him giving Catherton the cut direct. But the pompous lord deserved far more than just being dismissed.

The clip of Catherton's Hessians as he stalked from Ashford Hall rang through the empty house, and Damon could only exhale once the front door slammed in the duke's wake.

Payton was back from whence she came, and hopefully, that place did not overlap with Catherton's circle of acquaintances. Damon should be furious with Payton for putting him in such a predicament, yet he couldn't muster the energy to be upset with her.

No, anger was not what filled him, making his entire body heavy and sending his mind into a dark, deep dive.

Damon's head fell into his hands, and he squeezed his eyes tight against the coming pain he was sure to cause his children. His own discomfort at

Payton's departure would not compare to the agony of Joy and Abram's loss.

CHAPTER 23

PAYTON STUMBLED DOWN from the carriage and into Craven House—her sanctuary, her home, her place of utter rightness. Closing the door behind her, she leaned against the scarred wood as her legs shook beneath her and tears streamed down her face. Never did she allow herself such an unguarded moment of pure despair. She begged her heart to slow its beat and her face to cool. To make matters all the more daunting, she'd nearly run headlong into the Duke of Catherton during her final moments at Ashford Hall.

Thankfully, she was able to lower her head and scramble to her waiting carriage.

Now, she was home—her true home, though she was loath to admit it.

No one would be in residence at this hour. The women who lived at Craven House would be out and about for their day. Garrett would still be abed at the Albany.

Payton could only pray that Darla, their cook and housekeeper, was at the market and would not stumble upon her.

Her tears were useless and unfounded. Useless for the simple fact that no matter how many she shed, they would not bring about change. Unfounded because she'd known all along that her place at Ashford Hall was only temporary…a stepping stone of sorts until she moved on. Even if it had lasted several years, at some point, Damon's children would have been too old for a governess.

The position had been taken on a lark anyways—a means to escape Craven House.

And yet, here she was…

Back where she began without a shilling to her name and debt surpassing what she could hope to earn in an entire year of genuine work. Not that she'd fare so well again with her luck securing a suitable position.

"Payton?" Marce's familiar voice floated down the hall from her private office. "Is that you? What in heaven's name are you doing home at this hour?"

Her entire body stiffened, and she hurriedly brushed the warm tears from her cheeks, rubbing her palms down the front of her dress to dry them. Her eyes were likely swollen from crying, and her cheeks hot to the touch. One look at her and Marce would know something horrible had transpired.

"It is I, Marce," she called, praying her sister did not rush from her office. A moment or two, and Payton could compose herself enough to face her eldest sibling. "Give me a moment, and I will come see you. I simply must hear all about your travels."

She infused the last few words with excitement she did not feel.

Especially since Marce was always tight-lipped about where she went when she was away from Craven House. If Payton didn't know Marce so well, she'd think her eldest sibling had a secret family she hid from her brother and sisters—or perhaps a fine gentleman suitor.

It was an unspoken rule that they allowed Marce to keep that small part of her life hidden from them.

Would her sister give her the same courtesy?

I'll soon find out, she mused as she made her way down the narrow hall to the back of the house, a warmth infusing the abandoned corridor and teasing at her bare neck. Though Payton had visited the office several times over the last several days, it was different with Marce present. Calming…soothing…solid.

Tangible, in a way. If a feeling could be grasped and held onto.

It had been much the same when their mother had commanded the room.

Why had Payton fought so tirelessly to be away from the place, to stake her independence and leave it all behind?

No matter what transpired, who came and left their lives, they were always a family. Together. Craven House, its four sturdy walls and adequate roof, was their anchor.

If it were within her power, Marce always endeavored to make things right.

But how could her sister right something Payton wasn't convinced was wrong?

Everything with Damon—no, *the baron*—was too sensitive to be spoken aloud. What had transpired between them was just that: something for them alone. There was no remedy to the mess Payton had created for herself. No number of bribes or amount of intimidation could make any of it go away, disappear as if it had never happened.

Payton had gained an affection for Lord Ashford. She'd allowed herself to be drawn in to the point where she'd thought her value and worth far exceeded what it actually was. The baron had told her not long ago that he merely tolerated her presence, that she was replaceable. Why hadn't she heeded his words and kept her longings buried deep inside?

Instead, she'd allowed him to draw her into a false sense of security that had led to their intimate moment in the hall just outside Joy's darkened bedchamber.

Payton forced a smile to her lips—though inside, she frowned—and stepped into the red and gold office. Oddly, they were the same colors she'd nearly selected for the gown the baron had commissioned for her, but she'd settled for cream with a lace overlay. It would match the string of pearls Payton had borrowed from Sam before her sister wed and moved out of Craven House.

"How was your trip, dear sister," she said, lying on her favored lounge with more reserve than usual. So many times, her fits of anger or irritation had sent her casting herself heavily onto the chaise.

"It was..." Marce's brow furrowed, and the corner of her lips dipped into a grim frown. "Eventful, yet uneventful at the same time."

There was an openness in her sister's expression that Payton had never witnessed before. Her normally guarded demeanor seemed to have cracked ever so slightly.

"Is that a good thing?" Payton prodded.

"Only time will tell, unfortunately." Marce's blue eyes met Payton's. It was one of the few things they shared, a gift from their mother. Where Payton was tall and willowy, Marce was shorter with the curves of a woman; curves Payton could only dream of one day possessing. Payton's dark hair was a startling contrast to her sister's pale, curly tresses, though they favored the same long length. Marce smiled, but Payton knew enough to realize that her sister's thoughts were elsewhere. Her mind preoccupied with business not concerning Craven House. "What are you doing here? It isn't your day off."

There were so many ways Payton could answer

her sister's question. However, the stark truth would only bring her back to being the dependent babe of the family who needed everyone, especially her eldest sister, to care for her, to right her mistakes, and to coddle her as if she were a helpless child.

Payton lowered the back of her head to the lounge and stared at the ceiling above. For a moment, she stalled answering as she counted the cracks in the plaster and followed them to where they trailed to the corner of the room. If she were going to lie to her sibling, it was best not to allow Marce to see the truth in her eyes. "Oh, the baron decided to take the children on an outing. It was the perfect time for me to take an afternoon for myself."

It wasn't a complete lie, yet not an outright truth either. It *had* actually happened when Damon took the children to the museum. There was a glimmer of truth in her tale.

Payton longed for nothing more than to be open with Marce but doing so would equal giving up what little independence Payton had created for herself.

"Very good." Marce glanced down at the stack of work on her desk that had piled high while she was away from London. "However, I would not think Craven House would be your first choice of destination."

True enough. There had been no qualms made, no words minced, when Payton had demanded that Marce allow her to take the position as the Ashford governess. She'd longed for freedom, time to discover what life would hold for her without her family's crushing oversight, though her sister masked it as guidance.

"Only my first stop." Perhaps her last one, as well. What if she never had the means to leave her sister's home? She'd truly muddied everything up with Damon. The chance to go out on her own had been ruined by a single kiss, and then she'd left without so much as asking for a reference. Not that she'd settled on finding employment in another household as yet. Perhaps it was best she follow in Sam's and Jude's footsteps and secure a husband. The thought made her shudder. To go from her family's control to that of a husband was not what she longed for.

"May I ask you something?" Payton glanced over to see Marce reading over a document on her desk, clearly distracted. That suited Payton well enough, for Marce would be less likely to see her younger sister's dark mood and possibly allow slip something Payton had yet to know.

Her fair-haired sister set the paper aside and, for the first time, Payton noticed the heaviness—and exhaustion—in her sister's gaze. The subtle wrinkles that marred her pale skin at the corners of her lips and eyes.

"I suppose," her sister sighed.

"Do you think a person should wallow in their sadness indefinitely?" It wasn't what she'd planned to ask. "I mean to say, if something occurs, perhaps good or bad, shouldn't one look past it and plan what is to come next?"

It was what their mother had done her entire life. A man left her, disappointed her, treated her unfairly…she moved on. Madame Sasha, their mother, always had a plan. And a backup plan. She knew what she wanted, and she stopped at nothing to get it. Perhaps this was the reason their mother always seemed at peace with what had transpired in her short life.

"Is this about the baron and his wife's death?"

Payton thought about the question. "I suppose it is."

…yet, also so much more.

"Death—and loss, in general—is not something

so easily moved on from."

"And yet, Mother never floundered in despair."

"What does Mother have to do with this?" Marce's pensive stare settled on Payton, and for a split second, she was sorry she'd brought up the subject at all. "The baron could not be more different than our mother."

"It is just, all the time I've worked for Lord Ashford"—Payton had to still herself from calling him by his given name—"he's seemed lost in the depths of despair, unable to see any future for himself, not even to provide for his children." It had been the case...before their kiss. "He shuts himself in his study and ignores his entire household day in and day out. When he does venture out, he is irritable, gruff, and downright contradictory."

Marce's brow lifted. "But he is taking his children on an outing today."

"No—I mean, yes, but he will retreat once more, I am afraid." She'd nearly misspoken. "I am certain his wife meant much to him, and he's become a near recluse since she passed. He barely knows his children, and they know him not at all. I suppose my question is, how did Mother deal so wonderfully with loss? After your father died, Mother quickly purchased Craven House with her dowager settlement. She went on to have Jude and Sam...and, eventually, me. All this after losing her husband so suddenly. She did not hide away from us. She did not give up on life or her future, but she moved on. Why cannot others do the same, especially when they have been afforded the means to do just that?"

"What *means* does the baron possess that you think Mother lacked?"

"A title...healthy coffers...a nice home." She ticked off the list on her fingers. "And much more. He even has a sister in town, though she doesn't visit often."

"Mother had a title and a small allowance, though she lacked a home and had no relations to speak of. At least, none who would assist her and two small children." Marce sighed. "I do not think she so easily moved on."

Payton scoffed at her sister's absentmindedness. "Your father, Lord Beauchamp, my father, and the Duke of Harwich—and likely more that we never had occasion to meet. What of them?"

Lord Buckston, Marce and Garrett's father, had died long before Payton was born. Viscount Beauchamp, Sam and Jude's estranged father, had only been spied across a crowded ballroom and lurking in the shadows at Sam's wedding. Even Payton's own father, Nigel Samuels, was unknown to her. The only suitor her mother ever allowed near her children had been Julian Delconti, the Duke of Harwich, and after all these years, Payton had trouble bringing the lord's visage to mind as he'd disappeared as suddenly as the men who came before him.

Payton noted her sister flinch at the name Harwich, but she continued anyways. "Certainly, she must have loved them all at some point, but when they no longer fit into what she wanted in life, she moved on. I never noted her retreating into herself, she was never in the throes of despair or so sad she slept her days away. She was no stranger to the cruel realities of life…and society. But she had the strength to move on. I remember her always with a smile and a laugh."

"Yes, life is unpredictable. Many obstacles landed solidly in Mother's path; however, that did not mean she did not mourn each man when they left, or when she had to push them away." Marce inhaled deeply and let the breath out slowly, her eyes landing on something over Payton's shoulder. "Mother kept us close because family is the only thing that is certain. That did not mean she did not suffer immensely from bouts of loneliness. She was a single woman with a horde of children to raise and not many funds to do it. She did what she thought was best and, in the end, she suffered because she'd died, essentially alone. And you, Sam, and Jude suffered for never having the opportunity to know your fathers."

"I am certain there was a reason Mother kept my father away," Payton said with mild indignation. "And we know Lord Beauchamp for the fickle man he is. He told Sam he chose another woman, a suitable match, over his twin daughters."

"The fact of the matter is that Mother kept such a tight hold on us so she wouldn't be utterly alone." Payton saw the immense pain that entered her sister's eyes at admitting such a thing. "It is why I have never fought any of you when you set your mind to a future. Sam and Jude selected fine husbands, and Garrett moved to the Albany. When you came to me with the notion of taking a position in the baron's house, while I was hesitant to allow it, I acquiesced because I knew you were ready for such responsibilities. To be fair, I am looking forward to a future of my own choosing now that all of you have set out on your own."

"What will you do?" Payton asked, though her chest ached to think of a day when Marce would not be waiting at Craven House, her arms wide for Payton to return home.

"Oh, I have not given it much thought." Marce glanced back at the stack of papers on her desk. "There is plenty of time…plenty of time."

Once more her sister, while only a few feet away, was not at Craven House—or, Payton suspected, even in London.

"Do you think I made a wise choice?"

"You have made many choices, Payton," Marce said. "What choice in particular?"

"To undertake the position as the Ashford governess."

Marce's eyes settled on her youngest sister, and Payton couldn't help but lean closer as if whatever her sister said next would hold the key to solving all her dilemmas.

"You have been the baby in our family—" When Payton made to argue the term, Marce held up her hand to silence her. "I was referring to your age, nothing more. While I had my reservations about you taking the post—truth be told, I *still* have reservations—this is a time for you to spread your wings and discover what makes you happy. There is much to life that you were unable to explore while living at Craven House. I fear that is my fault for keeping such a tight hold on you. I think I found myself to be much like Mother in some ways."

The loneliness in Marce's eyes was enough to bring Payton nearly to tears. How had she never noticed her sister's isolation at Craven House?

"But none of that matters overmuch as you are doing well in the baron's employ and remaining out of trouble." Marce smiled. "I suppose my fears were for naught."

Payton longed to share all her troubles with her eldest sister, but something kept her from voicing anything. Perhaps it was Marce's exhausted slump over her desk or the hollow way she gazed across the room at her. Something was troubling Marce, and Payton would not complicate things any more than they already were.

She would have to admit at some point that she'd quit her post and would be remaining at Craven House indefinitely, but not today. Today, she'd allow herself some time to grieve—and readjust.

"I will let you return to your work." Payton stood and hurried to give her sister a peck on the cheek before departing the office to return to her private chambers.

Damon and the children would go on as they always did. Payton had never been part of their family despite everything. In quick order, he'd hire another governess, and it would be as if Payton had never been there. Her room, next to Abram's private chambers, would be filled with another woman's possessions. The baron would, hopefully, at some point allow his guard down and dine with the children, perhaps even go so far as to invite the new governess to his study after Joy and Abram found their beds.

Payton quickened her pace as she climbed the main stairs, keeping her head low as she passed Darla, their housekeeper. Only a few more steps and she'd be in the safety of her bedchamber.

Payton needed to focus on what she'd been meant to do all along: find her own future, forge her own path, and discover what happiness awaited her.

Her time as a governess had served her well to help her determine what that future would entail and the strength she'd need to achieve all she desired. Missteps, mistakes, and hardships would come her way. However, one day, when she found a home of her own, she'd look back and know it was all worth the journey.

CHAPTER 24

"MR. BROWN." DAMON strode down the hall after his butler. "A word, please."

The servant turned with an even smile, his hands clasped behind his back. "Yes, my lord?"

Damon sat in his study for nearly an hour after Catherton had left, worrying over Miss Samuels and whether the duke was skilled enough—or perhaps, *paid* enough—to have Payton located and brought before a magistrate. Until his plan solidified.

As the governess had so kindly thrown in his face, her personal dealings were not his concern. She was no longer part of his household; therefore, he shouldn't fret over her.

What he *should* do and what he actually did were two very different things.

"I would like to host a gaming night tomorrow evening."

The butler's brow rose in alarm. "It is not your usual night."

"Is that a problem?" Damon gritted his teeth, immediately regretting his harsh tone.

"Of course, not, my lord." Mr. Brown glanced past Damon, his welcoming smile returning. "Master Abram and Miss Joy, you are both looking wonderfully rested this morning. Mrs. Brown has laid out your morning meal in the back salon. The gardens are lovely right now." The man's stare hardened when he turned back to Damon. It was highly uncharacteristic of the butler to take any liberties with decorum. "I will arrange everything for the gaming night—tomorrow."

His butler certainly knew of Payton's resignation and departure…and he blamed Damon.

It appeared he also blamed Damon for changing his usual gaming night.

But he was committed enough to him and Damon's children to soften the blow by allowing them to dine in the sunny salon that was usually reserved for esteemed guests. Not that there had been any noteworthy guests in years—with the exception of Payton, that is.

"Thank you, Mr. Brown." Damon paused for a moment, wondering if his plan would be seen to fruition or bring Catherton to his boiling point. "One last thing."

"Yes, my lord?"

"Can you have a footman deliver this to the Duke of Catherton's residence?" He held out the personal invitation addressed to the duke and signed by himself. Damon had to convince Catherton his plot to chase down Payton would get him nowhere.

The butler collected the letter, followed it up by giving a curt bow, and hurried toward the kitchens. His bow was not as deep as it once was, and his hurried steps were more of a shuffle nowadays.

Once the butler had departed, that left Damon to face his children.

Alone.

"Good morning," he greeted, meeting them at the bottom of the stairs. Joy's hair looked as if it hadn't been combed in days, while Abram wore two stockings that didn't quite match. "May I join you for your meal?"

Joy giggled. "Of course, Father."

Abram ignored his greeting and pushed past his sister, starting for the back salon. "Where is Miss Samuels? I have something of grave importance to speak with her about."

Damon took Joy's tiny hand in his as they followed Abram. Her grip was tighter than he'd expect for such a young child.

He'd hoped to put off speaking about Payton's absence, at least until he could determine a reasonable explanation that did not include gaming debts and late-night kisses, not to mention scotches in his study. He couldn't bear the children laying the blame at his feet.

There was no denying that he was the cause of Payton's resignation.

Admitting as much to Joy and Abram was something he longed to avoid. It would be wise to find an explanation that fit his reasoning: that it was for the best that she'd left his employ. He would hire a new governess, perhaps one with a more impressive background in history, while Miss Samuels would find a household she was better suited to serve in.

"Miss Samuels has fallen under the weather," he said as they entered the back salon, the windows were open, and light streamed into the room, brightening every corner. He wished the morning sun reached within him, not only kissing his skin. "Is there something I can help you with?"

Abram halted and turned toward Damon, a hopeful glint in his eyes. "Do you know William Drummond?"

"The poet?" He searched his memory for any other Drummond, but none came to mind.

"Yes," Abram said as he sat. "Miss Samuels

thought it best I expand my educational goals and study poetry. I thought it nonsense, as there is little reason for a historian to study such things as literature; however, I promised her."

"And how are you faring at the task?" Damon pulled Joy's seat out for her to sit and then pushed it in when she was ready.

"Admirably, I assure you. Though I find literature is unlike history. Or science."

Damon took his own seat, and a footman hurried forward with an extra place setting for him. "How so?"

"Well, in the poem *To The Nightingale*, I suspect Drummond is not speaking of a feathered bird at all, but something wholly different…and scandalous." Abram's cheeks flushed red at his insinuation, and he glanced nervously toward Joy as if he'd misspoken in mixed company. "But I cannot think of any reason Miss Samuels would think I have something to learn from poets and their convoluted, misleading poems."

Damon averted his stare by filling his and Joy's plates with fruit tart pastries and plump cherries with pudding.

Pastries and pudding instead of boiled eggs and toast. There was little hope that the news of Miss Payton's departure had not already spread through the servants' quarters. Cook was coddling the children in preparation for the disappointment to come when they learned of their governess's departure.

"When will Miss Samuels be well again?" Joy asked.

"Soon, I hope," Abram replied, filling his own plate.

"I shall visit her after our meal." Joy turned to look out the window at the garden below. "Mayhap a bouquet of posies will brighten her day."

Damon's spirits sank further. "I am afraid Miss

Samuels is not at Ashford Hall. She is resting at her own home." At least Damon hoped she had a home to return to.

"Where is it?" Joy prodded. "After I fell into the pond and nearly drowned—"

"Do not be overdramatic, Joy," Abram chastised. "You merely swallowed a bit of water when you thought yourself an adequate swimmer."

Joy stuck out her tongue at her brother before continuing, "As I was saying, when I nearly drowned, Miss Samuels remained by my bedside. I should do no less for her. Isn't that correct, Father?"

Her shining, green eyes looked up into his, and Damon was hesitant to extinguish the light in the girl's face.

"That will not be possible." Damon shook his head, all his nerves failing him at Joy's upturned face. They couldn't be there to comfort Payton—Payton had left them. However, breaking his daughter's heart would be his undoing. "Miss Samuels' note said the sickness is contagious, and we mustn't visit for fear of falling ill ourselves."

The lie fell from his lips far too easily, though that did not stop the guilt from pooling in his stomach. At some point, sooner rather than later, he'd need to tell them the truth—hopefully, before they overheard the news from one of the servants.

Yet, Damon lacked the courage to speak the words, for when he did, things would be final.

He'd thought he would feel a sense of relief with Payton's parting. No longer did it matter what had transpired between them—and what hadn't. What had been said, and what remained unsaid. As was always the case, it was only him and the children. Their small family of three.

The children had gotten on well with Flora and her lady's companion the day before when they dined together. They'd appeared happy and content, while Flora had taken an interest in Joy's love of horses and Abram's habit of comparing anything and everything to a battle from years past.

In time, Damon would find a new governess for the children, and it would be like Payton had never come into his household. She'd been their governess for a mere six weeks. Certainly, that was not enough time for the children to form such an affection that they would mourn her.

This was what he wanted, after all. Damon had become far too attached himself, and that did not bode well for anyone.

Damon ate his meal slowly and in silence, waiting for the tension to release within him.

It did not happen.

He'd let Payton walk out of his house without even attempting to change her mind. He'd languished over the idea of going after her, but he feared it would only make matters worse and push her farther away.

Perhaps it would take time for normalcy to return, just as it had taken time for his children to latch on to their new governess.

Damon shook his head to dispel any thoughts of Payton, their kiss, and the draw between them that had grown so powerful he could no longer ignore it.

With time, the attraction and memories would fade until she no longer came to mind at all.

Much like...

Betrayal twisted his heart with a vise-like grip as he realized he'd gone nearly an entire day without thinking of Sarah, his loss, and the sorrow laced with despair that always followed.

How had he allowed his pain to lessen and slip away unnoticed? When had he begun to change without even realizing it was happening?

He couldn't focus on why his mind wandered to Payton nearly as much as it had been absorbed all these years by losing Sarah.

No, the children would be devastated by Payton's withdrawal, and it was his fault.

This time, he was determined to be there for them instead of shutting himself away in his study.

It was the one lesson he was more than qualified to teach them: people left, and life was full of disappointment, resentment, and anguish. It was a fact of life, and sometimes, there was no rhyme or reason to it all. It hurt. It changed a person. It left loved ones reeling in their wake; questioning their every decision, their every move, their every belief.

Perhaps he was to blame for allowing Payton to become such an integral part of their lives and standing by when she walked away. Since her arrival in his household, she'd been more than simply Joy's and Abram's governess; she'd been their constant companion, a friend and confidante. She'd spent countless hours with them in the schoolroom, having meals with them, doing Joy's hair, and selecting Abram's clothes.

Thankfully, Abram and Joy had believed his excuses—for now.

Damon had to accept that Payton was gone, as well. It was what she wanted. Which meant he needed to focus his time and energy on something other than the feel of her soft lips against his.

His gaming night…it had been his distraction for years.

Now should prove no different. He would help with the setup and organization alongside his servants. There was also Catherton and his acceptance of the invitation to take up space in his mind.

Mrs. Brown shuffled into the room, much like her husband had shuffled down the hall earlier, collecting their empty plates at the same time she pinned Damon with a sorrowful stare. A look that should have been reserved for his children, but the servant had turned it on him. There had been no witnesses to his kiss with the governess, except a sleeping Joy. No one had invaded their private moments in his study. Was it possible that Payton had spoken of their intimacy with another servant?

It would be wise to speak with the children about Miss Samuels, but he was still at a loss for how to tell them.

Today, he would act as if nothing had changed. Governesses had come and gone, some in quick succession. Miss Samuels was no different.

DAMON SLIPPED FROM Ashford Hall as soon as Mr. Brown had the carriage readied. He'd been able to avoid Joy and Abram the entire day, but when the sun rose anew, and Miss Samuels hadn't returned, they'd begged him to check on her. He'd been faced with either admitting that she wasn't returning or bending to the children's pleas.

It was just before lunch when Damon could resist them no longer and left, though he had no intention of seeking out Payton. She'd been clear that her decision was made, and her fury at his unappreciated meddling with Catherton had also been evident.

He'd had no choice but to throw himself on Flora's mercy and beg her to assist him in securing a new Ashford governess. When he hadn't heard back from her, he assumed she'd insist the children were ready to venture outside London for schooling. Surprisingly, Flora had sent a note saying she'd contacted Lady Devonshire, whose younger sister ran a school outside London that professed to training the most skilled governesses. Mayfield Academy. Lady Devonshire insisted that she'd write her sister, Miss Darby with all due haste and have several women journey into town to meet with Damon.

It hadn't been difficult to convince Flora to host the potential governesses at her home while Damon assessed each.

He was determined not to make the same mistakes he had with Payton.

His children's next governess would be prim, proper, and above reproach—and of a mature age. Her pedigree didn't matter overmuch as long as she did not admit to any vices or unsavory habits.

In another stroke of favorable luck, Catherton had sent his RSVP and would attend Damon's card evening. Things were back under control, and it would only be a matter of time before a new governess was secured, and Damon would convince Catherton to relinquish his quest to discover Payton's identity.

The journey through town to Flora's townhouse in St. James's Square passed in the blink of an eye, and before Damon was aware, he was ushered into the Wittenbottoms' salon where Flora waited with her lady's companion, Primrose. Damon hadn't known of the companion's existence before he dined with Flora and the children at Wexfector's.

He suspected that there were other aspects of his sister's life he was unaware of, just as he kept much from her.

"Good morning, Flora." He nodded before turning to her companion. "And to you, too, Miss Primrose."

Flora's companion hardly noted his greeting, her head bent low as she plied a needle with red thread through sheer white fabric, working on what appeared to be the petals of a rose.

"Damon," Flora greeted hoarsely as if she hadn't spoken in some time. "Miss Darby will be arriving any moment. Can I offer you a refreshment before they arrive?"

Miss Primrose set her stitchwork aside and hurried to the tea cart to pour two steaming cups before Damon could respond. She dropped one lump of sugar into each along with a quick pour of milk before returning to hand Flora and him their cups.

"Thank you." Damon took a nearby chair, selecting it because it did not directly face his sister but the windows at her left, affording him a view of the roof lines across the street where a chimneysweep lugged his pail and broom toward a waiting stack. "And, thank you, Flora, for assisting me."

"What happened to the dark-haired lass you hired last month?" she asked. He felt, rather than saw, her glare narrowed on him as if she were assessing him for weakness. "She was all the children spoke of the other day. What is her name?" Flora tapped her chin and glanced toward her companion.

"Miss Samuels."

"Ah, yes, thank you, Primrose." Flora returned her attention to Damon. "Whatever have the children done this time to send another governess running?"

Damon could not lay the burden at his children's feet this time, nor could he admit that it was his mistake that'd sent Payton running. "The decision was mine, as it were, not Miss Samuels'."

Flora stiffened. "I see, now."

Dread laced through him at the thought of Flora *seeing* anything where Payton was concerned.

"She was unqualified," Flora said with a confident nod. "I suppose I should have seen it long before this point."

Damon breathed a sigh of relief. It was difficult

to keep anything a secret in London; however, his connection to Payton would need to remain just that—a secret.

"I would not say unqualified, dear sister," Damon mused as if it were of little importance why Miss Samuels was no longer his children's governess. "Mayhap unprepared for such a daunting role. She is rather young herself."

"And rather handsome, too." Flora slapped her knee with a chuckle. "Girl should be setting her sights on finding a suitable husband before she grows long in the tooth. If you ask me, Damon, I'd say you did the woman a grand favor."

Damon wasn't asking Flora, although it was difficult to deny. Payton was at the age when a woman should be setting her sights on starting her own family, not watching after another's children. There was no need to close his eyes to visualize her with a dark-haired babe on her hip and a smile upon her face. She'd been wonderful with Joy, and supportive of Abram's rather eccentric tendencies. She would do the same for her own children.

His heart squeezed until his chest ached at the very real possibility that he would not see her again, let alone happy and content with a family of her own.

A soft knock sounded on the door, and they all turned when the butler entered.

"Miss Darby has arrived to see you, my lady," the Wittenbottom servant proclaimed.

"Very good, Vernon. Please show her to the green salon." After the butler had vacated the room, Flora turned to him with a smile. "I am certain Miss Darby will not disappoint with her selection."

She said selection as if the decision had already been made—a governess found.

"I do look forward to speaking with her choices."

"I doubt that will be necessary." Flora stood, Miss Primrose bolting to her feet to follow, but his sister shook her head. "Please wait here. Damon and I will see to Miss Darby."

Flora's companion sat on the lounge, and Damon longed to change places with the woman. "Yes, my lady," she mumbled.

Damon held out his arm for Flora, and they departed the room, making their way to the green salon. His sister, seemingly at ease, strode confidently at this side, while Damon had a sinking feeling that he was being led to the Tower.

CHAPTER 25

PAYTON SAT RIGIDLY in the high-back chair, her hands resting on the armrests on each side as she attempted to remain silent. Garrett, in opposition, toyed with the cloth napkin on his lap as they waited for Marce to join them for their meal.

Payton had been foolish to think that the situation she'd entangled herself in with Damon was the only debacle afoot. In less than two full days, she'd witnessed a parade of men coming and going from Craven House: Mr. Adams, who handled Marce's financial investments; a gentleman called only by his given name, Miles, who clearly worked in trade; and the tall stranger Payton had seen at a ball the previous year.

Something big was afoot, and Marce was tight-lipped as usual. Her eldest sister was also withdrawn and solemn, not seeming to notice that Payton hadn't left Craven House since she'd arrived the previous morning.

For brief periods of time, Payton had even been able to put Damon from her mind as she slunk around the house, hoping to overhear her sister and learn what was going on.

"Good evening," Marce said, her tone ringing

across the room.

Payton glanced at Garrett, taken aback by Marce's jovial mood after their difficult conversation the previous day, and the constant flow of guests in and out of Craven House.

"What has you in such fine spirits?" Garrett stood and pulled Marce's seat out for her to sit. "You were quite dour when last we spoke."

Marce retrieved her napkin and draped it across her lap, signaling for Darla to serve their meal—a light fare of duck soup, roasted pheasant, and fresh bread—before addressing them.

"I am never in a dour mood," she retorted. However, her tone rose a note. "My place as head of this family is one of great responsibility."

"Go on," Payton prodded, tiring of her sister's tendency to remain furtive when she suspected that Payton desperately wanted to know something. "Do not keep us in suspense. Who is the mystery man, and why have you been strange of late?"

"The man is of no consequence." Marce glanced down into her bowl of soup, and Payton feared she'd not say another word on the matter. "I wanted to share with you both that I am in the process of purchasing property near Kent. I will require your assistance packing up Craven House before it is time for the women and me to relocate with the servants."

"Moving?" Garett sat forward, knocking his water goblet over, rendering his food inedible. "You cannot."

Fear coiled in Payton's stomach. She'd never wanted to face the possibility of not having Craven House to escape to or what she'd do without Marce close—though she'd longed for it often enough. "Outside London? Where will I go when I need to"—Payton swallowed as both her siblings turned to her—"get away from the baron's hellions?"

"What of Jude and Sam when they return?" Garrett continued. "They will think we abandoned them. You will be gone, and they will have nowhere to go."

Marce held up her hand to silence Garrett. "Yes, I'm moving. Payton, you can just as easily go to Ellie's townhouse as this one. I will inform both Sam and Jude of the change. Besides, they are both wed now. They have no need to stay here, and neither do either of you."

Payton hadn't seen her friend—her *only* friend—Ellie, now Lady Ellington Chastain, since she took the position at Ashford Hall. How could she seek her out now only to beg for shelter?

"But—" they started in unison.

"This grand house is too much for me alone," Marce cut off their protests. "The new property is surrounded by open land with a beautiful garden and even a small lake for rowing."

Garrett pulled a frown of disgust. "You do not *row.*"

"Nor does she swim," Payton added.

"I think I would like to learn how to row—and swim. I've always enjoyed baths. Swimming cannot be much different." Marce paused, her shoulders straightening with assurance. "But that is beside the point. This new house will give the women I help a place to rest and heal from their pasts, and time to decide where to go from there. And it will also be somewhere you both can come when you need to be away from town."

"I adore town life," Payton argued, hollowly.

Marce snorted. "You enjoy the ready access to the gaming hells."

"London is my home," Garrett proclaimed, pushing his flooded plate away.

"Only because you've never known another"—

Marce sighed—"and that is no one's fault but mine."

It had been one of Marce's admitted faults from the day before. Payton wanted to dispel her sister's false belief. Both she and her other siblings knew the extent of Marce's sacrifices in raising them. They rarely agreed on many things, but now, especially after her time employed at Ashford Hall, Payton truly understood what her sister had given up to keep their family together.

"Regardless, shortly, Craven House will no longer belong to me, and I've chosen a fitting location with adequate space for everyone. You can choose to come with me or visit during the Christmastide season or whenever the time allows. That is your choice to make, but neither of you will instruct me on my course."

Garrett had the good sense to at least appear remorseful for his outburst, but Payton couldn't help but glare at her eldest sister.

"If there is anything of sentimental value here, I suggest you remove it promptly." Marce pushed away from the table and stood. Her fingers gripped the edge until her knuckles turned white. "I will bid you both good evening. I have much to attend to elsewhere in the house."

With a final hardened glare, Marce pivoted and stalked from the room.

"And she thinks I lack proper manners," Garrett huffed before draining his wine goblet and pulling Marce's plate to replace his ruined meal. "What plans have you tonight?"

"I will return to the baron's house and—"

Payton suspected her ruse while working admirably with Marce due to her distracted nature, had not escaped Garrett's notice.

His raised brow was enough to stop her lie.

"Lord Loughton is hosting a soiree this evening,"

he mused. "I have heard the Earl of Haversham will be in attendance, as well as Chastain and Maddox. The tables will be plump and ready for us to ply our skills."

Fear spiked within her, her palms growing moist at the possibility that Catherton could be in attendance, as well. Payton pondered the amount of money she'd be able to collect if such endowed lords were indeed seated in the card room. But a soiree? She hadn't attended a proper society event since before Sam and Jude were wed.

Images of the cream evening gown with its lace overlay hanging in her dressing closet came to mind. When would she have another excuse to don the dress? If Marce moved, Payton had no doubt that she'd have little other choice but to accompany her, and there were not many balls held in the rural countryside.

"When are you leaving for Loughton's?" she asked.

Garrett clapped his hands in triumph. "Ten o'clock sharp. There is little reason to arrive before the men at the card tables are rightfully and properly befuddled from drinking Drummond's fine brandy...unless you want to dance or some other such silly thing girls do."

If they'd been sitting next to one another and not across the table, Payton would have punched him in his arm; instead, she settled for throwing her piece of bread at this head. Garrett, swift as usual, caught the crusty lump and tossed it into her soup bowl, splattering the front of her gown and her exposed neck with duck juices.

Payton leapt from her seat, brushing the front of her dress with her napkin as Garrett chuckled.

"You beef-witted buffoon!" Her outrage matched the sound of her chair toppling over.

"You've ruined my dress."

"Do not whine," he chuckled. "You were going to change anyways."

"I do not discard my gowns every time I change, Garrett," she seethed. "I am not one of your wealthy consorts."

"Am I to act affronted by your words?" Garrett pressed his hand to his chest and rounded his eyes. "Miss Payton Samuels, I will have you know that the ladies who occupy my time have sparkling personalities and are superb conversationalists."

Her anger diminished as she tried to suppress her smile.

She missed Garrett's witty retorts almost as much as she longed to be a part of Joy and Abram's sibling banter.

"You are lucky I conduct myself with the utmost decorum, or I'd make certain the entire tureen tipped into your lap." Payton stomped her foot and turned, heading for the door.

"Ten o'clock sharp," he called as she neared the threshold.

She held her chin high as she flipped around to pin Garrett with her narrowed glare. "I'll be ready, don't you fear."

The deep rumbling of Garrett's laughter echoed through the house, drowning out her heavy footfalls.

Payton would have turned down Garrett's invitation to attend Lord Loughton's soiree were it not the perfect opportunity to put Damon out of her mind—and don the new gown he'd so aptly purchased for her.

PAYTON STARED AT her reflection in the mirror as she held the string of pearls around her neck and clasped the latch. The satin with the lace overlay hugged her body, creating curves that would rival Samantha's and enhancing the fitted bodice of the gown.

Her hair was fashioned in the only style she was able to achieve without the assistance of one of her sisters; the top pinned back with her long, dark locks twisted in a single curl that hung over her bare shoulder. She'd adopted the style two years ago when she saw a woman on a fashion plate with a similar face structure to hers. It highlighted her creamy skin and catlike eyes.

She'd even overheard a duke comment to his wife how rare and alluring she appeared.

Payton wasn't certain if the comment was meant to be a compliment or if she should feel offended; however, Sam had envied the proclamation for an entire fortnight. Soon after, she'd met Elijah, the Marquis of Ridgefeld, and her sister's jealousy had dissipated without another thought.

When Payton turned side to side, admiring the modiste's fine work, she wondered what Damon would think of the gown—was the color to his liking, was the cut pleasing to his eye?

"Humpf." His opinion didn't matter, couldn't matter. Not now. Not after everything. The tall clock in the hall below stairs chimed, echoing through the house, propelling Payton away from her looking glass and toward her dressing closet. She grabbed her ankle-length cloak and her matching beaded reticule before hurrying from her room.

She would not put it past Garrett to depart without her if she were not waiting in the foyer.

Grasping her skirts, Payton took the stairs two at a time before jumping down the final three steps, her slippers making no sound on the polished floor. Odd how old habits returned quickly when she was in her childhood home. How many times had Garrett chased her down these exact stairs? How many times had she raced up them to avoid being caught by Jude or Sam? How many times had she slunk into the shadows at the landing, eavesdropping on Marce below?

And now, her sister was so easily disposing of the house—their home—in favor of some property in the country.

What was Payton to do? Despite her small savings, it wasn't enough to support herself without Marce's assistance or finding another position. Moving to the country with her sister was an option, but it would not bring her any closer to the life she wanted. If she remained in London she would quickly find herself out of funds—and alone.

"Miss Payton?" Darla's stern voice halted Payton, and she turned toward the hall leading to the kitchens. "Do ye be know'n these two troublemakers?"

She gasped when she spied their trusted housekeeper holding Abram's collar and Joy's arm. Both children's eyes were downcast as if they'd received one of Darla's infamous reprimands.

"What are you doing here?" Payton knelt before Joy, lifting the girl's chin with her finger until her green eyes, shimmering with unshed tears, met hers.

"We—we—we," Joy stammered, sucking in her bottom lip to stop it from trembling.

"Caught 'em sneaking 'round the back and peep'n, I did." Darla released her hold on both children and set her fisted hands on her ample hips.

"I will handle them, Darla," Payton said, standing. "Thank you for bringing them to me and not Marce."

"They be honest and say they be look'n for ye." Darla's eyes softened as she glanced between the children. "The two of ye could'a been kilt or stolen off the streets."

"I am certain they are sorry for frightening you, Darla. Isn't that correct, children?"

Joy and Abram moved to Payton's side and turned to face the Craven House servant.

"We are very sorry," Abram said.

"We did not *mean* to be caught, only to visit our governess as we were told she was sick."

Payton noticed the sprig of flowers nestled in the pocket of Joy's pinafore.

"Her gown is awful pretty to be worn when ill, Joy," Abram hissed. "I shouldn't have let you convince me to come with you."

Sick? Was it a lie that Damon had told to put off telling the children of her departure?

"Be that as it may, I am happy you did accompany Joy, or something might have befallen her. London is a frightening place after dark."

"She would have fared well," Abram shrugged. "Mr. Brown caught us trying to saddle Father's stallion and had Digby and the stablemaster bring us."

"And what did your father say of your excursion?" she asked. She could not imagine that Damon would allow them to journey across London, after dark, to visit her.

"He thinks we are asleep in our rooms."

Joy sighed. "Mrs. Brown brought supper up to our bedchambers and said we were not to go downstairs until morning. Father is having friends over."

"Friends?" Payton asked.

"The ballroom was set up, as it normally is," Abram clarified.

"I see." The baron was hosting another gaming night. "So you slipped from the house unnoticed?"

Abram crossed his arms with a huff. "Those that care know where we are."

Payton's heart broke a little at the boy's words. There was a seriousness and a finality to his tone that no boy his age should have.

"Your father cares very much," she said. "For the both of you."

Darla tsked and ambled back toward the kitchen.

"We thought maybe he did, but since you've been gone, he hasn't been to see us, not even to check on our studies," Joy whimpered with defeat. "We thought that after you kissed Father he would change, even keep you as our governess forever. But when you left…we feared you'd had a row."

Payton stood frozen in the hall.

Their kiss? The children—or at least Joy—had witnessed their kiss?

"We did not want you to go—"

"Oh, dear one…" She'd heard Damon use the term on several occasions, and it came naturally to her lips. "You were not meant to see that."

"You and Father *did* have a row." Abram's chest puffed in reassurance, but it immediately sank when he realized the consequences.

"I meant our kiss. It was a private moment between your father and me, nothing more." Obviously, it had been nothing more to at least one of them. Payton didn't want to discuss her intimate moment with the baron with Joy and Abram. "How did you know where to come to find me?"

She'd always been careful when instructing Mr. Curtis to pick her up and drop her off several houses down from Ashford Hall.

"Oh, that was simple," Abram smiled. "Mr. Brown had you followed after you first started as our governess. He knew your directions."

Mr. Brown's words floated through her mind, "*My missus claims I sleep more soundly when all the household is accounted for.*"

Payton shouldn't be surprised that the Ashford butler had taken precautions to make sure she was safe, no matter where she went.

"Now, tell us, when are you coming back?" Joy demanded, her brow furrowing. "Or did you and Father really have a row?"

She wasn't certain what the right answer was. Damon had been adamant that he'd tell the children of her departure, but that apparently hadn't happened. It was understandable that he was hesitant to disappoint them. This would not be the first time their governess had left her position, nor would it likely be the last. With time, they would come to know Payton's replacement.

"Your father and I, and our association should not cause either of you any concern," Payton said, immediately regretting her attempt to distract them. Despite her words to the contrary, it was certainly their concern. She was their governess, and Damon was their father. If it concerned anyone other than Payton and the baron, it was Joy and Abram. "We should get you both home before your father notices you are gone."

And before Garrett—or worse, Marce—stumbled upon them.

"I told you, Abram, Miss Samuels and Father's kiss did not mean—"

"What is this?" Heavy footfalls sounded behind her, and Payton stiffened. "A kiss between my dear sister and Lord Ashford?"

Garrett's chuckle told her that she hadn't fooled him in the slightest with her recent stay at Craven House.

"Who are you, sir?" Joy's chin jutted forward.

"I am Lord Garrett Davenport," he replied with a gallant bow. "And you, my lady, are?"

"I am not a lady at all," Joy retorted, obviously

suspicious of Garrett. "Miss Joy Kinder. Lord Ashford's daughter, and Miss Samuels' charge."

"Very lovely to make your acquaintance, Miss Kinder," Garrett said, glancing up to wink at Payton. "However, since it has come to light that my sister has been linked romantically to your father, I think it best you call me simply Garrett, and I shall address you as Miss Joy." When the girl nodded in approval, he continued. "Tell me, Miss Joy, why have I not made your acquaintance at a ball or, mayhap a recital, before now? I certainly would have asked for a dance—or two."

Payton couldn't help but smile as Garrett spun his web of charm around the girl.

"I am only six," she preened, nervously tucking her blond hair behind her ear. "I shan't have my coming out for another ten years my father says."

"A pity, Miss Joy," he commiserated.

"But Father did purchase me a lovely gown like Miss Samuels wears—"

Payton set her hand on Joy's shoulder, ready to end their delightful chat and be gone before Marce saw the children. "I think we should return you both to Ashford Hall."

"No point, Miss Samuels," Abram said. "Father won't notice we are gone until morning at the soonest. Perhaps not even until our midday meal. He is busy with his card game."

"Card game?" Garrett asked. "Is that not what—"

Payton held up her hand, silencing what she knew her brother was going to say next. "We are headed to Lord Drummond's soiree. On the way, we will see Joy and Abram safely to their bedchambers and then be off."

"But—"

"No, Garrett." Payton firmly shook her head.

She would not allow her brother to convince her to remain in the baron's home. "Children, safely home, and then we are leaving. That is all."

"How do you plan to sneak in?" he asked.

Both children stared up at her, eyes rounded in question.

At least the conversation had moved on from her and Damon having a row.

"Mr. Brown was able to sneak them out, I cannot expect it will be difficult for me to see them back inside. Besides, Rigby and Mr. Brown likely already have a plan."

Garrett's eyes widened as he glanced between the children and back at his sister. "This Mr. Brown allowed the children out. Alone. At night?"

"I am as upset as you about this," Payton said. "But right now, we must see about returning them with all due haste."

"Father's coach is down the street," Abram chimed in. "Rigby walked us here to your home."

"Very good." Payton avoided her brother's cool stare. He'd been the one to tell her about the baron's gaming nights to begin with, and they'd attended a few nights together before she took the post as the Ashford governess. But she could not risk being seen by the baron. Their entanglement was over. He hadn't stopped her from leaving, nor launched any great protest. Not that she'd given him many opportunities as her anger over his meddling with Catherton had her seeing red. "I will ride in the baron's coach with the children. Garrett, you and Mr. Curtis will follow in the Craven House carriage. I will be in and out of Ashford Hall as quickly as possible, and we will be on our way."

Garrett pushed out his bottom lip and batted his eyes. "But—but—but, the baron's coach would be far more comfortable than our ancient, decrepit conveyance."

To Payton's utter disbelief, Joy stepped to Garrett's side and took his hand in hers.

"Yes, can he not ride with us?" Joy pleaded.

Payton turned to Abram, praying the boy would have some excuse that would curb his sister's request. She should say no. It was her right as their governess—former governess, as it were. When Abram only shrugged with a lopsided grin, Payton acquiesced. The important thing was that she return the children without Damon discovering they were ever gone.

"You will remain outside Ashford Hall," she said, pointing at Garrett. When he nodded, she turned to the children. "The pair of you will accompany me inside with no further questions. Understood?"

"Yes, Miss Samuels," they said, nodding in unison.

CHAPTER 26

THE ROOM FELT hollow and empty despite Damon's nearly two dozen guests. His coat stretched too tightly across his shoulders, his evening shoes cramped his toes until they were numb, and the strings holding his black and orange mask in place cut into the tender flesh above his ears. Why had he thought hosting a gaming night would take his mind off the dire circumstances that were his life?

He found himself scrutinizing every female guest that arrived—was her hair the right length and color, was she tall enough, did she hold her chin at that precise, defiant angle that was unequivocally Payton?

Damon nodded to his servant, signaling that the gaming should commence.

She wasn't coming. Why had he deluded himself into believing she would?

Neither had Catherton arrived, despite the acceptance of Damon's invitation. Having the pair at Ashford Hall at the same time was both unwise and reckless. The duke had been searching for Payton for over a week, and he'd no doubt spot her no matter what disguise she donned.

That did not deter Damon from watching the door for her arrival.

"My lord," a man with a solid blue mask and neatly trimmed golden hair called to him. "Join us."

Damon waved off the invite. He was no more interested in hazard than he was any card game.

He inclined his head to a couple as they took their seats at the whist table. Thankfully, the foursome was complete, and they wouldn't ask him to join them.

Mr. Brown appeared at the double doors of the ballroom, scanning the crowd until his eyes met Damon's. They nodded at one another, and the butler pulled the doors closed. The servants delivering refreshments entered through a side door that led to the servants' hallway and stairwell. When his Grosvenor Square townhouse had been built, the architect paid particular attention to making certain servants could come and go throughout the house without being noticed.

All it did was make Ashford Hall appear deserted when it was only he and the children in residence. Since Payton had left him and the children, the house had been too quiet. Too still. Too somber. He longed to hear Abram bickering with Joy, teasing her, or the pair playing a jest on their governess.

But the children had remained above stairs, quietly attending to their studies until Payton returned.

Damon sighed, gaining the notice of a man at the table before him who tucked his cards close with a scowl.

Why hadn't he allowed her to handle telling the children? Payton would have had the courage to tell them, she would have spoken the truth in a way they could've understood, and he'd never have had to lie to them. In her short time at Ashford Hall, she'd made everything better—including him. Damon had spent years hiding: from his life, his future, and his children; unable to accept losing Sarah. He'd built a wall so thick to guard his heart, he hadn't realized that he'd forgotten to breathe at some point.

Payton had been a breath of fresh air to his stale, cumbersome existence.

At some point, he'd taken his first deep inhale in four years. And he'd survived.

Moving forward without Sarah had been something he'd been unwilling to even contemplate. He'd set about remaining in the dark, empty place he'd entered after losing the mother of this children…and he'd done a marvelous job of it, too.

Until Payton.

She'd been the spark that set his darkened life ablaze—and he hadn't expected it. Hadn't seen it coming. Hadn't fathomed it was what he needed, what his life was missing.

She was what their *lives* were missing.

He was glad for the mask covering his face because if any of his guests caught sight of him, they'd realize the pain he'd kept buried for too long. He'd hoped to avoid further heartbreak, but all he'd managed to do was keep the pain and anguish inside so long that it had festered within him.

A group of men chuckled at the faro table near the doors, and Damon's stare lingered there. His way to escape. No one would notice if he slipped from the room. He could be in his study within moments, free of the watchful eyes of his guests, free to sink into his favored chair and lose himself in the dancing flames that licked the logs in the hearth.

Too many times, he'd lost hours—days even—watching the fire.

It had been nearly a month since he'd fallen into such despair.

Again, he could only blame Payton.

Blame or *praise* the woman?

She'd brought about a change neither his children, his sister, nor his servants could trigger, despite their years of trying.

And she'd done it swiftly, without Damon even realizing it.

Yes, she deserved praise, not blame.

In his own way, he'd tried to show her the appreciation she deserved by settling her debt with Catherton. How did she not see that he'd done it to help her, not to control or restrain her in any way?

The voices around him were made unintelligible by the pounding in his head.

He had been so bloody wrong—about everything.

He'd pushed his children away, denied them the love and affection they so desperately needed after Sarah's death. He'd limited his own emotions to the point where he lived in a constant state of despair. He knew no other way to make it through each day.

Yet, that wasn't wholly true.

Payton had shown him what things could have been like, had he not taken the path he'd chosen.

Anger, laughter, love…they were all possible, if he'd just give himself a chance.

Was it too late? Would Joy and Abram forever blame him for Payton's disappearance?

He needed to go to them now; tell them the awful truth and see where they stood.

Damon glanced at the closed ballroom doors, the panels sealing off his easy escape, closing him in, keeping him from doing what he longed to do: make amends with his children, and give them what they deserved.

Days spent strolling the museum. Nights at the playhouse. Endless winters at Falconcrest. Holidays in Bath or Cornwall. Afternoons horseback riding in the meadow by his country estate or promenading in

Hyde or Regent Park. Evenings by the fire, books in hand as the warmth from the hearth enveloped them. Morning meals in the salon overlooking the gardens while Abram and Joy bantered and bickered about their lessons, while he and Payton took pleasure in the children's passion for learning.

Payton? Tension laced his shoulders, tightening the fabric of his shirt across his back.

"My lord?" Mr. Brown had materialized at his elbow.

Damon glanced at his servant out of the corner of his eye, not taking his focus off the crowd milling about the room even though his idle musings still pushed for his attention. "Yes."

"Is all as it should be?"

"Of course," Damon huffed. "Why would it not be?"

"My lord, may I speak frankly?" the butler whispered.

Damon turned to face the man. "I always expect you to speak as such."

Mr. Brown's brow pulled low, and he lowered his chin, avoiding eye contact. "You are scowling, my lord."

Damon let loose a gruff chortle. "You cannot possibly know that. I am wearing a bloody mask."

"Yes, however—"

"Mr. Brown," Damon sighed, keeping his voice low to avoiding being overheard. "I have had a very difficult few days."

"I agree, my lord." The butler pivoted slightly to stand next to Damon, drawing far less attention from his guests than if they saw their host speaking privately in hushed tones.

"Has Catherton arrived?" Damon asked.

"No, my lord."

"No other uninvited guests either?"

When Mr. Brown stiffened at his question, Damon needed no further proof to know the servant had known about Payton's masquerading ways all along, or at least during her time employed at Ashford Hall.

Before the butler could respond, Damon continued, "Please inform me immediately if either occurs. Continue to make certain my guests enjoy their evening. I will be in my study if you have need of me."

He was in a distracted mood, and there was no reason to subject his guests to it. He was at Ashford Hall, yet longed to be somewhere else. Anywhere else, as long as Payton was close.

Making his way across the room, Damon didn't pause to speak with anyone, nor did he look away from the ballroom doors until he arrived at them as a servant swung the thick wooden door open for him to depart.

He pressed his palm to his forehead once he was alone—the noises from the ballroom muffled—and hurried toward his study. He didn't need to see to find the room. It was like a beacon that called him forward. A siren who sang until he was captured in her embrace.

Why had he thought a gaming night would work to distract him from Payton's absence? To diminish his feeling of responsibility for his current situation? To reduce his guilt over the loss his children would soon be forced to face—for the second time?

Discarding his mask, Damon slumped in his chair before the hearth, his head falling into his hands, all the while, his shoulders straining for freedom under the confines of his evening coat. He'd loved Sarah, and she'd left him. Payton had come into his household and won the children's hearts and brought light to Damon's life…and now she was gone, too.

His chest ached with emptiness.

It shouldn't hurt so much to be right.

Nothing in Damon's life had gone as it should.

He would do what needed to be done—for his children.

Come morning, he'd hire one of the women he'd spoken with at Flora's, or perhaps speak to the children about attending school away from London. Maybe they would thrive in an environment with other children, away from their disaster of a father and the shadowed memory of their mother. Even as his plan formed in his mind, the darkness that had encapsulated him so entirely before threatened to descend on him again, blocking out the light that had come with Payton's appearance in their lives.

He didn't want another governess, and neither would Joy and Abram.

Payton had healed their family. She'd shown them they could move forward, despite what they'd all lost. Honoring Sarah and the past they shared together did not mean forsaking his future.

Damon pushed to his feet, stripping his jacket away and discarding it on his chair.

Joy and Abram needed Payton in their lives.

Bloody hell, Damon needed her even more.

He couldn't—*wouldn't*—allow things to continue as they were. Another governess wouldn't do, and Payton returning to Ashford Hall as a simple servant was not what he desired. She wouldn't long for that either. He wanted more than Payton in his life to care for his children. He wanted more than to forget about her and move on. Damon had never been a man to move on easily—and for once, this would serve him well.

He only needed to discover what Payton longed for and hope it was the same as he desired.

He collected his discarded jacket, any thoughts of wallowing alone vanished.

"DON'T FORGET THIS." Garrett held his hand out the open door of the carriage, a cream mask with ebony strings dangling from his fingers. "You might need it."

Payton turned toward the children, eagerly waiting a few steps away before leaning back into the coach. "I am not attending the party."

"What if someone sees you?" he demanded.

"Everyone will be in the back of the house by now with the gambling underway," she hissed. "I will hurry the children in the front door and up the stairs to their chambers.

"Where did you find this?" As an afterthought, she'd had the mask made to match her gown, but after everything that had happened with Damon, she'd never thought to wear it.

When he didn't respond and only jiggled the mask, Payton grabbed it.

"Tsk, tsk, dear sister." Garrett waved his finger between them. "We both know that is not what is important here. Do don the mask, just in case."

"Very well," Payton said, moving away from the carriage and back to the children. "Are you ready?"

They both nodded, and the trio started for the front door.

She debated having the carriage drop them off in the alley behind Ashford Hall, but it was far more likely they'd be seen coming in through the mews than through the front door. The gambling would have begun an hour or so before, and the foyer and main staircase would be deserted. The only activity would be on the servants' stairs.

Mr. Brown was likely positioned close to the

front door, waiting for the children to return. Payton would certainly have a word with the man for allowing the children out after dark, unchaperoned except for the Ashford driver and footman.

However, when she opened the front door, the foyer was empty, although music and voices from the ballroom floated through the house. She urged the children in and up the stairs, turned to the right, and moved down the corridor to their rooms.

Joy's door came first after they'd passed the schoolroom.

Payton opened the door and ushered Joy inside. "I will see Abram to his room and then return," she whispered before pulling the door closed without a sound.

They took the few steps to Abram's door, and he walked inside without hesitation. "Good evening, Miss Samuels. I do hope to see you again soon. Forgive Father for whatever he's done to upset you."

Payton made to tell the boy there was nothing to forgive, but Abram gave her a sad smile before pushing his door closed, leaving her alone in the hallway.

Her own door was only a few feet farther down the corridor.

No, the room did not belong to her any longer. A new governess would take her place before long, and any remnants of Payton would be erased and forgotten with time.

Her lip trembled. Lifting her skirts with her free hand, she hurried back to Joy's chamber. When she entered, the girl had already undone the ties of her dress and was slipping her nightgown over her head.

"Joy," Payton called. The only light in the room came from a single candle and the dying embers in the hearth; however, there was enough warmth to last until the child found slumber. "You mustn't tell your father you came to see me."

"Will you be here when we wake?" the girl asked, ignoring Payton's warning.

She shook her head, turning to pull down the blanket for Joy to climb into bed. "No, Joy."

There was so much more she wanted to say: that she was heartbroken to be leaving them, that she would do anything to remain at Ashford Hall, that…she was sorry. But nothing else came.

Joy climbed into bed, and Payton tucked the blanket around her tiny body, much as she had the day the girl had nearly drowned in the pond, except when Payton glanced up, she did not meet Damon's watchful eyes across the bed this time.

"We don't want you to go. Not even Father, even if he did something to anger you," Joy mumbled.

Payton hesitated, knowing she needed to depart but unable to allow the girl's mutterings to go unaddressed. "What was that, Joy?"

There was no way Joy could know anything that had transpired between her and Damon beyond their kiss—she was only a child. Joy was too young to understand the heartbreak her father had lived through, or the future Payton wanted for herself. It did not include living as a servant nor being beholden to a man who overstepped his boundaries. Their discussion had made it clear that Damon hadn't anticipated her discovering that he'd settled her debt with Catherton. Could it be that he actually did not have any dark intentions with his action as he claimed?

"Abram and I heard Father." Joy's eyes grew heavy with unshed tears. "He was crying—in his sleep."

"Eavesdropping is very impolite," Payton said, easing herself onto the bed next to Joy. "You should not listen when you are not invited."

"We were not lurking about Father's door." She pushed up onto her elbows, leaning close to Payton in the soft glow from the candle. "He woke us up—last night."

Payton didn't want to hear any of this. She'd made her decision, given her notice, and was prepared to tell Marce of her failings and beg her sister to take her with her to the country. In the last few days, Payton had lost her position as governess and learned she'd soon lose the house she'd called home for all her life. Her future, the one she'd dreamed of for herself, was slipping from her fingers as the hours passed. A home of her own, the independence to live of her own accord, and find what would make her happy and content.

"If he was crying, it had naught to do with me—or you, for that matter," Payton replied. "Your father has lost much in his life. He's gone through things that most men would run from. He lost your mother and was left to raise you and Abram alone. That is a very scary thing."

Joy clutched her hands on the top of the blanket, allowing her head to fall back against her pillows. "But when you came…he changed. He went to the park with us, the museum, and took meals with us. Then you left—we knew you weren't ill—and he shut himself in his study again, didn't eat with us, and cried out in the night. It was like when I had my terrors, you came and comforted me. Someone should do that for Father."

Payton leapt from the bed as if it had caught fire, silently begging the girl to remain quiet…to not voice what they both knew to be true. Payton should be there to comfort their father.

"Joy, I must go." She could tell the girl the truth—she was afraid of the baron catching her at Ashford Hall—but she settled on a reason that was still true, though a little less to the point. "Garrett is waiting for me, and he is like a child. If left alone, he is sure to find himself in a spot of trouble."

Without thinking, she leaned down and placed a kiss on Joy's forehead.

"Promise me you won't do anything as drastic and dangerous as leaving home without telling your father again." When Joy nodded, she continued. "Your father would have been destroyed if anything had happened to you or Abram. Goodbye, Joy."

Payton inched toward the door as Joy shifted in bed, turning away from her.

Damon would not have been the only one destroyed if the children had been harmed.

With a sigh, Payton paused to tie her mask. She'd been upstairs for quite a while, and she prayed she wouldn't cross paths with Damon as she made her escape.

CHAPTER 27

DAMON STUMBLED FROM his study, moving away from the merriment in his ballroom and toward the front door that would lead him out into the night—and to Payton.

Few people had experienced the hardships he had during his life and the guilt that came with it knowing you held the blame. Except her. She understood the loss of a loved one and how difficult it was to find enough strength within yourself to love—and lose—again.

Love?

Yes, he cared deeply for Payton. He cherished her kindness to his children and her understanding for him. Surely, it could not have progressed to something as profound as love. He barely knew her, beyond their brief moments together. He was attracted to her; no man would be irrational enough to deny that.

What was irrational, was for him to even think the word *love* regarding a woman he barely knew, a woman who deserved more than an empty shell of a man who hadn't enough left within him to actively love his own children.

Pressing his outstretched hand against the wall,

Damon made his way to the front of the house.

He didn't know what to call the draw he felt for Payton, but if he could convince her to speak with him, they would figure it out—together. He would tell her all he should have confessed before—before he'd begun to push her away, before she'd discovered he'd paid her debt, and before she'd left.

Raised voices drifted toward him, and he slowed, pushing into the shadows to avoid being seen. The last thing he wanted was to be waylaid in the foyer when he desperately needed the solitude of his room. He wanted to be alone with his musings somewhere his servants wouldn't happen upon him.

"Unhand me!" a woman's voice growled.

"Your Grace, please," Mr. Brown pleaded. "Let the lady go. I will find Lord Ashford, and you can speak privately about this matter."

"This *lady* is a conniving swindler." The Duke of Catherton's furious tone was unmistakable. "Summon the magistrate now, and I will be pleased to meet with the baron when the magistrate arrives; however, she has been known to disappear. I will not release her until the authorities are called."

Damon pushed from the shadows, his head clearing as he stepped into the foyer.

Catherton stood below the bottom stair, his hand grasping a woman's elbow as she frantically tried to pull away. Mr. Brown attempted to push in between the pair.

The duke and his butler jostled, blocking Damon's view of the altercation. Who was the woman? Gowned and masked in cream, pearls at her throat, Damon didn't recognize her from the ballroom.

"Catherton," Damon's voice echoed off the high ceiling in the foyer. "Remove your hands from her before I have *you* removed from this house and thrown headfirst into the Thames."

Both men froze, allowing the woman to pull from Catherton's clutches.

Damon's heart beat rapidly before stopping. It could not be…but it was.

Wearing a cream evening dress with a mask to match, Payton's signature single mahogany curl hung over her shoulder, teasing the lace of her bodice. How he had not spotted her so clearly before, Damon would never know. Now, he saw only her—even with her mask as a guise. He blinked several times, but she did not disappear or morph into another woman. He knew the sparkling, deep blue eyes hidden behind her mask. He was familiar with the feel of her soft, lush lips against his. He could almost hear the melody of her laughter, or the dark tone of her voice when she was called to anger.

"Lord Ashford." Catherton straightened his coat and dipped to retrieve his mask from the floor. "Our thief has returned."

"She is not a thief," Damon seethed. "Her debt to you was settled. You have your money; therefore, there are no grounds for you causing a scene in my house."

Payton looked between Damon and the duke before turning to glance at the closed door.

There was nothing more he wanted than to ask her why she was here. Had she come back to speak with him or merely to gamble?

"I apologize," he confessed, holding her stare. "For the duke's rude behavior. You are free to leave."

"Over my bloody body will she be allowed to leave," Catherton thundered. "I have a grievance with this woman, and I will see it resolved."

He pointed his finger at Payton with each word, and Damon had the urge to prod the man in return. He took a step forward.

Footsteps sounded from down the hall, and Damon felt the inquisitive stares of his guests as they pushed closer to absorb any gossip they could overhear. The murmurs of the group left no doubt that his gaming evening would be the talk of the *ton* come morning light.

He didn't want that for Payton. She deserved better than to be exposed in the gossip rags.

Meeting Payton's eyes once more, Damon noted that they'd softened—even lightened in color— behind her mask. She should be terrified. Bloody hell, the duke was a fierce and formidable adversary. Yet, that was not what he saw in her eyes.

It was almost as if she regretted being caught by Catherton because of the impact on *him*.

"You should go," he whispered, notching his head toward the door. "Mr. Brown, make certain my guest finds her carriage and arrives home safely. Send Rigby as an escort."

"Of course, my lord." The Ashford butler cleared his throat, and Damon glanced away from Payton to see the servant nod upward. "If you will come with me, miss."

On the landing above, both his children stood staring down at him in utter shock—and outrage?

"Return to your rooms, children," Damon commanded. If at any time he desperately needed Joy and Abram to follow his demands, it was now. "I will come and check in on you in a few minutes."

He was satisfied when both blond heads disappeared, but he waited to hear the closing of their doors from above. His guests had fallen silent behind him, likely hanging on every word spoken, committing it to memory, and ready to retrieve it during their rounds of social calls the following day.

"I am not leaving," Payton said, gaining a gasp from the enthralled crowd and a scowl from Damon.

She turned away from him to face the duke. "I do owe you a debt and mean to settle it as soon as I have the funds."

"You owe him nothing," Damon countered. "I made good on what was owed to Catherton."

"Not before this woman fled your home like a thief in the night." Catherton took in the awestruck crowd lingering in the hall. "See this woman"—he pointed at Payton, who shrank back a step—"she lost a sizable hand to me, and instead of paying her due, she left. She is a coward and a con."

Damon turned to address his guests. "Please, return to the ballroom."

In the dim corridor, Damon watched as one by one, the ladies and lords of the *ton* exclaimed in horror, and their mouths rounded in Os of surprise as Payton began to untie the strings holding her mask in place.

"Don't!" It was all Damon could think to say. If the crowd learned her identity, despite merely being a governess in his household, she would never again secure a position in London or anywhere in England, for that matter. If the magistrate were summoned, she'd face far worse penalties for her crime than any proper lady would.

But his warning did nothing to stop her or even slow her as the mask slipped from her face, exposing her creamy white skin and her deep-set, catlike, blue eyes.

"Who is she?" a woman asked.

"I haven't the faintest notion," a man replied.

"Never set eyes on the girl before," another male voice mumbled.

Of course, they'd not know Payton. Perhaps there was still hope the matter could be settled in private without the magistrate.

"Let us take this to my study," Damon said.

"You have caused quite enough of a disturbance, Catherton." He turned to the crowd. "The spectacle is over. Please return to the ballroom."

When the duke nodded, the crowd dispersed quickly and, within moments, the musicians could be heard tuning their instruments.

Satisfied, Damon held out his arm for Payton, who gratefully slipped her gloved hand into the crook of his elbow. Her actions befuddled him, not to mention her unexpected presence in his home. They followed in the direction of his guests towards the ballroom but turned right instead of left when the corridor split.

The duke's sharp footfalls filled the corridor behind them with Mr. Brown's shuffle scurrying after them all.

Once everyone had entered his study, and the door was securely closed behind them preventing anyone from eavesdropping on their conversation, Damon offered Payton the seat behind his desk. If anything, it was to keep Catherton as far from her as possible. With a piece of furniture between them, Damon did not fear the duke laying a hand on her again.

"Your disturbance here this evening was uncalled for, Your Grace." Damon's tone left no room for argument. "You have insulted me, my guests, and provided ample gossip for the papers. I do not take kindly to such spectacles in my home."

"It was you who invited me, Ashford."

Damon faced away from Payton, keeping his focus on Catherton and settling the matter without another call for the magistrate. "I sent my invitation to make amends and secure your agreement that this entire matter was resolved. You are friends with my sister and her husband. I did not want any ill will between our families."

"Yet you, my lord, were hiding the woman in your home the entire time." The duke fell silent, but Damon would not refute his claim. "You thought you could fool me as she did. It is dishonorable and, despite making good on what she owed me, the debt is nowhere near being settled." His narrowed stare landed on Payton next. "I will have your name."

She stood behind Damon's desk, not taking the seat he'd offered her, and met the duke's glare without flinching. "Miss Payton Samuels of Craven House, Your Grace."

"Craven House," he scoffed. "I should have known."

To her credit, Payton did not appear wounded by his retort. She lifted her chin a notch and refused to break eye contact with Catherton.

"Lord Garrett Davenport's sister, are you?" When Payton only nodded, Catherton chuckled. "I should have noted your lack of pedigree the moment you removed your mask."

"You can summon the magistrate," Payton said, her voice cracking with defeat.

"Do not be impulsive, Miss Samuels," Damon said. If the magistrate learned of the incident, Damon would be helpless to save her. She'd be taken from his home and likely disappear, leaving him with little recourse. He wouldn't allow that fate to befall her. His temper flared for his part in bringing the duke back to Ashford Hall.

Once again, it was his failure that would cause others pain.

"How do you know the woman, Ashford?" the duke demanded, clasping his hands behind his back.

"She is—*was*—my children's governess," Damon offered, hoping the duke would take pity on her...or him. "At the time, I was unaware it was she masquerading at my gaming party. I settled her debt without her knowledge after I discovered her identity."

"And you did not summon the magistrate yourself? Interesting…" He stared between Damon and Payton, a slow smile spreading across his face. "What are we to do?"

"I am willing to hand myself over to the magistrate and accept my punishment," Payton muttered with contrition, stealing the breath from Damon's lungs as if he'd been punched in the gut. "As long as you leave the baron and his family out of the matter. I created this situation. Alone."

She was willing to sacrifice herself for him and the children? It was inconceivable and unnecessary.

Catherton had stalled calling for the magistrate this long, and Damon suspected the duke never planned to turn her over for punishment in the first place. No, he was the type of lord who took pleasure in doling out his own forms of punishment.

Unfortunately for him, he was unaware of the adversary he faced in Miss Payton Samuels…and the man who loved her.

Damon had no intention of leaving this room until Catherton knew the retribution he'd face if he tarnished Payton's name and family in any way—or worse, caused her to be detained by the magistrate.

CHAPTER 28

DAMON'S REASONING FOR settling her debt without consulting her became clear the moment the Duke of Catherton grasped her arm as she attempted to flee back up the grand stairs. Even now, behind the safety of Damon's massive desk with both men on the other side, the aching pulse in her upper arm from the duke's crushing hold reminded her that Catherton was not a lord to be trifled with. His face reddened further, and his nostrils flared even more when she proclaimed her willingness to take responsibility for her actions.

It was always bound to come to this.

She'd gambled when she hadn't the funds to make good on her bets. She'd misread the duke. More than that, Payton had underestimated his skill at the gaming tables.

She had wagered and lost.

And now she would lose far more than the freedom she coveted and the ability to make her own decisions.

She stood to lose Damon and the children, as well. It seemed all the more real and final, far more so than leaving the baron's employ.

Staring the duke directly in the eyes, Payton waited for his verdict, her outward confidence belying her racing pulse and trembling knees. She'd rather spend eternity in gaol without benefit of proper lighting or meals before she'd allow Catherton to see her weakness—or Damon to witness her losing the tentative grip she had on her fear.

All of Marce's savings would not buy her freedom from this situation. This was about far more than mere money…yet, she was at a loss as to what Catherton wanted from her.

Payton balled her fists at her sides, praying her flowing skirts hid them from sight.

"She was in my employ at the time, and it is I who should be held accountable for her transgression, Your Grace."

She couldn't bring herself to look at Damon as he spoke.

Why would he take the blame for her? Not many days ago, he'd basically told her she was replaceable, and that he merely tolerated her presence. She would have wagered on him in a heartbeat, and he could have turned her out onto the streets without a second thought.

Now, they were both willing to put their names and futures in jeopardy to save the other.

…and the children. What must they think of her after witnessing her confrontation with Catherton? She could only pray that they'd taken to their beds and had not heard the commotion.

A loud thump hit the closed study door with such fierce power that it rattled the latch.

"My lord," Mr. Brown whined. "I cannot allow you inside Lord Ashford's study. He is engaged in a very important meeting and has asked not to be disturbed. If you would like to wait in the ballroom, I will be pleased to—"

"I will not wait anywhere but where my sister is." The malice in Garrett's normally easygoing voice pierced through the thick, wooden door. "Move out of my way, sir."

The scuffle continued, and the latch jiggled as if Garrett were attempting to open the door while the butler was still blocking it.

"Is that the magistrate, Ashford?" Catherton demanded, stalking toward the door. "Your servant is denying him entrance."

Payton remained silent, her arms crossed, and waited for her brother to break through Mr. Brown or for the duke to wrench the door open from the inside. Her complicated situation was being made more complex by the moment. She hadn't told Garrett about her debt to Catherton or the baron having settled it.

The door burst open, and Garrett stumbled past the butler and into the room.

The duke's back stiffened. "Davenport?"

And Garrett's eyes rounded. "Catherton?"

"What are you doing here?" Catherton pivoted to face Damon, while Garrett met her glare over the duke's shoulder.

"I might ask the same thing." Garrett didn't wait for an invitation to join the fray. "Pay, you didn't return. I was worried."

Contrite was not a trait her brother exhibited often—or ever, really—but he was clearly apologetic for bursting in on them.

"Davenport." The duke focused on Garrett, pleased to have yet another adversary in the room. "Are you aware your sister owes me a hefty amount?"

"She owes you nothing," Damon interjected. "Her debt was settled. By me."

Garrett appeared amused, if anything, now that he'd seen for himself that Payton was whole and unharmed. "Lord Ashford," her brother said, ignoring Catherton's question. "It is a pleasure"—he glanced toward Payton and winked—"to make your acquaintance. I've attended your gaming night a time or two. Lovely gathering. My sister has spoken *fondly* of you and your children."

She wanted to throttle Garrett. He was acting as if he and Damon had been introduced amidst a ballroom and not in the study of her previous employer over a gambling debt. And to insinuate that she'd shared anything with her brother about the nature of her relationship with Damon had her cheeks flushing with embarrassment.

Damon appeared to be working through something in his mind, but Garrett continued before he could reply. "It was a pleasure meeting Miss Joy and Master Abram this evening. Fine-looking pair, I assure you."

"You've met my children?" Damon set his hands on his hips and glared.

Mr. Brown took the moment to clear his throat, gaining everyone's attention. "Is there anything else you require from me, my lord?"

"I demand the magistrate be called." Catherton's anger increased ever more.

"My dear sister," Garrett tsked. "Marce swore that bribing Mr. Newman to release Jude was the final time she'd rescue any of us from the clutches of the law."

"Ashford." Catherton stalked toward Damon until the toe of their boots nearly touched.

Garrett chuckled—chuckled!—placing his hand on the duke's shoulder. "As Payton's brother, and her eldest male relation, this situation is mine to remedy."

"I have settled the situation," Damon repeated. "Miss Samuels' debts were paid."

"This is not about money," Catherton seethed, spittle spraying the lapel of Garrett's evening coat. "She is a fraud, and I have half a mind to tell the magistrate that you, Ashford, are responsible for bilking your guests right alongside her. I am certain she cheated during our first game."

Garrett glanced at her, his eyes questioning. It hurt to think that he believed that there was a possibility she had cheated. Her younger self wouldn't have needed to ponder the decision, she'd have done anything to win, consequences be damned.

But she shook her head, hoping he believed she'd won the first game fair—just as she'd lost the second.

The last thing she wanted was Damon and Garrett arguing over who was responsible for the mess she'd created.

"Enough." Payton slashed her hand through the air before placing both palms flat on Damon's desk. "I lost at cards. Damon—er, Lord Ashford—settled my debt, but I am more than capable of accepting the consequences and also repaying the baron."

"That is not necessary."

"But it is." Payton needed Damon to understand that she could care for herself, or at least that she was trying to. Her family didn't think she could tend to her own life, make her own decisions. She'd taken her position as a governess to prove that she was no longer a little girl but a woman capable of caring for herself. Her stomach sank to think they could be correct.

"Catherton, there is not a magistrate in London who will take your words seriously when there is no debt left," Damon said. "Neither her brother nor I will allow a magistrate to be summoned, and I assume you will not relish the scandal that will follow if you are responsible for Miss Samuels being apprehended. Besides, I am certain Lord Garrett would never back your claim that it is Miss Samuels who lost to you. In fact, I believe it was I who lost to you. Perhaps the magistrate should be called for me."

"That is utter nonsense, Ashford," Catherton chortled. "It was this woman who I bested at cards, not you."

Damon glanced at Payton's brother. "That's not how I remember it happening, what about you?"

"Not close at all." Garrett shook his head. "I was sitting at the table. Couldn't believe my eyes. Catherton won a sizable hand, you paid him promptly, and Catherton left with heavy pockets."

"You were not there," the duke retorted. "And it was a woman who lost, not a man. There are witnesses to the fact."

"As I remember it, it is only Miss Payton that wasn't present." Garrett shrugged, filling Payton with a fondness for her brother. "I am certain any witnesses questioned will confirm the fact."

"You expect the magistrate to believe the word of a mere baron and a disgraced second son over a duke?" Catherton's hands balled at his sides as the vein in his forehead visibly throbbed.

"I can't believe he would be foolish enough to think we would lie about you winning..." Damon's voice trailed off, and Garrett clapped him on the back.

"I think it is time you leave," Garrett said, nodding to Mr. Brown. "Please show the duke out. If he has any other...concerns, he is free to take an audience with my eldest sister and me at Craven House."

Though Garrett and Damon had stepped shoulder-to-shoulder, blocking her view, Catherton could be heard breathing, practically seething with his rage. "This is not over."

"I think it is," Damon replied, gesturing to the door. "Mr. Brown, please show the duke out, if you would be so kind."

"Of course." The butler reached forward as if to grasp Catherton's elbow, but the duke shook off the man's attempt and departed, his footsteps ringing down the deserted corridor until the door slammed.

"Thank you for your assistance," Damon offered.

Garrett trained his narrowed stare on Damon as he stood a bit taller. "It was for my sister, not you, Ashford."

"Garrett," Payton warned. Why had his demeanor turned so quickly? Only seconds before, the pair had worked together to oust the duke. "Thank you."

"If that matter is settled, I think it is time we depart."

"Of course." Payton's head dipped as she stepped around the desk. "If you'll wait for me in the foyer, I would like a private word with the baron."

Garrett hesitated for only a moment before nodding and leaving the room. It did not escape her notice that he left the door open.

Payton walked slowly across the room, gathering her thoughts, and pushed the portal closed.

"Payton, I—"

"Damon, I—"

She smiled as the both stumbled over their words.

"What were you doing here tonight?" he asked.

She'd been foolish to think she could—or *should*—keep the children's excursion a secret from Damon. What if they attempted something similar again and it did not turn out well? She could never forgive herself.

"The children came to see me," she confessed.

"Came to see you?" His green eyes clouded with confusion. "I don't understand. How could they, I mean, even I was unaware of where you lived until a few moments ago."

She shrugged. "Mr. Brown had me followed one evening—for my safety. Rigby accompanied the children to my home. They were worried because I hadn't returned."

Damon averted his eyes, and she took a step toward him.

"They thought me sick, and that we'd had a row."

"I hadn't decided how to tell them you weren't returning," he admitted.

"They suspected you were lying to them and decided to check on me themselves." Payton willed him to look at her. "I would have made an excuse for my absence, as well. Besides, I was selfish leaving my position. The children need me far more than I ever suspected."

"It is not only Joy and Abram who need you. I do, too."

"But, I saw you…" She stumbled over the words. "You, the children, Lady Wittenbottom, and another woman…I saw you at Wexfector's. I assumed you were meeting with another governess."

He took her hands, stopping her from turning away. "I was, begrudgingly, having a meal with my sister and her companion. You said it would do the children well to spend more time outside the townhouse."

"I did?" she asked.

"Yes," he said, rubbing his finger along the back of her hand. "And I was uncertain what to do with myself—and the children—after everything that had happened between us."

"That is understandable," she confessed, her eyes drifting shut as the warmth of his fingers reached through her gloves. "It was the same for me."

"I had no designs on coming to care for my

children's governess," he said.

Her breath hitched at his confession. "And I had no plans to remain a governess for any longer than necessary."

"Allowing myself to care for anyone has been difficult."

His stark honesty kept her speaking, "I never meant to find a lasting place in your home. I took the position to show my family I could care for myself, but I…"

Admitting her deep affection for Damon—and his children—proved more difficult than anything she'd yet to do in her short life. His forthright words gave her confidence to continue and to hope he wouldn't push her away again.

"Damon." She swallowed, glancing down at their joined hands. Only a few short days ago, she would have scoffed at the notion of them standing so close. "I had a plan, and kissing you was not part of it."

"Kissing anyone was not part of mine," he retorted.

"What are we to do now?" she asked. He was a baron, and she was his children's governess, the illegitimate daughter of a blacksmith and an infamous London madame. "I cannot return to my place as Joy's and Abram's governess."

Saying the words aloud should have been freeing, they should have put an end to whatever was happening between them. She was no more fated to be with Damon than she was to be a governess, just as her mother had known her future did not mean wedding a man who could betray her in the end. Still, it did not stop her from longing to remain close to Damon—in whatever role she could grasp.

He placed his finger under her chin and lifted her face until their eyes met. "That is something we can both agree on. You cannot return to Ashford Hall as a governess."

Tears sprang up, threatening to slip down her face at the confirmation she should have been anticipating.

CHAPTER 29

DAMON HAD SPENT many years keeping everyone, even his children and sister, at bay.

He breathed because his body demanded it. He slept because his body required it. He ate because his body necessitated it. It would have been easier to cease all of it, or at least it would have been simpler before Payton walked into his life—their lives.

There was no doubt he could open himself to her, tell her all his deepest, darkest musings, give her the heart he hadn't known he still possessed, and she could still walk away.

Leave him devastated and destroyed as Sarah's death had: alone, terrified, and uncertain how to continue on—or *if* he wanted to continue.

Perhaps it wasn't his being alone that worried him most. He'd survived the last four years without anyone, but what of Joy and Abram? They deserved better than an absentee father. Truly, they deserved a mother who was still living. It should have been Damon who perished.

They'd gone after Payton when he was too scared to admit that he couldn't imagine living without her. How could children so young be so wise?

It was Joy and Abram who'd learned to press on, to grab hold of what they wanted and refuse to let go. That was precisely what they'd done while he reverted to his old ways: solitude and distraction. Anything to not experience the pain and anguish of loss once again.

"You cannot return as my children's governess," he paused, drawing on Joy and Abram's courage. "You are so much more than a governess, both to the children and me."

Her blue eyes clouded with confusion, and he responded by pulling her ever closer, allowing his fingers to move from her chin to her cheek. He hesitated for a single breath at the feel of her smooth skin, more perfect than the string of pearls adorning her neck.

"I don't understand."

Damon struggled for the right words, knowing if he misspoke, she could turn and walk out of Ashford Hall forever. She could disappear into the night, leaving him reeling in her wake. Every time he grasped on to a word, a feeling, they were overtaken by another, until his thoughts were scattered and disorganized.

"Payton, I need you." He shook his head, begging his mind to come together. "No, this goes beyond need. For many years, I've lived in such solitude that I forgot how it felt to need someone— not purely physical need, but emotional. Someone I can talk to, take my meals with, depend on when I am not feeling myself. Sarah was that person before, and I never, ever dreamed there would be another woman who so completely captured me. But this"—he placed his hand against his chest before moving it to rest on her bodice over her beating heart—"whatever this is between us, is so much more than anything I've ever experienced. No matter how hard I hid, how often I attempted to push you away, or the distance we created between us, we have found a way to return—to this moment."

"I shouldn't be here," she sighed.

"Yet, here we are." Did she understand as he did? "You were never meant to be a governess. I was never meant to meet you, long to know you, or to kiss you."

On the word *kiss*, Payton took the final step until they stood so close their breaths mingled.

"You still want to kiss me?"

"With ever-increasing fervor," he confessed. Damon lowered his head until his lips were a mere inch from hers. He knew if he closed his eyes, he could imagine with vivid detail how her lips would feel against his. Yet, that was no longer enough for him. Dreaming of her—them—together was no longer enough. Had *never been* enough he realized. "But…"

"But you cannot?" She glanced away, her chin lowering in defeat.

"Not until I've said everything I need to say," he replied. "And then, only then, it is you who will need to decide if *you* want to kiss *me*."

She took a step back, and his hand slipped from her shoulder.

His confidence fell with her retreat.

It could not stop him from speaking. He needed, *they* needed, his honesty before they moved forward, and she fled, no matter the outcome. Acceptance or rejection. This moment was worth a thousand years of sorrow and despair.

Payton was worth Damon risking everything. He had to know if she cared for him, too. "When I settled your debt with Catherton, it wasn't because of any scheme to have you beholden to me. The duke was determined to find you, and his methods of punishment are rumored to be vile. I could not allow him to learn your name. Not because you worked in my household. It had nothing, and yet everything to do with your place here.

"I saw the way you treated my children, interacted with them, and knew you were what's best for them," he confessed. "I couldn't stand to lose you because of some wager you'd lost. It didn't matter why you were here that night. It only mattered that you remained here, at Ashford Hall, with my children. You have given them more than I was able to in years. To be honest, I was jealous and captivated by your relationship with Joy and Abram all at the same time."

"They want the same connection with you," she said. "They want—*need*—your love and attention."

"Until you came into our lives, I didn't know if I had any love to give them." As he spoke, the pieces— all the fragments of his being—started to come together. "With you here, giving them the love I couldn't, it was enough. It was more than I'd ever hoped for until I realized I longed to be a part of it, too."

Payton turned, walking slowing to the lounge by the hearth. As she pivoted back toward him and sat, her cream skirts flared around her legs. It was difficult to ever envision her in the simple, everyday attire of a governess again. She was every inch the lady: poised, graceful, and stunning.

"I envied your connection with my children." Damon sat in the chair across from her, knowing he should give her space—the opportunity to listen without having him so near. "After—after—" He couldn't repeat the words. Sarah and her memory shouldn't be a part of his attraction to Payton, yet they were unequivocally intertwined. There was no future for him—or for them—without his past.

"After I lost Sarah, I was resigned to exist as the lost soul I've been all these years. Eating, sleeping, breathing…but not living. I feared she'd taken the best part of me with her."

Payton's stare moved from her clenched hands back to his face. Damon expected to see hesitation, discomfort, or possibly irritation in her eyes, but what shone back at him was something akin to compassion. Could this woman understand all *he* was struggling to grasp?

"The best part of you, the two best parts of you are sleeping upstairs," she whispered. "The best parts of you came in search of me long after they should have been safely in bed."

"Mayhap they know me better than I can ever hope to know myself." Damon massaged the back of his neck. "What I am attempting to explain, though I'm making little progress, is that it wasn't your relationship with my children I coveted. It was the way they embraced you. And you, them. It was as if the three of you were a family. A family I wasn't part of…and I've greatly missed being part of such a unit."

"Family is very important, Damon." She leaned forward toward him. "When all is gone, family is left. I am uncertain what I would've done without my siblings after my mother passed away. I can only imagine the pain of losing your wife."

"Family?" he muttered, an unmistakable question in his tone. "After Sarah, I had my children and my sister. Joy and Abram were young, I should have been there to comfort them, but I could think of nothing comforting to offer. My sister thought that moving on, marrying again, and returning to societal life would make me whole again. Was she right?"

He held Payton's pitying stare. He hadn't anyone but himself to blame for being reduced to needing someone so much he accepted their pity.

"Partly, I think yes, and in so many ways, no."

"Have I failed everyone?" Damon asked. He couldn't move past the fact that he'd failed his children, displeased his sister, and betrayed Sarah's memory. The determination to push everyone who depended on him away had been overpowering for so many years, he wasn't sure how to let it go, to even begin to allow his children back into his life. They were his children, yet they'd attached themselves so readily to Payton, a stranger, not many weeks before.

Could he blame them? He longed for Payton to remain in his life, as well.

Would he go to the lengths Joy and Abram had to keep her?

CHAPTER 30

PAYTON WATCHED AS uncertainty, despair, remorse, and hope battled within Damon, and she wasn't certain which would win out. However, she did know it was a victory better achieved if won by his own volition. It would do no one any good if she made the decision for him, if she dissuaded his misguided thinking, or attempted to soothe his conscience.

It would be easy to tell him how she felt, what she would do; though what if he came to resent his decision later?

His choice, and the risks involved had to be his own—and unwavering.

It couldn't be decided during a moment of weakness or out of guilt or remorse for her present circumstances or his past hardships.

Payton wanted to believe she was worth more than her position as a governess—to both Damon and his children. That their brief times of privacy had been more than a man still in mourning for the loss of his wife and only in need of an ear to listen and a woman to care for his offspring. She needed to be sure that he saw *her*, not her value as his children's caregiver, but noticed and valued her as a woman. She couldn't replace the wife he'd lost, nor the mother Joy and Abram barely remembered. Payton hadn't the first idea how to even begin to be either of those people.

"Do *you* feel you've failed?" she asked. "Your children are healthy, your servants and their families respect you, and your home is one to be admired. Perhaps it is not everyone else you fear disappointing but yourself."

She knew this because it was the same for her. The future she'd planned would arrive or fade away but would not have any effect on her family. Marce would be content to have her close for all her years though Payton knew she longed for a life of her own. It was Payton's personal success she feared failing at.

Disappointing herself, not others.

He remained silent, though she saw the battle growing once more within Damon. "You came and accepted, loved, and cherished my children in a way I've never allowed myself. You stepped into the role I was unprepared to fulfill."

Was. *Was* unprepared to fulfill.

"What about now?" Her breathless whisper filled the space between them.

"They may very well reject me," he confessed. "But I can no longer allow my fear to stop me from trying."

"They would never turn away from you, Damon." She slipped from the lounge to kneel before him, her cream gown of satin and lace crushed and wrinkling under her knees. "Just as I, despite my anger over your high-handed manner, could never reject you."

Taking hold of his hands—strong, capable hands—Payton raised them to her cheeks, their warmth infusing her with a sense of urgency. She needed him to understand how much he meant to his children, her, and his entire household.

"Favorably, you have the benefit of time." His thumb caressed the skin of her face. "The children are young, and I suspect they would forgive you anything. They have only you, no one else."

"That is not true," he sighed. "They have you."

It was Payton who broke their eye contact. "Yes, but I am no longer their governess."

"What you've done tonight shows you care," he replied. "In my need to be distracted, I was oblivious to their longings, their hurt. But they went to you, and you came even after everything that had happened between us. You saw them home, safely."

"I did as any person would."

"No, you did what someone who loves them would do," he countered.

"I do love them." At some point, they'd both reverted to whispering as she leaned closer, her hands settling on his knees while he continued to trail his fingers along her flaming skin from her cheek, to her jaw, to her neck. She trembled under his touch, longed for him to never withdraw his hand. In this moment, she would gladly remain forevermore. "…and you."

The declaration slipped from her lips unbidden.

As the words hung between them, the seconds of silence stretched between them as everything around them faded. Payton could not think of the crowded ballroom down the hall, or her brother waiting in the foyer, or what ploy Catherton would employ next to seek his revenge.

It was only her and Damon. There was much she'd gambled on in her life, but never again would she wager so carelessly with her baron.

She loved him. Despite everything, she was in love with Damon.

Could he love her in return?

Something broke within her, freeing her from

everything that held back her words—her emotions. It wouldn't stop her if he didn't love her in return, as long as he knew that she loved him.

She'd spent her entire life believing that one was only free and unburdened if they remained in control and were beholden to no one. It was how her mother had lived. No one could hurt her because she was in control of every aspect of her life—her children, her home, and her business.

Her mother had been wrong.

Everything Payton had believed was wrong.

She'd never feared risking herself financially, but now she had to risk the independence she'd fought so hard for by offering her heart to someone who might not think her love worthy enough to let go of his past and embrace a future together.

Yes, she was in love with Damon.

No amount of distance or time would ever change that.

Now that she'd laid all her cards on the table, no matter the consequences, she could move on with no regrets or thoughts of what might have been.

His hand slipped away from her cheek, grazing her collarbone before grasping her gloved fingers. At the same time, his stare fell away from hers.

This was the risk of her admission. Payton was familiar with taking risks. She took them every time she entered a gaming hell or sat down at a card table. Sometimes, she won. Other times, she lost.

After so many years, she was uncertain if her wins outweighed her losses.

When his head fell forward, and his shoulders slumped, she feared she'd have yet another thing to add to her loss column.

"I love you, too, Payton." His utterance weighed more than a thousand stones, and his head hung with more despair than she'd ever seen before. "I am not certain when it happened or how it all began, but I can no longer deny it. Not to myself or to you."

When he looked up, the sadness and despair in his eyes were heartbreaking.

It should be a moment of great happiness—for them both. A time they would remember all their days to come; however, something held Damon back.

If she loved him and he loved her, she could not reconcile the wretchedness that settled over him. It was as if admitting his affection for her was not the difficult part of it all but only the beginning.

Payton was well aware of the outcome of her admission.

Seeing the dejected air about Damon had her wishing to take it all back.

"I've held onto the reasoning that love means eventual hurt, heartbreak, and loneliness. I shuttered myself in my study for all these years in a failed attempt to stop myself from hurting and make certain my children never experience a loss like that of losing their mother again." The words tumbled from him, some rushed while others were pronounced with such slow deliberateness that Payton wondered if he were in control of himself at all or if some invisible force had taken over. "All I did was keep the pain and loss fresh in their minds because they lost me a bit more and more each day. When you entered our home, you were not the only stranger. I knew you that first day as well as I knew my own children. Without you, I never would have learned of Joy's love for horses or Abram's love of books and history."

Payton suspected that wasn't true; however, she remained silent, fearful that he'd stop talking, and their time together would come to an end without the answers she so urgently needed.

Her brother was waiting in the hall for her, and they would depart.

If she were taking advice from her sister, Sam would have advised Payton to stand up and leave. If Damon came after her, his feelings were genuine. But if he didn't, then it would be necessary for her to move on without him or the children.

If she'd sought out Jude for her wisdom, she would have suggested nothing so dramatic. She would tell Payton to remain all night, speaking with Damon, if that's what it took. Even if the conversation continued, talking in circles around what they both truly needed to discuss. Running was not an option— was not as noble as facing her fears and conquering them. Success or failure was not the important part.

What of Marce? Sometimes, Payton suspected she knew the least about her eldest sibling, despite their significant time spent together over the years. Their mother had died so many years ago that Payton sometimes had a difficult time remembering Marce was her sister and not her mother. Her eldest sibling would do something in the middle, Payton thought. She would not run and expect a man to chase her. Neither would she remain in a situation that was stagnant.

No, Marce Davenport would discuss the important matters at hand. She would face it head-on and allow everything to work out the way it was supposed to. She would do what was best for her future.

Winning, or losing for that matter, was irrelevant when Payton didn't know the game or how to play, let alone the stakes.

"I'm ready to let it all go." He exhaled, and Payton could almost trick herself into seeing it all go.

"What does that mean?" she dared ask.

Damon stood, holding out his hand for her to take. When she did, he helped her to her feet.

"It means, I am tired. Tired of merely existing,

tired of hiding who I am and what I want to the point where I don't recognize myself. I am tired of distancing myself from my children, and, mostly, I'm tired of allowing life to pass me by. Thinking I either don't deserve anything better, or that I am somehow betraying Sarah by any small attempt at happiness. No matter my excuse, I'm done with it."

"And what, exactly, do you want, Damon?" Her body tensed, anxious for his answer yet leery of it, as well.

His lips pressed into a firm line as if he were actually pondering the question for the first time. "I want to explore the museum and parks of London with my children. I want to journey to Bath and perhaps Scotland. I want to frolic in the meadows surrounding Falconcrest. I want to fall asleep reading tales of adventure…on that very lounge."

He paused, and Payton's excitement dissipated to apprehension.

"Is that all?" She should be content, happy even to see how far he'd come since they met. He'd gone from a man who avoided his children at all costs to genuinely enjoying their company.

"It is not all I want," he said, pulling her securely into his embrace and bringing his lips to hers. However, he didn't kiss her. Instead, he halted, his mouth hovering close to hers. Their breaths mingled; his, rich and warm, fanned her cheek and neck. "I want you, by my side, through it all."

Of everything Damon could have longed for and desired, Payton was fearful it wouldn't include her. He'd opened himself more than she'd ever thought possible, and it was only fair that she do the same. "I want all those things, too."

Payton had lived her life one card game at a time, and she'd been known to cheat at them because she did anything to make it to the next stepping stone, her next goal, her next stop to where she wanted to be.

Perhaps it was past time she stopped long enough to determine if she'd already found everything she'd spent her entire life searching for. While she'd been plotting and planning, she'd misguidedly neglected to see what was right in front of her.

Damon.

Life wasn't about moving forward, forging ahead until you found the green meadow you sought. It was about finding the right person who stood by your side and letting the paradise you longed for grow around you.

She held Damon's stare, and a thousand unspoken musings passed between them: apologies, regrets, promises, and…something she didn't quite understand.

Before she could ask, his head dipped, and their lips pressed together.

Suddenly, it didn't matter. Nothing mattered but the feel of Damon's lips against hers, his hard body pressed to her soft curves, his scent of lavender and citrus mingling perfectly with her floral aroma. Neither attempted to overpower the other to take control.

They merely reveled in an unspoken harmony that had always been present.

His kiss was reserved just as he was, yet the distance between them disappeared. His arms held her so tightly, Payton wondered if he thought she would vanish from his embrace. Did he not realize that his solid hold on her was the foundation she'd lacked her entire life? With him close, there was no room for her to flounder. There was no possibility of failing.

In his arms, she was no longer the wounded child seeking happiness on the horizon, only to gain that distant point and find herself unfulfilled yet again. No, there was nothing better awaiting her somewhere else, no matter how far she traveled or how many people she left behind.

In that moment, as their lips danced to an unsung melody, Payton realized she'd found everything she'd been searching for—and so much more.

CHAPTER 31

DAMON HAD SPENT so many years dwelling on the unfairness of everything around him that he'd nearly allowed the most perfect thing to walk out of his life. He'd spent so many years drowning in despair that he'd almost missed the opportunity to pull himself from the turmoil.

Drawing Payton ever closer, he reveled in the feeling of her pressed against him even as a longing stirred within him that had lain dormant for so long. With it, he expected a spike of betrayal to pierce him, the overpowering need to retreat to his solitary life, and a heartbreaking realization that he would never have anything more.

He'd loved, and he'd lost.

Loss was a natural conclusion to love.

It had always been the way of things. Or was it?

Damon breathed in deeply, pulling back slightly from their kiss. Her responding moan made him confident that even if loss one day came, this love was worth exploring, knowing, and accepting.

And sharing, with his children and all of society.

"Payton…I…" Damon kissed her parted lips, both her cheeks, and her forehead as his fingers released their hold on her. She'd confessed to wanting the same things as he did, yet how that future would look was still indecipherable to him. She needed to know that when he said he wanted her by his side, he wanted all of her. Finding the words to tell her that was nearly impossible, however, as he was afraid to speak the wrong words…feared ending this moment. "I want you in my arms from today until forever."

"I hadn't imagined it would be what I wanted, yet here we are," she mused, a smile lighting her face.

"I did speak the truth earlier. You cannot return to Ashford Hall as my children's governess," he whispered. He stroked her cheek and down the length of her neck as he gazed into her eyes, content to be lost in their blue depths until his last breath until he noted the light dim and her stare cloud with confusion. She shivered under his touch, and his body naturally responded. "When you return to my home, it will be your home, as well."

"Damon." She shook her head, and her gloved fingers tightened on his forearms. "Are you certain?"

"For so many years, I've been uncertain about every aspect of my life," he confided, brushing a wayward curl from her cheek. "My days have passed without consequence, my nights indistinguishable from my days, and my thoughts as unpredictable as the rains across town. I neither knew where I was going or from whence I came. I've been adrift, with no land in sight"—he pulled back, needing to say his piece yet fearful she wouldn't understand—"and you were the beacon sent to rescue us all. So, when you ask if I am sure, I can say that, without hesitation, I have never been so very certain of anything in my life.

"You have not only blessed me with a second chance at life, but you have also brought it to Joy and Abram. No longer will they live a trivial existence shut in this townhouse with a reclusive, unworthy father. Even if I do not deserve better, my children do."

Her eyes watered as her fingers fisted in his shirtsleeves. "Damon, you deserve happiness as much as any person. Life, like luck, is a fickle thing, or so I've learned. Despite your misfortunes, that does not mean you are unworthy of contentment and peace."

He searched her stare. "Perhaps. However, I want far more for myself. I want love."

"And I want to be the one loving you." There wasn't a moment's hesitation, she did not avert her gaze nor wilt in his embrace. "Damon, though I hadn't realized it, I have spent my life in search of something. Every day looking to the next...until I found you. I tried to focus on what came next. but it always led back to you and the children." It was then that she looked away, her stare moving to the floor. "I must admit, there have been times I longed to end my attraction to you."

"I have resisted, as well." There would be no more lies between them, no more half-truths, no more hiding. "I would do things differently if I had it to do all over again."

"How so?" she asked.

"I would have spoken to you at my gaming parties long before you came to work in my home." He'd noticed her on many occasions, though always kept his distance. Not only from her but from everyone.

"I likely would have rebuffed your advances, my lord."

His brow raised in surprise. "Why ever would you do that?"

"It is not the brooding lord sulking about the edges of his ballroom I have found myself longing for, but the man—the father—you truly are."

"Just as I did not know I could come to love a lady, a gambler in masquerade. However, I most certainly cannot live without a woman who can comfort my daughter when her night terrors threaten to overtake her. A woman who challenges my son and cares deeply for his studies." It was more than all this. Their love could not be all because of the children. "I found myself falling in love with a woman whose temper got the best of her on more than one occasion, a woman who wasn't afraid to stand up to me, a lady who could soothe my own lost soul."

"You were never lost, Damon, just as my searching was useless."

He shook his head, unable to believe her.

"We were both exactly where fate meant us to be…"

Payton pushed to her tiptoes, her arms twining around his neck as she pressed against him.

Another truth he'd come to realize was that there was nothing more natural than having Payton in his arms and he, without a doubt, would do all in his power to keep her there.

"Miss Payton Samuels." He tilted his head back, needing to gaze into the dark blue pools of her eyes when next he spoke. "Would you do me the great honor of becoming my baroness, my wife, and my children's mother?"

She fell back a step, her hands coming to cover her mouth before dropping to her sides.

Damon smiled, his heart surging when his happiness was mirrored in her.

This woman, this lady he'd chosen to love, was everything he'd waited for all these years: strong, confident, and willing to wager everything for what she believed in.

"Do say yes, Miss Samuels." Joy's tiny voice squeaked from behind them.

When they both turned, they were greeted by three bright smiles: Joy, Abram, and Payton's brother.

"What say you?" Garrett asked.

"Unconventional, indeed. However…"

PAYTON GLANCED BETWEEN Damon's beaming face and the expectant looks of her brother and the children. There was not a thing about her day that had gone as planned, and Payton was overjoyed by that.

She'd returned to Ashford Hall to see the children safely home.

She hadn't planned to seek out Damon nor be confronted by Catherton. The last thing she'd wanted was for Garrett to be entangled in the mess she'd created for herself. But, suddenly, his presence meant everything.

The last vestiges of her planned future fell away as images of a new course settled around her, mirrored in the shining faces of those who she'd come to care so deeply for. Damon, his children, as well as the entire Ashford household. She'd misguidedly thought she could walk away from it all and move on—move forward. The truth was, there would be no moving anywhere if Damon weren't by her side.

Damon placed his hand on the small of her back. "Children, Miss Samuels is likely overwhelmed. I think it is best you both return to your chambers and give us a moment of privacy. Lord Garrett, would you be so kind as to see them to their rooms?"

Garrett nodded and proceeded to usher the children from the study, despite their pleas to remain.

Did Damon think she was opposed to being his wife? Did he bid Joy and Abram leave because he did not want them to remain and hear her turn down his offer of marriage?

Her pulse quickened. "Children. Wait, do not leave."

Garret, Joy, and Abram halted, turning back to the room.

"Come inside," she bid. "My answer affects you as much as your father."

Payton steered the children toward the lounge while Garrett remained close to the door as if debating if he should stay, as well.

"Lord Garrett?" Joy called, holding her hand out to him. "Are you coming?"

How had it taken weeks for her to win the girl's heart and only an hour for Garrett?

Payton lowered herself to the lounge, the children settling on each side of her with Garrett and Damon taking the chairs across from them.

This discussion was not solely hers, nor would this be the last time she'd need to consult others because, despite her longing to select her own future, with her answer, she would be affecting the lives of each person sitting around her.

Her life would no longer be her own.

Her life was to become *their* life.

"Joy"—she took the girl's hand and turned to her brother—"Abram. How would you feel if I was to wed your father?"

Their opinion carried an equal weight to Damon's. Their future would never be solely based on her and Damon, but the four of them. Wasn't that what family was about?

"Will you still study ancient history with me?" Abram asked.

"Of course."

"Will you continue to put us to bed?" Joy's rounded, green eyes stared up at her.

"I would want no one else charged with the task." Payton kept her tone gravely serious. Her own decision, while made up in her mind, could be easily swayed if either Joy or Abram objected to the marriage.

"You wouldn't have a day off any longer?" Abram's question came out in a rush.

Payton couldn't help but chuckle at Abram's question. "No, I would not."

She risked a glance at Damon, whose eyes were locked on her. Her breath hitched in her throat, and she silently pleaded for the children to have no objection to her wedding their father.

"Would you buy me a pony?" Joy's voice was as serious as Payton's.

"That is a decision for your father, not me," Payton answered.

The little girl shook her head. "If you wed Father"—she paused, tapping at her chin—"then you would be my mother. *And* mothers can decide to purchase ponies for their daughters, correct?"

"Very true," Garrett chortled. "Mothers can do anything fathers can do—most times, better."

"And while Father is busy," Abram cut in, "a mother can take her children to Spires Reading Room without permission."

Payton could only nod. Never in all her years had she ever envisioned herself a mother. However, being Joy and Abram's mother would be a gift far beyond anything she'd ever imagined.

"If Father takes us to the museum again, you will always come?" Joy squeezed her hand.

"If Payton agrees to be a permanent part of this family," Damon said, "she will always be close.

"Also, you will have three aunts—and an uncle." Garrett fiddled with his cravat, puffing his chest. "If either your father or my sister refuses you anything, we shall step in and make everything right."

Joy leaned forward and exchanged a silent look with her brother before turning back to Garrett. "We have an aunt already, and she makes nothing better."

"Well, I can assure you both that anything that will irritate my youngest sister will bring me and my other sisters great joy."

"Garrett," Payton chastised. "Do stop. Next, they will be asking for trips to the New World and ancient artifacts."

"Samantha is wed to an explorer, and Jude to an antiquities collector," he mused. "Neither would prove impossible. Actually, I'd very much enjoy being an uncle. Do I appear an uncle to either of you?"

Garrett made a spectacle of turning his head from side to side, showing off his angular profile.

"With a haircut, I do believe so," Joy replied with a giggle.

"Whatever is wrong with my hair?"

"It hangs over your collar," the girl snorted as if his need for a haircut was evident to everyone.

"If you do not mind," Damon said, "I have yet to hear Payton's answer."

"Damon." She glanced between everyone in the room, her eyes not lingering on anyone until they met Damon's. "I could think of no better fate than being your wife—and the children's mother."

Payton couldn't take her eyes off Damon as her answer sank in, and his last lingering doubts disappeared. The many burdens he'd born for so long dissipated, and his eyes lit with happiness. The shadows that always lingered around him dissolved, leaving behind not a broken man but a lord capable of loving once more despite the heartbreak of his past.

"Father," Joy said, clapping her hands in excitement. "I think you should kiss Miss Samuels now."

Payton barely noticed her brother standing and taking both Joy and Abram's hands and leading them from the room.

The door shut almost noiselessly in their wake, leaving Payton and Damon alone.

As if she'd done it a thousand times before, Payton stood and walked into Damon's waiting embrace. Lifting her chin, she accepted his kiss.

All this time, Payton had believed she could gamble her way to a happy, content life with some sleight of hand but it was only by putting all her cards on the table before Damon, the man she loved, that she could truly win.

EPILOGUE

London, England
December 1820

PAYTON PAUSED OUTSIDE of the Craven House drawing room's open double doors and breathed in deeply. The aroma of freshly baked marmalade tarts and plum pudding remained from their evening meal, giving the entire gathering a festive air. After they'd dined as a group, she'd excused herself under the guise of fixing her hair and straightening her skirts.

This being the eve before her wedding day, not a single lady present had cause to question her reasons for stepping away from the gathering for a few moments of privacy—each of her sisters had done the same before they gave themselves completely to their husbands.

That was all she'd allow herself—a few brief moments alone.

The gathered crowd awaiting her in the drawing room was a diverse lot, indeed.

Yet they all had one thing in common: they loved her...or Damon.

Many of their guests loved them both.

How things had changed over the past eight

months was something akin to magic. Damon had gone out his way every day to show her how grand their life would be together; however, Payton hadn't needed the reassurance at all.

Fingers gripped her elbow lightly. "Is all as it should be?"

Payton glanced up to see Damon by her side, a place he rarely left since the night he'd confessed his love, and she declared hers in return.

"Yes, very much so," Payton said with a smile and turned back to take in the room. Everyone had yet to notice her, and she was fine with having a few moments to take everything in with Damon's comforting presence by her side. Her life—its path and the future she'd intended for herself—had changed since she'd met Damon and his children— until she barely recognized anything. Including herself. "How is Flora acclimating to my expansive family?"

"I believe she is quite taken with the Dowager Lady Cartwright and her support of boarding schools, especially an all-girls school in Canterbury," Damon sighed. "It has the most preposterous name. However, Lady Theodora appears to enjoy the school immensely."

"Miss Emmeline's School of Education and Decorum for Ladies of Outstanding Quality?" Payton couldn't help but chuckle. The name was pretentious and nearly too long to say without pausing to catch her breath. "Theo enjoys the school very much. Simon and Jude traveled to Canterbury to collect the girl for the Christmastide holiday—and our wedding."

"I certainly hope no one is giving Flora any reason to rekindle our conversations about sending Joy and Abram away to school," Damon grunted. "However, I am overjoyed Lady Theo could join us."

"I think we should be far more concerned with

Abram departing with Sam and Elijah on one of their worldly expeditions." Payton risked a glance up at Damon before they both turned in Abram's direction where he sat with Simon on one side and Elijah on the other. Her sisters' husbands had far more in common than either realized, despite their character differences. An explorer of historical sites and a collector of artifacts, Abram could not have been in better company, especially when he learned Lord Cartwright, Jude's husband, visited Oliver's Bookseller on many occasions.

Damon wrapped his arm around her back, settling his hand on her hip. It was a gesture she'd grown accustomed to quickly and missed when Damon wasn't close. "I think we can both agree that between Canterbury and India—or Africa—we'd settle for the journey that kept him in England."

Payton remained silent on the topic. She had no doubt that, one day, Abram would use his talents for history to explore the world, discovering long-hidden treasures. And his father would do nothing to stop him.

At that moment, the Dowager Duchess Harwich, or Anastasia as she'd begged for Payton to call her when they met several months prior at Marce's wedding, looked up and gestured for her to come and sit. Payton smiled and nodded before she and Damon entered the room, drawing more attention than she was comfortable with. She'd never been one to blush and bluster, but the increased notice she'd gained since she and Damon had announced their betrothal had been daunting.

Payton took in Marce's glowing smile as she made her way farther into the room.

It had been an utter shock to learn of her eldest sister's intent to wed the Duke of Harwich and move to his family estate; however, Payton had learned quickly how difficult it was to be away from the man she loved. It had made Marce's departure from Craven House all the more comfortable, knowing she wasn't deserting their home but creating a new one for herself and the duke—and the children who would no doubt follow.

For once, her sister wasn't sacrificing her own happiness for her family.

Payton sat on the lounge next to the dowager duchess and across from Lady Wittenbottom and the Dowager Lady Cartwright, who had Joy on her lap, despite the harsh glare of envy coming from Flora. Could Damon's sister finally be realizing her grave mistake of treating her niece and nephew as little more than inconveniences to be shipped away?

"Payton"—Anastasia patted her hand—"you have returned, and not a moment too soon, I must say. Explain to Lady Wittenbottom, my dear, that I gift every family member with a new horse. It is the way of things. And Miss Joy and Master Abram will be no different."

The Dowager Lady Cartwright vigorously fanned her face as Flora's cheeks reddened.

"A horse?" Joy bounced up and down, nearly tumbling from Lady Cartwright's lap. "Of my own?"

Lady Theo pushed to her knees from her seat on the floor, smiling broadly at Joy. "Yes, of your very own. Lady Harwich brought my horse to London for my fourteenth birthday. Her name is Polly and she is a beautiful grey mare, though she has developed a bit of an attitude as of late. I adore her!"

When Flora glanced between Payton and over to Lady Cartwright, they both could only shrug.

The conversation brought to mind Payton's disbelief when she'd arrived at Hadlow Estate for Marce's wedding to find a horse waiting for each of her siblings. It had been unexpected and rather odd to discover that the Duke of Harwich's mother had known of all of them since they were young babes.

"Horses, you say?" Damon inquired.

"Oh, Father!" Joy slipped from Lady Cartwright's lap and bounded over to Damon. "Do say I can have one. Please, oh, please, oh, please!"

Damon's face grew stern, but Payton noticed the smile he worked hard to suppress. Another oddity she'd become accustomed to in recent months. The baron was not as dour and reserved as she'd suspected. "It was my understanding that you had your sights set on a pony, not a horse."

Joy's little face scrunched. "A pony is only a small horse. I am nearly a grown woman, Father, and what fine London lady rides a pony about Hyde Park?"

Laughter filled the room, coming from every corner as the men drifted toward Payton, Damon, and the gathered women.

Her chest swelled with a fullness that she'd never experienced before, despite having such a large, close family. It brought her even more joy to see all her siblings happy, content, and thriving—just as her mother had predicted.

And she…she was done searching.

There was nothing outside that very room Payton needed or would ever long for.

She had her family—and all those that had become family over the last several years—Damon, and his children.

Come tomorrow, they would be *her* children.

They were all perfect because she'd chosen them…and they, her.

Come tomorrow, she would return to Ashford Hall, not as a governess or a gambler, but as Damon's baroness.

A family.

Her family.

The one thing she'd rebelled against since her youth had been the only thing to make her happy in the end.

"Miss Samuels." Abram sat on the floor at his father's knee and looked up at her. "Did something make you sad?"

Payton pressed her hands to both cheeks, brushing away the tears that she hadn't realized she'd shed as she pondered how to explain her overwhelming elation to the boy.

"I am not sad at all," she said, keeping her voice low as others continued to talk around them. She glanced at Damon to find him staring at her. When he reached over and clasped her hand, she continued, "I was thinking about all the remarkable things I almost let slip by me, and I am so thankful your father and I came to our senses before it was too late."

"We wouldn't have let you slip away." Joy climbed onto her lap, and Payton noticed that all four of her siblings watched her intently, especially Marce.

Yet, her eldest sister did not look at her as if assessing her every move as she'd done for most of Payton's life, but almost in a reverent way. Did Payton possess something her family had feared she lacked? Whatever the look meant, Payton would not fret over it nor allow it to dampen their festive mood.

"Well, children," Damon said with a clap of his hands. "It is time for bed. We all have a very busy day tomorrow, and I would not want either of you to miss a second of it. We should be heading back to Ashford Hall."

"But, Father…" Abram whimpered.

"We cannot depart yet." Joy pushed from Payton's lap. "Do you not remember?"

Payton stared between the children, each donning mischievous grins as they hurried from the room. Damon wore an identical smile. He released her hand and stood, as well, making his way to the door.

"What is afoot?" Flora squawked. "I do not like surprises."

"I am certain it is not anything to do with you, Lady Wittenbottom," Lady Cartwright hissed, her brow drawing low.

Payton watched in stunned silence as the children returned, Damon trailing behind them. They each clutched the end of a small, rectangular box with a purple bow on top.

"What is this?" she asked, eyeing the delicate box as Abram attempted to pull it from Joy's grasp. However, the girl was not to be thwarted and held tight to her end as the pair halted before her. Their mirrored smiles, blond hair, and green eyes were so much like their father's.

Abram cleared his throat. "Father instructed us to get you a gift"—he glanced down resentfully at the box—"and I insisted on a book detailing the merits of the Egyptian aquatic military, but—"

Joy elbowed her brother, all while keeping her fingers tight on the box.

"Ooof," Abram grunted.

"Children," Damon prodded. "The hour is growing late…"

Joy focused on Payton at the same time she pulled the box from Abram and stepped forward. "While I do not agree with Abram's choice of gift, I do very much believe Father was correct when he said—"

Affection shone in Damon's eyes when he spoke to Joy. "What I said is not important, dear one."

Payton glanced up to see a light blush stain Damon's cheeks before he cleared his throat and looked away.

There would be plenty of time in the coming days to discover what exactly Damon *had* said, but for now, Payton took the small box from Joy as the child bounced with excitement.

"A gift, for me?" The box was smooth to the touch with the simple bow on top. "Shall I open it?"

"Yes," her siblings called in unison as Joy nodded vigorously, her blond hair tumbling over her shoulder.

"I cannot imagine what could possibly be in this box," Payton mused, turning it over in her hands.

"Well, it is not a book on the Egyptian military," Abram grunted. When Damon gave him a stern glare, he continued, "Though I suspect you will like it all the same."

"I am positively certain I will love it."

"Open it," Joy giggled.

Payton stared around the room as all eyes settled on her and the gift in her hands. Any other time, she'd have wanted a spot of privacy for such a precious moment, but as she took in everyone squeezed into the drawing room of Craven House, Payton was confident the moment was developing perfectly.

They were a family—all of them.

Payton had found her place.

A place she'd never long to move on from without Damon, the children, and her family by her side.

Nothing *far better* awaited her anywhere.

She would thrive. They would all thrive.

Together.

She took in a deep breath and opened the box. Nestled inside was an emerald, the shade identical to Damon's, Joy's, and Abram's moss green eyes. The stone was set in a gold pendant with a delicate chain. The light from the chandelier above and the sconces on the walls made the gem glitter and sparkle.

"It is lovely," Payton said, releasing her breath.

"Father says you should wear it tomorrow," Joy gushed, squeezing her hands before her. "I helped pick it out."

"No," Abram refuted. "You wanted that dreadful pink stone. I selected the emerald."

She glanced up to see Damon smiling at her over Abram's shoulder. "The necklace is beautiful, and I can see both of you in it. May I wear it now?"

When Damon nodded, new happiness banishing the sorrow that had marred his face for far too long, Payton stood. Everyone in the room followed suit, calling their farewells as they departed the room until it was only Damon and the children with her.

Garrett poked his head around the doorframe and called to Joy and Abram. "Miss Joy, Master Abram, come along. I heard that Cook has a special treat for the pair of you waiting in the kitchen. Lady Theodora is already on her way...you do not want her to get all the surprise, do you?"

Both children scampered from the room after Garrett, their laughter ringing through Craven House as they made their way to the kitchen, leaving Payton and Damon blessedly alone.

Payton bit at her lip to suppress her smile and turned to allow Damon to clasp the necklace around her neck. She couldn't help looking down as her gloved fingers stroked the emerald pendant that nestled above the neckline of her gown.

"What did you say?" she asked, knowing her question could not wait another moment.

She turned as Damon attempted to hide his sheepish grin. "I am not certain what you—"

"Joy said she agreed with what you said...about the gift..." Her chest seized as she waited for his reply.

He took hold of her hands, and she noticed them trembling slightly, but he did not look away.

"I told them the emerald pendant was the perfect gift because it sparkled—just as we now do since you've come into our lives." He paused, and she searched his stare, knowing there was more, but uncertain if she could hold back her brimming emotions long enough to hear it.

It was her turn to tremble. "Oh, Damon. You've brought me peace and happiness I never imagined for myself. I love the children—and you—with all my heart."

Damon pulled her close, his eyes never straying from hers as he lowered his head and their lips met.

The tightness in her chest from moments before unraveled, giving her a sense of freedom she'd always longed for but never allowed herself to grasp.

She pressed against the hard length of his body as her gloved hands ran through his hair. All the while his lips moved against hers, parting as his tongue slipped along her bottom lip, causing her to shudder once more as the passion within her blossomed, driving her ever closer to him.

Freedom wasn't a place, but a person.

This man before her.

Damon Kinder.

She pulled away, staring up into his sparkling eyes—more alive than she'd ever seen them—and Payton knew, without a doubt, that Damon had been the man she'd searched for her entire life, without so much as realizing her true heart's longing.

"Damon," she sighed. "I love you with everything I am. I never knew joy and love such as this could exist, let alone one day be mine. I will live every day making certain your eyes sparkle as brightly as my pendant."

"With you close, there is nothing that could

eclipse the love and light within me."

As he pulled her to him once more and claimed her smiling lips, Payton could almost hear applause coming from the corridor, but as his mouth moved against hers and burning desire pooled within her, the sound faded—until there was nothing but Damon and her.

And the promise of the family they would create, along with Joy and Abram.

Together.

AUTHOR'S NOTES

Thank you for reading *The Gambler Wagers Her Baron*
(Craven House Series, Book Four).

If you enjoyed *The Gambler Wagers Her Baron*,
be sure to write a brief review at any retailer.

I'd love to hear from you!

You can contact me at:
Christina@christinamcknight.com

Or write me at:
P.O. Box 1017
Patterson, CA 95363

www.ChristinaMcKnight.com
Check out my website for giveaways, book reviews, and
information on my upcoming projects,
or connect with me through social media at:

Twitter: @CMcKnightWriter
Facebook: www.facebook.com/christinamcknightwriter
Goodreads: www.goodreads.com/ChristinaMcKnight

Sign up for my newsletter here:
https://bit.ly/2t6MhwV

**For more information about
the Craven House Series, turn the page!**

CRAVEN HOUSE SERIES

MEET LONDON'S MOST SCANDALOUS FAMILY!

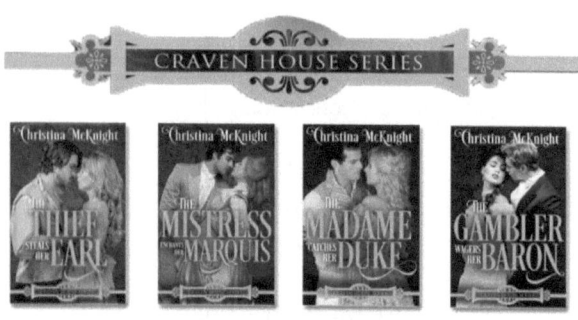

Available in print and e-book
christinamcknight.com

The Madame Catches Her Duke
Book 3
Now available

THERE'S A FINE LINE BETWEEN
LOVE AND HATE.

Despite being thrown from her home and stripped of her place in society at a young age, Madame Marce Davenport is proud of what she's accomplished with her family and the notoriously scandalous Craven House. Except it's all built on a lie. When an arrogant duke strode into her home years ago, offering her a way to keep the brothel open, she agreed to his game of deception. But now that her siblings have found their happiness, Marce can finally live the life she's always wanted: one that embraces the truth. And that means severing ties with the man who has claimed too many of her days—both in reality, and fantasy.

Rowan Delconti, the Duke of Harwich, has been angry for so long: at his father, at the woman who broke apart his parents' marriage, and at the children who won is father's love. He's determined his mother won't be unhappy again—even if it means pretending to be married to Marce, so that his mother will think he's found love in his life. But the beautiful madame fuels his fire like no other, and the charade starts to feel all too real.

When Marce and Rowan's secrets finally come to light, their passion may not be enough to staunch the hurt of the past. Can two people who were so wrong for each other, realize they've been right all along?

London, England
February 1820

MUCH HAD CHANGED for Marce Davenport in recent years. As she paced the warm, soothing office that had once been her mother's treasured sanctuary at Craven House, she listened for approaching footsteps, shrieks of laughter, or even the angry shouts of her bickering siblings. However, nothing could be heard.

The house was shrouded in utter silence, something Marce had never thought possible.

No door slammed on its hinges above stairs.

The constant clang from the kitchen was no more.

Even the endless pounding up and down the steps had ceased.

For the first time in all her life, Marce was unequivocally alone.

The deep feeling went far beyond the physical to a daunting mental solitude that threatened to drag her down. The silence echoed inside her, filling her with more of the aching emptiness that had slowly overtaken her as the years passed. She was an outsider within her own home—a woman whose lies had distanced her from everyone she loved.

The most damning part was that Marce's siblings had become so accustomed to her aloof nature they didn't realize the secrets she held inside. They saw her quiet reserve as simply her way, not as the sad loneliness it was. They mistook her domineering fortitude regarding family matters as her way of controlling them. However, they didn't notice her grasp on the strings gradually slipping away as the years came and went.

If her siblings heard her sobs in the dark of night, they did not ask what haunted her.

It was her burden to bear—alone.

She glanced at the missive on her desk; the familiar, heavy-handed script summoning her and instructing her to be ready for departure at precisely noon and not a moment after. The carriage would arrive with no one but a driver to escort her the two hours to the Whisper Hook Inn on the outskirts of Welling in Kent.

The same as it had for nearly eight years.

Eight long, lonely, solitary years.

At least in that regard, there was comfort in routine.

With four siblings underfoot, and a household brimming with other *guests*, lonely should be the last emotion Marce felt. Alas, her burdens were not something she spoke of with anyone, especially her family. It was *her* obligation to care for Judith, Samantha, Payton, and to a certain extent, Garrett, her brother. And that was what she'd done during the many years since their mother's passing—without complaint, hesitation, or remorse. Never had they need worry over finances. Never had they gone hungry or spent a cold night without a fire in the hearth.

Marce had done all she could to see to their education and proper upbringing.

Finally, it was Marce's turn to find happiness.

Or risk going mad.

With Jude and Sam properly wed, and Payton, her youngest sibling, having recently taken a position as a governess, Marce was free to explore her own options for the future. Perhaps complete happiness would always elude her, but contentment would suffice. At twenty-eight summers, Marce would be firmly classified as *on the shelf* by society. Thankfully, she had no aspirations to be part of the *beau monde* of London, a group that had shunned her mother and turned their backs on Sasha's orphaned children.

No, a cottage on the cliffs of Dover or a modest house in the wilds of Cornwall were much preferred to the hustle and bustle of town life—as long as room allowed for the many women who sought Marce's help in improving their lots in life.

She moved around the desk her mother had favored. The private office was atrocious and overwhelming, even to Marce, with its gold and red décor—Sasha Davenport's favorite hues. As an ode to her mother, Marce had never altered the room, keeping it as it was before Sasha's death. Originally, the space had been a comfort to her and her siblings. A place where they found solace and truly felt the presence of their mother, though she was long departed from this world. But in recent years, it had become Marce's personal prison, filled with deception and the secrets she kept hidden from her family.

All manner of things she was ashamed to be a part of—so much so, she'd never gained enough courage to speak of it to anyone.

Yet, she'd spent years with no other choice. Her family came first, even before her own needs and wants.

The tall clock in the foyer chimed. Twelve times. Its familiar gong echoed through the empty house— one still bouncing off the walls and shuddering down the corridors as another began. Peculiar that only a few short months before, Craven House had been filled with such boisterous noise the peal would have gone all but unnoticed in the midday commotion.

Glancing at the small trunk packed with the requisite necessities for a weeklong trip, Marce waited once more. For the sound of anything besides the gong of the clock and the quick, erratic thump of her pulse.

Nothing.

Silence.

Empty—except for the remorse that filled her and the lies that surrounded her.

She sighed.

Odd that she longed for the time when her siblings would rush into the room and question her about where she was off to, where she planned to spend her time away from Craven House. Was she relaxing in the rejuvenating waters in Bath? Or perhaps she found peace and quiet in Brighton, along with a turn about their fashionable shopping area? Would she please bring them back sweet treats? They would laugh and jest about how Marce spent her time away. She'd even heard envious whispers shared between the twins, Jude and Sam, regarding her frequent jaunts outside of London. And in turn,

Marce would tell them, in her stern, motherly tone, to mind their own business and keep their noses from the gossips.

Where Marce went and what task she was entangled in was far darker than any of her siblings suspected—and something Marce was loath to speak of.

The deal made with the Devil himself nearly eight years prior was her own personal secret…and the prison that kept her trapped.

Rowan Delconti, the Duke of Harwich, was certainly close to the beast who ruled Hades with his midnight-black hair, intense green stare, and massive frame—not to touch on his arrogant demeanor and lofty opinion of himself. If she so much as dared open a book about the master of the Underworld, there was little doubt the drawings of the creature would resemble the duke in every way. She remembered the way he'd appeared that first time; how he'd strode into her office, all arrogance and confidence, and demanded his due. Had they met under any other circumstances, Marce would have found his forceful demeanor thrilling and refreshing.

As if on cue, the chimes quieted, and a knock sounded on the front door of Craven House.

The duke's carriage had arrived to collect her.

Darla, one of only two servants employed at Craven House, hurried from somewhere deep in the house to greet their *guest*.

Quickly, Marce moved to the cabinet behind her desk and retrieved the small box that held a stash of money *in case* anything unexpected happened during her time away from London. It was always best to be prepared, as opposed to being caught off guard as she'd once been. With the box securely under her arm, she scribbled a hasty note for Garrett and Payton in case either came home while she was away. Jude and Sam, both newly wed, were traveling with their husbands—Jude to Canterbury to visit the young Lady Theodora at her boarding school, and Sam away from England entirely. Lastly, she placed the duke's summons in the side drawer and used the long key around her neck to lock her desk in case anyone thought it wise to snoop about in her private correspondence.

Marce longed for the day she no longer had to think of every minute detail—*in case*—for fear she'd be discovered.

Part of her wished to leave the key on her desk and hope someone discovered her secrets…only then would the trappings fall away, shedding light upon her deceptions.

Instead, she left the note addressed to her siblings face-up on the desk and grabbed her traveling trunk, slipping the box with her money inside before halting once more.

The house, especially this room, had given her solace for most of her life. This was the only place she'd ever felt safe calling home. The rooms and halls were filled with memories—Jude's first steps as a babe, Garrett's horrible years attempting to master the flute, Sam's many years of teasing Payton for her sullen behavior, and Marce overseeing it all.

This was their home. It had taken years for Marce to adjust to life at Craven House—and truly come to think of the residence as a *home*—especially after everything she'd known was stripped from her when her father died.

No longer was Craven House a temporary place where her family resided.

But now, it was all to be gone—stripped from her—very soon. Yet, in a way, it was long overdue.

While sad, Marce could not muster the expected sense of loss at knowing that everything she prided herself on possessing would shortly be in another's hands.

Less competent hands, unfortunately.

One source of regret over her duplicitous life coming to an end was present. Her family. This was their home, too. Sam, Jude, and Payton had been born within the walls of Craven House and had known no other home.

The time would come when they learned of Craven House's fate.

And what of the women she helped in London? Travel accommodations would need to be secured, as well as a house large enough to serve as a refuge. Marce could not—*would* not—abandon them, no matter the hardship it caused. Her family had lived many years helping those less fortunate, and Marce would not end that now, no matter the appealing lure of absolute freedom.

A light knock sounded on the door, and Darla opened it enough to peek her head in. "A carriage be here ta fetch ye, Madame."

"Thank you, Darla." Marce smiled to cover her cringe. *Madame.* It was only fitting that the proprietress of a brothel be addressed as such, even if it had been many, many years since Craven House housed such scandalous activities.

Nonetheless, she was known as Madame Marce—and her mother before her, Madame Sasha. The *ton* had a long, detailed memory.

Perhaps she could outrun her reputation if she traveled far enough. Would Cornwall do, or would she need journey as far as the distant corner of Scotland—or perhaps across the Channel—to find a reprieve from her family's past?

Marce would dwell on the matter later. For now, she had a carriage waiting to take her to Kent.

When she focused on the door once more, Darla had disappeared, slipping as soundlessly away as she'd arrived.

Marce adjusted her hold on her traveling trunk

and walked toward the foyer, careful to keep her pace unhurried to hide the mounting dread that increased with each step.

It was not every day a woman told a duke to go to hell—consequences be damned.

With her head held high, Marce departed Craven House with only a slim hope she'd be allowed to return.

"Your carriage," the driver called, pulling the coach door wide for her.

With this servant, and the several that had come before him, she was never Madame Marce, nor even so much as Miss Davenport. He only held the door for her to enter at Craven House and exit the carriage at the Whisper Hook Inn.

She was simply a chore that could be assigned to any random servant. Collect and deposit her as if she were naught but a bag of sugar needed for afternoon tea, or a gown needing collection from the laundress.

Perhaps she, at some point, had acquiesced to her role as such and began to think of herself in the manner in which the duke treated her—as something of little import.

The time had come for that to change.

She may have shed the trappings of her noble birth long ago and nearly forgotten her status as the eldest daughter of Lord Buckston, a marquess; however, she had not fallen so far that she believed herself as insignificant as a bushel of sugar.

"Sir." Marce halted before stepping up into the waiting conveyance, making certain to keep her tone level. This was not the man her years of pent-up frustration should be aimed at.

He was but a messenger.

"Yes?" He cleared his throat, keeping his stare trained on her feet.

"I need to make a stop before departing London." She pinned the driver with a hard stare even though he'd yet to lift his gaze to hers. Would he deny her request? Would he load her into the carriage and ignore her demand?

"His Grace will not be pleased if we are tardy," he mumbled, his eyes finally meeting hers.

"It is a gift—for the duchess." It was Marce's turn to avoid his gaze as she admitted the truth of the matter. She was in no way seeking to delay or displease the duke, only curry favor with the duchess. "I must pick it up from the bookseller on Piccadilly."

"Certainly." He nodded, his stare focusing on her feet once more.

Without another word, Marce handed her trunk to the driver to stow in the boot and entered the carriage.

As they pulled out of the Craven House drive, Marce stopped herself from glancing out the window and watching her home disappear in her wake. Neither would she waste precious time dwelling on the looming task awaiting her once she arrived at the Whisper Hook Inn. Her decision had been made— and Marce would allow nothing to alter her course.

Available in print, audiobook, and e-book now!

ABOUT THE AUTHOR

USA TODAY Bestselling Author Christina McKnight writes emotional and intricate Regency Romance with strong women and maverick heroes.

Her books combine romance and mystery, exploring themes of redemption and forgiveness. When she's not writing, Christina enjoys trying new coffeehouses, visiting wine bars, traveling the world, and watching television.

Email: Christina@ChristinaMcKnight.com
Follow her on Twitter: @CMcKnightWriter
Keep up to date on her releases:
www.christinamcknight.com
Like Christina's FB Author page:
ChristinaMcKnightWriter